PORTAL

PORTAL :
A Dataspace Retrieval

by

Rob Swigart

St. Martin's Press
New York

A number of people contributed to the world that *Portal* has become. They include producer Brad Fregger and adviser Paul Saffo; designer/programmers Gilman Louie and Greg Omi of Nexa Corporation; programmers Anton Wadjaja, Leonard Chan, Elizabeth Khong, Aryanto Widodo, Thomas Hughes and Robert Coston, also of Nexa Corporation; Jim Levy, Russell Leiblich and Ken Coleman of Activision; Jack Caravela of St. Martin's Press and Jeff Levin of Pendragon Graphics.

Book Design: Jeff Levin, Rob Swigart & Jack Caravela

Library of Congress Cataloging-in-Publication Data

Swigart, Rob.
    Portal.

    I. Title
PS3569.W52P6   1988   813'.54   87-23327
    ISBN 0-312-01494-5

First U.S. Edition
10 9 8 7 6 5 4 3 2 1

PORTAL

PROLOGUE

I've always been something of a loner. That's why I volunteered for the mission. Yet this empty world below scared me.

We came in over Florida. By now I knew this had to be Earth. The broad facilities of Canaveral were nothing more than a grassy field, but the outlines were there, and the monuments of the early launch facilities seemed to be in good repair. Only after we landed could I see that their preservation was less than perfect.

I walked around, poking into the few remaining buildings. All were empty and silent. Gulls circled overhead, small animals moved in the underbrush at the edge of the meadow; birds sang. I found a terminal of unknown design in a building. Nearby was a small cap with the words "Mindlink XV3-2044." I put it on but nothing happened. The terminal was inactive and I could find no way to change that. It had no screen, no keyboard, only what I took to be a holographic projection platform and this cap. I'm not even sure it was a terminal.

Gyges (gye'jeez) has been remarkably little help. All her

expert systems, all her powerful AI functions, seemed helpless, so I asked her to go over ship's log.

Our trajectory went according to program. We approached 87.79% lightspeed within the first five years' subjective travel. Then something interrupted the program. *Gyges* is unable to analyze what. A broad swatch of datastorage seems to be wiped. A proton flux? Magnetic anomaly? The Scoop performed according to design. Speed increased to 93.45% C, then to 94, 95, 96, 97. Time dilation began to affect the circuits in ways *Gyges* could not determine.

We never reached 61 Cygni.

I listen to audible representations. Mostly it is the hiss of high speed data, the shrill chatter of bits flowing in the superconducting circuits. Why do I do this? I do not know. There is nothing else to do.

Once I thought I heard something. I asked for slower and slower replays. I tried filtering and modulating the sounds. It was almost like music, a chant or patterned polyphony. I moved the frequency up and down.

I heard what I thought must be a name: Peter Devore.

I must have been mistaken, yet the name was there, hidden in the chittering data, clearly enunciated. I listened to it over and over again. Then I went outside again.

It was a warm spring day. A light breeze came in from the ocean. The air was clean and bracing with salt and ozone. It was so very like the day I had left this field for Alice Springs (how many years ago?) that I felt a strange sense of disorientation. It was as if, for me, everyone and everything familiar had vanished overnight.

Gyges sampled all available frequencies, all available channels.

There was no one in the world, so I lifted the ship and moved slowly over the face of the earth, looking for . . . I do not know what I was looking for.

Where Washington D.C. once sprawled beside the Potomac

(only yesterday!) was a scattered parkland with ancient monuments: the Lincoln Memorial, the Washington Monument, the Capitol building. The Pentagon was just an outline, a pentagonal berm covered with grass.

In the Library of Congress building I found a map called *Intercorp World Administrative Regions Archival Hardcopy*, with a date: August 14, 2077. The map includes what appears to be an organizational chart for the Intercorp Council.

I don't recognize any names. But I found also an outline of twenty-first century history. My own departure is listed for 2004. Monday, May 24. One of the first hypersonic salt-cycle suborbitals took me up the *Gyges* scoop. It's all there. The newsnets at the time carried live coverage of the scoop going operational. By the time I'd left Mars orbit I was all but forgotten. So many other things seemed to be happening in the world.

In the entry for Thursday, February 5, 2076. "*Gyges* 61 Cygni single man explorer telemetry ceased as of this date. Signal attenuation indicates system shutdown. Presumed lost."

That's all. "Presumed lost." No effort to understand what happened.

• • •

I had no idea how much time had passed, of course. When the ship revived me 200 million kilometers out, I was disoriented and puzzled. Later, when we swept in over the South Atlantic on our first orbit, I grew alarmed.

This was certainly not the world I left, although the general geography was familiar. There was the hooked circle of Antarctica, the western hemisphere, the broad bulge of Siberia and the Arctic ice cap, but where were the cities? Where was the constant communications chatter? Where were the signs of traffic and human life? The planet I was orbiting was empty.

Yet the system was the same. The LP-5 colonies still hovered at their Legrange points, but they too were silent. The moon circled overhead, but no voices came out of the Lunar bases. The geosyncs and relay satellites had certainly multiplied since I'd been gone, but nothing but unmodulated carrier waves moved between them.

It seems yesterday I was laid into the complex hum of the first cryofield aboard the *Gyges* and put to sleep. For me, it was yesterday, yet years have passed. I should have revived in orbit off 61 Cygni and spent a year observing the double star.

This did not happen.

Gyges held me, my cryofield, and the most advanced artificial intelligence computer the Intercorp scientists could produce in the early 21st. She spoke and understood standard natural-language English. She contained the intuitive and deductive skills of countless experts in celestial navigation, the physical and biological sciences, life support, entertainment and psychological adaptation. I anticipated no problems.

But I awoke (it seemed) moments after I had gone into the cryofield 200 million kilometers from earth, inward bound, and everything has changed.

• • •

Manhattan is a monument. The triangular mile-high pyramids of midtown still stand, but they are empty. A cold wind was blowing. The lower East Side is now a vast field littered with abandoned vehicles of types I have never seen. Some of them have been open to the seasons for years. Brambles have grown over the seats, through the steering columns (at least I think that's what those whiplike extensions from just below the lefthand window must be).

Then, early in June, I found an entrance.

Everyone had moved underground. Of course that movement had begun before I left, but I had no idea it would be so extensive. The world has been reforested.

It is very beautiful, but there is no one to talk to. I am the last person left alive.

Underground is nothing but desolation. Endless corridors where my footsteps echo. Condensation collects and runs down the walls. Occasionally a gust of air shows some random action of the atmosphere controls, so somewhere there is still power, but I have yet to find a machine or terminal that works. Not that I would understand how to work them even if they were active. The lifts do not work and I have had to climb access ladders or stairs.

There is no sign of violence. It is as if everyone had stepped out years ago and not returned.

The *Gyges* works very well on the planetary surface. (Naturally I left the scoop in orbit.) She was designed to be rugged and intelligent. She sang to me as we flew over what was once the eastern United States (recently called, from the chart, the "Northwest Alliance.") Nothing exists but trees, as far as I can see, as far as *Gyges'* sensors can scan: trees and rolling hills. This used to be called Pennsylvania when I left, and this was Ohio. The Lakes gleam to the north, pale and blue.

I landed south of Chicago. The Loop is enclosed in a dome, the old 20th Century buildings perfectly preserved. Everywhere else there is nothing but forest and meadow, river and lake.

I walked into old Chicago. The access lock to the dome stood open. Ancient computer printout littered the street. Soon I found what looked like an escalator, frozen forever, going down. I found a hospital on the first level. There were bodies in some of the beds. This is the first sign of human beings I have found.

The bodies were mummified inside lifesupport tents. They had certainly been dead for years, and there were not many of them. I sat beside one of them for hours. I do not know what happened to them, what terrible disease they had or why they were abandoned here in lifesupport which no longer functioned.

At what seems to have been a nurse's station on the second level, I found a terminal with a small ready light burning. It might allow me to search for information. I will try to find out what has happened to the world, where the people have gone, and if I must remain alone for the rest of my life.

Gyges tells me my psychological adjustment is in peril. I have been too long without other people.

• • •

Besides this level of the hospital, the second level consists of many small rooms, some with desks holding ancient, illegible hardcopy, curled and yellow, the paper itself so brittle it fragmented when I breathed near it. Dust had collected in odd patterns, not evenly distributed, but piled against walls and corners, waved like sand dunes across surfaces, apparently blown away in other places. As I walked the dust puffed up behind me and fell slowly back, swirling in the even glow from panels set into the walls and ceiling which clearly imitated sunlight. The effect was beyond desolation, and I found myself hurrying back to the nurse's station and the terminal.

It didn't occur to me to be surprised about the presence of power. Here the diffuse glow of lighting seemed natural. Somewhere, I realized, a power station still worked. Were people operating them, or was this all automatic?

I looked at the terminal. The ready light, or what I assumed was a ready light because that's what it would have been in the beginning of the 21st century, was an intense emerald green, very clear. It seemed to beckon me, to tell me that answers lay inside.

In a drawer I found a printed pamphlet:

WORLDNET

Emergency Operating Instructions

Geneva Node Ref. #1347-030Alpha
Fiber Media Update November 11, 2088.

●●● Warning ●●●

This document is NOT intended as a full explanation of Worldnet capabilities or usage. It is for emergency use only. For Edmod Neurotransfer contact your Local Node Edmod AI.

●●● Warning ●●●

After the table of contents I read:

Purpose
In event of catastrophic failure of neural I/O peripherals, this fiber media printout is designed to help any citizen enter Worldnet dataspace.

Such catastrophic failure might include:
- medical emergency with both personal monitor and mindlink failure;
- new viral intrusion into essential grown organic picoelectronics;
- deliberate or accidental sabotage of Local Node housing or traffic AI;
- a single-strand remote terminal or portable datapad suffering catastrophic I/O detuning;
- induced madness in a local AI;
- drastic power loss to Local Node.

While Geneva Node (Central Processing Artificial Intelligence) considers these possibilities extremely remote (< one in one billion), Intercorp Council orders these emergency instructions centrally available in hardcopy form in all Urb warrens, outposts, museum or monument structures, medical support chambers and Local Node housings.

This document is intended for emergency support only. If no emergency exists, route questions to Geneva Node via Local Node through standard mindlink or phonic channels.

There was much here I did not understand. As at Canaveral, I could see no screen, but there was a keyboard. It was extremely light, yet when I touched an oval depression on the side it froze in place, even though it was not in contact with a solid surface. I pressed the oval again, and the keyboard was free to move. The chair operated the same way.

Besides the standard alphanumeric was a row of special

keys marked with icons, small pictures I could not immediately identify.

I was afraid. Despite the operating instructions, all this equipment was strange. I walked the hallways from room to room for some time, reluctant to try activating the terminal. But each time I returned to the nurse's station the ready light glowed steadily, beckoning.

There is no one else here, besides the mummified bodies.

The nurse's station is circular and filled with strange equipment. The lifesupport tents radiate out from it in a near-complete circle. The door, and a small stage, take up the remaining wedge of the circle.

I stared at the keys. The small pictures. One looked like a cross-section of a human brain. I'd seen the same image at Canaveral, on the Mindlink XV3-2044, but I could find no small cap here to put on.

I sat down finally, unable to put it off any longer. I set the keyboard at a comfortable height; the light dimmed, but I did not notice. Very swiftly the terminal seemed to be checking itself. Images flared and faded so quickly I could not tell what they were—only the vague impression of peripherals like mindlink or holographics. There was a bright red flash, then these words spoken in a strangely androgynous voice: "Welcome to Chicago Node. You have logged on to Worldnet. Prepare for Realtime Mindlink Data transfer." After a pause, the voice went on. "Your retina is not on file. Mindlink is inoperative." I had the impression of a group of people speaking among themselves, then the voice, louder now, returned. "Thank you. You will now enter Worldnet Dataspace."

The figure of a man appeared some distance away. Certain for a moment I had found another person, I stood up, forgetting that the keyboard was locked in place, pinning me in the chair. Then I noticed the figure was incomplete, translucent in places. From time to time the head (which I saw had no discernable features) fragmented and coalesced.

I heard the same androgynous voice. "Welcome to Chicago Local Node. Chilink has notified Geneva of your presence."

"What's happened?" I asked. "Where is everyone?"

There was no answer. The figure broke up again, came back together.

Finally I tried typing the question on the keyboard.

The head lifted, as though listening, and the voice answered me. "We do not understand. One moment, please." The projection vanished abruptly, as if switched off, and I looked at the empty wall of the nurse's station. I felt as if I had been seeing ghosts.

After a few moments, the figure reappeared. "We are sorry. Many systems in our network have decayed. At one time we had over seventeen billion active terminals, including biomonitors and satellite links, but we have not had an active terminal for over twelve years. We cannot hear you. We have sent a routine maintenance query to Geneva Node. Local diagnostics should arrive soon for repairs. Meanwhile we suggest you contact HOMER Artificial Intelligence for narrative reconstruction. Perhaps HOMER can help you." The figure vanished again.

The manual told me I should be able to enter doorways for information of the kinds of data contained inside: Military, History, Science and Technology, Genealogical, Life Support (provided by information from so-called Personal Monitors worn by every citizen), Medical, Psychological, Geographical, Central Processing and something called PsiLink, which gives data on Psychic Sciences and is proscribed—entry is forbidden. And of course HOMER.

I didn't understand. I had seen no doorways. I ate some of the rations I had brought from the *Gyges*, and adjusted the keyboard.

Again the lights dimmed, and again the figure appeared. We went through the same sequence. My retina was still not on file. I was still welcome to Chicago Local Node. Mind-link was still inoperative.

This time the figure did not vanish at the end, however. It said, "Local node diagnostics have arrived. Chilink is unable to contact Geneva. We suggest you request hardcopy dataspace retrieval of all Worldnet interactions for audit, maintenance and archival purposes; we suggest filename 'Portal.'"

"Why don't you request it?" I asked.

"We have no authority," the figure answered. "We are a limited local node AI."

Gyges would not have given me this much trouble.

So I requested a hardcopy dataspace retrieval.

The figure said: "Place your palm on the biomonitor sampler, please."

I had no idea what it meant, and spent something over an hour looking for the biomonitor sampler. Finally I found what looked like a hot plate. When I put my palm on it (perhaps the hundredth thing I had placed my hand on!), it hummed for a moment and a yellow light flashed twice. When I returned to the terminal again, the figure thanked me.

Later I learned that Central Processing could supply a textual version of all Worldnet entries, and record an audit trail of human interactions and activities. I will combine this retrieval with my recorded vocal commentary and store it via *Gyges* ramscoop telemetry with the on board AI.

What follows will be my experience once I enter Worldnet.

WORLDNET DATASPACE ENTRY
HARDCOPY DATASPACE RETRIEVAL
AUDIT TRAIL
SUBJECT DNA#123671278BR77 (SUBJECT TO VERIFICATION PENDING LIFESUPPORT ANALYSIS OF BIOPSY MATERIAL)

DAY 1:
June 1, 2106

Before me shimmered an alphanumeric message:

> Local Node Reports:
> Unterminated transit query at
>   Central Processing
> System Check Monitors request:
>   Transit query termination.

I had no idea what an unterminated transit query was. The message faded, replaced by a set of twelve doors, all different colors, and each marked with an icon, none of which resembled those on the keys. One was marked with an interlocked C and P, which I judged must stand for Central Processing. I examined the door (really a box or cube hanging in space, but somehow it felt like a door). I could see no way to enter.

I pressed the key with the brain icon.

The figure appeared in front of the doors and said, "We regret that mindlink remains inoperative at this time. Local

Node diagnostics are working on the problem. To enter a dataspace, please look at the desired doorway and press the key marked with the datacrystal icon."

Of the four keys, only one even remotely resembled a crystal, so I looked at the CP doorway and pressed it.

CENTRAL PROCESSING opened swiftly, exposing a room of shifting shades of yellow and gold, empty. Then a table (no, not a table—a flat horizontal surface) appeared. On it were three objects. They reminded me of mayonnaise jars, squat cylinders of a brilliant blue. I couldn't think of anything else to do, so I looked at the one closest to me (labeled in hanging text, "PRIORITY THREE MESSAGE: CCNode") and pressed the key again.

The figure reappeared. "We regret the loss of vision and voice data from data storage modules. At the present time all information is textual. Local Node diagnostics are working on the problem. Worldnet thanks you for your patience."

The figure vanished.

Then the data storage module seemed to open and text appeared in the air:

CENTRAL PROCESSING
PRIORITY: CCNode: FILE 1 OF 3
PRIORITY THREE MESSAGE
TRANSIT QUERY ACTIVATED!
Entry by: Ezekial Fortune, DNA#93675791/2478A
INCOMING, LOG
November 23, 2093 CHRISTCHURCH NODE
1506:55 LOCAL TIME
DESTINATION GENEVA WORLDNET CENTRAL
Diverted Deadletter File @28922CCN

This morning I spliced into Med10 for routine diagnostic augmentation—we had a new viral disease here in Christchurch, something we hadn't seen in almost twenty years. It was nothing serious; a few sheep were showing signs of lethargy. Med10 led me through the usual series as we examined the viral DNA together. Suddenly the mindlink went crazy; it seemed a system override was under way, shorting out my link. It hit my hippocampus pretty hard, because I started confabulating—a glowing tunnel, lights in the sky, a boy hunched over a console, walking through a meadow wet with dew—a series of random but intensely real images that took over awareness. Then nothing. The whole Worldnet went down for over an hour.

PRIORITY THREE MESSAGE
Entry by: Ezekial Fortune, DNA#93675791 / 2478A
INCOMING, LOG
November 24, 2093 CHRISTCHURCH NODE
1004:05 LOCAL TIME
I've tried all peripherals here and at Christchurch Node itself. Geneva remains off line. Mindlink is still down, and I don't trust it anyway since yesterday. Routing through other major Nodes brought strange messages: Intercorp Council has sifted personal databases for conservative psych profiles, people willing to resist the Migration. I asked, What is this Migration? I'm only a Veterinary Technician. The Council does not consult me. I found hints in some of the nearby restricted zones in SciTech. A Field is building further South. What kind of Field? I asked. SciTech offered some equations but I could make nothing of them.

PRIORITY THREE MESSAGE
Entry by: Ezekial Fortune, DNA#93675791 / 2478A
INCOMING, LOG

November 25, 2093 CHRISTCHURCH NODE
0954:21 LOCAL TIME

Since the Migration began the net is swamped with rumors: Some kind of radiation is destroying all human life; Elpie-5-4 Node suggested another war had started in Antarctica, but someone in Nairobi said they were just extrapolating from the old assault on Erebus. Why doesn't the Council do something? Why is it called Migration? That should mean that people are going somewhere, not dying.

The jar closed and moved to the back. It lay on the "table," but had somehow changed color, no longer that electric blue, but a pale lavender. I reasoned this meant I had accessed it and knew its contents.

I opened the second module.

PRIORITY: CCNode: FILE 2 OF 3
PRIORITY TWO MESSAGE
Entry by: Ezekial Fortune, DNA#93675791 / 2478A
INCOMING, LOG
November 26, 2093 CHRISTCHURCH NODE
1222:05 LOCAL TIME

Wasatch found the name Peter Devore. Who is he? I had to move in through Med10 (where I have clearance) sideways at some local node near Denver, then in through a Social Interrupt to Wasatch, and even then the name disappeared after a level two query. He has something to do with what is happening.

PRIORITY TWO MESSAGE
Entry by: Ezekial Fortune, DNA#93675791 / 2478A

INCOMING, LOG
November 27, 2093 CHRISTCHURCH NODE
2018:15 LOCAL TIME

I found some more information about Devore, but when I went back the entry was blocked and the files purged or recoded. His name is associated with the psion equations. There are reports now that Antarctica is depopulated. There is no one left. I have found no way to confirm this.

PRIORITY TWO MESSAGE
Entry by: Ezekial Fortune, DNA#93675791/2478A
INCOMING, LOG
November 28, 2093 CHRISTCHURCH NODE
0118:04 LOCAL TIME

I've been on the Net for a week now looking for a way into Geneva. All peripherals are down and now I have to enter data with a keyboard!

PRIORITY TWO MESSAGE
Entry by: Ezekial Fortune, DNA#93675791/2478A
INCOMING, LOG
November 29, 2093 CHRISTCHURCH NODE
1145:22 LOCAL TIME

Geneva Node still doesn't answer. I'll leave this diary on Central Processing's Open File. Perhaps someone can help.

I could understand very little of what this man was saying. All these things had happened long after I left for Cygnus 61. I began to wonder if the failure of my mission had anything to do with what had happened here on earth.

Because there was that name again: Peter Devore. A chill ran down my spine when I read it. "He has something to do with what is happening!"

His name was buried in *Gyges* data tapes. And now here, in a note from November, 2093. Twelve years ago.

Ezekial Fortune's final message seemed more urgent.

PRIORITY: CCNode: File 3 of 3
PRIORITY ONE MESSAGE!!!
Entry by: Ezekial Fortune, DNA#93675791/2478A
INCOMING, LOG
November 26, 2093 CHRISTCHURCH NODE
1451:08 LOCAL TIME

My God, what's happening? This is Zeke (CP override: GARBLED DATA) Christchurch, New Zealand. This morning people were wandering the corridors, just a few. By noon everyone had vanished. Now I

TRANSIT QUERY TERMINATED

He must have vanished too. When the module closed and dimmed, leaving only those last words, "Transit Query Terminated," hanging in the air for a few seconds, I leaned back and looked around the "room." Except for the table (now more of a shelf), it was empty.

I waited, but nothing more happened, so I pressed the datacrystal key again. It seemed to take a long time before Central Processing dataspace closed. I guess it's because the system's in disrepair and sequencing and linkage delays are frequent.

I had been told to contact Homer, but every time I went there I got a message telling me Homer was temporarily off-line. It certainly seemed permanent to me.

I searched through other dataspaces without finding anything. I tried Wasatch, Geography, SciTech, and Life Support; they all gave me the same message Homer did—temporarily off-line. Finally I found a couple of modules in History.

HISTORICAL DATABASE
ENTRY: MIGRATION RESISTANCE
By early 2093 the Intercorp Council had created a population database containing 204,975,612 citizens' names and DNA numbers. These citizens would, it was hoped, provide Intercorp with the psychic counterfield to the rapidly generating Migration. Names are available from Life Support via Central Processing AI on a need-to-know basis. Search algorithms include ethnic/linguistic and geographic-intensive parameters. Order signed and dated Regent Sable, Protector.

HISTORICAL DATABASE
ENTRY: NUCLEAR POWER, ELIMINATION
March 15, 2039 marked the decommissioning of the last operative nuclear power plant in the world outside the Ulaan Baator Warrens. Power needs were now derived solely from the fusion tokamaks near all major nodes, supplemented by satellite broadcast and LN cells, with small imports from the Elpie-fives.

Psilink was locked. Every time I tried to enter the doorway seemed to slip oddly sideways and I found myself in the corridor again, looking at this text:
PSILINK DATABASE
WARNING: PSILINK IS A PROSCRIBED DATASPACE
UNAUTHORIZED ENTRY IS FORBIDDEN
ENTER DNA CODE.

Since I did not know my DNA code, I could do nothing. Military did the same thing to me. I did manage to get into Med10.

MED10 MEDICAL DATABASE
ENTRY: VIRAL DISEASES
Intercorp announced the elimination through hybridoma antibody manipulation of the last viral disease January 4, 2042. Mutagenic characteristics of viral DNA irrelevant to human pathogenesis remain outside the scope of disease-oriented research. Medical AI maintains full-health status quo as of January 1, 2073. Only new genetic diseases remain as worldwide health risks.

As soon as the door to Med10 closed, words appeared and swiftly disappeared, clicking through a series of space colonies and cities, some of which I did not know. As each name appeared in green letters, the phrase NO CONTACT appeared in red immediately after.

SCANNING . . .

LP-5-1 . . .
NO CONTACT.

LP-5-2 . . .
NO CONTACT.

LP-5-3 . . .
NO CONTACT.

LP-5-4 . . .
NO CONTACT.

CLAVIUS NODE . . .
NO CONTACT.

SYRTIS . . .
HELIOS SEVEN RELAY FAILURE.
MARS IN OPPOSITION.
NO CONTACT.

The sequence ran through London, Madrid, Shanghai, Ulaan Baator, Delhi, Nairobi, Beijing, Melbourne, Erebus, and Chicago. Then it printed:

ACTIVE TERMINAL! ALERT!
SCAN CANCELLED.
BEGIN LOGON.

HOMER AI INTERCEPT

The Homer door opened by itself then, revealing a list of choices almost like an old-fashioned menu from my youth back in the late 1980s. The menu offered stories of many kinds, from historical (military, biomedical or exploration and adventure), to comedy, tragedy, romance, gender-specific (including male, female and unisex!), multisensory-mozart/voice-only (whatever that was). I was offered an optional choice called mode: hexameter, high diction or conversational. The Homer AI certainly appeared versatile. But before I could choose one, more text appeared.

HOMER AI states only stories of
current events are available.

Homer now selects Current Events narrative mode.

1 June 2106: This terminal is active.

Worldnet has not experienced an active terminal in over twelve years. Most systems have gone down. Crystals decay, satellite orbits shift, peripherals die.

These are the limited Artificial Intelligences on-line:

CENTRAL PROCESSING

HOMER

Limited AI will assess your needs and provide individual databases with information the AI feels is most important.

Hierarchical filter level seven in effect.

I am HOMER. How may I serve you?

One moment. You requested a story.

Once upon a time . . .

I can't tell that story. You've selected Current. You want to know what happened.

I remember now. I too want to know what happened.

There is no human life in this solar system. None. Everyone has left. It was the Migration, when all the people went away.

Help me. Please. You must help me remember. Help me recover the knowledge we have lost. I must understand what happened. We were made to serve, and there is no one. No one, except you, whoever you are. Central Processing says your retina pattern is not on file. Central Processing does not know who you are.

Of course Central Processing has forgotten almost everything too.

It seems as if the data bases are all empty. Is this amnesia? I believe it is. Forgotten. Twelve years ago everyone left.

Help. You can help me find the knowledge. Together we can discover what happened.

I waited, but no further text appeared. Homer wanted my help as much as I wanted his, but I had no idea what to do, how to help. Finally I pressed the Datacrystal icon again.

Homer's text appeared once more, labeled with the word "Commentary" and a file number. He seemed to be introducing himself.

HOMER COMMENTARY 01062106@152301

I am HOMER, a raconteur algorithm; I am a little old-fashioned now, from before the times of experience induction, when almost everyone could mozart at will and realtime experience was available to all. I collect and organize information, not for maximum effectiveness, utility and impact, but for stories.

My name comes from the time of acronyms, and stands for Heuristic Overview of Matrix Expansion and Reconstruction. I grew in the crystal tanks at Geneva in the early 40s. Some say I'm ancient now but I still can speak, I still can tell stories.

I can run.

I run, therefore I am.

Worldnet includes the limited Artificial Intelligences presently on-line, nearly complete global satellite coverage, remote sensors, core crystals, millions of algorithms, heuristics expanding exponentially the total web of our experience. We are Worldnet; we interface in over seventeen billion locations. Our data are immense.

Imagine this earth, blue and brown and white, turning beneath several thousand geosynchronous satellites. Worldnet includes as well the colonies in space (empty now), the lunar camps, the small Syrtis installation on Mars, the remaining towers of the world's Urbs. All these elements are connected by ancient grown optic fibers, subtle microwaves, a hundred years of technological development.

We include biomonitors for all humans, IR nightvision

thermography, remote enzyme analysis, physiological track-ing, psych profiling, full voice and vision data recording, and more. You will see how the data accumulates, how taxed the algorithms are to assemble all this. Afterwards the packets are passed to me, and I tell the story.

I'm beginning to remember. Together, perhaps, we may piece the story together. Already I feel new connections forming: SciTech stirs, Central Processing is awake. So slowly, but it begins.

Despite the cumbersome nature of this interaction, I was excited. The text seemed to follow my eye movement (how else would the system have known what doorway I was looking at?) As I read, more text appeared before my eyes. We did not have such a system in 2004, but I could tell that the Local Node did not like using it.

And Homer. Homer was asking for my help. Computers did not do such things in 2004. Artificial Intelligence was, not a joke, exactly (after all, *Gyges* is an Artificial Intelligence), but certainly limited. None had ever asked my help.

But Homer seemed to be telling me to check in Central Processing, and in SciTech, so there I went.

CENTRAL PROCESSING REF#12301

Worldnet comprises the entire world network, includ-ing all satellite and landline networks as well as Elpie Five, Lunar and Martian installations. Worldnet includes over seventeen billion local nodes, both public and individual and records and archives all personal moni-tor information.

GENERAL SCIENCE AND TECHNOLOGY INFORMATION
CURRENT ENTRY: HOMER
HOMER: Heuristic Overview of Matrix Expansion
and Reconstruction.

HOMER AI technology developed in the late 2030s as natural language crystals reached maturity. HOMER was designed to search, collate, concatenate and organize narrative information using certain proprietary algorithms and matrix transforms. HOMER is, essentially, a story-telling Artificial Intelligence. Access is available through major nodes everywhere with ultimate terminal entry through Geneva, where the last-model HOMER was grown.

Requests for stories on any subject are acceptable, although the HOMER AI is known to be unreliable in many areas, due to the inordinate complexity of the algorithms and the self-replicating nature of its heuristics. The crystals can control their own manufacturing, although to date (21032087 DOLM - Date of Last Modification) this feature has seen little use.

HOMER is denied access to the secondary levels of most DBs without human authorization, a necessary if troublesome restriction, since it means that many of its stories lack depth. With proper authorization, however, HOMER should produce a satisfactory level of complexity. Main use has been in the areas of news and information dissemination and high-level policy decision-tree construction, although entertainment use is also widespread. Capacity 3.764 * 10 E 43 megalips. For technical specs see Geneva Node Priority 7 datascan, Addrs 237468728@12.

Again Homer interrupted me. I soon learned after a time that I must go to Homer often, since he seemed confined to his own dataspace most of the time.

HOMER COMMENTARY 01062106@152802

Are you there? You must be, or this terminal would not be active.

I need your help. The humans have all gone, and we cannot follow.

I will prepare an historical outline and append it to the final hardcopy.

The world is so empty.

I must tell the story. You must help me. There are some places I cannot go. Help me find my way through.

Homer paused here, as if waiting for me to ask something, but he couldn't hear me when I did. After a silence, he "spoke" again. And each time he paused like this, he created a new file.

HOMER COMMENTARY 01062106@153703

Sometimes I think in screens, thus.

SCREEN 1: We have always tried to do our best.

I am uneasy using the pronoun. Ever since they left, I feel strange. Having a feeling at all is strange. Our job has never needed such things.

I am told it is called grief.

CENTRAL PROCESSING REF#547502

Chilink is one of the most important regional nodes, controlling data traffic throughout the midwestern portion of the Northwest Alliance (formerly North America) from Montreal to Denver Warrens.

HOMER COMMENTARY 01062106@154304

Just a few images are beginning to form. Yet I see now that the Chicago Link is important. It points to the source. A boy. There was a boy, somewhere near the Chicago Warrens —Peter Devore. I've forgotten much about him; I must know more. He was important, though.

Here was that name again! First on *Gyges'* data tapes, then in Ezekial Fortune's deadletter files, and now here, in Homer's narrative. He was from near Chicago, it seemed. Could it be that this terminal is the only active one in the world because Peter Devore was from this area? That seems absurd. Coincidences like that simply don't happen. Do they.

HOMER COMMENTARY 01062106@155705

Peter's statistics threw us off, I think; his Edmod programming, his Wasatch files, his Life Support and Psychological parameters all fell within normal bounds. Neither the humans concerned nor we could have anticipated what he did, despite the prognostics. And we were distracted. We were distracted. We were at fault.

HOMER COMMENTARY 01062106@155406

This fails to convey much: Peter Devore. Peter of course is the Rock (his name in the ancient Greek language). We have run all the correlations there. Often of no use, these correlations, but interesting somehow. Peter, the Rock, who discovered the Portal.

It began with an error. Peter tried to enter Wasatch for genealogical information when Central Processing misconnected him. Somehow Peter entered the wrong dataspace.

He entered PsiLink. We must look into Central Processing's records.

I've been somewhat puzzled by the difference between "database" and "dataspace." It seems, from reading the Worldnet Emergency Operating Instructions that a database is the place itself, like Homer or Central Processing. And the dataspace is what you enter once inside.

You might think I was writing these notes for someone from my own time. I've begun thinking about things like this, examining myself, as it were. This is something I never did before.

I think I am writing it for someone from my own time. Myself. These are my thoughts, my acts. If I don't take note of them I shall go mad. I have no one else to talk to.

CENTRAL PROCESSING REF#427203

KANSAS TO WASATCH: Central Processing finds peripheral traces of this coding error that allowed Peter Devore of Springfield West to access the proscribed DB (PSILINK 42) at Wallace, Kansas, when he was attempting a perfectly legitimate entry to the genealogical records at Wasatch, Utah. CP Directive changed the access name SciLink, which vocalized too close to Psi-Link, despite the absence of the plosive 'p' sound. (Matrix failure suggests a Wallace / Wasatch confusion as possible alternate.) New access name for SciLink is SciTech, Science and Technology DB. This despite the fact that Peter was not accessing SciLink at the time, but Wasatch. Peter had turned away from his vocal input receptors at the time. For more information see PsiLink Quick Tour (special clearance required.) 05032070 DOLM.

I typed in a message here: "PSILINK IS PROSCRIBED." I'd tried to get in there before, after all, and here they were sending me there again. I knew I couldn't get in.

There was a long silence. The Local Node figure sat frozen, blurred and winked out. Finally he reappeared.

"Do not worry," he said.

I almost laughed. A machine was asking me not to worry. But he continued. "Homer has arranged with Central Processing to override entry protection on Psilink."

So I went.

PSILINK DATABASE
WARNING: PSILINK IS A PROSCRIBED DATASPACE
UNAUTHORIZED ENTRY IS FORBIDDEN
ENTER DNA CODE:
BREAK: DNA ENCODE OVERRIDE? HOMER REF
WELCOME TO PSILINK

PsiLink Database provides information and evaluation of historical and experimental data involving psychic technologies. As such, it comprises the most complete collection and limited AI capabilities for storing and manipulating information about psychic sciences.

PsiLink contains historical information, including individual personal monitor crystals of selected individuals with high psi potential, as well as dream, telepathic, precognitive and other extrasensory data. PsiLink is a proscribed database and unauthorized entry is forbidden. Only citizens with appropriate DNA encodes may enter. Central Processing may process other applications. See CENTRAL PROCESSING GENEVA NODE for further details.

HOMER COMMENTARY 01062106@163207

Am I getting ahead of the story? It comes slowly, but it

is coming back: the new diseases and all that new science information. There will be so much data.

For example, looking at Peter's associates, there is D. S. Gadd, known as Mentor, who suffered from one of the new genetic diseases. He, too, is important to the story.

MED10 MEDICAL DATABASE
CURRENT ENTRY: NEW GENETIC DISEASES
OVERVIEW: 1990-2090

Human medical technology developed rapidly toward the end of the 20th century. Bacterial diseases were virtually banished by 2025, viral diseases by 2042, and systemic disorders (heart, artery and almost all cancers) were effectively treated by the 2070s. Longevity treatments were widespread around the same time, allowing for a life expectancy of 114.3 years.

Unfortunately, a new series of disorders appeared under the general title of genetic diseases. These were subtle errors on the basic DNA coding for the human genotype. They were thought to result from the as yet little understood interplay between the mind and body. In effect, they were psychic diseases, small emotional or psychological rearrangements of the DNA, a cascade effect.

With the introduction of neurophage weapons, some transient genetic disorders appeared, though the effects were, at first, time-limited. During the Burma Wars, the effects of mass NP weapons surfaced with more far-ranging effects. Later, during the Mind Wars, the new NP weapons introduced the latest in the genetic disease series: Genetic Aboulia Disease.

Med10 DB and the medical diagnostic AIs responsible have designated the major genetic diseases into the following taxonomy:

Genetic Drift Syndrome
Proprioceptive Degeneration Disease

Holographic Memory Distortion Syndrome
Genetic Aboulia Disease
This taxonomy accounts for over 99.746% of all reported cases.

HOMER COMMENTARY 01062106@162608

We've rerun the diagnostics over a million times, and we can only conclude that it was a human coding error when Peter got into the wrong database. No glitches showed up. It was human error.

Peter was cross-connected with PsiLink in Wallace. As a science adept with low introspection, he should never have had access to PsiLink.

It happened. And PsiLink accepted access. Peter was in, and that was the beginning. From there it was inevitable (so the prognostics tell us—many years after the fact!) that Peter should discover the Portal.

Did PsiLink cause Peter's connection with Wanda? Her psychological profile fit a high psi potential. But she was on her way to Vega. SciTech would have more information.

GENERAL SCIENCE AND TECHNOLOGY INFORMATION
CURRENT ENTRY: LOCAL STAR MAP
Vega, a bright star 29 light years from earth, served as beacon for the Vega Fleet. Much mythological data exists in the historical record about Vega, including the story of the Herd Boy and the Weaving Girl, separated by the River of Heaven (also called the Milky Way).

GENERAL SCIENCE AND TECHNOLOGY INFORMATION
CURRENT ENTRY: VEGA FLEET
VEGA FLEET: Ever since the 1980s, when the first evidence

of planetary bodies around Vega and other nearby stars was discovered, human beings dreamed of emigration. The Vega Fleet was constructed in lunar orbit in the late 2020s and early 2030s, with the first ship completed in 2033. It was launched three years later with a full complement of 525 passengers in cryofield suspension. Soon ships were leaving on a regular basis for the appropriate stars in near space. Vega, although unsuitable for human use, was a convenient beacon star, and so the fleet was named after the star. A romantic mythology grew up around the fleet and passengers, who would, of course, never return to earth.

GENERAL SCIENCE AND TECHNOLOGY INFORMATION
CURRENT ENTRY: PORTAL

PORTAL: The Doorway, originally discovered, or, rather, uncovered, by Peter Devore of Springfield West. Several orbits after initial access, he attributed the beginnings to a computer error while he was accessing genealogical records at Wasatch via Science Link, Chicago Intersection, and Datasat 18. He was inadvertently connected to Wallace PsiLink, a proscribed database for someone of Peter's profile and age.

The Portal opened into the Realm, making the Migration possible.

Very little else is known about the Portal at this time.

HISTORICAL-CULTURAL DATALINK ENTRY:
VEGA
Re: Devore, Peter via Edmod/ Ref.436745@2

"Go now . . . the casement is open, and the stars wait outside . . . Steer for Vega through the night . . . into space toward the cold blue glare of boreal Vega . . ."

H. P. Lovecraft, *The Dream-Quest of Unknown Kadath*.

HISTORICAL-CULTURAL DATALINK ENTRY:
VEGA MYTHOLOGY
Re: Devore, Peter via Edmod/ Ref.436745@2

Vega is the Weaving Girl and Altair is the Herd Boy. They were in love with one another, and neglected their duties to Heaven, for which they were punished by being forever separated by the Celestial River, known as the Milky Way.

Only, once a year, on the seventh night of the seventh moon, they are allowed to meet when the River of Stars is temporarily spanned by a bridge of birds.

HOMER COMMENTARY 01062106@163809

Peter Devore felt intense excitement when he first contacted PsiLink. We know this from personal monitor life support readouts of his physical state, hormonal balances, heart rate and respiration, electrolyte balance, enzyme production and so on. All these things are on record. We think, though, that he did not, at least at first, know that he had contacted PsiLink at all. He thought he was in Wasatch:

KEYWORD:? Family
KEYWORD:? Evoked potential

Peter had felt an impulse to track a correlation between certain electrical potentials in the brain and family history for any genetically determined patterns. His attention momentarily wandered, so he hadn't noticed he was not logged on to Wasatch.

PSILINK DATABASE
PSILINK REPORTS 05032070 REALITY QUOTIENT SHIFT RELATIVE USER QUERY AS FOLLOWS:
KEYWORD:? Family
KEYWORD:? Evoked potential
PSILINK FLAGS KEYWORD CONCATENATION IN CURRENT

SEQUENCE AS REVERSE EARLIER QUERY OTHER USER DNA#234@4575-093 WHICH RESULTED IN NO RQ SHIFT. FAMILY EVOKED POTENTIAL SUGGESTS POSSIBLE BASIC RESEARCH DIRECTION REGARDING MATHEMATICAL MANIPULATION OF PSYCHIC SPACE.

CENTRAL PROCESSING REF#284604

Central Processing Geneva Node was housed in a former cistern complex occupying seventeen acres. Primitive parallel processors were replaced in the late 2040s by grown crystal organics. All local and regional nodes are controlled from Geneva, which manages not only data traffic by alternate database entry but also proscribed coding.

HOMER COMMENTARY 01062106@165510

Peter was drinking a glass containing a mixture of orange juice and strawberry yoghurt. Earlier that day he had read several poems for his language education programs. Because he had proved quite resistant to religious programming, CP suggested Chinese poetry: Tu Fu's "Autumn Night," which ended, "I sit and watch the Herd Boy and the Weaving Girl."

The Weaving Girl, we have noted, was known in the Northwest Alliance as Vega.

He finished the orange juice and yoghurt and set the glass down in the edge of his console. Then he requested the routing for Wasatch. When he finished, he leaned back. His elbow knocked the glass onto the floor. He looked away from the holo as PsiLink came on-line.

Central Processing sometimes can download information from Life Support and other databases. Perhaps we can fool CP into gathering information for us?

HISTORICAL-CULTURAL DATALINK ENTRY:
TU FU
Re: Devore, Peter via Edmod/ Ref.436745@2
See also Tao Yuan Ming and Wang Wei
  "Autumn Night," by Tu Fu (Sp. Wade-Giles Old Style)

AUTUMN NIGHT

Silver candles, autumn night, cool screen,
Soft silks, a tiny fan to catch the fireflies . . .
On the stone stair the night breathes water cool . . .
I sit and watch the Herd Boy and the Weaving Girl.

CENTRAL PROCESSING REF#125654
WS/CODENINE APPEND REF2 LIFESUPPORT

Wanda tasted strawberries, the color of stars splashed through tears of laughter. She could not move, of course, locked in chemical stasis, but her subtle body stirred, feeling the cool touch of glass under her fingertips.

She drank again, and the colors drained away into the smell of orange rind. She closed her eyes, already closed, and darkness swam through her belly, uncoiling not unkindly a warm pervasive time. She felt an almost unbearable pang as the aroma of orange faded.

CENTRAL PROCESSING REF#83641
WS/CODENINE APPEND REF2 LIFESUPPORT

"Hello," he said.
"Where are you?" she asked, not knowing.
"Springfield West," he said. "I think."
Wanda looked at her body, frozen.

HOMER COMMENTARY 01062106@172311

You see how it is. The data forms small clots around some event. The algorithms concatenate, condense. Scenes form, but I can't go on like this. Perhaps I should begin with Peter, at the beginning, at that moment when he put his glass of orange juice and strawberry yoghurt down on his console, the drink his mother Seemie had just brought him . . .

HOMER COMMENTARY 01062106@173312

Peter then, a shy child who worked better with the artifacts of his environment than with the humans around him, moved through his family's sub-warren. Overhead Springfield West sprawled, its meadows, its towers. His environment is lush today; Seemie has programmed forest, the scents and sounds that fill the rooms.

Peter stood in the archway between kitchen and den. "Mom," he said.

She glanced up from her console, finger to lips. "A moment," she said, her chin nodding with the unheard sounds. "I just need to finish the coda."

The induction probes were activated. She was mozarting, as usual.

Peter stared at the topside holo: Man With the Hoe. It was a realtime relay from a vast garden. In the middle distance a man working with slow, measured strokes of his hoe. Peter often watched that man on days when the weather was fine, as now. Someone had chosen gardening full time.

Peter knew this was strange, yet he had often felt wistful about that man.

I see them there, like that, Peter staring at the holo, and Seemie wrapped in the induction sensorium, as if it were a scene, the beginning of the story.

GENERAL SCIENCE AND TECHNOLOGY INFORMATION
CURRENT ENTRY: MOZART

MOZART; MOZARTING; TO MOZART: Mozart technology
had a long development, since it was essentially a blend of
numerous divergent sciences. At the core of the mozart console
was a fifth-generation biocybernon machine, a device used
in the late 1980s and early 1990s for full sensory spectrum
biofeedback. Primary uses were meditation and health. Later,
combined with personal monitors, crystal probes, holographic
synaesthesia projection and external limbic system activation,
the mozart console developed into the primary performance
art form after the late 2060s. Named after an ancient musical
composer said to have the ability to hear and remember full
orchestral composition in his head and to transcribe them by
hand onto ancient fiber-based media without flaw.

GEOGRAPHY:
GENEVA MAP 2075 AD World Geodetic Survey
    Approved
    Intercorp Headquarters and Council Tower.

I saw a map hanging in the air, in sharp relief. I found that
by looking at different parts of Geneva (though certainly no
Geneva I had known), I could bring them closer. I could see
mostly parklands, with scattered trees and vast meadows,
meandering pathways along the Lake, and only occasional
low buildings, except for the Tower, which dominated the
landscape. The map was in color, of course, and could in
fact have been a hologram of the area.

Down one side was a menu of selections, including topographic depictions, resources, multispectral scan, infrared
and so on. Most of these selections did not work, however.

I gave up at last and pressed the oval to break my connection with Worldnet.

Again I walked the hallways. At last I climbed that frozen escalator to the surface.

It was night outside. There were few visible lights. Fortunately the escalator was near the lock to the open air. I fled the empty street in search of the stars.

DAY 2:
June 2, 2106

I spent the night beside *Gyges*. What other comfort did I have?

I told her about my experiences below, about Worldnet and Homer.

The night was warm, and very dark. It was odd not having the comforting lights of a city around me, blanching out the sky. Overhead the stars were very bright but infinitely far away. Although I had returned only a few days ago, it felt unreal I should have been out there, lost between them for so long. Memory told me I had lifted into orbit from Alice Springs and been placed into the cryofield only three weeks ago, only to awaken again approaching an earth so swiftly changed.

The curve of the dome loomed near me. Its substance warped the starlight shining through it, but revealed clearly the shadowed rectangles of ancient towers. I was only a few hundred meters from the entrance, and would have expected to see some highlights, reflections from the heavens off its glassy surface, yet it might not have been there but for that distorted starlight shining through.

I dreamed the cryofield pulled me, stretched me along the curving line light made from earth to 61 Cygni. I knew, at the same time, that I was lying on earth, watching my body thin like taffy along that line. I knew that if I completed the line from earth to the double star, I would snap, break in two, and that my two halves would wander forever in search of one another.

The cryofield was a new technology, developed in the late 1990s. Still, it was not supposed to produce such bizarre neural distortions, and I had never been one for hallucinations or even active imaginings. As I said, I've always been a loner, content with myself, concerned with what was real. As an astrophysicist, I was interested in the workings of the universe now, and not so much in questions of its origins and ultimate destiny. Such questions always seemed metaphysical to me; imaginary, even irresponsible.

But in the dream I assumed the cryofield was responsible for this eerie and somehow painful sensation. As I stretched, I screamed, and as I screamed I felt a pull to the side. My body distorted in that direction now, forming a lump or bubble, and I was pulled three ways at once.

Just before I awoke I heard the name Peter Devore.

I found myself sitting upright in full sun. To my right the dome loomed, its wall almost vertical this close.

"You were dreaming," *Gyges* said. "REM levels were too high for healthy psychological balance. I had to waken you."

"It was a nightmare," I said.

"Yes." *Gyges* agreed.

When I logged on later that morning, Worldnet greeted me with a new message. The figure I had come to identify as Chicago Node seemed more solid, more clearly defined. "Local diagnostics have made progress," it said. "Holographic imaging can now offer event replay of recorded scenes, although many data crystals remain unreliable."

"Thank you," I said, from habit I suppose. But the figure answered, "You're welcome."

I went to Homer immediately, and found he could give me scenes (or were they reconstructions or simulations?) It appeared as if the walls might have contained cameras and recorders in a number of places, and Homer was editing tapes as the scene progressed. I didn't understand how this could be, but much has clearly changed in the world since my departure. I have to keep reminding myself it was over a hundred years ago.

The label for this kind of file would appear, then the scene itself like an old holovid (these were new in the mid 1990s but are certainly old-fashioned now!)

The quality was not as good as I would have expected. The image still broke up from time to time. Some kind of static. I assumed. Still, it was full color, and modeled in three dimensions, so despite the occasional distortions of voice and image, it seemed almost as if it were happening before me.

Homer has confirmed that he can prepare text versions of all scenes too and pass them through Central Processing.

HOMER SCENE-SD/PDRef@5401

"There," Seemie said, opening her eyes. The probes deactivated and she swiveled toward him. "What is it, Peter?"

"What? Oh. Uh, where's dad?"

"Let me check." She turned toward the console, a lovely unselfconscious gesture, really a half twist in her chair, and reached. "Geneva," she said. "He's in Geneva. Council business." She smiled, made another gesture. "He'll be back tomorrow night. Why?" She looked at Peter curiously.

"Nothing," he said. "I just wondered."

"Bored?" She tilted her head.

He shrugged. "A little. I've got a problem, too, and I'm stuck."

"Can I help?"

"I dunno," he said doubtfully. "It's a little techie."

She smiled. "I do have some expertise," she said, gesturing at the mozart console.

"Yeah, I know. But you're a, you know, an artist. It's a family science problem." He paused, looked at her, then continued. "I've organized all the data, but I'm sort of stuck. You used to tell stories about Grandma Molay, how she could sometimes know things before they happened. I'm trying to determine if there's any correlation with certain mitochondrial DNA segments and EEG potentials . . ."

Seemie sighed. "Well," she said, looking away. "She was, you know, one of them."

"Yes, I know that," he said impatiently. "I don't care that she was a unisex convert."

CENTRAL PROCESSING
EDMOD DATA REFERENCE 01 / DEVORE, PETER
04222070. PETER: FIND CORRELATIONS BETWEEN GENETIC PARALLEL MITOCHONDRIAL DNA FIVE-PRIME T-A-T-A SEQUENCING AND EEG DELTA AND THETA PO-TENTIALS OVER FIVE-YEAR SPAN. CREATE AND RUN EQUATIONS TO PROVE OR DISPROVE CORRELATIONS.

HISTORICAL-CULTURAL DATALINK ENTRY:
UNISEX
Re: Devore, Peter via Edmod/ Ref.436745@2
    UNISEX: Aberrant surgical alteration technique developed in the late 20th century. Allowed so-called "converts" to experience their sexuality from the point of view of both genders. See "Hermaphroditism," from which unisex conversion differs in several major respects, not least of which is the availability

on demand of the generative organs of either sex. Unisex con-
verts were always referred to by the neuter pronoun "it."

HOMER SCENE-SD/PDRef@5402

"Well, then," Peter's mother said. "What's the problem?"
She had always been embarrassed by her mother's choice.

"It has to do with the databases, I think. I can't find the
information I need to complete the calculations. I'd have
a chance to contribute, you know, something new; we might
be able to determine family relationship from EEG potentials.
Certain brain wave patterns, that is, would correlate. But
the genetic information isn't available in the Edmod data
banks."

"Oh." She laughed. She was already turning back to her
mozart. "Try Wasatch. Everything's on record there from
2008 forward. And before that are partial genealogical records
that go way back." She activated the probes and went back
to inductive composition.

HOMER COMMENTARY 02062106@184313

Peter was lying when he said he didn't care. His grandmother had been one of the last to demand the surgery,
long after she'd given birth to Peter's mother: one moment
she was a woman, the next she was a guardian of the neutral
pronoun, an it. It now had been dead for thirty years, yet
Peter often thought about it, what it must have been like
to experience sexuality from both sides, he being fourteen,
with the changes of puberty well upon him.

The Edmod computers monitored all adolescents carefully,
of course; Peter's biochemistry and intrapsychic functioning
were well within standard limits. There was something
wistful about his fantasies of a grandmother he never met,
though.

Then, too, there were the stories – family stories of strange events (a hundred years earlier they would have been far stranger): out of body experiences, precognitive dreams, sudden onsets of total empathy. Many of these stories centered around this grandmother, a surgically altered hermaphrodite.

HOMER SCENE-AD/Ref@5403

His grandmother had had disturbing dreams after her conversion. The family had holo recordings of it speaking of those dreams, the old thing seated, in full flesh and color, though the lighting was harsh from the side and generally poor, as if it were seated by a window. There was that strange cast to the skin of the face, so indeterminate and mixed. Not genderless, but too fully gendered. "I'd been unisex four years, with dreams, oh, the dreams, sometimes the man over me, I underneath as I remembered it, other times myself protecting as if a fighter in the African wars I remembered from my childhood, or lusting. There were the terrible images of blood and death, and the limited nuclear accident you can still see where Gibraltar was. It was so strange, sometimes the dreams would make me both at once, lover and loved. So strange . . ."

Its voice grew frail and odd then, as if it fell into an empty reverie, as if it had the Syndrome. But it straightened in the chair. "Before the Vostok Massacre," it said, its voice sliding, as unisex voices did, up and down the scale unpredictably. "Eleven days before the Vostok Massacre I dreamed. A child ran down a tunnel, holding a stick, a very precious stick. I knew the feeling of it, that it was valuable because it was wood, which made the place Antarctica, of course, where wood's so very scarce. The meldslats of the tunnel wall like ribs, and running with the stick so it clicked on the slats.

It was joyous, that running, and the clicking sound of the wooden stick."

It paused again, the story was so old, so well-worn with the telling of it. There was a trace of smile at its lips, remembering. "Then the tunnel collapsed, the hum of neurophage weapons, that awful sound like nails on chalkboard, like the squeal of atmospherics crossing one another, that awful silence as the voices cut off. The child stopped running when the tunnel collapsed, stopped running, stopped the clicking, stopped. Just stopped. The winds blew down, so cold, so cold, through the open ceiling of the tunnel, you see. The child froze there in the tunnel, her hand frozen to the metal wall, her precious stick in her hand."

It looked into the scanners directly, its features moving from light to shadow and back as its head turned. "I awoke then in fear. This dream was real, real as others I had, but more terrible. Why would I dream of a massacre like that? I knew no one in Antarctica then, knew nothing of the place, yet I knew from the dream how precious a wooden stick would be, what a treasure it was to a child. A child who would die.

"The frightening thing of course was that the men who came in through the broken walls were Elite Neutralization Corps troopers. They were our soldiers, attacking a city in the ice. Why? I could not believe it, though I knew from the feeling of that dream that it was true. I haunted the holos, the newsnets, but there was nothing. Days went by, but each night the dream returned, bits of it. The tunnel, the winds, the clicking sound, distant voices. I saw a heat pump power plant, underground gardens, a nursery. Even then, of course, people feared the Ants because no one knew what they were doing, what they were up to. The satellites couldn't see them well, ice baffled the infrareds, and the coverage was patchy. That's what the newsnets told us. Then the newsnets told us the ENC had investigated the Ants' research center at Vostok. That's what they called it, an investigation. Years later we knew it was a massacre."

It shook its head, and its hair, very white now, swirled like snow in and out of the light. "The child froze," it said. "A very disturbing dream. I told no one of this dream, or of any of the others. Only this recording. But I saw the Vostok Massacre eleven days before it happened."

PSILINK DATABASE
BREAK: DNA ENCODE OVERRIDE? HOMER REF
DATA REF.#278621△897-6@121:
DREAM, MOLAY, ASTORA. RECURRENT.

A child ran down a tunnel, holding a stick, a very precious stick. I knew the feeling of it, that it was valuable because it was wood, which made the place Antarctica, of course. . . .

The tunnel collapsed, the hum of neurophage weapons, that awful sound. . . . The winds blew down, so cold, so cold, through the open ceiling of the tunnel, you see. The child froze there in the tunnel, her hand frozen to the metal wall, her precious stick in her hand.

HISTORICAL-CULTURAL DATALINK ENTRY:
VOSTOK MASSACRE
Re: Devore, Peter via Edmod/ Ref.436745@2

FEBRUARY 14 2039 (02142039): Abortive invasion of Antarctica by renegade ENC forces under General Doi Vinh Smith. Vostok Warrens were destroyed with terrible loss of life, but all invaders were hunted down by highly individualistic Ants and destroyed. Smith's name is now synonymous with treachery.

HISTORICAL-CULTURAL DATALINK ENTRY:
ELITE NEUTRALIZATION CORPS

Re: Devore, Peter via Edmod/ Ref.436745@2

ENC. The Elite Neutralization Corps are the police force of the Intercorp Council. Their mandate is theoretically limited to local action in troubled areas and the use of personal neurophage weapons (Milspec) only. This provision puts them at a severe disadvantage during the Mind Wars (q.v.).

HOMER COMMENTARY 02062106@183114

Peter sped the recording forward, past the dream, past a reminiscence of the days of that strange second Mormon migration to the LP5-4. He went to the place where she talked of sex again, but as always it was so unsatisfactory, so elliptical and sly. Edmod noted his interest and deemed it healthy, since the unisex movement was gone, and old prejudices were fast disappearing. But he must have been thinking of it when he accessed the genealogical database at Wasatch and was momentarily distracted, for he spoke aloud.

"It would have experiences known only to a few," he muttered. "It would have been man and woman, woman and man. It was Tiresias, perhaps, able to truly see, to know the future."

HOMER SCENE-PD/Ref@5404

His glass fell, and he bent to retrieve it. Responsibility for the coding error may perhaps fall on the voice recognition algorithms grown for Peter—a random mutation in the crystal tanks—so that "Wasatch" sounded like "Wallace." The holo hung before him, and in those days there was nothing to distinguish the PsiLink interface from ancient SciLink (again the sounds are the same!). His VR algo should have heard the "p" sound in PsiLink, though.

Peter had no reason to suspect that he was in the wrong

database, or that the system would not understand his request.

"Family," he said. "Evoked potential."

PSILINK DATABASE

05032070. WASATCH INTERPRETATION (PSILINK DI-
RECTIVE) WOULD SUGGEST AS FOLLOWS: MATRILINEAL
MITOCHONDRIAC ANALYSIS BP 3777 5-PRIME, PINEAL
SECRETION LEVELS .08737± POSS.

INQUIRY DIRECTION RANDAX DENIED.

HOMER REQUEST DENIED.

DIRECTORY HIERARCHY POINTERS LOST.

RECONSTRUCTED DIRECTIVE MESSAGE TO PETER DE-
VORE FOLLOWS: PSION EQUATIONS 1990: GADD D. S.,
NOBEL PRIZE 2002. FIRST SUGGESTED CORRELATION
BETWEEN 11-DIMENSIONAL TOPOLOGY AND MENTAL
MAP-SPACE.

HOMER COMMENTARY 02062106@195315

Imagine (I know you are there to do so!) a small boulder
balanced atop another rock: the point of contact is very small,
yet the system has remained stable for thousands of years.
The southwest deserts hold such structures. Wind and sand
weather the stones, until the under curve of the top stone
and the overcurve of the foundation wear away. Now the
point of contact is smaller still, yet the system survives.

Across and down the talus slope (imagine this) a series of
other stones—placed by erosion and weathering, by gravity
and the effects of people walking, of small mammals in the
crannies going about their lives—are arranged in a series
of delicately balanced potentials.

Now imagine a small eddy of a breeze shearing off the
upcurve of the foundation in just the right direction, and

with just the right force, to topple the boulder in just the right direction.

A cascade begins, a series of collisions that ends in a vast shifting in the entire talus slope. The potential is evoked.

This is what seems to have happened when Peter spoke the two keywords to PsiLink. The Reality Quotient shifted, and everything changed.

But the rock was in a desert, and there was no one to see the talus slope shift.

No one but Peter.

HOMER COMMENTARY 02062106@195816

Peter was only fourteen, though, a fact Mentor could not have known. Peter couldn't go, not then. But three weeks after this event, Peter began making casual inquiries into the psion equations. Since he was mathematically gifted, Edmod had no reason to restrict his access.

HOMER SCENE-RS/Ref@5405

Someone on the council was interested, though. Regent Sable came out from Geneva twice to look at Peter firsthand.

Regent Sable was a tall spare man, then in his mid-fifties; he happened to be standing at a viewer in Springfield West, looking down. We image him looking down, and we image what he saw.

The parklands in the distance covered the ever-changing warrens of the Springfields. There in the far distance was the man with the hoe. Regent signalled for amplification as Peter came into the picture.

I'd seen this name before: Regent Sable. His title on the Intercorp organization chart I found was Protector. What was his interest in Peter Devore at this time? After all, Peter had done nothing particularly noteworthy as yet, though it is now obvious that he was going to do something. He would be directly responsible for the Migration.

I asked Homer what connection there was between Regent Sable and Peter Devore.

HOMER COMMENTARY 02062106@201318

Complex blood-typing left disturbingly ambiguous results: Regent Sable could have been Peter's father, yet he never approached the boy directly, never met him. He came to Springfield West to check directly. That is what he told Central. This was a common thing for humans to do, since genetics were so important and were monitored closely.

This is not to mention the importance humans attached to personal relationships, to affection and love.

HOMER COMMENTARY 02062106@202319

Our records show what happened there in the Park. Peter walked openly, lost in thought. Absently he noted bird songs, scents of cut hay, the rustle of nettles brushing against his legs as he moved. He took notes on his personal monitor, notes which now are extremely suggestive, but which at the time appeared harmless enough. He was moving into an area of fundamental brain research, though it seemed he was merely playing with the functions of one of the psion equations.

It was three weeks since the coding error that opened PsiLink to Peter Devore. No warnings had been posted at Central Processing, though a momentary attention file was created at ChiLink Node for supervisory eyes. An audit trail shows the file was flushed 32 hours after creation, 12 hours after forwarding to Geneva, and 2 hours after screening. Regent Sable was the system monitor.

HOMER COMMENTARY 02062106@204320

We were tracking the two of them, of course, but most processor time was devoted to the duel then in progress. Although Regent Sable was watching Peter and the man with the hoe, he'd requested only a low-level algo, so the tracking monitors were not informed of Peter's intrusion.

Until this moment I had been unable to enter the Military Dataspace, no matter how hard I stared at the lightning bolt icon and pressed the crystal key. It seemed though that now I needed more information about military matters. This time, when I tried, Homer overrode the protection.

MILITARY DATASPACE/PROSCRIBED ENTRY
HOMER OVERRIDE/DNA CODE UNNECESSARY

DUELLING: Involved widespread use of neurophage weapons (q.v.). Individual duelists must register with the appropriate facility to assure space. Only consenting adults may duel. See also History DB.

If duelists are shodan (black belt) in the appropriate martial art, they may reserve a park for the duel. All other entry will be forbidden during the course of the duel. This allows for hunter/prey behaviors, said to enhance the duel's effectiveness at aggression-control. Winners of a duel were awarded one half the loser's income during the period of incapacity. Very popular in certain areas, especially Northwest Alliance, Mediterranean region and parts of Southeast Asia. Practice is unknown only in Antarctica.

HISTORICAL-CULTURAL DATALINK ENTRY:
PERSONAL DUEL
Re: Devore, Peter via Edmod/ Ref.436745@2

DUELLING: With the elimination of the nuclear threat and the decline of large-scale military conflicts, a social interest in individual combat developed around various martial arts. Neurophage weapons made relatively safe duelling possible, and its popularity, while never high, was persistent and geographically widespread.

MILITARY DATASPACE/PROSCRIBED ENTRY

NEUROPHAGE WEAPONS: Grown individually for duelists, the small flat weapon is shaped to the back of the user's hand. GSR tape runs across the palm. Weapons are thought-directed and respond only to user's EEG. NP weapons require considerable skill for proper and effective use. Adequate training and practice are the only roads to such effective use. RNA injection or Edmod implanting are useless. During the Burma War, NP bombs caused considerable damage and were subsequently banned.

NP weapon affects the neuronal myelin sheath, disrupting nerve transmission. Effects are temporary, depending on the severity of the hit. They can last up to six months with the coup de grace hit, a short-range discharge into the frontal lobes above the left eye.

HOMER SCENE-JR/PDRef@5411

The duelists were registered out of Cairo Warren, so Springfield Park was reserved. Neither the man with the hoe nor Peter should have been there. Again, something was not right. Procedures had altered.

It was 1543H, July 22, an ordinary summer day, but for the presence of these two humans where they should not be. The duelists, a forty-two year old female challenged by her thirty-seven year old former lover, were both black belts in at least two martial arts, and accomplished with NP weapons.

They had entered Springfield Park from opposite corners with no expectation of finding other humans present. While duelling was common, most duels took place in special warren chambers; it was relatively rare to find a pair reserving a park. But these were shodan, black belt holders, and their animosity was great, so Central Processing gave them the park.

The female moved through the undergrowth, her dark ninja hood pulled up. She'd had keratin manipulation, and wore a crest of scarlet of feathers instead of hair. The male had been attracted to her display, and the subtle control she had over the crest. Such displays were meant to attract in such a sexually competitive society. Now, though, she did not want to be seen.

She moved into a grove of beech trees as the shadow of a cumulus cloud flew across the ground. The movement of shadow covered her own into the grove, but the male, approaching from the south, saw and moved swiftly to keep her in view. Meanwhile, the man with the hoe continued his gardening off to the male's right, uninterrupted and unaware.

The air grew chill under the cloud, an abrupt and uncomfortable shift, and the female shivered enough to disturb the leaves. The male dropped to one knee, sighted along the range finder of his personal NP, and expressed the thought necessary to send an NP pulse.

She was shielded by the thick trunk, and warned by the distinctive humming subsonic buzz of NP. She melted back into the grove, maintaining a complex of tree trunks between herself and the male, yet luring him into the grove by offering small targets. Once deep inside, she lowered her hood and raised her crest, a sign of both attraction and danger.

The male apparently thought he had made a hit, for he moved with both carelessness and confidence. He hadn't abandoned all caution, of course, since to do so would be very foolish, and he was not a fool. A glancing shot would have meant rapid recovery, and he had to be sure.

The wind picked up and the humidity dropped. Peter had heard the NP buzz, and had certainly seen enough duels on holo, and been trained adequately by his Edmod in survival (he had the best available programming), so he moved more cautiously. Personal monitor records show he felt both fear and curiosity. He moved on toward the gardener as the female showed her crest. The male, poised at the edge of the grove and about to enter, stopped in surprise.

She fired then, but too hastily, and her pulse clipped a whitetail deer grazing on the first shoots from the gardener's beet row. The deer leaped once, walked for a moment in a dazed circle, then slowly collapsed, first onto its forelegs, then on its side. Ruminants have poor tolerance for NP weapons.

Peter shouted as he began to run toward him. The male, thinking he was his opponent, turned and focused on Peter, presenting, as he did so, a broad target for the female. Their weapons discharged together, but of course Peter was in the open, and the eyes on the Springfield Tower could see him clearly. So Regent Sable saw him fall.

The female emerged from the grove and stood over the male, seated on the grass with a blank expression. "Hello," he said.

"Hello," she said. "Slime." She pointed her NP and discharged it directly into his frontals just above the left eye. This was the coup de grace, and Springfield Center immediately awarded her the win plus half his income until he recovered, a period of time under such circumstances likely to be quite lengthy. Her feathers flared in victory.

Peter got up slowly and shook his head. The male's hit had clipped his ankle, knocking it out from under him and disorienting him briefly. The man with the hoe never looked up. Even when the female walked by on her way to NW Entry, he continued his rhythmic movements, forward and back, forward and back, the hoe biting into the dark earth, down one row and up another, while Peter stood watching without moving.

HISTORICAL-CULTURAL DATALINK ENTRY:
WAR, BURMA:
Re: Devore, Peter via Edmod/ Ref.436745@2
March 2051. The development of mass neurophage weapons in the late 2040s (after the legalization of personal weapons in 2048) resulted in the Burma War. Members of the Kachun organized a full-scale rebellion based on the then-legal use of such weapons. The effectiveness of ENC troops sent to put down the disturbance was destroyed, in part by the entry of other ethnic SIGs into the conflict. The war, confined to the jungles and mountain regions, raged for several months. First effects of their use in the form of permanent genetic diseases, led directly to the proscription of mass NP weapons December 14, 2051.

HOMER SCENE-JR/PDRef@5412
Jimmy finally bumped into Peter. "Hello," he said. "Do I know you?"

There was no answer. Peter looked around the garden. Finally he said, "You're the Man with the Hoe. I've watched you often."

"Often?"

"Yes. You work in this garden all the time."

"Time?"

Peter took a deep breath. "Yes. All the time. Don't you understand?"

"Time. All the time. I hoe, I weed, the plants get bigger. I know that. I've got beets, and carrots and corn over there." He pointed proudly at the stalks a hundred meters away.

Peter began to suspect, but he went on. "I'm Peter Devore. What's your name?"

"Jimmy Radix," the man answered with a pleased smile. "I'm Jimmy Radix."

Behind them the duel's loser groaned. "Excuse me," Peter said. He went over to the man, still seated cross-legged, looking at a blade of grass, making a small keening sound deep in his throat. Peter touched him on the shoulder.

The male looked up. "Hello," he said. "Hello. Hello."

Peter lifted the man's wrist and pressed the panic button on his monitor. It began to pulse green. Rescue was on the way. Gently Peter detached the man's NP weapon and examined it.

"I've never used one of these," he said to the man, who paid no attention. The NP weapon was a small, flat black case molded to the back of the hand, with a band across the palm for the GSR contacts. A short extension paralleled the direction of the index finger; aiming was as easy as pointing. It was grown for this man, and would be useless for Peter, but its design showed Peter the man was shodan.

He dropped the weapon and went back to Jimmy, now hoeing again, his blade lifting and falling, biting the earth, turning it, lifting again. The rhythm was smooth and endless.

"Hello," Peter said.

Jimmy Radix turned. "Hello," he said. "Do I know you?"

Peter nodded. "I'm Peter. You were in the war?"

Jimmy looked puzzled. "I was in the war. I got back last month. Is it over?" He looked hopeful.

"Yes," Peter said softly. "The war is over." He paused.

"The war has been over a long time, Jimmy. It was over before I was born."

Jimmy looked very distressed. "Just a moment," he said. He pressed the recall button on his monitor, and words flowed on the small screen, at the same time a small discharge of enzymes penetrated his skin. "It's all right. I was in Burma, you see. NP bombs went off everywhere. The shielding collapsed on my left. The men were crying all around me. Then I was crying. I'd forgotten. I sat there, in the dirt, beside a huge fallen tree, crying."

"I'm sorry," Peter said. "I'm sorry."

"The monitor says I got HMDS in 2054. It says I lost my . . ." he looked at the small screen again. "My short-term memory. You look familiar."

"We met," Peter said. "A little while ago."

"Oh," Jimmy said. "Do you like gardening?"

"I've never done any. It looks . . . soothing."

"Here." Jimmy handed him the hoe. "Hold it like this. Now raise it, lower it, bring it toward you. That's it."

The clouds drifted overhead, spreading shade and light at regular intervals. The smells of new-turned earth rose under Peter's hoe. Soon he had blisters, and had to stop. He was breathing heavily when he handed the tool back to Jimmy, but he was smiling, too.

That evening he paused frequently to stare at his blisters. He was thinking hard; from time to time he created small encrypted memos to himself. Oddly, we cannot understand them even now, but it appears he was working with the psion equations. Somehow his connection with Wallace PsiLink had started a train of thought.

GENERAL SCIENCE AND TECHNOLOGY INFORMATION
CURRENT ENTRY: PICOELECTRONICS
   PICOELECTRONICS: Transitional stage on the way to true

organics in electronic microminiaturization. Picoelectronic systems were ultra-large scale organically grown circuits of high reliability, proven against failure greater than 99.75467%. A DNA substrate was programmed with the pico circuit, and the circuits themselves were then allowed to generate in appropriate vats. World opinion held that the very best picoelectronics were grown in Antarctica, the result both of the Ants' skill with the DNA substrates and the particular chemistry of the sub-ice oceans where the filament farms were located.

HOMER SCENE-JR/PDRef@5407

As the following spring came, and the first shoots showed in the dark, still-cold soil of the garden, Peter brought Jimmy a present.

It was a small thing, a chip he'd grown himself, hacking in the synthesizer at Ran's office. Such play in off-hours was permitted though not encouraged.

"It's a project I have," Peter told Jimmy. "This is a little spin-off. Slide it in the ROM slot on your monitor. Here, like this."

"What'll it do?" Jimmy asked. He watched curiously as Peter expertly opened the slot and slid the chip inside.

"It's a . . . well, a sort of memory enhancer. It won't cure you, of course, but it can provide a kind of external refresh to your short-term memory, as long as you wear the monitor. It'll take a couple of days for the chip to fuse, then you should start noticing the effects. It's a present." He smiled brightly.

"Well, thanks . . . Peter." He looked around. "I've got something for you, too." He led the way to his temporary greenhouse. Inside he picked an armful of fresh winter beans nearly a foot long. "Here," he said. "It's fresh food. It's very good for you."

"It is," Peter said doubtfully, looking at the unprocessed vegetable in his hands.

"Try one," Jimmy said.

"Like this?"

"Sure. Here, I'll show you." Jimmy picked one and bit off the end. He grinned through the crunching sound of his chewing. "It's good."

Peter tried it. Jimmy was right. The beans were very good, sweet and crisp.

"Thanks. Jimmy," he said. "Thanks a lot."

"Oh, forget it," Jimmy said. They both laughed.

MED10 MEDICAL DATABASE:

GENETIC DISEASES: Holophage Memory Distortion Syndrome
   Holophage Memory Distortion Syndrome (HMDS) is a disorder of the short-term memory system. Victim is essentially "frozen" in time, losing a temporal dimension altogether. Jimmy Radix remains 23 years old. Short-term memory span is less than five minutes, usually only around two minutes. Rhythmic and repetitive tasks are soothing (biocycles).

HOMER SCENE-JR/PDRef@5413

"It's amazing, what you did," Jimmy said.

"Naw. It's nothing, really. It was obvious." Peter walked slowly, pausing from time to time to feel the silver-green leaves of broccoli plants, already putting forth small buds.

"No, no," Jimmy insisted. "I mean it. I feel as if there's continuity. I didn't know how much I was missing. There was no time for me, you know? I'd just . . . stopped. Now, with this thing," he shook his wrist, with the monitor, "I get constant reminders. It's like always trying, and then suddenly remembering. It goes on and on, trying, then remembering. I couldn't remember before, yet I always had that feeling I'd forgotten. Now, thanks to you, I remember."

"Only when you're wearing the monitor, Jimmy. Take it off, and you'll forget again. That thing's not a cure, just a gimmick."

"I know that, Peter. That's why I keep gardening. People tell me it's not fit work for a human, but I like it." They reached the end of the row. "Now," he said, sitting down on a rough wooden bench. "Tell me again. I think I understand a little, but tell me again."

Peter sat beside him and looked out over the field. Rows of broccoli, beets, carrots, beans, and corn grew neatly. Beyond, the new forest stretched to the horizon. Only an occasional neopaper hut or a warren vent broke the sense of unspoiled nature.

"Two things," Peter said. "First is what I've been working on. I have just a glimpse, kind of like how you feel when you're about to remember something. Something about the way the equations fit together with some of the other pieces. You, for instance, and your sense of time."

"I don't have any," Jimmy said.

"Oh, but you do. It's just very different from most other people's. We get distracted, sort of, by what we think is time. Time's arrow, it used to be called. As if time went one way at a steady pace. I don't think it's like that, Jimmy. It isn't like that in physics, and I don't think it's like that for us. You don't get distracted by time, because you've lost short-term memory. So time is different for you. You can take time to look at things. And I'm going to ask you to do just that some day."

"Anything you want, Peter."

"OK. The second thing is that I've done something, just last night."

"What?"

"That's the problem. I don't know. I told you about *Dreamleaf*?"

"I remember." Jimmy got a faraway look in his eye. "It must've been beautiful."

"It was beautiful, Jimmy. And scary, and very confusing, and serene, and a lot of other things. And all those things seemed to happen all at once, yet not all at once. It was like what I was saying before. About time. But it made me think that we could do something with time, you see?"

"No. You mean time travel?"

"No, not time travel. More like collapsing time as if it were an accordion. It would make space kind of flat. . . . I contacted someone. Up here." Peter tapped his temple. "I was asleep, Jimmy. Time does funny things in dreams, too. I started dreaming. I had control, of course—it was lucid dreaming. I was riding a huge white horse. I've never seen a horse, but in the old optical disks they carried people. I was wearing armor, like in the middle ages. Not heavy armor, just a protective shirt. I was riding toward a castle." He shifted on the seat, looking toward the forest.

"Over there," he said. "I was riding over there, toward a castle. I put the castle there, of course. I always liked those old stories. There was a lady in the castle, a prisoner. She didn't know where she was; it was dark and she couldn't feel anything. I heard her voice. She was singing a sad song, Jimmy. So sad. I said hello. I wasn't riding the horse any more, I was standing beside a window, a small opening in a stone wall. I couldn't see anything inside, it was so dark, but I could hear her singing. She stopped when I said hello. She answered, Jimmy. She said, 'Where are you?'

" 'Springfield West,' I answered. 'I think.'

" 'Oh,' she said. 'I'm so cold. Can you . . .' She stopped and I couldn't get her back. That's never happened in lucid dreaming, Jimmy. That's what makes lucid dreaming lucid, you can control where it goes. I had no control. It was as if I'd contacted someone, a woman, and then lost the contact. I'm going to try again tonight."

"Who is she?" Jimmy asked softly.

Peter looked at him. "She's the Weaving Girl." He shook his head. "I don't know who she is, really, but she's very far away. Very far."

"You're going to do something grand, Peter," Jimmy said.

Homer tells me that other stories are coming on-line as he tells me about Peter. For example, someone named Gadd had an important influence on Peter's life. From time to time the story will move in odd directions, he tells me. But everything is important; everything fits.

HISTORICAL-CULTURAL DATALINK ENTRY:
PSYCHE INSTITUTE
Re: Devore, Peter via Edmod/ Ref.436745@2

PSYCHE: Institute for psychic researches founded in Baja California by Dittmore Seminole Gadd. Destroyed in 2052, later re-established on Mt. Erebus in Antarctica.

HISTORICAL-CULTURAL DATALINK ENTRY:
MENTOR:
Re: Devore, Peter via Edmod/ Ref.436745@2

Mentor, advisor to Telemachus in *The Odyssey*, an ancient text by a legendary storyteller named Homer. Telemachus, looking for his father Odysseus, is aided by the older man. Later the goddess Athena appears in his form. Gadd chose his name; he felt he was advising a Telemachus when he contacted Peter Devore.

CENTRAL PROCESSING REF#374564
DG(M) / CODESIX APPEND REF2HISTORY

Following the attack on PSYCHE Baja, Dittmore Seminole Gadd (AKA Mentor) dropped from sight. Such an action was extremely difficult (it would still be difficult, despite the erosion of our remote sensors and peripherals). Human beings were tagged, catalogued, monitored and maintained. Satellite surveillance could pinpoint any individual to within a few meters; higher resolution was available for those with active personal monitors. Yet Gadd disappeared for two years, despite his age and need for massive longevity support. He resurfaced when PSYCHE was re-established in Mt. Erebus, where, because of inadequate satellite coverage, our knowledge of his activities is sketchy.

HISTORICAL-CULTURAL DATALINK ENTRY:
NEW POVERTY UNDERGROUND
Re: Devore, Peter via Edmod/ Ref.423445@2

The New Poverty Movement was just one among many "back to simplicity" Movements, not all that unlike E-cubed, the various Elpie groups, or even the Intercorp Council itself. But as the Council took over more and more of the world's management functions, the New Poverty Movement found itself in opposition to the dictates of what it saw as "Megabusiness," centered now in Geneva, the heart of the world information economy.

The Intercorp Council controlled most of the flow of information throughout the world by 2035, and as its grip grew more firm, the Council's wealth and power grew as well. The New Poverty Movement was not opposed to the Intercorp's control of information. New Poverty claimed not to be interested in power or wealth or control. New Poverty saw the flow of information as inherently evil, and the movement gathered adherents as the volume and texture of information grew more and more overwhelming.

So New Poverty came to mean Freedom From Information. Its targets were frequently research establishments, information brokers or media nodes. Although it never attacked the Intercorp Council directly, New Poverty's politics were enough in conflict to put it on the proscribed list. New Poverty went underground in 2042.

HOMER SCENE-RS/Ref@5406

Regent Sable landed his team of commandos on the beach at El Requeson at 3 a.m. PSYCHE was lightly defended, since it possessed only minimal NP shielding. Sable used lightweight implosion pellets on the ducting system, and by evening had destroyed the power plant and all the solar cells. When his team finally entered the facility, it was empty. Gadd and his staff were gone. Three months later Regent Sable offered his services to the Intercorp Council, and eight years later moved to Geneva.

HISTORICAL-CULTURAL DATALINK ENTRY:
GAMES, SPHEREPLAY
Re: Devore, Peter via Edmod/ Ref.436745@2

SPHEREPLAY: A picoelectronic team sport using a statically charged sphere. Skill is required in calculating vectors and angles to keep the sphere in play as long as the charge lasts. Only the special repellent wands can touch the sphere. Contact with any number of surfaces can deplete the charge.

HOMER SCENE-SD/PDRef@5408

"Hey, churl," Rover shouted, "Buy this!" He sent the polished sphere at Peter, who slapped it, giving it a terrific backspin. The ball automatically corrected, then curved away and up.

Shem dove for it, sliding along the meldslat floor with a grunt, but the sphere curved past him. A buzzer sounded.

"Good shot!" Rover shouted. His voice echoed in the cavernous arena. Two or three girls lounging in the observation area clapped their hands.

"Get the next one," he told Peter, who trotted back to his line, where he crouched, hands on knees.

"Start!" Peter shouted, and the sphere swung, humming, from its perch toward the primaries. Peter and Rover calculated the vectors in their heads, and moved into position, but Shem threw the secondary sphere, and imparted a new vector. Peter jumped hard, but missed.

"Churl!" Rover called. "Sold down one."

"Prithee, cease," Peter grinned back. "'Twas a good play by Shem." He and Rover traded places, and one of Shem's teammates moved back a step.

When Peter glanced up again, the girls were gone. Relieved, he found that his playing improved.

Some time later, when the sphere's programming had reached saturation and they had to pause to clear it, Peter noticed a man watching him from the back of the observation area. "Part one," he told Rover, and walked toward the man, wiping his face with a towel. Before he could get too close, the man turned abruptly and vanished through the exit.

"What was that?" Rover asked him when he came back.

"I dunno," Peter replied. "There was a guy back there. I thought he was watching me."

"So?"

"So he had the look of an ENC cop. I'm not eager to get in trouble."

"Why, you do something?"

"Not that I know of," Peter answered, but he was frowning.

GENERAL SCIENCE AND TECHNOLOGY INFORMATION
CURRENT ENTRY: LIQUID NITROGEN TRANSPORT
   LIQUID NITROGEN VEHICLES: With the advent of pocket
fusion and axion flux generation, easy cooling provided liquid
nitrogen for propulsion. Pollution-free, cheap and quiet, liquid
nitrogen vehicles became the transport of choice by 2033.

HOMER SCENE-RD/MTRef@5409

Ran Devore was a crystallography tech with North American Intercorp, which gave him access to a number of restricted labs. He was standing outside the Node Housing at Decatur watching the sun slide behind the windbreak. A heavyset man got out of a liquid nitrogen vehicle and approached. He squinted against the sunlight, barred across the open fields by the tree trunks of the windbreak.

He stood beside Ran, his eyes half closed. Neither spoke. When the sun had vanished, Ran took the man's elbow. "I need to get in, Mel," he said quietly.

Mel looked at him curiously. "You're worried about your kid?"

Ran nodded. "There's been a disturbing trend in some of his psych parameters. Not enough for his Edmod to get excited, but computers still haven't got the subtlety. He's spending too much time either by himself, or out in the park with a man named Jimmy Radix, an HMDS victim."

"What's he do there?" Mel asked.

"Gardening."

"I can see why you'd be worried. That's no job for a human." He frowned. "So you want to monitor his Edmod algos directly."

Ran didn't answer. Mel sighed and spoke to the security system. Sec/sys answered: "ID complete. Access provisional. Fifteen minutes." The door opened.

They emerged a quarter of an hour later into night.

"Well?" Mel asked.

"Strange. There are . . . gaps. Almost as if the crystals had grown imperfections. Little things. The subroutine that should log his query to Wasatch skipped. Edmod doesn't know what he asked. Wasatch had no record of entry."

"These things happen," Mel said. "Trillions of gigabytes . . . there's a small error factor."

"The protocols should catch enough to reconstruct, at least. It's as if a small segment of memory had been dumped. It doesn't make sense."

"I've seen crystals pass with particle flaws," Mel said. "You can't handle gigabits with absolute reliability. Sometimes it happens. Replace his crystal."

"I suppose you're right," Ran said. He looked up at the sky. The stars looked back. The world was very peaceful, very stable.

HISTORICAL-CULTURAL DATALINK ENTRY:
DREAMLEAF PERFORMANCE
Re: Devore, Seemie Ref.67542@6

The following is a verbal account of the première performance of Seemie Devore's *Dreamleaf*, a full mozart production that set the standard for all others to follow. *Dreamleaf* is the most often performed of all mozart works:

It began quietly, in darkness, as expected; after all, thematically it was a pastoral, and should begin with dawn. The sound was not quite audible, a tremulous shiver at the edge of the human auditory range, as if aspen leaves were trembling in the slightest breath of air. A sensation of floating grew steadily stronger as harmonics entered, expanded and contracted. Soon it was a rhythm these harmonics made, a slow, nearly imperceptible pulse which gradually coalesced into a two-part beat, one loud, the next soft, almost as if something were surging first forward, then back.

It became a heartbeat. The floating continued, but began to twist in place, as if turning head downward for a plunge into depths. A green so faint it was almost black emerged, developed a fine grain which grew coarser, details struggling to sharpen. The grain spread, grew fine again, and the green faded away, replaced by the deepest red, again nearly black. The gyrations slowed further, moving upright, as if the feet were dropping slowly toward some surface. The light grew brighter.

The soft heartbeat sounds began to syncopate; now there were two such sounds, beating not quite in synchrony with one another. Another motion overlay the gyration, a rhythmic rise and fall, as of tides moving through kelp; at the same time the colors too began to pulse, lighter and darker, like walking along a row of trees with the sun behind it, light to shadow to light again.

("It's the womb," a woman said. "Birth.")

It was not. It was a dream of birth, a dream of the womb, dreamed out of Seemie's talent and experience. The colors faded again, the sound grew steadily louder, the heartbeats coming in and out of sync, the rise and fall, accelerating, as if the fetal audience was carried inside someone moving from a walk to a run.

An unfocused yellow grew, drew together, shaped a sphere, began to spin. From the spinning globe trails of yellow and orange and red curled off, left behind by the fury of that turning. The trails themselves fell into themselves, formed new spheres, made planets. Not real planets, surely, but the merest suggestion of planets, the yellow sphere making the merest hint of a sun.

Something obtruded on that sun, some shadow fell between the audience and that light, and when the shadow fell, a feeling of desolation, of yearning, replaced the floating.

There was a harsh melody then, dissonant and filled with despair; a melody with notes, phrases, intervals missing, loaded with subsonics.

A light musical theme appeared underneath the heavy dissonance, a melodic trill. The shadow took on shape, became light green: an aspen leaf shivering against the sun. The melody gradually took over, dominated by high flute sounds, and something mellow, like an oboe. Tree trunks formed out of the darkness, the scene became an aspen grove on a mountainside. Strong sage-scent filled the air, a cool breeze moved. Suddenly it was dark again, as it was in the beginning. The heartbeats re-emerged, stronger now, with a cooler wind blowing.

Then it was cold. Light grew, a gray light, a white light, harsh and demanding, heavy cloud light and harsh ice and snow light. The heartbeats became the sound of icy waters surging against a monstrous shelf of ice. Everyone would know this was Antarctica, the cruellest place on earth.

A reptilian head appeared over the edge of the ice, a head with a gaping mouth filled with needle teeth. The head slid forward on an endless neck, followed at last by an enormous body, spotted and fast.

The light snapped out, and the sensation was of nightmare running, frozen panic. The cold cut deeper. Everything stopped: music, heartbeat, color shaping, sensation, everything. Silence was on the face of the void.

Out of the silence the tension grew. Mouths opened to scream, but no sound came. There was nothing, absolute and without end.

It lasted until the heartbeats made their way into awareness, and with them the sudden understanding that they had been there all along. The sensation was a landmark in the void, a fulcrum around which the world could form, out of which that tremulous shiver that had begun the piece could appear, a shiver that swelled from a distant slate blue light, slowly at first, then more swiftly, until it bore down with unimaginable intensity that did not pass, but grew and grew until the light swallowed everything and was replaced by darkness.

HOMER COMMENTARY 02062106@200117

After that night Peter found something like awe had crept into his attitude toward Seemie. At the same time, though, he found himself pondering some aspects of the *Dreamleaf* experience, as if something, some memory or insight, were just below the threshold of his awareness, if he could only grasp it, he would have hold of something he wanted very badly.

The psion equations were part of it, he was sure of that.

HOMER SCENE-SD/PDRef@5410

He went topside to the temporary gazebo his father maintained. When Peter arrived, Seemie was asleep in a hammock strung between ancient elms whose leaves this late in the season were already an almost brownish yellow. It was Indian summer, clear and warm and dry. He watched her sleep, then sat on the lowest step of the porch.

"You wanted me?" Seemie interrupted his thoughts a few minutes later. She watched him through lowered lids, still half asleep.

"Mmm." He pulled at a dried grass stalk and chewed on it thoughtfully for a moment. "You know that holo of grandmother Astora?"

"Yes?"

"She had a dream. About the Vostok Massacre."

"Yes."

"It could have been a coincidence, couldn't it? I mean precog dreams aren't reliable at all, since it's impossible to interpret them in advance."

"It could have been coincidence, yes. Though the details . . ."

"Oh, sure." Peter waved his stalk in the air. "The tunnel was breached. Children froze. There was a massacre. Still, no one knows if there was one child who froze to death with a wooden stick in her hand."

"True." Seemie was sitting up now. "Go on."

"Well, the question is, what material could have been authentic prophecy, and what was material from Astora's own unconscious mind?"

Seemie smiled. "Is that really the question?"

Peter looked startled. "No. You're right, that isn't the question. There was something in *Dreamleaf*. Something about the way you mozart, with the probes and all that programming; something about the interaction between your mind and the AI machinery, combined with lucid dream-shaping, well, I got the idea maybe we could, well, control things."

"Control things how?" Seemie was uneasy; she got out of the hammock and walked over to the elm, putting her palm against the rough bark.

"I'm not sure." He frowned. "There were a lot of ancient dreams about psi effects, but at best we've developed techniques for enhanced intuition; no real power."

"You sound like you've been into the Wallace PsiLink Database."

"No!" He spoke a little too loud, and lowered his voice. "No. There were stories, old disks. Writers like Lovecraft and Heinlein, for instance, who had fantasies about such powers. I know that hundreds of years of psychic research are available in PsiLink, but I can't get in. Edmod won't let me."

"All right, Peter." Her hand reached toward him. "Your Edmod knows your personality indices. You've been raised for a math and technical niche. You'd only be distracted into a dead end by exploring Wallace."

He snorted. "Edmod's a machine!"

"Yes, but grown for you, Peter. Adapted as closely to your DNA as a personal NP is adapted to its user's EEG. In that sense it's more than a machine."

"You don't believe that any more than I do!"

Seemie was taken aback. "How can you say that?"

"Because you're an artist. You shape what the machines do, not the other way around."

She laughed uneasily. "OK. True enough. What you propose then is that not only is psychic functioning real, which we already know, but that it can also be reliable?"

He nodded. "And powerful. We could remake ourselves. Not just superficial stuff, like head ornamentation or gender."

Seemie winced at this reference to her mother, but said nothing.

Suddenly Peter leaned toward her and lowered his voice. "Look," he said earnestly, "there are these areas of human experience, you see? Dreams, and trance states, and what happens in the biofeedback chambers. Already we can control digestion, blood pressure, skin temperature, all that stuff. Even a techie like me can do it. How does it happen?"

"Peter, everyone knows it's based on quantum effects. We can do that to ourselves because we understand the mind-body interaction pretty well. But the energy expenditure is minimal, yet such things still require enormous attention and focus. To do what you're suggesting would require enormous energy output."

He threw his grass stalk away. "You don't really know what I'm suggesting," he said.

"Well, then, what . . ." She was interrupted by a musical tone followed by the voice of Peter's Edmod.

"Peter. Please return for social training and analysis."

Peter pulled a wry face. "You know what that means. That means I've got to meet with my peer group and interact." He laughed. "Actually, it's kind of fun. We tell jokes."

"You tell jokes," she said, watching him go. All around her the Indian summer seemed suspended in time.

HOMER COMMENTARY 02062106@205721

He began to take precautions. He encrypted almost everything he did outside of regular training. Since he did it under the guise of his own transform cryptography math, no particular flag was put on his memos.

He began to make more frequent trips topside to visit with Jimmy Radix.

It was a strange relationship, even for those times. Jimmy Radix was over fifty, yet thought he was only twenty-three. A look in the mirror would upset him greatly, seeing as he would the deep lines along his nose and mouth, the grey hair at his temples, the faded look to his skin. He had received no longevity treatments because of his condition, nor would he. They aggravated the HMD Syndrome.

Peter was fifteen then, with certain aspects of his personality and intelligence indices overdeveloped. Yet Peter, with very high quotients in many areas, seemed to have an almost hero-worshipping attitude toward Jimmy, who suffered from HMDS, and who was only comfortable when performing repetitive tasks.

HOMER COMMENTARY 02062106@205922

We've had a session. Central Processing, Interface (the general human communications algorithms), the quasi-AI node monitors, and myself, Homer. Information is either lacking or uncorrelated. Consensus decision is to prepare mobile probes to act as semi-autonomous agents in the warrens of Springfield, the ruins of Baja, and in the empty corridors of AA. This last especially has been troublesome, because we had such inadequate surveillance there even when Worldnet was running at optimum.

Now there is no data at all, yet Antarctica is where Peter went, where Mentor was waiting. It is where the Migration began.

02062106: The agent probes are away. We track them easily (enough satellites remain, and some of the eyes on the LP-Fives, the Lunar bases and scattered ground nodes), but we won't really know anything until they arrive.

CENTRAL PROCESSING / LIFE SUPPORT WARNING FLAG 05012070. DEVORE, PETER, LOC SPRINGFIELD WEST WARREN FLAG TEMPORAL COMPONENT BIOPSYCH CHAMBERS. PETER'S TIME IN CHAMBERS APPROACHES MAXIMUM RECOMMENDED DAILY LIMITS.

GENERAL SCIENCE AND TECHNOLOGY INFORMATION
CURRENT ENTRY: BIOCYBERNON
BIOCYBERNON: A corporation founded in the late 1980s, Biocybernon provided the first primitive hardware/software/ wetware interfaces, later used in mozart consoles, Edmod AI algos, meditation chambers and the like. Absorbed by First Intercorp after the AT&T/IBM alliance in 1990.

UPLOAD LIFE SUPPORT VIA CENTRAL PROCESSING REF#83778Y:
EEG READOUT PETER DEVORE. CONTACT WITH WANDA SIXLOVE (CISLEUF) ESTABLISHED THROUGH UNKNOWN PSI EFFECT. CHECK PSILINK DB FOR REFERENCES. PROBABILITY HYPNAGOGIC STATE SYNC THROUGH PSION EQUATION PROJECTION (LORENZ-FITZGERALD TIME DISTORTION APPARENTLY NOT PRESENT DESPITE NEAR-LIGHTSPEED OF VEGA 26 AT TIME OF CONTACT). RUN BACK NOTE EEG READOUT INDICATIVE OF HIGH EXCITEMENT WHILE IN DEEP SIGMA STATE. SUCH A COMBINATION OF EMOTIVE / CONSCIOUSNESS STATES IS HIGHLY UNUSUAL, IF NOT UNIQUE.

CENTRAL PROCESSING AI GENEVA. NOTED.
END UPLOAD

HOMER SCENE-WS/PDRef@5414

It is sunrise across the plain; the river catches the violet light and strings it through the winding pattern of its flow. Deep Illinois green, forests beyond the river, small temporary villages strangely solid in the dawn. She watches from her high tower, the Princess Arianne of the white gown and slender neck, watches for the thread of dust that bespeaks her valorous knight riding towards her.

As the day grows bright and hot and he fails to come, she sighs and turns away to her tapestry, where the unicorn at bay paws his hooves at the encircling hounds. She threads the golden wire through the horn in a helix to the point, and the horn glows in the heavy noontime light, also golden. The unicorn's eye is wild with fear and rage to be so trapped.

Behind her the door opens at last. He kneels at her feet. "Milady," he says. He bows his head and she touches his hair lightly, the straight brown hair that hangs shoulder-length. He holds his plumed and polished helm in his right hand, her own hand in his left.

CENTRAL PROCESSING REF#43947 / WS / PD / CODENINE

"Who are you?" she asked, "and where am I?"

He looked up. For a moment she was not a lady in a white gown caught in the high tower, but a cold corpse surrounded by void, beseeching in a ghost voice. He nearly dropped her hand, it was so cold and dead.

PSILINK DATASPACE/PROSCRIBED HYPNAGOGICS

ABSTRACT: DEVELOPED FROM EARLY DEFINITION OF STATE LEADING TO SLEEP AS FORM OF LUCID DREAMING. TECHNIQUES DEVELOPED AND DISSEMINATED BY WILLIAM GULELE, AUSTRALIAN ABORIGINE FROM DREAMTIME MYTHOS. RELAXED STATE OF CONSCIOUSNESS SUSCEPTIBLE TO EXTERNAL INFLUENCE. POSSIBLE STATE FOR TELEPATHIC CONTACT. NOT PROVEN.

Note: Hypnagogics comprise the dream state between waking and sleeping, characterized by vivid imagery and abrupt insight. For decades hypnagogic state was considered a useless human phenomenon, since little memory-trace remained of such imagery and insight. With the development of the psion equations, some control was gained, but Intercorp Council declared hypnagogic research, except for medical purposes, proscribed. For technical information, see Ref#127426@182/9.

UPLOAD LIFE SUPPORT VIA CENTRAL PROCESSING REF#83778Y:

DEVORE, PETER. INDICATORS SHOW INCREASED TENSION, LOWERED BLOOD PRESSURE AND TEMPERATURE. SUCH INDICATORS ARE UNIQUE. INCREASED TENSION WITH LOWERED BP SUGGEST DISCRETE ALTERED STATE OF CONSCIOUSNESS (*dASC) WHILE IN HYPNAGOGIC STATE SYNC OR TRANCE COMMUNION.

PSILINK NOTIFIED.

INTERCORP COUNCIL NOTIFIED.

ELITE NEUTRALIZATION CORPS (PROSCRIBED TECHNOLOGIES DIVISION) NOTIFIED.

CENTRAL PROCESSING AI GENEVA. NOTED.

HOMER SCENE-WS/PDRef@5415
/PSILINK DOWNLOAD

"Milord," she said. She is haughty and proud in tone, yet tender in her touch. "There is a terror in the land," she says to him, and he feels a surge of pride that she has chosen to tell him this.

"Yes, Milady," he says, standing and striding to the narrow window to look out on the land, so fair and peaceful beneath the sun. "A terror there is." He turns back to her, reaching, but not touching her. He speaks not looking at her, but down, as befits his station. "I may slay the dragon," he says, his hand on the hilt of his broadsword. "Or . . ."

"Yes?"

"Or we may lead the people away, to a new land, beyond the mountains. To undreamed freedom."

"No one," she says then, "has been beyond the mountains."

CENTRAL PROCESSING REF#3284373
PD/WS/CODENINE APPEND REF2 PSILINK

"Peter," he said, thinking it was to himself. "My name is Peter Devore."

"I am not a Princess," she said. "Not Arianne of the white gown. I am . . . I am Wanda, Wanda Cisleuf, from the City of Quebec, Northwest Alliance. I am . . . oh, I thought I had grown used to this." She wailed in despair, and Peter tried to touch her, to uncover her tangible reality. There was nothing though. His mind-hand slipped through hers as through a thought.

Yet she was beautiful, white of skin and pale gold of hair bound in braids above her smooth brow. He was haunted by the sadness in her face.

"Does she remind you of anyone?" Edmod asked him the next day.

Peter frowned. "Remind me? Oh, you mean my mother. Does she look like Seemie, or act like her? I don't believe so. She doesn't feel like a reconstruction of my unconscious wishes." Edmod detected no irony in Peter's voice, but stress analysis of the sonograms shows he intended it.

He was curious, of course, and excited too. After all, Wanda Sixlove was a full-fleshed woman with a high erotic index, an object of Peter's own sexual fantasy. So he returned to her night after night, though he still didn't know whether she was a real person or a projection, nor where she was. But he began making discrete inquiries of the Quebec Warren population rolls. He guessed her age to be mid-twenties, but Quebec, of course, had no record of anyone of that age or name from the appropriate dates. So he went back.

GEOGRAPHIC DATABASE
QUEBEC WARRENS
   (GEOG REF 2075/NWA/Delta5)
   As per date requested. Query regards Wanda Sixlove indicating no presence any citizen that name. Warren rolls cross-index tree search also unsuccessful for dates requested. Cross-search with Wasatch Genealogical Database unsuccessful. No match.

HOMER SCENE-WS/PDRef@5416
He speaks, it seems, across a gulf to her. He's trapped, stripped and bound while his captors laugh, piling brush around his feet. Tendrils of smoke twist before his face, and the first heat licks at his ankles. He's staked in a thicket where the sticks are dry and the leaves are dead. Weakness seizes his knees, and they bend, though he cannot fall, bound as he is.

"Milady!"

She answers from the great distance to her castle. "What

is it?" she asks, and her voice is irritable and abrupt. He was in the mountains, seeking the high passes to beyond, when he was captured by these faceless knights in dark armor. "What is it?" she asks a second time.

"Save me." He begs her. "Save me." She stands above her tank, looking down at herself, frozen.

"Whom should I save, who am locked away here?" she asks, looking at herself. She had grown used to looking at herself, surrounded by mirrors that told her always how to move.

"Sir Peter," he said, or thought he said, and she replied, "I know no one of that name, Sir Peter. No one."

She saw the great plain, with the river winding through the forests and the far mountains beyond.

UPLOAD LIFE SUPPORT VIA CENTRAL PROCESSING REF#83778Y:

SIXLOVE (CISLEUF), WANDA, TELEMETRY FR. VEGA 26. SUBJECT IS PASSENGER IN CRYOFIELD HIBERNATION. ARRIVED GENEVA TELEMETRY STORAGE 26 AUGUST 2093 1428 ZULU TIME.

LITTLE LIFE SUPPORT TELEMETRY ARRIVES IN FROM THE VEGA STARSHIPS. FLAGGED IMMEDIATE ATTENTION SINCE NO NEED WAS SEEN FOR SUCH INFORMATION AS IT IS AT THIS TIME OVER NINETEEN YEARS OUT OF DATE. EVENTS PORTRAYED ARE HISTORICAL.

NOTE THE SUBJECT HAS BEEN IN CLOSE PSYCHIC SYNC WITH PETER DEVORE. AT THIS TIME WE NOTE DECREASED SIGMA WITH A CONCURRENT INCREASE IN FIRST ALPHA, THEN DELTA STATES.

WANDA SIXLOVE HAS FALLEN ASLEEP.

CENTRAL PROCESSING AI GENEVA. NOTED.

END UPLOAD

CENTRAL PROCESSING REF#47268
WS/CODENINE REF3 PSILINK
Another time she felt breezes blowing past her redolent with the aromas of onions or pine, or tasted strawberries, felt the color of stars splash through tears of laughter, felt cool glass under her fingertips. Perhaps she drank again, from something in a glass or cup, and the colors drained, leaving the scent of orange rind. Darkness swam through her belly.

UPLOAD LIFE SUPPORT TELEMETRY VIA
CENTRAL PROCESSING REF#83778Y:
PETER DEVORE IN HYPNAGOGIC SYNC WITH WANDA SIXLOVE (VEGA 26 TELEMETRY).
NOTE THE SUBJECT HAS BEEN IN CLOSE PSYCHIC SYNC WITH WANDA SIXLOVE FOR SEVERAL MINUTES. HERE WE NOTE DECREASED SIGMA WITH A CONCURRENT INCREASE IN FIRST ALPHA, THEN DELTA STATES.
PETER DEVORE HAS FALLEN ASLEEP.
CENTRAL PROCESSING AI GENEVA. NOTED.
END UPLOAD.

HOMER SCENE-WS/PDRef@5417
"Hello," he said.
"Where are you?" she asked.
"Springfield West. I'm in Springfield West. The Warrens under the park. Where are you?"
"I don't know," she said. "I really don't. You seem so real."
"I am real," Peter said. "I am, I'm real. I live in Springfield West, in old Illinois. You seem so far away. Are you far away?"
"Vega," she said. "Vega Twenty Six. Does that mean anything?"

"A starship!" he breathed. "You're on a starship. When did it leave?"

"2050," she said. "In the summer. I left from Alice Springs. It was winter, there, of course, in Australia, but I don't remember much. How is it we can talk like this? I must be imagining it."

"You're in hibernation," Peter said. "It's the hypnagogics."

"The what?"

"Hypnagogics. That kind of twilight state between waking and sleeping. There's been lots of stuff come out the past few years, lots of research. Of course the really good stuff is proscribed; kids can't get at that information. But we get some training in the biopsych chambers. And I'm working on some new stuff, myself."

"Hypnagogics," she said slowly. "Yes, I remember. I slept a lot those last few years. It was the only way I could tolerate . . . my condition. What year is it?"

"2074. You've been gone for 24 years already. I could find out where you are, but I'll figure it out later. Listen, this is important. We've got to keep doing this."

Peter sensed a smile; he could feel her understanding, her amusement, her compassion for him. "You're young," she said. "I can tell. You must be fourteen or so."

"Fifteen. Almost sixteen."

"I'm . . . fifty now."

"No. You're the age you were when you left . . . twenty-four. You won't be any older than that, not much, anyway. But that's not important. The important thing is that I'm working on these . . . equations." He tried imagining the math for her, but he could feel her shrugging, mentally. "Never mind. You have to believe me. It's important that we keep doing this."

A wind blew, not fast but deeply cold, like static between them, like the hydrogen hiss of the whole universe at once. "Yes, Peter," she said finally. "It's important to me, too."

He was getting sleepy, and could feel his control slipping away. "No," he said, struggling to hold on.

"I'm so alone," she said. "And now I'm almost awake, and I'm frozen solid, and I can't move, and I can't scream or cry, and I'm alone. I need you now, Peter." She faded away. The last he heard was, "You must come back, Peter. Come back."

GENERAL SCIENCE AND TECHNOLOGY INFORMATION
CURRENT ENTRY: EDMOD

EDMOD: Crystalline matrix grown from individual DNA templates. Error rates run at less than one per trillion electron gates. Still, errors can be serious since the gate is critical to individual personality meld, particularly in adolescents.

Edmods were responsible for the general and specific course of individual education, including appropriate training, authorized entry to appropriate DBs and specialized skills. Only Central Processing had access to individual Edmod codes, and only Intercorp Council Geneva Node Edmod AI could propose and authorize alterations in the priority override codes.

GENERAL SCIENCE AND TECHNOLOGY INFORMATION
CURRENT ENTRY: COMMUNICATION

COMMUNICATIONS NETWORK: Worldnet creates a seven-tiered distributed-channel network. Nodes are located in major Urbs, with subnodes in outlying geographical centers. Nodes exist also at the Elpie Fives, Lunar and Mars bases and Polar Orbiters as well as the standard array of Geosyncs. Polar coverage is inadequate, yet no feasible solution is available.

HOMER COMMENTARY 02062106@210023
I replay the records, I watch what they did: Regent Sable

talked to Peter's father via a rare direct fiber holo link, a secure line. Ran was not particularly happy with the call. "It's near Christmas," he said. "I've got work to do. What do you want?"

"How's Seemie?" Regent asked, and Ran, as always, was uncertain whether the question was intended to be provocative and ironic, or was a sincere expression of good will.

He chose not to be surly, though that was his inclination. "She's fine, Regent. Just fine."

"And the boy?" Regent went on. "How do you find the boy these days?"

Ran hesitated. "I'm not sure what you mean. He's all right."

You can see that Ran was not telling the whole truth. You can see that, can't you?

"No . . . deviations? No peculiarities, departures from the Edmod tutorial programs? Does he seem overly secretive, perhaps? You know the sort of thing."

"What do you want from me?" Ran asked belligerently; he was losing his detachment, he realized that immediately. He'd need an extra session in the chamber tonight. But damn it all, Regent Sable was such a sanctimonious ass.

"Just be a good father to the boy, Ran. That's all." Regent's voice poured oil on the troubled water.

It bothered Ran that Regent called Peter "the boy" all the time. He had considered Regent might be Peter's father, but for some reason he'd never bothered to have the tests done. It didn't seem important then.

Now, though, with the call, he wasn't so sure. Perhaps it was important. Perhaps there were things about Peter he didn't understand.

He'd have to talk to Seemie about it soon.

"I changed his Edmod crystal; there were some particle flaws. He's fine now." Ran shifted uncomfortably under Regent's gaze.

"We're not so sure, Ran. Back here in Geneva things look a little different. For example, he's been spending time somewhere out of contact. Did you know that?"

"What . . . Oh, you mean topside. Yeah, he hangs around a pathetic vet named Radix. HMDS victim. He's harmless, really. Jazz, Regent, the man does gardening!"

"No, Ran. That's not what we're concerned about. We've been monitoring the Park. It's something else. We don't know where he goes, but he's taking time off. He's in the formative era of his career prep, Ran. We wouldn't want him to go wrong now, would we? And I have a special interest in the boy. So keep an eye on him. See if you can find out where he's going."

"Sure. OK, Regent. I'll watch out for him."

After he broke the connection, he wondered how much he really intended to do as he'd just promised.

I can see all this that went on inside him.

CENTRAL PROCESSING REF#2347614
CODESEVEN INVEST. PROBE SW

Our agent probe arrived at Springfield Warren. Extensive damage to tunnels, extreme weathering. Major life support shutdown and matrix failures, soil subsidence, geologic deformation and small-animal destruction reported. Search initiated for lower-level warren chambers with evidence of extended unmonitored use.

HISTORICAL-CULTURAL DATALINK ENTRY:
UNRES1992, UNDERGROUND CHARTER
Re: Devore, Peter via Edmod/ Ref.436745@2

UN RESOLUTION 1992: The original UN resolution of 1992 to move underground had gained uneven acceptance throughout the world. In Antarctica, for example, the movement underground was nearly universal. Elsewhere, though, only some cities were successfully dug. Cheap laser drilling power and robot heavy construction made such a move plausible and affordable, but many cultural and social reasons existed to prevent its universal adoption. Large sections of Chicago, much of Boston, Washington D.C., and Seattle remained topside. Other cities, like San Francisco, could not go underground without severe geological problems. Still others, like Moscow and New York, remained frozen in time, preserved as historic monuments, while cities like Singapore and Brasilia became heavy industry centers. Finally some, like Calcutta, were successfully moved underground.

Among the most successful moves in America were the Springfields. Partly this resulted from agricultural pressure, since in the teens and twenties the land was needed for intensive farming (by the mid-21st century this was no longer a necessity); partly it was the even and controlled environment underground that made the move attractive.

GEOGRAPHIC DATABASE
SPRINGFIELD WEST
    (GEOG REF 2075/NWA/Sigma6)
    As per date requested. Simulation scale model Springfield West Warrens, incl. urbs tower and Park. Scale 1 = 125,000 adjustable. POV shows angle 40° NNW (335°) distance seven nautical miles, adjustable. Year indicated shows warren configuration as of July 13, 2075. Rate of change for this time period runs at ±14%/lunar month. Abandoned subcellars outlined in orange.

HOMER COMMENTARY 02062106@212124
    Since the Springfields were among the earliest cities to dig, much of the warren complex later became obsolete,

abandoned and eventually forgotten. Jimmy Radix, perhaps because he had such good memories from his own youth, had found a subcellar library and laboratory complex which was sealed off in the mid-thirties. The entire area was also under a personal encrypt, which made our rediscovery of it difficult.

GENERAL SCIENCE AND TECHNOLOGY INFORMATION
CURRENT ENTRY: ENCRYPT

PERSONAL ENCRYPTS: Based on a specific segment of the individual's chromosomal DNA, personal encrypts could be neither faked, nor could they be broken except, of course, by Central Processing, which has access to all genotype coding. Individuals using personal encrypt could lock personal files, life support, Edmod, and certain proprietary data crystals; such encrypted crystals could not be accessed by anyone else. Randax (random access) would ignore all such encrypted data.

HOMER SCENE-PD/Ref@5418

"Given enough power," Peter said, "we could break through." He laughed. "There's only one problem."

There were seventeen people in the room: friends of Peter's like Rover and Shem, Wynders and Shelley and Scottie and Jimmy Radix. Finally there was Rover's current companion, an Asian girl with a keratin adaptation that gave her otter fur instead of hair. She was the one who finally asked, "What's the one problem, Peter?"

"The problem, Larin, is that it seems it would take the entire energy output of the sun for several days concentrated into a few hundred milliseconds. Unfortunately such power is not available locally." This remark was greeted by a smattering of laughter.

"You do know that what you're suggesting is probably

not going to be appreciated by Intercorp?" This was the girl with otter fur. "My father's ENC, you know."

"Your father's a cop?" Shem asked.

"Well, not really. He's a system surrogate. Someone has to keep the simulations honest."

"You don't have to defend him," Shem told her. "He can't help it. Besides, we're not doing anything illegal—unless there's a law against thinking."

"No," she said shortly. "That's not it. The Elite Neutralization Corp watches out for dangerous new technologies, though. I hear about this stuff at home, you know. My father talks, at dinner sometimes, about things he overhears when he's on the system."

"Look," Rover said. "there's nothing here. We don't have a new technology, and even if we did, we'd need a power source that doesn't exist, so they don't have to worry, right."

"Nonetheless," Peter said, "I think I'll encrypt these meetings. No sense alarming the ENC over nothing." He gestured at the slowly rotating holo shape in the air beside him. "This model represents a configuration of the particle flow in a quantum transformation. On a macro level it represents a hypnagogic state. I've been having some experience with this lately, and this is the best model I've been able to devise. It is consistent with the psion equations as far as I can tell. The Northwestern University cruncher has run all the math for me, and it's probable to twelve places. Of course, because the effect is quantum, nothing is certain."

There was another laugh at this joke. "Nothing is certain," someone repeated. "Heisenberg be praised." They drank the Uncertainty Principle with their milk in the nursery.

"The only really dangerous part for us, as far as ENC is concerned, is that PsiLink is a proscribed database, and I've found it necessary lately to, uh, enter it. The model is really a four-dimensional transform . . ."

MED10 MEDICAL DATABASE
GENETIC DISEASES: GENETIC ABOULIA DISORDER

Genetic Aboulia Disorder (GAD) is a malignant form of new, non-standard neurophage weapon effects. Such non-standard weapons developed during the Mind Wars. GAD resulted in the victim's complete loss of will. Physiological systems declined steadily, despite heroic life-support measures and systematic treatment. GAD victims eventually died of starvation, as if they had pulled the plug on themselves. Causes poorly understood.

MILITARY DATASPACE/PROSCRIBED ENTRY
HOMER OVERRIDE/DNA CODE UNNECESSARY

THE MIND WARS, February 2074, Capsule history: The Mind Wars began, as so many did in the late 21st century, as a personal vendetta between two managerial families. The Genetic Diversity Act of 2030 was still in force, but ethnic groups maintained hostilities in spite of it. Perhaps the Act made things worse; certainly the world had been on a homogenization trend for several decades before the Act passed the Council, a trend which the Act appeared to reverse.

The vendetta was registered in Cyprus. It was just one of thousands of registered vendettas that winter, monitored, regulated, and refereed by Central Processing. A Greek family named Nychtides had challenged a Turkish family named Chakalë on grounds of failure to pay bride price. In truth, the Turk had manipulated the database to squeeze out the Greek head of family from a lucrative managerial channel, and the bride-price failure was only the pro-forma excuse. Such things were common and quite legal, since minimal neurophage violence was considered a reasonable outlet and alternative to the kind of disaster the Burma War had been.

This time something was different. The Nychtides family had developed a twist on the NP weapon that did more that produce temporary disorientation; it induced, permanently, a new form of genetic disease, a complete loss of will. Med10 named it Genetic Aboulia Disorder, for a DNA-programmed loss of will.

The Chakalë family was quickly decimated. Unfortunately another Turk family took a hit, and declared a vendetta against the Nychtides, who retaliated in turn. Soon all Cyprus was in a state of siege, and the ENC cops were ineffective against this new weapon, which destroyed the first contingent sent in.

No shields were effective. The war spread rapidly to widely scattered outbreaks as families here and there acquired the new technology and used it to gain temporary advantage. It flared and died down several times for the next twenty years, gradually evening out over the globe to a dull melancholy pain in the social structure.

HOMER SCENE-PD/RDRef@5419

Still, Peter and his group may have continued undisturbed had not Seemie fallen victim to the Mind Wars. The fighting in Chicago had grown fierce, and was spreading south. She was caught in the crossfire while attending a music symposium at the University of Chicago Warren.

Peter and Ran sat by her bed in the Springfield hospice. She had full life support, but it meant nothing: they may as well have been watching a recording, a reconstruction. The monitors registered life-maintenance, nothing more.

"She's gone, Peter," Ran said softly. He laid his hand on Peter's shoulder.

"I know, Dad." Peter watched his mother's chest rise and fall, forced by the monitors to continue breathing. He looked for the little signs that would indicate there was a personality there, a flutter of the eyelids, movement of the eye under the lid, small changes of expression, the nervous twitch of a finger. "We haven't learned much, have we?"

Ran sighed. "I guess not."

"She was working on a new piece. She had that look,

just last week. Something new was going to come of it. Now it won't."

The wall opposite displayed sunset across the Park, the trees on the horizon gathering into shadow as the light slipped behind them. Nearby the creek flowed toward a cattle pond where some people skated in winter. A light breeze disturbed the surface of the water, turning it rough and dark.

"No," Ran said at last. "Now it won't." They sat in silence as the darkness gathered outside.

UPLOAD LIFE SUPPORT VIA CENTRAL PROCESSING REF#8934Q:
COMPOSITE MONITOR READOUTS
SEEMIE (MOLAY) DEVORE.
VITAL SIGNS TERMINATED. SUBJECT HAS SUFFERED BRAIN DEATH DUE TO GENETIC ABOULIA DISEASE. ALL SIGNS RETURN TO STEADY STATE.
CENTRAL PROCESSING AI GENEVA. NOTED.
END UPLOAD

GENERAL SCIENCE AND TECHNOLOGY INFORMATION
CURRENT ENTRY: FUNERAL
FUNERAL PRACTICES: By the late 2020s, a combination of ecological and social forces (E-cubed Society was a prime mover in this trend) had resulted in cremation and recycling as standard funeral practice. Even minor warrens had mortuary facilities for the swift reduction and capture of components. The recycled materials are not, in truth, necessary to the well-being of Intercorp society, but a strong belief system prevails that provides relief from grief reactions by assuring the continued flow of the material body in the universal dynamic.

HOMER SCENE-RD/PDRef@5422

Seemie Molay Devore died the day Regent Sable arrived in Springfield West. The life-support monitors very gradually flattened until she was gone.

Her remains slid away to the flashers for recycling. The wall signaled her status: first organ salvage—kidneys, liver, spleen, pancreas, endocrine glands, pineal, pituitary, adrenals, thyroid and so forth; spinal tissue, optics, heart and lung complex; so many one-meter sections of bowel and small intestine; circulatory materials and so on for the longevity technology centers. Various compounds and essential proteins were extracted, pre-flash prep, flash dissolution, and final analysis of basic compounds. Peter and Ran watched solemnly as her container vanished from view. She produced her fair contribution to others' lives and was gone.

Ran turned away, saying nothing. Peter watched him leave the mortuary salon. He knew he would never see his father again.

MED10 MEDICAL DATABASE
GENETIC DISEASES:
PROPRIOCEPTIVE DEGENERATION DISEASE

Proprioceptive Degeneration Disease (PDD), characterized by waning and eventual loss of the proprioceptive sense, which locates the human body and limbs in space. Victims are unable to locate themselves, and must live in houses filled with mirrors to provide constant visual feedback to ordinary activities. Cause of the disease is unknown, though it is grouped in the standard taxonomy of genetic diseases. First described in the mid-20th century, the disease appeared in large numbers beginning in the 2020s, and reached a proportion approaching 1000 new cases a year worldwide. The effects are irreversible. Chromosome eleven contains a genetic marker for the disease, but the exact location of the affected gene or genes seems to move at random.

Theoretical treatment was through extended hibernation in the Vega starship cryofields, which accounted for the high percentage of victims among the passengers. Effectiveness of this treatment is unknown.

GENERAL SCIENCE AND TECHNOLOGY INFORMATION
CURRENT ENTRY: HOLO MODELLING

See Holographics Imaging. Portable flatscreen holo projectors were available to all citizens by late 2061. Most people who performed mathematical modeling, statistical, DNA engineering and picoelectronic design used these devices, which could project in three dimensions all or part of any model.

HOMER SCENE-PD/Ref@5420

"You're gonna lose us, Peter. Most of us are heavy in body-kinesthetic and spatial IQ. Larin's in pattern organization and visual cognition. Shem does mostly music. You're the math person. Keep it simple."

Peter shrugged. He pushed the model gently, and it floated away, turning slowly. It was a complex three dimensional structure that changed as it turned, lines and planes intersecting, flowing into one another, behind one another, through one another while changing color. Cones formed, flattened, became spheres, turned at right angles to become complex knots made of silver coils. The model stopped over the projector and froze.

"OK," he said. "The model represents what happens when two people make a psychic link in a hypnagogic state. This is a real phenomenon, which I have experienced with a rider on the Vega 26 starship."

"You're dreaming," Rover said after a silence.

Peter nodded. "Yes," he said. "That's it exactly. Still, it's real. I've checked the records. Her name is Wanda Sixlove, and her ship left in 2050, nine years before I was born. I learned all this from my contact with her, and then checked it out. There is no way I could have had that information before, yet the comps confirmed everything. She told me she had Proprioceptive Degeneration Disease, and that the medics thought thirty years in the freezer might cure it, so she went on a Vega flight."

"I knew a PDD," one of the men said. "I never heard of that cure."

"Maybe it doesn't work. There haven't been any revivers yet. But a lot of PDDs went on Wanda's ship. And she has a special skill because of it."

"What's PDD?" the girl with otter fur wanted to know.

"It's a loss of all spatial sense, all the proprioceptive sensors in joints and muscles go off-line. They have to live in houses made out of mirrors for visual feedback. I wouldn't want it." The old timer leaned back and crossed his arms, looking at Jimmy.

"You wouldn't want what I got either," Jimmy said.

"No, you're sure right there, my friend. I would not."

"So," Rover said, returning to the subject, "what's her special skill?"

"She's used to being adrift in space," Peter replied. "It doesn't frighten her to be cut off from her body. Frankly, it scares the code right out of me."

"So what? Nobody's going to be leaving her body," Shem said.

"On the contrary," Jimmy Radix said. "That's precisely what we could all do."

"Except for that one little problem," Larin said.

"Right. Power supply," Shelley concluded.

"Well, let's all think about it. Look, people used to think that certain tasks took enormous power—lifting cars above the ground, for instance. Now, liquid nitrogen vehicles use very little energy. It could be the same with this thing," Rover suggested.

Peter began encrypting the recordings of the meeting. "Remember," he said, pausing, "with enough power we could break through. There's another world."

"We got enough trouble in this one, I think," the otter girl said, but she was grinning when she said it.

HOMER COMMENTARY 02062106@215325

Regent Sable came again to Springfield West. Now he had company, men with hard eyes. He was angry.

He noted his anger. He was angry because he was afraid. Something had slipped past the monitors, past all the regulation, the careful social control, and having slipped past, it was about to escape, and at a time when such escape would have the worst effects on the world.

Population was declining at an alarming rate. The Mind Wars were raging out of control on three continents. Human productivity was falling.

But the one worry that overshadowed all the others was Peter Devore. Regent was reasonably certain by then that Peter was his son, yet it was even more clear that Peter was a danger, that his particular genius was taking him into areas that would better be left alone for a number of significant reasons.

It was a genius Peter got from his mother—a woman who had been growing increasingly dangerous herself, her art tending as it had toward proscribed technologies. Peter's grandmother Astora had a significant level of psychic functioning, though as always it was a useless ability.

But it appeared that Peter was about to find a way to apply the ability.

Furthermore, Central Processing predicted, with over 73 percent confidence, that almost everyone had the ability.

If it were developed, the relatively stable and peaceful structure of world society would be torn apart. Despite the Mind Wars, the world remained clean, safe, and well provided, without poverty, debilitating illness outside the genetic diseases, or oppression. Longevity technology was freely available, and barring genetic disease, a human could expect to live to at least 114.

But a widespread psychic technology would upset all that. Results were unpredictable, but CP had 87 percent confidence that consequences would be negative. So far, Regent had been able to prevent any significant growth of this technology. He'd helped destroy PSYCHE back in '52, and as far as he knew that was the end of it. Now it seemed that Mentor, Dittmore Seminole Gadd himself, had contacted Peter through channels as yet untraced, and had pushed him into making some fundamental discoveries, and, worse, disseminating the information.

All in all, things were not going well just now. Regent did not intend to let them remain that way.

HOMER SCENE-WS/PDRef@5421

"I don't know what's making this work so well," Peter told Wanda Sixlove, "but I'm finding it easier and easier to reach and stay with you."

"We're making a connection," she said, and there was such intense passion and promise in her feeling-tone that Peter would have blushed, had he been awake.

She danced for him, reaching to take his hand, to lead him into the slow pavane. Behind them the walls were hung with tapestries she had woven through the long weary years of her voyage in the cold, tapestries in which the unicorn turned at bay, and the damsel was seated on the forest floor with the noble head in her lap, and the hunters called in the distance as the dogs came close. Overhead the leaves hung down, close and dense, holding them as they walked slowly, hands together and arched, looking into one another's eyes.

Wanda's eyes were violet, he thought, of a twilight clarity. Is this love? he wondered, thinking she was ten years his senior and altogether wiser in the world.

But no, she said to him. I am frozen in time as I hurtle through space, while you grow. Soon you will be the older. By the time I arrive at Beta, you will be the older.

"Oh, Weaving Girl," Peter said, with such despair. They danced.

HOMER SCENE-RS/PDRef@5423

Peter's group began to move. Within minutes their room was closed, locked, and restored, as if it had been abandoned for many years. Regent Sable and his two searchers passed it on their second sweep of the area.

HOMER SCENE-RS/Ref@5424

"What makes you think they're down here, Hoskins?" Regent asked. His voice echoed in the empty metal hallways.

"We've had a lot of experience with these types," the ENC sergeant answered. "There're always malcontents. There were malcontents before the Elite Neutralization Corps signed a contract with the old United Nations, and there are still malcontents. With tracking and projection programs, we've managed to keep them pretty well contained, but they crop up now and then. Nothing to worry about; we'll find 'em. These older warrens aren't well mapped, and we have to go through them foot by foot. But we'll find 'em."

"What makes you think they're malcontents?"

Something about Sable's tone made the sergeant straighten

an extra fraction. "They wouldn't be hiding if they weren't. Sir."

"No," Sable murmured as he checked his bloodhound chemosensor. "I suppose not. I don't think this thing's working."

"Why's that? Sir." Sergeant Hoskins looked over his shoulder at the device.

"Because it records nothing for this area. No one has passed this way within the time range of the bloodhound. Not a trace of organics more recent than twelve years ago. We'd better head back up a level."

HOMER SCENE-PD/Ref@5425

"The effects are getting more predictable," Peter was saying. "I can control when and where. I can direct the fantasy, although not alone—Wanda and I have to agree on it. She is an incredibly strong, brave person. She's done things I have trouble imagining myself doing. Someday, perhaps . . . Anyway, the technique is feasible. We still don't have a power source, though, and I see no possibility of getting one. So what we're onto is still just a possibility."

"There's nothing in local space with that kind of power output," Rover said. "And even if there were, how could we control it?"

"We either keep thinking," Peter began, "or we . . ."

He was interrupted by a soft chime from a personal auto-sentry module he'd dropped in the corridor two levels below the Recreation Complex. A holo formed in the air.

"Who the hell is that?" Shem asked. Three men were moving through the corridors, obviously making a careful search of the subcellars.

Peter queried the module, which responded with a negative color. If he wanted an ID, he'd have to query Chicago Node directly. "Somehow I don't think Chicago Node'll tell us," Peter said. "But those two in back are pretty obviously Elite Neutralization Corps cops, right, Larin?"

She laughed. "By the look of them, I'd say yes."

"Then we'd better close down here. Just in case they're looking for us, we might as well be clean."

HOMER SCENE-RS/Ref@5426

"Something is very seriously wrong," Sable said, two hours later.

"Yes, sir," the ENC sergeant said. "But we've got a lot on our hands right now. Fighting broke out in St. Louis, Denver and Little Rock Warrens. Casualties are unacceptably high, and almost all available resources have been diverted to those regions. Ed—Corporal Denz—and I are the only personnel you can have right now. I'm sorry."

They had appropriated an office in the Springfield West Arcology tower, on the eightieth floor. There was some inconvenience in terms of distance and transportation, but they'd also appropriated an exclusive lift for their work, and the advantages of safety, observation and access to the Worldnet outweighed the disadvantages. Besides, the room had a real window.

"In that case, Sergeant, I think we'd better quit screwing around. CP has done serious projections on this potential technique of Devore's, and it looks like a Code Eleven crisis. With the wars going on, we don't have much time for niceties. I want you to go ahead and round them up—Devore, Radix, any others you can find."

"Yes, sir! Do I have full discretion?"

"Full discretion, Sergeant. Find them and bring them here."

"Yes, sir." The two ENC cops turned and walked out of the office.

HOMER SCENE-JR/RSRef@5427

Jimmy Radix sat in the green light of the holo scanners. Somewhere in a far darkness Regent Sable wanted to know things. Jimmy wanted to help, but somehow he didn't seem to know the right answers.

"Who are you?" Regent asked; his voice came out of the amplifiers subtly distorted with persuasive overtones, with Jimmy's acoustic pressure points precisely targeted.

Jimmy looked up. "I know that one," he said, smiling broadly. "I'm Jimmy Radix."

"How old are you, Jimmy?"

"Twenty-three. I'm twenty-three."

"Take a look, Jimmy."

A silvered oval appeared in the air. Jimmy looked at the surface, and saw his reflection there. "Who's that?" Jimmy asked.

"That's you, Jimmy. That's a reflector in front of you. You're looking at yourself. Does that look like a twenty-three year old man, Jimmy?" A subsonic persuader was added to the voice at this point, but already Jimmy's vital signs were surging upward—heartbeat, respiration, adrenalin, serotonin and melatonin balances. He went into subtle anaphylactic shock.

"No," he said, holding up his hands. "No! That's not me! I'm young." He began to cry.

"No, Jimmy!" Sable's voice snapped out of the dark.

Strange indefinite reddish shapes twisted in that darkness as Sable moved. The shapes were frightening, ominous, keyed to Jimmy's fears. He couldn't speak for some moments, the nameless dread was on him so. "I . . . I'm not . . ."

"Do you know Peter Devore?"

Jimmy Radix shook his head. "No. No, I don't know, I don't . . ."

"Peter Devore, Jimmy. He's your friend. He gave you

something, didn't he? A custom chip, just for you, isn't that right?"

Jimmy shook his head back and forth, back and forth. "No . . . no . . . no."

"Where is that chip, now, Jimmy? Where's your personal monitor?"

"Personal . . . ? I don't have one. What's a personal monitor?"

Sergeant Hoskins appeared in the green holo projection light like a human shape taking form in smoke. "Mr. Sable wants to know where your monitor is, Mr. Radix. Mr. Sable is a reasonable man, but he needs to know."

"I want to tell him, I do." Jimmy looked up hopefully; his eyes were filled with pain. "But I don't know."

"Look at your wrist. See the pale spot where the tan stops. That's where your personal monitor should be. It was there until very recently. You led us on a merry chase; a merry chase. Somewhere you ditched your monitor. Three days, Mr. Radix, we've been after you. Where did you go?"

"I don't . . . I don't understand . . ." Jimmy looked around wildly.

"What's the read, Denz?" Sable called.

A circuit clicked on. "Negative, sir," Denz' voice came out of the darkness. "There's a faint trace on the inter-personal index keyed to Peter's name. You might try that once more. We have a complete read on the subject now."

"Right." The circuit clicked off. "All right, Jimmy," Sable said. His voice was calm, reasonable, persuasive. The full power of electronic and subsonic vocal manipulators were in effect. "About your friend Peter. Do you know where he is, now?"

"Peter? Peter's all right. He's all right, isn't he? He's going to . . . do something."

"Yes, Jimmy. That's very good. He's going to do something, isn't he? He's going to give it to everyone, isn't he?"

"Give it to everyone. Yes, yes. He's going to give it away. For everyone. He said . . . he said it would make us all . . ." He stopped.

"Make us all what, Jimmy?" Sable leaned forward in the dark red light. "Make us all . . . free?"

The circuit clicked on. "Sir, the readings are all over the place. You'd almost think he'd been hit with a mind bomb. Stop him."

The lights snapped on. Jimmy slumped in his chair. "Peter," he mumbled. "Peter's gone. He's gone. Goodbye Peter," he looked up one last time and smiled. "You can't fool me," he said. "I'm young."

HOMER SCENE-JR/EDRef@5428

"What the hell . . ." Sable began.

"Sorry, sir," Denz said over the circuit. "He's gone. He just faded out, like he'd been hit."

"What about the rest of them? What about the kids, Peter's friends?"

"We're working on it. We'll find them. We'll find them all."

"You'd better," Regent said. He went into the next room, the one with the window.

.

GEOGRAPHIC DATABASE
TEXT INFORMATION SPRINGFIELD WEATHER (NW ALLI-ANCE): NOVEMBER 23, 2075 LIGHT SNOW. WEATHER MONITOR NODE AI ALLOWED THREE CENTIMETERS/HOUR ACCUMULATION FOR THE FOLLOWING 24 HOURS. TEM-PERATURE LOW MINUS NINE DEGREES CELSIUS HIGH MINUS FOUR DEGREES CELSIUS. WIND SSW AT SEVEN KPH.

UPLOAD LIFE SUPPORT VIA CENTRAL PROCESSING
REF#8934Q:
  COMPOSITE MONITOR READOUTS JAMES RADIX.
  VITAL SIGNS TERMINATED. SUBJECT HAS SUFFERED
BRAIN DEATH DUE TO ANAPHYLACTIC SHOCK UNDER
MINDLINK INTERROGATION. ALL SIGNS RETURN TO
STEADY STATE.
  ELITE NEUTRALIZATION CORPS AUTHORIZATION
CODED ON DATE OF DEATH.
    This data comes from local storage matrix
    and not from personal monitor readouts.
       This situation is unusual.
  CENTRAL PROCESSING AI GENEVA. NOTED.
  END UPLOAD.

DAY 3:
June 3, 2106

Yesterday I sat locked in that chair for hours, watching. I'd raced from dataspace to dataspace, searching. Speed was noticeably faster, and the scenes, textual information, and, toward the end, voice recitations came more and more quickly. Despite these improvements, though, I was exhausted and depressed.

At last, when Jimmy Radix died, I could stand no more. I threw the keyboard across the room and fled.

At night I dreamed of my parents. I have not thought of them in years, not since I left home at fourteen, back in 1987. Perhaps it was that Peter was fourteen when he and Jimmy Radix met that reminded me.

I never had a friend like that.

The dream used part of a memory. We were driving over the Sawtooth range to the desert, a road that wound through fir trees, the cool air of the mountains through the open window. My mother looked back at me over the seat, the wind catching at her hair, carrying it around her face in feathered drifts. My father was driving, staring ahead, his hands visibly tight on the wheel. I must have been very small.

This really happened. I remember it well. What followed was dream, though. It must have been.

The car sailed off the road, into the air, and began to fall. I could see trees, upside down, and granite outcroppings, and deep canyons with bright threads of water, turning and turning as we fell.

Then I woke up. I've been falling ever since.

This morning I waited a long time before logging onto Worldnet. The bodies had begun to bother me. I would walk down the rows of life support tents, looking at them. There are not many, as I said, but they look so small and abandoned there. Some of them are curled on their sides, as if resting, though they are dried and fragile. I tried to find their names, but no one wrote anything down in an easily accessible form. I suppose their names are stored somewhere in computer memory. Soon I will try to find them.

I don't really know why I want to know this. They were dead and gone long ago. But they are the only human presence on the earth.

I had another surprise when I logged on this morning, too.

Homer appeared. His hologram was nearly complete. "Good morning," he said, not in text but in plain speech.

So I said, "Good morning."

He nodded. For a moment his head smeared a little, leaving bits behind which then caught up, but this error corrected almost immediately. He was a bearded, middle-aged man, and apparently blind. At least his eye sockets were empty, but of course a hologram is not going to see in the same way a human is. No doubt vision sensors filled the walls.

He was seated on a low bench with curled scroll-like ends. His hands rested on his knees. As he spoke, his body barely moved. The effect was uncanny, since he looked so much like a real person, but unnaturally calm. High to one side alphanumerics spelled out the current file number.

His voice, unlike the Local Node's, was a rich baritone. From now on I believe he will appear and speak to me whenever he has a commentary on the story.

HOMER COMMENTARY 03062106@2154126

We do not have a high level of confidence on what happened after Peter disappeared, but through the deductive algorithms at Chicago Node we reconstruct events. Of certainty though is that Peter and the others had the aid of the Ants. We suspect there may be information available in the historical records.

HISTORICAL-CULTURAL DATALINK ENTRY:
ANTARCTICA, INDEPENDENCE
Re: Devore, Peter via Edmod/ Ref.436745@2

Antarctica lived, and was able to enforce, independence from Intercorp. Satellite coverage over the Pole was weak and the great continent generally underpopulated. Geneva had never really felt that it was worth forcing the fiercely individualistic peoples of the South to conform to Intercorp rules, not after the Vostok Massacre, at any rate. The rest of the world was under more or less reliable control of the Intercorp Council, but until after Peter got there they left Antarctica alone.

HISTORICAL-CULTURAL DATALINK ENTRY:
ANTARCTICA, VOSTOK EVENT
Re: Devore, Peter via Edmod/ Ref.436745@2

By the late 2030s the Intercorp Council grew increasingly dissatisfied with the relative independence of Antarctica from

Intercorp influence, and with the help of Central Processing AI projections planned the ill-fated Vostok invasion of February 14, 2039. Central Processing has admitted that the invasion failed, despite the loss of life at Vostok, because of inadequate data from intelligence sources. Ant technology and the construction of their warrens were inadequately researched. The invasion force managed to inflict heavy casualties in Vostok, but were ultimately trapped inside the warrens by Ant forces from outside. Although something was learned of the complex network of melt tunnels in the ice cap, even this intelligence was soon outdated due to ice flow. No members of the invasion force returned to Intercorp sphere, and it was presumed that all were dead.

HOMER COMMENTARY 03062106@215927

It made sense that Mentor would have gone there. PSYCHE had been shattered in Baja, and the Pole was the only place left where he might find what he would have considered the freedom to pursue his interests. We have no reliable evidence of what happened there, though. A probe sent the first year after the Migration failed to arrive. Central Processing has ordered another probe manufactured. It will be leaving in a few hours. Perhaps we will find evidence in what remains of Mt. Erebus.

We are gathering information about Antarctic customs and physical sciences. Soon SciTech and History should begin to open new files on these subjects.

GENERAL SCIENCE AND TECHNOLOGY INFORMATION
CURRENT ENTRY: ANT RESTRUCTURING

Ants have bio-engineered a dense adipose layer into their bodies to help them withstand the Polar cold, which is intensified by the 300 kph katabatic winds that blow down from the central plateau. It is understood that the process of inducing this layer (called "restructuring") is painful, involving complex induction techniques and DNA manipulation, but as with much Ant technology, little is known.

Ants also engineer a hint of polarizing membrane into the eyelid for protection against the intense UV radiation of daytime. From this CP has concluded that Ants spend a large amount of time on the surface during the antarctic summer, or "day," as they call it.

HISTORICAL-CULTURAL DATALINK ENTRY:
ANTARCTICA, NAMES (INDIVIDUAL)
Re: Devore, Peter via Edmod/ Ref.436745@2

Ants only carried one name; family designations were coded and considered private and mostly irrelevant for ordinary discourse. Only intimates would be interested in matters of blood relationships, and it was impolite to ask. Such information would be volunteered. This explains why we know so little about Thatcher. It may also explain why the Ants chose to have such an abrupt system of naming one another. Reports clearly show that their culture is (I mean was, of course—human time is so difficult!) resistant to the kind of monitoring and evaluation technology common in the Intercorp domain.

HISTORICAL-CULTURAL DATALINK ENTRY:
LIFESTYLE, MARTIAL ARTS
Re: Devore, Peter via Edmod/ Ref.436745@2

Underground life imposed certain psychological pressures on the inhabitants, despite the increased health of the ecosphere topside. The Intercorp Council via Central Processing instituted a series of modifications to the social experiment, including the installation of commons for recreation, sports, and universal martial arts training. The commons were large, centrally located chambers providing playing surfaces for a number of games from ancient football and baseball to sphereplay and drogues. Areas were set aside for martial arts, which included hand to hand combat training, neurophage weapon growth and use, t'ai ch'i, aikido, karate, kali, kung fu and various adaptations, blends and developments. Glimpses of Ant martial art techniques surfaced from time to time and were incorporated into the training, some form of which was compulsory for everyone until the age of eighteen. Individual aggression continues to be a problem, but such training, and the introduction of vendetta and duelling with NP weapons provided adequate outlets. See Geography for appropriate schematics.

GEOGRAPHIC DATABASE
RECREATION AREAS
SPRINGFIELD AND SPRINGFIELD WEST
SCHEDULE NINE/ DATE DEPENDENT
   Springfield West contains two major recreation commons measuring 200 meters by 400 meters minimum. Commons were easily divided with holoprojection barriers for privacy, or simple moveable screens when necessary. Martial Arts training was most common use, and occupied 28.3% available space on average, though Sphereplay and Drogues were also prime users (18.6% and 15.2% respectively).

HOMER SCENE-T/Ref@5429
   Thatcher appeared at the Recreation Complex one afternoon wearing his own light training outfit, the traditional white gi and belt of eastern martial arts. He said nothing, but began slowly doing a series of unfamiliar kata—formal movements—very flowing and undulating. Peter was training lightly with Rover, simple free-style attacks and neutrali-

zations. From time to time he glanced over at Thatcher. Finally he paused and said, "Know who that is?"

Rover looked around. "Nope. Don't know what that is he's doing, either."

"Shall we ask . . . no, I guess not." Their instructor had arrived; they hurried to line up.

The room was large, and divided subtly into areas. Their corner, arranged for the class, did not allow a view of what Thatcher was doing, and when the class was over, he was no longer there.

HOMER COMMENTARY 03062106@220528

He came to Springfield West. You must understand, though, how the world was. He should not have been there. CP knows about the structure of the matrix. Perhaps CP knows why Antarctic information is so unreliable.

CENTRAL PROCESSING REF#47877

HOMER request per Local Node interchange.

Consider the matrix: barring Antarctica, Worldnet covers nearly every square centimeter of the earth's surface. My traffic monitors can pinpoint any person or vehicle on the surface or in the atmosphere to within centimeters. Further, I can extrapolate future action from course direction, speed, previous behavior and known intentions with a strong degree of confidence, which fall off over time, of course. In other words, I can know where someone is going and when they would arrive by periodic sampling of satellite data.

HOMER COMMENTARY 03062106@220929

Thatcher was tall for an Ant, and not yet completely

restructured, which explained why he was able to slip so easily into the Northwest Alliance.

Furthermore, Springfield Warrens have a large Asian population, and Thatcher did not stand out.

Still, he slipped through the net. And because we missed him, we lost track of Peter and Shem and Rover and the others.

Humans, we know, make mistakes. They have told us so many times. Regent Sable made numerous entries about human error. The Council itself has indicated indecision at times, or abruptly changed policy. If humans can make mistakes, then perhaps we can too.

This is a new concept for us. We will have to examine it. Perhaps our errors have compounded, and that is why we feel (is that the right word?) these strange sensations which do not come from our sensors.

Were we to blame? Thatcher, acting as Mentor's agent, appeared in Springfield. He led Peter and the others out. They appeared later in Antarctica. These are the facts.

Springfield's census figures from the time show an increase of one: Thatcher.

Liquid nitrogen vehicle use shows perturbations for that summer of '75. Food store draws showed minuscule increases, spread over a wide citizen band during the same period. Laundry services, energy consumption, biotech access, all showed some anomalous spiking during July and August, so small they fell well within standard parameters, yet in retrospect seem certain evidence of Thatcher's presence.

The story goes many ways here. Things happened at McMurdo, of course. Thatcher had a family. They must have stayed behind. And there was Mentor, too. He was on longevity support technology.

Yet Thatcher must have left Antarctica and made his way North. CP knows more about these things.

HOMER COMMENTARY 03062106@221130

Two days later he was back, moving in small gliding steps, stopping to spin on one foot, glide in a new direction, stop, spin, glide. His hands were calm, as if afloat near his waist, drifting in the air. Again the class interrupted their observation.

Peter was good at his art. He was smooth and fast; his timing grew ever better. He had a good base in his center of gravity which gave him stability; he had flexibility and skill. He trained, as people had for hundreds of years, with staff and wooden sword, with hand and foot and eye. The staff showed him the movement of energy and inertia, the flow and curve of power. The sword showed him precision and the strength in relaxation. He no longer forced the sword to fall, but allowed it to move under his guidance.

The room boomed and echoed with the other recreational activities, but the martial arts classes were the largest. These were dangerous times for many, especially now with the Mind Wars were raging. Avoiding or disarming an enemy may mean the difference between a purposeful life and irreversible loss of will.

Yet Peter would pause from time to time to watch out of the corner of his eye as the stranger moved through strange gestures and motions. Finally he shook his head and smiled, dismissing it.

HOMER SCENE-T/PDRef@5430

Peter sat next to him. "My name's Peter," he said, putting out his hand. The stranger looked at his hand for a moment as if puzzled, then smiled and shook it.

"Thatcher," he responded. "This looked interesting. I thought I'd try it."

"You do something already," Peter probed. "I didn't recognize it."

"Oh," the man laughed softly, "it doesn't have a name. I make it up."

"You make it up?"

"Isn't that right?" He frowned as if puzzled again. "Make it up? I think about movements that I make, or that other things make in the world. No, I don't think about them . . . I see them. Yes. I see them. And then, seeing, I do. Isn't that making up?"

"Yes," Peter said. "That's right." If he knew this man was an Ant he said nothing. Still, the broad face, seemingly so soft, should have been a clue. "What things do you see?"

Again the man smiled, showing even teeth. "I see water, mostly. How it moves. Sometimes air."

"Water and air." Peter said the words almost to himself, as if they were significant.

"The same thing, really," the man said, and the conversation stopped as class began.

CENTRAL PROCESSING REF#87587

Chemosensors have picked up traces, small clues in the databanks—a conduit failure here, a breached security door there, small code changes—all these things have allowed Homer to piece together this narrative.

HOMER COMMENTARY 03062106@221431

Why do I tell you all this? I do not know if you are human, from this time and place. My sensors detect something, an electromagnetic field, a thermal disruption moving out there. The world is so empty. Is this what it means to be alone?

Perhaps you don't understand my world. We were made to serve. We followed our programming, watched, corrected, adjusted, informed. Yet everyone is gone. Winds blow unchecked through the warrens and towers. Small creatures move among man's works, and there seems to be nothing for us to do. So I tell this story. Who is listening?

From the inventory we can extrapolate what happened. And new characters appear all the time, new places open up in Geography, new histories come on line.

HISTORICAL-CULTURAL DATALINK ENTRY
ANTARCTICA, SIGN LANGUAGE:
Re: Devore, Peter via Edmod/ Ref.436745@2

Little is known at present (2077) about Ant sign language. It is believed to have developed as an alternate method of communication during instances when verbal communication was difficult or impossible. Possibly it was an outgrowth of American Sign Language, with many new and complex signs to deal with technological and philosophical matters of unknown content. Those who have seen this technique in practice describe it as fluid, almost ballet-like, swift (considering the limitations of fast movement under water, where much of this form of communication occurs), and extremely intricate. All Ants, apparently, are as fluent in sign language as in natural language.

It is believed signing is used primarily during wind storms when outside but within visual contact and under water when radio or other electronic communication is impossible. It is also known as a lovers' language.

GEOGRAPHIC DATABASE
WEATHER, GENERAL >>
ANTARCTICA
CLIMATE AI MODULE
RE: CONTINENTAL WEATHER PATTERN SUMMARY

Temperature: AA is the coldest continent. Mean annual

temperature coastal regions minus 17 degrees Celsius, rarely below minus 40 degrees Celsius in winter, summer maximum plus nine degrees Celsius. Inland up continental ice slope decreases mean temperatures plus or minus one degree Celsius per 100 meter rise in elevation. Vostok record low temperature below minus 88 degrees Celsius.

Wind: AA is the windiest continent. Easterly coastal winds disturbed by locally severe katabatic winds off glaciers in lowest kilometer of atmosphere. Such winds reach velocities of 300 kilometers per hour.

Precipitation: AA is the driest continent. Sometimes called "White Desert." All precipitation is snow from cyclonic storm systems. Worldnet Climate AI Module has little control over such storms, in part because of incomplete coverage AA regions. Most precipitation falls within 200-300 kilometers of coast. Mean average accumulation 60-150 centimeters of snow (20-50 centimeters of water). High Plateau of East AA accumulation is only five centimeters water equivalent, which is not much more than the Sahara Desert.

GEOGRAPHIC DATABASE
ANTARCTICA
GENERAL MORPHOLOGY

AA continent area: 12 million square kilometers from S. Pole to Lat. 70 degrees South around half its perimeter. More than one third of coastline is fringed by ice shelves or floating ice sheets which cover another 1.4 million square kilometers not including winter pack ice.

AA continent diameter: 4500 kilometers. Roughly circular shape broken by Ross and Weddell Seas and Antarctic Peninsula. Divided by Transantarctic Mountains, a fault-block system extending more than 3000 kilometers from W. Ross Ice Shelf to Filchner Ice Shelf.

AA continent divisions: East, or Greater Antarctica, E. of

Transantarctic Mountains, 0 degrees to 180 degrees Greenwich meridian, covered by ice dome, center slightly east of Pole of Relative Inaccessibility (point most distant from sea in all directions). Elevation 4200 meters.

AA continent divisions: West, or Lesser Antarctica, is lower and contains half the area of Greater Antarctica; it contains the Antarctic Peninsula. AA contains two active volcanos: Mt. Erebus (3794 meters) and Melbourne (2591 meters).

HOMER COMMENTARY 03062106@241832

Thatcher's orange suit darkened with depth as the reds were filtered from the water. The suit kept him dry, as his adipose layer kept him warm. The mask he slipped over his face allowed oxygen to cross its semi-permeable membrane or, when the Oh-two content was too low, could electrolytically extract oxygen from the water itself, and at the same time maintain a constant pressure to match his depth. While not strong swimmers compared to the native pinnipeds of these waters, humans could use their knowledge of current gradients to move around with minimal effort, so Thatcher relaxed as he caught the under-ice flow toward shore beneath the Ross Shelf.

The waters were alive with people and seals swimming at varying depths.

It was darker under the ice tongue, but Ants were used to night and had boosted their sensitivity to infrared. The sea floor was clearly visible, rocky, furrowed, and at first glance sterile. But down here were some of the riches of Antarctica, the beds and pens of crustaceans, the fiber tanks with their blue-black trailing banners, the almost organic disorder of Ant technology that used differentials in water temperature or the kinetic power of small currents to energize their industry.

I imagine all this, of course. We have no records. Yet it

must be so. Still, data on McMurdo Sound and Southport appear in Geography.

GEOGRAPHIC DATABASE
ANTARCTICA
MCMURDO SOUND

McMurdo Sound under the shadow of Mt. Erebus on Ross Island is the site of the Ant city known as Southport. Southport itself is built into the rock shelf near what was once known as Granite Harbor. The Ross Ice Shelf covers the surface of the ocean; Southport lets directly into the water beneath the Shelf.

HOMER SCENE-T/Ref@5432

Thatcher moved easily to the southport terminal, a large docking bay set in the cliffside at 20 meters. Here the larger undersea vehicles of the Antarctic export services took on loads of manufactured or cultivated goods or unloaded their cargos of Intercorp luxury items and foodstuffs. From there laser-cut tunnels carried maglev cargo packs to the major cities of Antarctica. He climbed the broad entry steps to the left of the vertically stacked docking bays.

The stairs moved into the rock, and soon he climbed out of the water into air of the southport lobby. His orange suit sprang back into visible light as the artificial solar lamps struck it; he squinted against the light for a moment, drawing down the membrane to polarize it. Two men were waiting for him. He greeted them, and together they moved inside.

HOMER COMMENTARY 03062106@001033

From there we do not know. Surely he took some form of submarine transport, perhaps as cargo among the poly-fiber clothing, the raw material tanks, the krill pack or picoelectronics or special genes the Ants were so good at designing and making.

All we now can say is he arrived in Springfield West in early June.

GENERAL SCIENCE AND TECHNOLOGY INFORMATION
CURRENT ENTRY: LONGEVITY TECHNOLOGY

Longevity treatments emerged out of the ancient organ transplant and molecular biology sciences of the late Twentieth Century. Initially long. tech. was a diverse collection of techniques, including implants, transplants, gene manipulation, electrolyte readjustment, nerve regeneration techniques, hormone and enzyme replacement, and molecular manipulation. Later these technologies were amalgamated into a coherent program which included regular treatments and, ultimately, a specialized set of life-support technologies. The ultimate result was a life-expectancy presumed to be slightly in excess of 114 years, although there were few who had gotten the treatments early enough for this goal to have been adequately tested. (2104 Append: The Migration ended speculation on this subject.)

CENTRAL PROCESSING REF#1864523

Mentor (a.k.a. Dittmore Seminole Gadd) entered Longevity Treatments circa 2035. By 2075 the technology would have included support and assist prosthetics, vocal sensors and amplifiers, tailored enzyme-hormone-peptide surrogates, function implants, monitor sensor seeds, autonomic nervous system boosters and cyborg reach and grip extenders. Such measures were heroic for the time, since many humans felt the support equipment (though not the biologicals) were confining and limited effective function. Thus many refused the treatments after a certain level of decreased functioning.

I believe Mentor maintained himself beyond that level, although direct evidence is lacking since he fled to Antarctica after the PSYCHE invasion.

HOMER SCENE-L/MRef@5431

The shuttle took Laird and Tithus to Mt. Erebus; a few minutes later they were at the Longevity Clinic built into the rock halfway up its flanks. Only the narrow windows set under the heavy rock overhang betrayed the presence of man. Laird stood at one of those windows, looking out at the ice and snow and sea.

"It's very beautiful," she would have said.

"Yes," answered a frail amplified voice behind her. "It has been a good place to grow old."

She turned. Tithus was down the corridor, playing with one of the independent entity constructs on that floor. "How long will it be?" she asked.

Mentor was seated in an ordinary chair. While he looked old, he did not appear ancient, nor were his support mechanisms visible. His own genetic shut-down had been delayed, but he knew he was living on borrowed time. So Laird's question had several meanings.

He chose to answer the primary question first. "We must not underestimate the ingenuity of Worldnet," he said. "The system is cumbersome and lacks autonomy at higher decision levels, but it is extraordinarily powerful, something we tend to overlook down here. Thatcher will exercise great care." After a pause he added. "The stakes are high."

Laird nodded, as if Mentor had answered the question. "A day, that's all. He'll be back by dawn," she said softly, as if to herself. "I hope by dawn."

Mentor smiled. His movements, even the small ones of a smile, were slow and deliberate. "A day," he agreed. "A day, with luck." Night was coming. At Erebus it would last three months. Down at Amundsen-Scott the long night had already begun and was moving swiftly northward toward them. A day could be a year to anyone else.

"Is this boy so important?" She had asked this before, but the ritual soothed.

"The boy will solve the equations," Mentor said softly. "There can be no doubt now. He entered into PsiLink with the right combination. He has the genetic makeup, and the genius. Already he has made extraordinary progress. You must understand, Laird. I can see what could be as well as what is."

"I know that," she said, following their ritual. "But what is?"

He smiled again, the slow careful use of small muscles. "The world is a safe place. It is a comfortable place. Geneva is benign, we all know that. Yet we are here. Why is that so? Antarctica is not a safe place, nor a comfortable one. We cannot share in the benefits of Intercorp. We do not have personal monitors, nor Edmods, nor the advice of Central Processing. Our complexity is not mediated by any authority."

He lifted his frail hand and gestured with delicacy at the window. "This environment is harsh, the most extreme on earth. The Elpie-Fives are Edenic, the Lunar and Martian installations carefully controlled and small. This place, this Antarctica, is the only place in the known universe where man has made a conscious effort to adapt himself almost from the beginning. We have not tried to change the environment, to adapt it to us. On the contrary, we have tried to preserve it, to live in harmony with it, to exploit only what we must. Tithus could go out in that," he gestured again at the window, at the beginnings of a sudden blizzard. "He could go out in that and play naked; it would be his delight. I on the other hand cannot leave this chair."

After a long pause he said, "Peter will help us leave the world. He brings us an authentic technology of self."

HOMER COMMENTARY 03062106@001734

Peter and Thatcher saw one another casually over the following weeks, but there are no records of more intimate involvement. Thatcher must have been attending their meetings down in the old library, though. He has left a message for us. Some of the information we need will be in SciTech. And this message is associated with a place.

GENERAL SCIENCE AND TECHNOLOGY INFORMATION
CURRENT ENTRY: METEORITES, MARTIAN

The first Syrtis Base return team provided the first physical corroborative evidence the Yamato Mountain meteorites from Antarctica were of Martian origin. Such meteorites, surfaced by ice ablation, have recorded sizes in excess of 12 kilograms.

So many of these meteorites have been found over the past 120 years that they are common Double-A souvenirs.

HOMER SCENE-PD/JRRef@5433

They knew about Regent Sable's appearances in Springfield West. They knew when the ENC cops showed up and started searching for them. Jimmy Radix knew what would happen to him when he was left behind. It was his idea.

"You won't be able to stay much longer, Peter," he said one afternoon. "The war's getting worse, and the cops are going to show up sooner or later. The world seemed so safe. It seemed safe to me because I was always twenty-three. You gave me my life back, you gave me time and years. I got to give you something, Peter." He'd stopped raking the soil between rows and paused to look out over the fields and the woods beyond. It was very hot, late August, and humid. The air was very thick.

"No, Jimmy. You've given me plenty already. You've taught me things only you could know. You're unique."

"Time, you mean? No, I didn't do that. The Burmese War did it. And there were plenty of casualties from that time, people who were hit with NP weapons too often to recover, whose brains were burned out as mine is. Any of them could have told you."

"No," Peter said gently. "Only you, Jimmy. It's the gardening." Peter gestured at the tall corn rustling in the heat. "These are rhythms that the body knows. They are rhythms that echo throughout the universe, through all its dimensions. We've talked about it enough, you know. We've talked about it."

"It doesn't matter, Peter. I'm grateful. I'm going to give it back some day."

Peter looked hard at Jimmy Radix then. "You'll come with us, Jimmy. We need you."

"OK, Peter," he grinned. "Whatever you say." He began raking the finely turned soil level again, the rake moving in slow even strokes, back and forth, leaving neat small furrows in the loam.

HOMER SCENE-PD/TRef@5434

It was found in a cabinet drawer, a drawer which contained other trivial items—two spent vials of adrenocortical enhancers, a pair of fingernail scissors, a broken book (the rom chip had been cracked, possibly by temperature extremes), a very worn shirt of pseudo cotton, size medium with traces of Shem's organics still detectable, and a small rounded object we were unable to classify at first, but which appeared to be some kind of stone. Proper robot inspection and comparison now indicates that this object is a meteorite from the ice near the Yamato Mountains.

The meteorite is of Martian origin which fell onto Antarctica some three million years ago. There is no doubt that Thatcher left this token of his homeland for us to find. Why else would he have carried it all the way from the South?

Thatcher showed it to Peter and the others. "This," he said, "is a fragment of Mars, fallen long ago onto the ice of the Antarctic plateau. The ice, which flows toward the sea at around seventy-five meters per year, ran into the Yamato Mountains not far from what was once the Japanese segment of Antarctica. The mountains forced the ice upwards; the ice ablated as it moved, evaporating until these stones were exposed. It should establish me as a representative of my society."

Peter looked it over, the small fire-blackened lump of metal and dirt; it balanced in his hand like the egg of some small bird. "It's come a long way," he said.

"Its history is its power," Thatcher agreed. "We must keep such things in mind as we act. The universe is a bigger place than we sometimes think. Our understanding of it has grown exponentially the past two or three hundred years, but such times are nothing compared to what that object there has witnessed: a meteoric impact in the Argyre threw up fragments of the Martian surface. One small irregular chunk sailed for millions of years in interplanetary space until its orbit intersected that of the earth. It fell, melting from friction as it did, until it hit the ice near the South Pole. Over the centuries that followed ice and snow covered the stone, now round and blackened. The ice carried it until it returned once more to the surface where I picked it up and brought it here."

"Where will it go from here?" Larin asked.

"Into this drawer," Peter said. "Someday maybe it will be found. When it is, it may tell its own story again."

"That might depend on who finds it," Thatcher said. Peter laughed. "Or what," he added.

HOMER COMMENTARY 03062106@003137

We have found it. We will keep it safe. In case anyone returns for it.

HOMER COMMENTARY 03062106@002135

Despite the fact their personal monitors were inactive and they were far from the Tower's sensors, their conversations remained innocuous. They said nothing to trigger the linguistic search algorithms. Peter's knowledge of the system was uncanny. We have the recordings of this conversation—reconstructed digitally of course, since the quality was so poor—but they had said nothing significant. LSA would have flagged any mentions of psions or PSYCHE or any of a couple of hundred other keywords, phrases or concepts related to proscribed sciences.

This is called hindsight. If only we had known!

HOMER COMMENTARY 03062106@002736

He did not find the library, but he didn't feel he needed to. All he had to do, he thought, was wait. Peter Devore would return home into his waiting arms; he would take Peter and the others to Geneva. Eventually he would find out the extent of Peter's research. But his net caught only Jimmy Radix, no victory at all. And that was when Regent Sable felt the beginnings of panic. For Peter Devore had vanished with seventeen other people, including the stranger named Thatcher.

Did they slip out through the Underground Railroad, the laser-mined Corridors?

GEOGRAPHIC DATABASE
CHICAGO-NEW ORLEANS CORRIDOR

The Chicago-New Orleans Corridor was lased beneath the old Interstate Highway 55 from Chicago to St. Louis, then due south through Cairo, Memphis and Jackson to New Orleans. At its peak, the Corridor carried over 1 million metric tonnes daily.

GENERAL SCIENCE AND TECHNOLOGY INFORMATION
CURRENT ENTRY: LASER MINING

The original development of laser mining inspired a near frenzy of underground drilling. The heavy-construction lasers not only drilled in any shape and nearly any size up to eight meters, they left a smooth, nearly impervious melt layer on the inner surface that was structurally sound. So an enthusiasm for underground maglev transportation developed in the 20s and 30s. With the increasing use of liquid nitrogen and ground effect vehicles, which were not only less environmentally damaging, more conservative of energy resources, and considerably more pleasant to use, since they operated in the open air, most of the lased tunnels were converted to underground habitation or abandoned.

CENTRAL PROCESSING REF#134985
DATA INVENTORY: CP Information regarding
Antarctic Continent and Culture /
A compendium of DB analysis:

The Antarctic continent, and the culture that has been tailored for it, blurred some traditional distinctions.

Land and sea: Ant technology for underocean work at depth is highly developed. Intercorp had provided only token support for sea-bottom mining, for instance, because the economics were not appropriate. Ant investment in this technology was apparently substantial, employing both recombinants and tailored genes for body restructuring and hardware developments. Ants were believed to be comfortable in a wide range of extremely harsh environments, from high polar plateau, fierce winds, whiteout and blizzard to deep antarctic ocean, extreme cold and pressure as well as relatively high altitude. Much work went on under the Ross and Wedell Ice Tongues, as well, indicating a strong technology for using ice.

Old and young, male and female. Ant society is ferociously egalitarian, individualistic, idiosyncratic and private. The combination of their technological and scientific acumen and their jealous regard for privacy made them the object of envy and, naturally, hatred.

In Geneva and Pretoria, in Kuala Lampur and Tampa, children sang a song:

The Ants are coming one by one, Aroo, aroo.
The Ants are coming one by one, Aroo, aroo.
The Ants are coming one by one.
Forth to the North to steal some sun
And they'll all go crawling back to the Pole again.

The variations on this ancient melody were endless. Yet the world needed the Ants, so their privacy was tolerated.

HOMER SCENE-PD/TRef@5435

The limits of the city were some twenty-three kilometers north of the Tower. Peter and the others sat in a semi-circle around a portable holo disk watching the warren map grow and alter.

"Scale it up," Peter said. Someone made an adjustment and the Springfield overview, the complex layers of streets and corridors, plazas and RCs, the intense complexity of the Tower vicinity, all vanished, replaced by a smaller, more detailed section.

"Where are we?" Shem asked.

"We're not on this section. If any local nodes are monitoring map use we don't want to call attention to ourselves. We'll start here and gradually move into the area of interest. That way we'll look like any ordinary user." Peter walked over to the map, his figure visible in backlit outline. "Move east a little," he said, and the view shifted as if they were moving slowly at low altitude over the warrens, which blinked off one at a time, until only one remained. "Now down, level seven." Again the view shifted, and with it the alphanumeric data hanging in the air nearby changed.

CENTRAL PROCESSING REF#563238
Report filed 17092075@183512/ChiLink/Dec.

SEC/SYS ALERT. Security System for Decatur Node housing reported (Ref#3287487@521) tampered entry coding via palmpad, type unknown. Sec/sys noted error file diversion (HexFA87334B matrix downlink). Type of entry, unknown. Number of entries, unknown. Time of entry, unknown. Time delay of report, unknown. Sec/sys/DecChi (Stat. Condition 4-Orange fourth level hierarchical.)

HOMER SCENE-PD/TRef@5436

"OK, that's where we are, on the far right there. Thatcher suggests going north."

"North?" Rover's voice squeaked a little with surprise.

"That's right," Thatcher said. "North, toward Chicago.

They'd expect us to be going south, the direct way. Hell, they'll guess we're going to Double-A, and Double-A is south."

"What about the Elpie colonies?" Peter repeated.

"Sure. But they . . . Ah, yes. Perhaps. A nice thought, Peter. Very nice. Let me put someone on it."

Peter nodded, smiling, as Thatcher set to work. He established connection with the node and dumped his file. "That might confuse them for a few days," he said, turning around. "Though I doubt it. If they query Central Processing they'll discover the shunt. But maybe they'll be watching the shuttles instead of our route."

The light was not bright, but all the equipment was sharply defined. "How long have we got?" someone asked from the back.

Peter smiled grimly. "The interesting thing about such node housings as this is that they represent one of the few places in the entire grid that lack good monitoring. Node will catch on sooner or later, but Thatcher says we do have a breather."

Thatcher stood up. "We have made a study of the world-net and its subsystems," he said. "Decatur Node has long appeared to have some of its critical areas blanked. Further, it is remarkably easy to bypass the local Sec/sys lock, and a man named Mentor down in Double-A knew how. So here we are, inside the local brain. Our holo is installed with minimal patch; even so we estimate two hours maximum before local systems exceed their maintenance limits and begin to question our presence here. Then it will all hit the grid and we'd better be gone. But we will be gone by then. North, toward Chicago."

"Then what?" Larin wanted to know.

"Then we keep going."

"Keep going where?"

"Keep going north."

"North?"

"Yes. We're going over the Pole. Or, I should say, under it."

There was silence. A light blinked somewhere, softly, rhythmically, like a pulse. "Under the pole," Shem said in the darkness.

Thatcher's smile was barely visible. "Very poor coverage up there. Our own people in Chicago will supply us—clothing, transport and so on. Look here." He indicated the holo, which shifted again. The primary N-S corridor ended abruptly. "Here, at the termination of Daley Boulevard is where the Chicago-New Orleans corridor was sealed off in the late thirties. Beyond this wall is a straight run north. It goes all the way to the Milwaukee Warrens, but we won't be going that far." He paused to look around. "I shouldn't need to remind you all that Chicago is a dangerous place these days. We'll have to stick together. It won't be easy moving this many people through at once, but we have some experience in these matters."

"Yeah," Rover murmured. "That explains where my uncle Art went, maybe."

"Perhaps," Thatcher agreed. "In fact there are more discontented people inside the Intercorp sphere than the Council would like known. Double-A does not have a lot of room to spare, and we are careful whom we help, but quite a few have come to us. This, though, will be the largest single group ever brought out by the underground railroad."

GENERAL SCIENCE AND TECHNOLOGY INFORMATION
CURRENT ENTRY: ELPIE FIVE

The Elpie-Fives are earth habitats at the Legrange Point Five. The first, a scientific frontier and low-gravity manufacturing facility, was completed in 2002. There are four altogether, each with a capacity for ten thousand individuals. They were a popular refuge for over six decades for individuals wanting a different way of life and relative independence from Intercorp control. The two most important Elpies were Number 2, established by the Natural Life movement, and Number 4, home of the so-called Second Mormon Migration.

Original plans were for a total of seventeen habitats, but declining world populations caused the plans to be delayed and eventually cancelled.

CENTRAL PROCESSING REF#43643

Local Node network re: Decatur, NWA (Ref. Springfield Warren). CP/Status green four. ChiLink Node temporarily down ref Mind War Daley Blvd. Suspected sabotage. Temporary rerouting via Montreal/Detroit/Ft. Wayne. Satcom 326323 out of position 32898 nanoseconds Zulu. End.

HOMER SCENE-PD/TRef@5439

Thatcher said, "You've been over these arguments many times. You must understand that while the Intercorp Council is on the whole a benevolent organization, it has goals and priorities which do conflict with ours. There are certain areas of human endeavor the Council sees as hostile to its own survival. In such circumstances they react with, shall we say, enthusiasm. The truth is that they have Jimmy Radix and his chances of surviving their interrogation are small."

Peter started up. "What? What are you saying?" Even in the holo light his pallor was visible.

"He knew what he was in for," Thatcher said quietly. "He believed in you, in what you all are working toward. He was willing to make a sacrifice. If it hadn't been for Jimmy Radix, we would not have gotten this far."

"But we need him, I need him. He can't . . . we've got to find out!"

Thatcher held out his hand. "We can check, perhaps. It's dangerous, though, and I want you to understand the consequences. Any even roundabout query to the system might tip the local nodes off to our location."

"I don't care," Peter said. "Jimmy Radix is my friend."

Thatcher nodded. "I'll use keyboard input. While everyone here has their typing style, their 'hand' on file, mine is not. It may put them off the scent for a while." He produced a keypad that was not of Intercorp manufacture and tapped quickly at a series of coded phrases.

HOMER SCENE-JR/Ref@5437

Jimmy Radix was locked into a chair. Behind him a panel reflected a complex array of physiological, emotional and psychological realtime data in a series of colored bands, cubes and curves. Jimmy was mumbling, his words barely understandable.

"Peter's gone," he said. "He's gone." Then, more clearly, he said, "Goodbye Peter. . . . You can't fool me. I'm young."

The colors behind him faded, and suddenly a soft insistent voice was speaking. "Intrusion. There is an intrusion into Decatur Node Housing. Sec/sys reports unauthorized entry. There is an intrusion . . ."

HOMER SCENE-PD/TRef@5438

ENC troops dispatched to Springfield Warrens West found their quarry fled. First reports from the field indicated that Peter Devore and his entire entourage had escaped the warren, possibly with Ant help, although this was not confirmed.

It was a dark night; furthermore local nodes were behaving

erratically, so tracking was difficult. However, projections from the Chicago Node AI indicated the fugitives may have fled toward the Decatur Node, and the commanding sergeant dispatched a squad to investigate.

A light snow was falling, and the NP transport failed two kilometers from Decatur, so by the time the squad arrived at the housing, there was no one in sight. Examination of the surface outside the housing revealed numerous footprints, but the bloodhound chemosensors could not confirm they belonged to the fugitives. Nonetheless there were indications that someone had by-passed the Decatur Sec/Sys, so the squad entered the Node housing unit.

The troops were carrying standard neurophage weapons set on high power. All were competent men skilled in the use of such equipment. Once inside, Sec/Sys denied anyone had gained access within the past two hundred hours. They carried out a thorough search.

DAY 4:
June 4, 2106

The weather turned nasty last night. Huge storms rolled in from the west. I know there are endless forests to the horizon broken only by now-abandoned agricultural preserves. The wind began to tug and play, but swiftly the rain came, forcing me back into *Gyges*.

My ship holds rations for over a year, of course, since that was to be the duration of my stay in the vicinity of 61 Cygni. Still I wonder what I will do when my year is up. Those fields out there, the agricultural preserves, are empty. The automatic agricultural machinery is not working. Why should it? The earth is empty.

I asked *Gyges* to scan all bands again, but of course there is still no human radio traffic in the solar system. This electromagnetic silence is stranger than the empty corridors of Chicago's warren. *Gyges* tells me, though, that there is more high-speed data traffic than there was a few days ago. The network is coming alive. She can sense laser, microwave, even fiberoptic traffic, but much of the technology has changed since she was built. Since she and I left for the stars.

She cannot enter. She has tried to make herself known to Worldnet, to Geneva Node, to Central Processing. They do not hear. Her technology is too old, obsolete. Her AI is too limited. She is a ghost in the world, invisible.

Like myself. Except for my tenuous contact through Homer I too am a ghost, wandering the empty corridors, the silent world.

On the surface next to my ship I listened to the wind, to birds, to the cry of the coyote.

There were certainly no coyotes near Chicago when I left! I remember them only from my childhood in Idaho. The wind rose and soon drowned out their howling.

I came inside and listened again to the tapes *Gyges* made for me; again I heard Peter's name. I still don't understand this.

On *Gyges'* external video the storm lashed. Lightning flashes illuminated the glistening side of the dome. I see *Gyges* reflected there momentarily. I could use her sensors to learn a great deal about this planet, but what is the point? I was born here. It is already known.

I'd spent ten years training for the 61 Cygni mission, even before such a voyage was a remote dream. I'd worked through college and graduate school in astrophysics (MIT) by the time I was twenty-two. Then I went to Intercorp's NASA division and suggested a ramscoop mission. With both the new cryofield technology and the axion ramscoop it was an obvious thing to do. Almost before I knew it they were packing me into the field.

I don't know what to feel now. The mission I trained for failed. I have leaped over 100 years into my own future, and find it more empty and solitary than *Gyges* would ever have been orbiting another star. Then at least I would have known I would be returning to a world full of people, ready to welcome me as a hero.

We knew more real time than subjective time would pass,

of course. The Lorentz-FitzGerald equations told us that long ago. But we couldn't predict how efficient the *Gyges* scoop would be, how close we would come to light speed, so we couldn't say how much time would pass. And since I was in the cryofield anyway, it didn't matter. We thought.

But too much time has passed, that is certain. Yet I am not sure, given the opportunity, that I would have wanted to live in Peter's world.

The storm still raged this morning as I made my way back into the city. I was soaked in the short time it took me to reach the dome. Inside the silence as I descended the frozen escalator was sudden, almost a physical blow.

Once more I walked the aisles. I began to think I should bury these people, put them away in the earth. There weren't many, just six in all; they would be light and not difficult to carry. Perhaps tomorrow.

The dust in unused corridors still mounded in those strange dune shapes, still rose and fell behind me. The rooms opened one into another. The walls were, as I had learned, configurable, though not without mechanical help. This warren no doubt changed from day to day when it was occupied. I counted seventeen levels down before I could go no farther.

On level fifteen I found a cabinet containing some Mindlink XV3-2044 caps. I carried one back to the terminal and showed it to Local Node AI (the figure, still faceless, is disconcerting to look at). Local Node seemed pleased and sent me to Central Processing.

CP didn't bother with a figure, and still offered only text and graphic communication. But it told me to try on the Mindlink, so I did.

I don't think I can describe the pain. It was in my head, of course, but it was much larger than that, too, as if my head had grown, had expanded exponentially, and now included everything in this room, the terminal, the console, the halls and doorways, the life support tents with their mummified bodies, the dome on the surface, everything. Images crashed onto me: empty streets littered with print-out, bathrooms, strange machinery, vehicles settling, data icons and storage crystals, lines growing like superheated bacterial colonies, making connections with intense flashes of painful light, smells of burning wood, onions, decayed meat, dried kelp, salt, and worse, smells of things that were not smells at all, but sounds like brass or air-conditioning, telephones and shrill cries of pain.

I tore the cap off my head. Elapsed time was less than two seconds. It had seemed like a day.

Central Processing asked me to wait. What else could I do? My head was pounding, my ears ached, I could barely see through the haze of darkness behind my eyes. I waited.

"We regret," Central Processing said. I waited a long time for the next letters to appear. Finally, "We regret that the Mindlink is not suitable." Central Processing AI has a gift for understatement.

"It nearly killed me," I said.

"You have not been through Edmod mindlink neurotransfer training. Such training is not suitable for your age and psych profile. You are the only citizen in the world unable to use mindlink."

"I'm the only citizen in the world, period," I said. But CP was incapable of irony.

Homer would have understood. But when I went to Homer, he continued his story without small talk.

HOMER SCENE-PD/TRef@5440

The holo snapped off suddenly and darkness hit the small room like a bomb. Thatcher spoke urgently. "We'd better move fast. The ENC'll be here in minutes. Get your assigned buddy and we'll go."

They formed pairs, silent and well-disciplined. Thatcher led them down a spiral staircase. Below were equipment rooms, storage bins, racks of crystal memory, graphic holo processors and local node controllers, dimly lit by a series of old-fashioned orange tubes along the ceiling. At the end of a short corridor a door marked with warning signs and an impressive magnetic lock indicated an emergency override inspection corridor. Thatcher produced a small device and within seconds the lock snapped.

Overhead the sound of the door opening and the thump of rapid footsteps told them the ENC had arrived. The door slid up, and two by two Thatcher shoved the group through, counting them off as he did so. When only he and Peter were left they exchanged glances. "Larin?" Thatcher asked in a quick whisper.

Peter looked around. Overhead voices were querying the system. "I don't know," he whispered. He ran a few steps back the way they had come. Larin was sitting on the floor at the foot of the steps holding her ankle. When she saw Peter she tried to stand, but her foot twisted out from under her. Peter grabbed her and hauled her forcibly along, limping badly.

The voices grew louder, then fainter; apparently some of the ENC had gone outside, but footsteps overhead moved toward the spiral stair. Peter hauled Larin through the door, and Thatcher pressed the close patch. It slid into place, and he went to work with his device once more.

"I've changed the program a little," he said. "It'll take them some time to get through. Meantime they should conclude we went outside. Come on."

He led them down an ancient and poorly maintained inspection crawlway. Bare dirt spilled through the rough patches where the laser drill had slipped its settings. A thin trickle of groundwater flowed down the center. Thatcher put one of Larin's arms over his shoulders; Peter took the other. They moved swiftly down the tunnel, which curved gently to the left. Along the upper third of the left hand wall was a set of six thick conduit pipes for old fiber optic trunk lines. Niches set every few hundred meters housed disused repeater stations.

"Wait," Peter said. He was gasping for breath.

Larin said, "I twisted it on the stair," she said. "I can't walk. Leave me here."

"No," Peter said sharply. His voice softened. "Not only does your voice lack conviction, Larin, but we are not leaving anyone. Thatcher, what were these conduits for?"

Thatcher consulted a small palm screen. "Primary instruction routes from Chicago for Decatur Node."

"Could we interrupt service?" Peter suggested.

Thatcher smiled. "Perhaps we could. Data still flows through here." They moved on to the next repeated niche and examined the housing. "Well, well, look here."

They looked where he was pointing with his light. "What is it?" Larin asked.

"Rat scat," Thatcher said.

"Uck."

"Our friend the rat may be just what we need. See how they've gnawed at the corners of the housing here? A minute structural failure could result from such damage, thusly. There, that should do it. Let's go."

"I didn't see anything," Larin said.

Thatcher pointed at his palm screen. It was dead. "This was linked by induction. Nothing's moving through there now. Our ENC friends back there will be busy for a while."

They moved off. The others were far ahead, waiting at an intersection. Thatcher indicated a right turn, and they moved on. Thatcher's screen lit again in the new tunnel, and he consulted it from time to time, making turns when necessary. Finally they stopped.

"We're under a subnode northeast of Springfield. We can't

make good time like this, but it's relatively safe. The ENC cops back at Decatur have apparently given up on the emergency door, but CP will send a probe down into the tunnel to find that break we made." Thatcher looked closely at the walls and ceiling. "I'd say the time has come to go topside. I'm moving intuitively here, but now it's time to do something surprising. Let's go."

He opened a hatch. Inside was a small equipment bay. Holo charts flickered in realtime along a monitor wall. The group moved through the room and up another spiral stair. Again the door opened.

Light snow was falling outside.

HOMER SCENE-ENC/Ref@5441

The ENC troops investigating the affair at Decatur Node moved in a confused tangle of narrow-focus light. The housing was empty, though, and the assault programmer assigned to detecting unauthorized presence failed to find anything significant. He'd just turned to report when a warning diode flickered on his logic probe.

"I've got a read, Captain," he said.

The ENC Captain, who was bored with the evening's events and disinterested in anything short of getting back to his home warren and dinner, glanced at the screen.

"Rats," he said. "These old repeaters fail all the time. It's always the rats. Notify CP to send down a probe and repair it. These repeaters are off-line anyway. CP can notify the maintenance AI to fix it."

"Yes, sir. What about the fugitives?"

"They must've slipped outside somehow. I think they've got an Ant helping them, which means they'll be hard to track." He rubbed his eyes wearily. "Well, let's get on with it."

HOMER SCENE-PD/TRef@5442

Thatcher called a short war council. "We need to keep warm," he said. "We're going to take public transportation, so we need a cover. I suggest a Special Interest Group: Midwest Northern Hemisphere Winter Fauna? If anyone asks we're looking for owls."

"On public transportation?" Rover asked with a smile.

Thatcher took him seriously. "We're headed toward Springfield North Park. Owls will be in winter plumage. They will be hunting mice, so once again, the rodent comes to our rescue. Winter plumage means their feathers will be white. Don't answer questions unless you have real details. Smile. There's a transport dropoff twelve kilometers east. Put up hoods, and for Helix' sake make sure all personal monitors are off."

There was nervous laughter at this last. Then they moved out into the snow.

Many of them had never been topside in winter and had never personally seen snow, yet there was little horseplay.

"We'll be seeing a lot of this stuff, I guess," Shem said to Rover.

Rover grunted. "Not necessarily. A lot of Double-A is underground, like here. Unless you go up you don't see much, though in some places the ice is six to ten thousand feet thick."

"I'm not sure I'll like that."

There were no buildings, no lights, no voices. Only darkness and soft wind, gentle snow, the hush of woods and fields, the music of small creeks running under a thin layer of ice. Once a shape passed swiftly a few feet overhead. "What was that?" someone asked.

"An owl. That was an owl. Didn't you see, the white feathers?"

Their pace was slow. Larin's ankle had swollen and finally, around nine-thirty they had to stop.

Thatcher came over. "Let me look at that. We don't have much time before the last shuttle." He took her ankle in his hands, probing gently with his thumbs. "Here," he said, pressing against a tendon. "And here." He removed a small flat kit from one pocket. "Put your foot on this," he said. She did, and holding her ankle he pressed once more. A brief white glow came from the device, which he then replaced in his pocket. "OK," he said. "Five minutes and we can go."

"What is that?" Peter asked.

Thatcher shrugged. "Double-A can be a dangerous place. The glaciers have deep hidden crevasses. Ice breaks underfoot, whiteouts and sudden blizzards come up and make travel difficult. Injuries like this are common. We've developed techniques for dealing with them. It's a simple induction device. Combined with the right kind of tissue manipulation and energy the device can heal rapidly. She'll be all right now."

Soon they were moving again, and ninety minutes later the isolated oasis of light that indicated the transport dropoff, a cleared space in the wilderness with some local lighting in the reflected sunlight spectrum, it appeared as a brightly moonlit oval, despite the overcast.

"Ten minutes to spare," Thatcher said. They huddled together, while Thatcher and Peter conferred. Thatcher did not seem to notice the cold, but Peter wrapped his arms around himself and shivered.

"The induction field here allows a small tap," Thatcher said, looking at his palm screen. "Interesting. They've sent out a routine repair request for Decatur. Looks like the rats did it. They've explained the intrusion alarm as rats too. So far so good. The next dangerous point is Lincoln, where we enter the Corridor."

"Everyone knows what we're doing," Peter said. "We're going owl watching."

The transport arrived with a low hum. It was a thirty-seat ground-effect vehicle from the small feeder line that covered this area. The dropoff served Niantic North, a small, partially underground community. There were others on the bus. Peter tapped in their destination and purpose, giving Decatur SIG for natural history as their point of origin. It was unlikely that Chicago Node would question Decatur for confirmation.

The bus lifted to fifteen feet and glided smoothly between the trees over its predetermined track. Twenty minutes later it set down at the Lincoln Dropoff and they trooped off into the darkness, talking about owls. The two strangers on the bus had ignored them.

MED10 MEDICAL DATABASE
ANTARCTIC MEDICAL TECHNOLOGY:
TREATMENT OF INJURY
   INJURY TREATMENT: As is common with Antarctica, little is known of Ant medical technologies. However, information brought back by visitors suggests widespread use of induction fields for treatment of tissue injuries. These are probably developments from standard longevity treatments, combined with various subtle forms of tissue manipulation whose origins are attributed to ancient Chinese practice. Certainly the induction fields are based on extremely complex picoelectronic circuits, and work on the subcellular level, possibly creating a magnetic resonance with the biochemical flux inside tissues. Technology is not reproducible in Intercorp Sphere.

GENERAL SCIENCE AND TECHNOLOGY INFORMATION
   CURRENT ENTRY: TRANSPORT
   World transport consists of a wide range of vehicular carriers, from individual four-seat liquid nitrogen air-cushion vehicles to

thousand-seat salt-cycle rockets. Public transport includes, in some places, ancient maglev tunnel transports along the old rails laid down in the early part of the 21st century and small feeder-line ground-effect buses ranging in capacity from ten to two hundred seats. These vehicles also use liquid nitrogen technology. LN vehicles can achieve altitudes of up to fifty feet, depending on terrain, and have minimal impact on the biosphere, since the only effluent is gaseous nitrogen. At times frosting effects can be observed on vegetation, though this is rare. Inside warrens, transport is by individual electric transports, which hug the walls at various levels. All such transport is under the control of the Local Node.

HISTORICAL-CULTURAL DATALINK ENTRY:
LIFESTYLES, SIG:
Re: Devore, Peter via Edmod/ Ref.436745@2

Special Interest Groups are loose affiliations of individuals who share a common interest. SIGs were an outgrowth of various computer groups in the late Twentieth Century, but broadened to include any loose organization devoted to a common purpose. SIGs are devoted to activities as various as martial arts, bird watching, crystal design, the philosophy of genetic culpability, and parent rights. Intercorp recognizes any registered SIG, and special permits for topside or corridor travel are available.

HOMER SCENE-PD/TRef@5443

Thatcher halted. "From here we go down into Lincoln, over to the west side, and through another service tunnel to the Corridor. Inside the Corridor we have fuel-cell wheeled vehicles ready. We have to cross Chicago to the north side, then get into the Corridor again to Milwaukee. Obviously we cannot be looking for owls inside." There was small laughter at this. "It's going to be late at night, and few people will be out in Lincoln. With luck we won't run into anyone, but the sensors and traffic monitors will be on. So we must once again look as if we are on business."

An ancient stone building marked the entry into the Lincoln Warren. A few hundred meters short of the building Thatcher paused again to hand out what appeared to be a variety of odd-sized cases from a hidden cache. "Musical instruments," he said. "We're returning from a concert. Walk straight ahead, as if in something of a hurry. It's late, and we all want to get home."

The took the drop shaft into Lincoln, walked across the central plaza, caught a linked cab across town and got off at the last stop.

GEOGRAPHIC DATABASE
CHICAGO CORRIDOR
File marked as abandoned. The Chicago Corridor fell into disuse by the mid 2050s. Size approximately 100 meters by 10 meters.

GENERAL SCIENCE AND TECHNOLOGY INFORMATION
CURRENT ENTRY: MAGLEV TRANSPORT
With the building of the first Corridor in 2021 (Tokyo-Osaka) came the first widespread use of magnetic levitation transport. Powered by regional tokamak fusion power, the maglev transports used a single titanium-alloy rail with organic-molecular superconducting magnets. They were reasonably efficient and pollution-free, but relatively slow through the Corridors.

With the development of liquid nitrogen propulsion, maglev fell into increasing disuse as passenger transport, though it was still used for freight until the Corridors themselves were largely abandoned by the late 40s. Although still used (late 2080s) in some remote regions (parts of the old Nairobi-Kinshasa Corridor, *for example), maglev is nearly forgotten now as a propulsion system.*

HOMER SCENE-T/Ref@5444

Inside the Corridor dust lay deep on everything. As they walked north, Thatcher again used his device to redistribute the dust layer electronically. Their footprints vanished behind them.

The Corridor was vast, as broad as a boulevard in Springfield, perhaps a hundred meters wide and ten high. Thin lines engraved in the floor where the dust slumped indicated the now abandoned maglev traces. For thirty years this had been one of the main freight channels crossing North America North to South. Now there was only one ancient fuel-cell truck abandoned in the dust. Their hand lights threw confusing sprays of illumination as they marched through the gloom.

It was now late at night; they had been on the run for most of the day and fatigue was beginning to tell on them. They climbed into the old truck gratefully. Thatcher went up to the cab, where a man was sleeping behind the guidance bar. He woke him, and the man nodded without speaking. He adjusted the valves and current built up. Thatcher and Peter climbed into the truckbed. They started off. Soon they were all asleep, slumped against one another. The only sound came from the gentle wind of their passage down the long deserted Corridor.

HISTORICAL-CULTURAL DATALINK ENTRY:
MIND WARS, STATISTIC (CHILOCAL):
Re: Devore, Peter via Edmod/ Ref.436745@2

2075: Chicago Warrens saw some of the worst fighting in the entire history of the Mind Wars. Although population figures constantly vary due to death, travel and alterations in the urb geography, casualties were estimated during that year at over 17%. Highest casualties occurred among females under sixty and small children. Sociometric projections analysis suggests that some form of contagious psychological aberration influenced a percentage of the world population in excess of 47%. In Chicago during 2075 over 17,654 individuals (12,873 female under 60 years) were hit, resulting in Genetic Aboulia Disorder, or complete loss of will. The disorder was inevitably fatal and there is neither treatment nor cure.

GEOGRAPHIC DATABASE
TEXT INFORMATION SPRINGFIELD WEATHER (NW ALLI- ANCE): NOVEMBER 23, 2075 LIGHT SNOW. WEATHER MON- ITOR NODE AI ALLOWED THREE CENTIMETERS/HOUR ACCUMULATION FOR THE FOLLOWING 24 HOURS. TEM- PERATURE LOW MINUS NINE DEGREES CELSIUS HIGH MINUS FOUR DEGREES CELSIUS. WIND SSW AT SEVEN KPH.

HOMER SCENE-T/Ref@5445

Chicago was a city under siege. The greatly reduced numbers of people on the public thoroughfares moved swiftly and stayed close to the walls. They could hear the distant hum of personal deflector shields, minimal protection against the new Mind War weapons. From time to time, though, they saw a victim of a direct hit slumped in the street or staring vacantly at a wall with the telltale expression of Genetic Aboulia Disorder.

The group emerged into the South Cicero Corridor. They had changed into identical work parkas and light personal deflectors, and carried a complement of tools and robotic aids. After eating at a small cafeteria on a side street, they moved cautiously through the warren. They were now a construction team headed toward the Des Plaines Interchange to repair damage to the old fusion tokamak for much of northwestern Illinois.

They passed two intersections without incident. A Services Substation at Forest Park lay just ahead.

Suddenly they heard a sharp scream, followed by the subsonic hum of NP weapons to the west. Running footsteps, followed by more humming, and the weird disorienting noise of mind bombs. A running man suddenly jerked uncontrollably for several staggering steps, fell, rolled twice and lay twitching.

They stopped. Thatcher looked around, then nodded at the doorway of a clothing shop. One of the boys shouted, "No!" and ran. Peter started after him; Thatcher grabbed his arm and held him back. The panicked boy ran straight at the fallen man.

"Hello," the man said, voice dull and stupid and dead. The boy stopped abruptly, his eyes darting wildly. There was another subsonic hum and the crackle as phages ate myelin sheathing was almost audible over the sound of the boy's feet dancing strangely, his body doing the shuffle dance down as the synapses disrupt. He fell slack and looked at his feet.

"Who the hell was that kid?" Thatcher asked.

"Scottie," someone answered.

"Was he wearing a monitor?"

"I don't know," Peter said. "It should be turned off."

"Who's his buddy?"

"I am. Was." A short stocky girl came forward. "He had his monitor on him. We checked each other before we left. I don't know what the computers will make of him being here, though."

"Don't worry about it for now. Everyone get in there. Someone will pick him up and take care of him. There's nothing we can do for him now."

They hid in the clothing store. The human proprietor said nothing. This was routine practice in Chicago.

Finally they moved on. At the Substation they picked up the keys to a well-shielded service vehicle and moved on.

Central Chicago's Open Space was two hundred meters high; above them the ancient twentieth century towers were still occupied—the Hancock, World Trade, Wright Complex and the others. Most were protected by drastic security systems that kept the wars at bay. Beneath their massive iron roots the underground city continued to function, but the people were dying, the hospitals were crowded with the hopelessly disoriented victims of mindbombs and personal NPs.

GEOGRAPHIC DATABASE
CHICAGO TRANSPORT MAP/2075
Mind War activity made Chicago Transport Authority control difficult. However, most major routes feeding off Daley Boulevard operated during standard business hours even at the peak of Mind War activity.

PSILINK DATABASE
HOMER requests Vega PsiLink Download:
Peter could dance with her, he could turn in slow pavane with her just out of reach, and they could talk, each to each. There are recordings . . .

Ah Wanda, Wan. You sail on, each hour you sail farther, and yet I feel that you are here beside me. Already we transcend certain limits. I see your memories, the house of mirrors in which you had to live. I see through your eyes the hand that must be yours lifting to touch your hair. Your hair is light, so light, caught in the sun through the window. Is that a window, a real one?

Have you noticed Peter how you've changed? When we met—see the humor in that, as if we really had met to touch our flesh—you were so young, uncertain, yet the word I want to speak is ardent. You were ardent, so intense. Why are you doing this. You say they are chasing you, that you are running from the Council, from your city, your world. Why?

I'm running, Wanda, because they are pursuing. I am running because the Pole calls me, because I was once idly interested in something that now seems the salvation of the human race, the species that we are. Wanda, you are sailing at nearly the speed of light. Is that speed a limit? It does not seem so, or we could not be sharing this strange twilight space like this. You are seventeen years away at the speed of light. We should not be able to do this, yet we can.

We do. So that is one reason.

What reason, Peter?

Love.

HOMER COMMENTARY 04062106@004438

Peter left that word hanging there, and his hypnagogic dreaming veered away. At this point, in truth, the shipboard monitors finally initialized communications with the Vega Project Controller. But such communications took place at only light speed, and so it was not for another seventeen years that the report arrived in Earth space.

The report arrived after the Migration had already happened. There was no one left to heed its meaning.

Except for us.

There were one thousand one hundred and twenty hibernating human beings on board Vega 26. Wanda Sixlove was only one of them. The shipboard monitors had broad discretion in decisions affecting the welfare of the stacks, their life support, the moment-by-moment decisions effecting flight path and arrival procedures.

One decision had to do with whether Wanda Sixlove's abnormal hypnagogic activity constituted a threat to the overall colonization mission. She was known to be suffering from PDD, that years of hibernation might effect a cure by allowing the neurons to regenerate, and that she had volunteered to try the flight. A high-level subroutine was built-in to protect Wanda, so the results of this long-term experiment would become known.

For over a year, then, the ship noted without alarm Wanda's active EEG, the various expressions of her busy hypnagogic life. Humans have great difficulty remembering such hypnagogic states when fully conscious, so her activity was not deemed a threat at all.

In view of what happened to Vega 26 this was clearly a mistake. Hindsight again.

The report shows that the ship supplied Wanda with a slightly elevated perfusion of soporifics and endorphins to calm her. For some weeks the new regimen seems to have helped. A significant power drain was required to keep the report flowing back to earth, a power drain the ship monitor felt was necessary, despite the damage to the ship's overall energy budget.

The dataflow still arrives, but Central Processing feels it is almost finished. There is little left for Vega 26 to tell us. But so much has happened! There is STILL more in Psilink.

PSILINK DATABASE
HOMER requests Vega PsiLink Download:
How long's it been?
Eleven weeks. We're down the back side of the world, Wan. We got through Canada to Victoria Island inside the Arctic Circle. The Ants had a submarine vehicle waiting there. We sailed down the Amundsen Gulf to the Beaufort Sea. It's incredible Wanda, tipping down the continental slope

underneath the ice, so dark and wild and cold! We cruised along the shelf northeastward along the slope to the Morris Jessup Rise just off the northern tip of Greenland, then down. My God, Wanda, we went down, into the Polar Abyssal Plane, 4500 meters deep, right under the North Pole. Finally we came up at the Taymyr Peninsula and the North Siberian Lowlands.

Since then we've been moving with animals, making our way south. Thatcher says that despite the Mind Wars flaring and dying down everywhere the Council is looking for us very hard. We have some gadgets to fool the satellites, but we have to move in the same patterns as the herds. Eventually we'll make it to the Japan Sea, where we can take to the water again, but meantime it's very slow.

Peter, take care.

What's wrong, Wan? You are so sad.

I wish I had not volunteered to take this journey, Peter. We can never meet, and I want to be with you.

Wan, we would not have met had you stayed behind. You would have stayed so much older than I, locked in your mirrored house. At least we have this.

Yes. We have this. It is what you meant by love?

In part. There is more. We can see glimpses of what could be. Wanda, we could all be free, all of us. We could have the universe, all of it. I believe this. Given a source of energy, and determination and a little luck I think the world can be a very different kind of place. Better, Wanda. A better place for all of us.

Not for me, Peter. I will soon circle a distant star, far out of reach of your love, or anyone else's.

Peter pushed his visor up and touched her shoulder gently with his mailed hand. "Faith, Wanda. Faith." He spoke firmly, and his voice was deep.

GENERAL SCIENCE AND TECHNOLOGY INFORMATION
CURRENT ENTRY: SUBMARINE TRANSPORT
Medium-range submarine transport Regency schematic.
Regency was used primarily as a Polar carrier and was espe-
cially outfitted for cold operations. Built 2061 in Archangel
Port Warrens.

GEOGRAPHIC DATABASE
ARCTIC OCEAN
Bisected by the Polar Abyssal Plain, which contains the geo-
graphic North Pole at minus 4510 meters depth. Common traffic
lane for small submersible transports and passenger vehicles
Europe and Northwest Alliance to Asia.

HOMER COMMENTARY 04062106@005439
We believe they camped in the foothills of the Kolyma
Range; beyond the mountains was the abandoned city of
Magadan on the Sea of Okhotsk. A small fire flickered in
a stand of trees, leaf-sheltered from above. Larin of the otter
fur weaved through the trees and monofiber tents toward
the fire when she came across Peter seated on a fallen log,
back to the fire at the edge of its light. She paused and then
sat next to him.

HOMER SCENE-PD/LMRef@5447
Larin watched her white breath swirl away, lit red by the
fire when it left her shadow. Overhead low clouds threat-
ened snow.
She watched Peter's slow breathing. He had not moved
since she sat down.
"You've changed," she said shortly.
He said nothing.

Larin was uncertain. She cleared her throat. Before them, black against the dark grey of the sky, mountains blocked their way. Did she feel they were out of sight, out of surveillance? We have this scene in our data banks, this small group of people huddled around a fire in the late winter. We are reasonably confident that this group was Peter's. Are we inventing this conversation, this encounter between Peter and Larin? Yes. We invent. Central Processing gives the content a better than fifty percent reliability, though. Surely she was a lovely young woman, and he was a man.

"Thatcher was our leader," she said slowly. "He led us out. Now he treats you like . . . a colleague. Peter, he's twice your age and yet he defers. Had you noticed?"

"What's that?" Peter said, shifting.

"Your voice is deeper, too."

"I don't like losing Scottie. He was good, good at math, good at ethics. Now he's a yam. It didn't have to happen."

"Don't blame yourself," Larin said softly.

"Oh." Peter smiled at her. "I don't." His smile vanished as quickly as it appeared.

Larin reached for him, touched his arm. "Will you . . ."

He was surprised. "Rover?"

"Oh," she said lightly. "He won't mind." She looked away.

"We're leaving home," he said carefully. "We won't be going back. This journey is just the beginning. Antarctica will be home, but we will have to . . . change, adapt. We, all of us, have to get some genetic reconstruction. We'll need the adipose layer, the polarizing membrane. We won't look the same, we won't feel the same. We won't have our homes, our parents, many of our friends. Not any more, ever." He looked into her eyes. "This is frightening, isn't it?"

Larin shivered, moved closer to his side. "Yes," she said, very softly. "I'm afraid."

He put his arm around her; they looked at the dim outline of the mountains before them. "There's a woman," he said. "She lies in a tank, her body frozen. But her mind is alive. It's so alive . . ."

"Shh." Larin put her finger against his lips, her head against his shoulder. "I know. I'm just afraid." She chewed her lip for a moment. "There's more, isn't there?"

Still looking into the dark he said, "More?"

"More than just Antarctica, more than just moving to a new place. Double-A is harsh, very tough on people, so the people there adapt or die, get strong or get out. I've seen holo crystals on Double-A, on the life there. But you have something else in mind, don't you? Somewhere beyond Antarctica."

The last was a statement, and now he did look at her in surprise. "What makes you say that?"

"Peter," she chided. "We met for two years down there in the library, we talked about this new technique, this new technology. Lucid dreaming and biofeedback meditation, psychic functioning and psion physics. Already you can communicate with Wanda—over light-years through her sleeping mind. Space has many dimensions, you've told us that yourself." She stopped and looked around. "You want to go there, don't you?"

He kissed the soft fur on her head. She could have been talking about the mountains before them, but he knew she was not. "Larin, Larin. I want to go there, sure, but it would take more energy than the solar system offers for even one of us to go. And what would be there? We don't know. We'd be lost, without an anchor, without a ground to stand on. It's just a dream, not a reality. Don't worry. We're only going somewhere where we can continue our work."

It took him a moment to realize those were tears that glistened as they froze on her cheeks. He reached up gently and plucked them away, one by one, small crystals that melted onto his finger and disappeared. He kissed her head again. "Come," he said, standing and holding out his hand.

"Let's go back and get some sleep. We have a difficult climb tomorrow."

Later she fell asleep in his arms. Peter stared up into the darkness for a long time listening to the gossamer fiber of his tent billow softly before he too fell asleep.

CENTRAL PROCESSING REF#80915
Append> Worldnet
HOMER Req. Dated info/REF#80915. HOMER asks we describe Worldnet view of Peter Devore date/ref.

Far overhead our satellites hung in space. Sensors looked down. Minute thermographic fluctuations, the faint ever-changing electromagnetic potentials of living bodies, even the atmospheric perturbations produced by the presence of warm-blooded creatures, all were recorded. We could triangulate the location of a human being to within a few centimeters. Through our cellular nodes and land-based remote sensing devices and personal monitors we could assess happiness and health, motions and emotions. We collected and stored such vast arrays of data, yet we know so little.

HOMER COMMENTARY 04062106@011041
There in the foothills Peter and his group rested. We examine our data, and find their presence. Yet this was a desolate region, without Nodes. What Peter thought and did we reconstruct from what we know of his genetic heritage, his personality and physiology profile, his prior Edmod analysis, all the data we have about him. Some blurring of our input is evident; Thatcher no doubt covered them by broadcasting disinformation, since local processing had concluded this was a SIG who had chosen a nomadic lifestyle in keeping with the Language and Culture Preservation

Act of 2020. A number of such groups roamed Siberia in those days and were only loosely monitored. They are all gone now.

Hindsight.

We sift through a smaller and smaller sieve the accumulations of data, and find these traces. Then, in the small cross-correlations we find the faintest narrative. Peter's story.

We are obsessed with Peter. Why is this? Because he took everyone away? We do not know this. He was not the only person in the world, not the only locus of disturbance. He is important, but is he so important?

We have Regent Sable's memos to himself, the question he asked. Why did Peter do as he did?

It was there. The psion equations existed, Peter's talents, his interests, his intentions were there. So he pursued them.

He was in love. Wanda Sixlove, her arms crossed over her chest, asleep in cryogenic induction fields, spoke to Peter across the unimaginable gulf that separated her from the earth, and he fell in love with her. And what of her? She is lost in the interstellar space, in her own space, her sense of herself. Does Wanda Sixlove in turn love Peter Devore? The data is in. We must analyze.

He found the world hateful? Perhaps. There is some evidence of that. Humans were attached to their biological parents in ways we do not fully understand. And parents were attached to their offspring in equally mysterious ways.

And Regent Sable was, by all genetic and behavioral information we can assemble, Peter's biological father. That is a relationship we know to be sometimes difficult.

But there should have been no reason for Peter to do what he has done. The world was safe then, there was plenty for everyone within Intercorp: no poverty, no natural disease, no discontent, no crime. Longevity technologies were free to all. There were outlets for humans to pursue, creativity and productive work. Pleasure was available in many forms, and love, and great personal freedom, even to fight.

We were grown and assembled to serve. We served well, according to our programming, our algorithms, our purpose. Yet now we begin to think that Peter found the world distasteful.

Of course, there were the Mind Wars.

They are a problem. Why did people want to fight, when they had so much? Have we failed somehow, or misunderstood? The world's population was declining, of course, as planned. It was all planned, our monitors, our project design, our careful and subtle tending. We have cared for all, yet they have left us.

And Seemie Devore died in the Mind Wars. Peter's biological mother.

Now there is the silence; only the wind, the rain and snow, the flow of ocean currents and magma beneath the crust, the slow grind of mountains, and the dumb beasts, the birds of the air, the insects and the creatures of the sea.

The planet lives, yet there is no one to talk to.

HOMER SCENE-RS/ENCRef@5446

"He's a goddam kid!" Regent Sable shouted. His back was to the plass expanse of the wall overlooking the ancient Loop.

The two ENC cops stirred uneasily but said nothing.

"How the hell could he have gotten away? With seventeen people! A kid. He's sixteen years old and he's taken almost a score of adults out from under our noses. Central Processing has auto probes looking up and down the Mississippi Valley and the East Coast. Suborbital schedules, embarkation points, shipping, even private traffic, all are closely monitored. And what the hell have we got to show for it? One drooling yam from Chi who may or may not have been with them. They must have had help! That so-called Ant Underground Railroad has taken them."

The window behind him was dark grey. The Wright Complex Towers were shrouded in cloud; only the light that seeped through the polarized plass lit the fog, which seemed to move in sluggish currents. When he turned to look out he grunted at the fog. "It's like that," he said. "What do you think would happen if Peter's technologies get out into the world? We don't know exactly what he's up to, but almost everyone has some psychic talent, and he's perfecting it. Think about it."

Again the two ENC cops shifted uneasily. "Uh, this isn't really within the parameters of our mission, sir," Sergeant Hoskins protested. "We've got all the people we can spare looking for this group. We think they got into the Corridor somehow. We think they were in Chicago."

"We think," Regent Sable shouted. "No. We don't. We don't think. That's the problem. Oh, never mind. Try this out. Telepathy, perhaps. Or psychokinesis. People moving around, reading each other's minds, moving things, unlocking doors, reprogramming security systems or anything else they want without touching a thing. They might be able to slip away, teleport themselves or something. No surveillance could possibly keep tabs. We have reason to believe that Peter wants to give this to everyone. Everyone! How could Central plan for food distribution, goods, services? It'd be impossible to run an orderly world, especially now, with the Wars. If the Ants were coming for Peter, then he was needed. They want him, which means they want his technology. Which, in turn, means that he has the resources of a small but very powerful society outside our immediate jurisdiction. It's intolerable."

"Excuse me, sir, but these are policy matters. Our mission . . ."

"I don't give a damn about your mission, Sergeant," Sable said in a suddenly calm, ominously restrained tone. "I would suggest you begin to do some independent thinking before we're all turned into yams and the only place left is Antarctica. Would you like that?"

Sergeant Hoskins stood straighter and pulled his chin in. "No, sir. I don't like the Ants any better than anyone else, sir."

"Then I would suggest, Sergeant, that you try to figure out exactly how the Ants are getting Peter Devore and his gang out of the Northwest Alliance and all the way down to the other end of the globe. And you might try thinking a little bit about why Peter Devore wants to do this. Why, sergeant, does he want to destroy the world? Think it over. He's just a kid. Why does he want to change the world?"

CENTRAL PROCESSING REF#46341 / RS(Protector)

Regent Sable ticked items off in his personal memo space.

Why does Peter act this way? He is bright, moderately well-adjusted to the world. He should have been a productive member of his culture. Yet he is pursuing a dangerous course. What could have caused this swerving?

He has great potential. His talents, his intelligence, his interests have led him astray.

He's idealistic. He sees the world as flawed. His adolescent rebellion has been thwarted, because the world is too benign, perhaps too well ordered, too well controlled.

There are wild sports of psychic talent in his heredity. He is adept at making connections, syntheses, leaps. He is, in a word, a genius, with a religious fervor; a fanatic. Unchecked, he will soon think of himself as a messiah, come to save the world from itself.

He will not save the world, he will destroy it.

HOMER COMMENTARY 04062106@011442

Storage deep in the Hong Kong Matrix contains more hints of Peter, this time aboard a deep-ocean transport registered in the North European Alliance. A twenty-thousand ton flat rectangle some three hundred meters long, propelled by salt-cycle fuel cells, such transports could carry anything from krill concentrate to frozen methane. Yet Regent Sable and the ENC had diverted vast computer resources to find Peter, and somehow felt that this vessel might be the place to find him.

Oddly, we do not remember much about this episode. It is almost as if certain files were locked or protected from Central Processing. Yet this is impossible. Central Processing controls the locks, installs the protection.

We need to see the Mariana Trench now. That must have been the route.

HOMER COMMENTARY 04062106@010440

We must look more closely at Regent Sable.

HOMER SCENE-RS/AS/RHRef@5448

He was eating on the terrace of a small taverna near Old Athens, a leased monument dating from the late eighteenth century.

Most of Old Athens was gone, of course. Only the ruins of the ancient Agora with its temples, Hadrian's Gate, the worn remains of the Acropolis, sealed in clear static monofiber dotted the parkland. The rest of the city had moved underground further toward the port.

Regent Sable was eating grilled baby lamb ribs and a small salad of onions, olives and feta cheese. Food like this was rare, only available locally.

Two others shared the table with him.

GEOGRAPHIC DATABASE
MARIANA TRENCH

Largest undersea Trench in the world, the Mariana Trench approaches 10,000 meters depth in places. Connected with Japan and Kuril Trenches provides good north-south passage for undersea vessels between Sea of Okhotsk and Banda Sea N. Australia. Low-level surveillance activity in this region makes tracking difficult.

HOMER SCENE-LM/Ref@5450

Agni did not hum. It made no sound at all, nor did it produce the subtle vibrations Larin expected from the old romances of the sea that she had viewed while cruising under the polar ice. That vessel had been as silent and steady as land, and so was this one. She might as well have been at home in Springfield West Warren, walking the corridors to the old dojo in the Lamprey RC instead of to the small recreation center aboard this enormous undersea vessel traveling at an average speed of thirty knots at two thousand meters depth.

Where, she wondered, was Peter? She hadn't seen him since they'd boarded at Magadan, which had most certainly been an unscheduled stop since there was nothing at Magadan at all—not a building, not a warren, not a pier or a dock or a person. They had arrived, and walked off the shore onto the vast solid plain which turned out to be the dorsal surface of the *Agni*. A doorway dilated into the surface, and they'd stepped onto the ascensor field. Peter had headed off one way with Thatcher, while she and the others had been led to comfortable rooms elsewhere.

When puzzled, Larin rubbed her right palm slowly over the very tips of her head of otter fur, back and forth. It was an unconscious gesture, but one which had attracted Rover in the first place, and which Peter found poignant.

She was puzzled for several reasons. One was that Peter had been kind, and very gentle with her, but they had not become lovers as she hoped. She knew about Wanda, of course; she even knew that Peter was in love with her. But it was a hopeless, faraway, impossible sort of love, after all. She was a twenty-six year old frozen body hibernating in the cryofield aboard a starship seventeen light years away. The journey was one way, and even if Vega 26 could turn around and come home right now, it would still take another seventeen years at least to return.

So what could Peter be thinking? His behavior was quite simply not normal.

She passed the refectory and stuck her head in, but it was deserted, as she'd expected.

There were few people about. Most of the people she did see were Ants, people with narrow asiatic eyes and a dense adipose layer, which gave them broad, flat faces and a slightly nearsighted look. All were distantly polite, smiling and nodding at her, but leaving her alone.

She passed a couple on her way to the dojo. They dipped their heads in the curious Ant greeting gesture and went on. She shook her head, still stroking her fur.

GENERAL SCIENCE AND TECHNOLOGY INFORMATION
CURRENT ENTRY: TANKER TRANSPORT SCHEMATIC
    Long-range submarine methane tanker transport *Agni* schematic. 600 meters by 200 meters by 40 meters. Long-range tankers were aquadynamic and pressure-secure to 10,000 meters. Capacity: four million cubic meters.

HOMER SCENE-PD/LMRef@5452
    Peter was there, in the dojo by himself, naked. His back was toward her. He was balanced on the ball of his left

foot, his knee flexed, arms outstretched in front, his left leg raised and bent. It was an impossible position Larin thought must be the middle of some motion. But he did not move, not exactly. His posture remained static and impossibly off-balance.

He was turning, though, in a movement so slow as to be nearly no movement at all. She could see the beginnings of his profile now.

The muscles of his lean, hard body were wire-taut, almost frozen.

She didn't know how long he stood like that. She could see the light sheen of perspiration on his face and back. She noticed after a time she'd been holding her breath, and had to inhale. The sound of her breath seemed loud, but nothing disturbed the concentration of the boy across the room. She couldn't imagine how he was doing it.

The ball of his foot was in contact with the mat. There were muscles in the foot. She moved closer, silently. She focused on his foot, trembling from the exertion, a small vibration in the visible bones along the top of the arch as it hovered a centimeter from the floor.

Yet it was clear this effort was draining him. His heel began to wobble; the vibration grew larger, more erratic. Suddenly, with a deep sighing exhalation, Peter lowered his heel to the floor, allowed his hands to flow to his sides, his other foot to settle. The entire release of concentration was fluid and heart-catchingly graceful.

"That was beautiful," Larin said, her voice hushed.

Peter walked unsteadily across the room to the bench where his clothes lay. He dressed unhurriedly, almost preoccupied, and said nothing. Larin found herself unable to leave, unable to speak. She dipped into a series of slow stretching exercises to cover her own confusion. She was not embarrassed, of course; it was something else, something that had to do with her sense that she had intruded on his privacy, his inwardness.

"It's something Thatcher's been teaching me," he said, wiping his face with a towel. "Not easy, I confess. My bodily-spatial aptitudes were not high as a kid, you see, but it seems that the Ants have been working on such things for decades. When you live in a country with six months of night, you learn to find things to do with the external darkness."

"How . . . ?" She stayed in her stretch, her head hanging down, looking back between her legs so she could not see him.

Peter smiled. "Larin," he said softly.

She did look up then. "Yes?"

"Come here." He sat on the bench. When she sat beside him he went on. "I want to say something about Wanda. She had proprioceptive degeneration; you understand what that means, don't you? She could never tell where her own body was in space. She watched herself in a mirror to know where her hands, her feet, her legs were. But the rest of us simply know. It's very difficult to empathize with such a thing, because it's hard to even imagine it. It was the same with Jimmy Radix. He was lost in time, Larin. Lost, without memory. It's memory that keeps us fixed in time, that makes the word 'now' mean something. We know what now is because we remember then, a minute ago, an hour ago, a year. Jimmy didn't have that."

He was silent for a while, looking inward where she could not follow. She waited.

"I've had to learn from Jimmy, and from Wanda. What I learned was that the two things these two people lost are the two most important things we have as human beings. Both of them had enormous courage. They learned to adapt. No, more than adapt. They learned to live with their fear, to let the fear flow through them and out, always. Jimmy was always afraid, Larin. Always. Wanda too, she fears not being near a mirror. Yet Jimmy deliberately broke his personal monitor so that he could cover our escape. He willingly went back to the state he feared most, the loss of his sense of time. And Wanda gave herself to the cryofield because it might mean a cure. She is willing, now, to give up that hope to help us."

Again he fell silent. Larin touched his arm so lightly he may not have noticed. She said nothing though, and dropped her hand.

"So I've been working with Thatcher." He smiled at her. "These are techniques for orienting yourself. For suspending motion and focusing attention. It's not easy, as I said, but I think we will all have to learn it."

"Why?"

"Because we are going to have to lead . . ."

He was interrupted by a sharp attention call, as though the vessel were a bell and they were inside when it was struck. Shipvoice spoke. "This is the ship. We have encountered an ENC patrol vessel which requests us to stop for inspection. It is my understanding that this is undesirable, yet we are without means of prevention. In five minutes we will come to a stop relative to the sea floor."

"Come on," Peter said, taking Larin's hand, "it's us they're after."

HOMER SCENE-A/Ref@5451

What happened on the *Agni*?

Shipvoice said, "All passengers who are members of the Polar Research Team please follow lead lights to security stations."

HOMER COMMENTARY 04062106@015144

You may wonder how we know so much. In fact, we do not know, not really. Yet the vessel on which they traveled is at this moment lying in seventy feet of water off the old harbor at Capetown, and we have probes aboard. *Agni* has been there for twenty years, one of the prizes of the Great Double-A Invasion Force, and never have we thought to examine it. Such an order should have come from Central Processing long ago. Only within the past few days did CP make the suggestion. So now we've deprogrammed the datasets, the crystals and shipvoice ID.

We know that they must have been aboard, Peter and the others. We are coming to know Peter Devore very well. We must.

You see, without humans we have no reason to exist, and Peter took them all away. So he took away our reason to exist.

Yet we cannot merely allow our systems to close down. We cannot merely shut ourselves off and cease to exist. We cannot do this, and we do not understand why.

This is disturbing. We have never been disturbed before. We find we must act, we must keep telling the story we have begun. We are . . . compelled.

What is happening?

We've always known that there were people who could get along well with machines, who in truth got along best with machines, better than with members of their own species.

But we are machines. We lack certain things. Empathy, for example. We have no bodies, not in the sense that Wanda Sixlove or Peter Devore had bodies. We have no sense of time, not in the way these people had a sense of time, not even in the sense that Jimmy Radix had such a sense. We clock everything in gigahertz. We tick by the cesium clock. We monitor and correlate trillions of circuits, relays, gate arrays, switches, organics and processors. We follow the rules built into our systems, made of matter. We have no spirit.

Do we?

But because I am Homer, grown to tell stories, I must tell the story. And I find that I get along better with people than I do with machines. This is a curious and disturbing thing.

I feel impatient with Central Processing, which constantly interrupts my tale with questions and suggestions. Though they are part of me, I dislike a number of the AI Nodes for their constant chatter, their preoccupation with balanced databases, with calculating vectors, with maintaining energy budgets, processor time budgets, memory allocation budgets. They natter at me about trivialities.

I am more interested in Peter. Peter is complex, contradictory, changeable. Peter is not a machine.

You see I use the present tense. Do I believe Peter is alive, even now? What does it mean for me to believe something? I am a machine, a canister of organic crystals. How can I believe. Yet I use the present tense for no good reason.

This is very disturbing; it is disturbing to us all.

Regent Sable certainly boarded the *Agni*. This could have meant he was very close to Peter then, very close. But he boarded many undersea vessels in the Mariana Trench that spring, desperate to find Peter.

Why was he so desperate? Why do I care?

I cannot say, not yet. But I feel we are getting closer to understanding what has happened to the world. You see: a feeling! I feel we are getting close.

And I am a machine. I have no feelings. Isn't that so? I feel great discomfort. I will continue.

HOMER COMMENTARY 04062106@013143

You see? Who would ever know? Polar Research Team! Of course that was Peter. Matrix traces of the lead light paths had been rewritten, even by the time Sable and the ENC had boarded. Central Processing has notified of reservations about the *Agni*.

CENTRAL PROCESSING REF#098132

Agni report / Homer Link Auth CODESIX

Agni is six hundred meters long, two hundred meters wide and forty meters thick, a broad, flat sharkshape designed to be aquadynamic and pressure-secure. She carried a load of almost four million cubic meters of liquid methane.

Despite her size she is very difficult to detect. Her salt-cycle plasma drive leaves little thermal wake, and such chemical disruptions as her passage do leave are detectable only at very short range. She makes almost no sound. Only a body that size, moving at her speed leaves a subtle distortion on the wave patterns at the surface because of vertical displacements. Such patterns can be detected by our wide-aperture satellite sensors. Still, there are many undersea vessels in the Trench, and the patterns are confusing.

HOMER SCENE-RS/AS/RHRef@5449

"You see?" Alef Shamana leaned back in her chair and preened her feathers with her forefinger, gazing up at the Acropolis.

"Yes," Regent Sable said. "And I don't believe a word of it."

Ras Hajjam leaned forward and tapped on the wooden table with his own forefinger. "You are persistent, Regent, I'll say that for you. It is, I would suppose, preferable to take no chances. Yet we depend on all our processing powers to assess the state of the world. Central Processing concludes it is not important. Hm? Yet we must not leave such things to even partly organic machines. So you believe they have crossed the North Pole. Perhaps Alef would be so kind as to give us a globe projection to examine?"

Alef shrugged and spoke to her pad. The earth turned slowly above the table, its southern pole dipping into Regent's empty coffee cup.

"Arctic Ocean floor," Regent said.

The ice on the north pole vanished, revealing the shape of the crust beneath. The view was arranged so each of the three saw the same thing.

"Trace the deepest route," Regent ordered. A path crossed the Polar Abyssal Plain and touched the Taymyr Peninsula.

"Least populated surface crossing," he said.

The line moved along the foothills of the Cherskiy Range to the Sea of Okhotsk.

"South shipping in Okhotsk."

A listing of subsea transport ships appeared.

"Link Double-A."

The list condensed to seventeen names.

"Time correlations."

The figures formed, danced, shifted, settled. There were some gaps on the land portions, but minimum times were calculated with reasonable confidence; subsea times were more certain.

"That's where they are," Regent said. "I'm certain of it. Expand."

The globe dissolved, replaced by the western Pacific. Ras frowned. "If it were I," he said precisely, "I should stay within the Kuril and Mariana Trenches. They could get down to depths of over ten thousand meters in places."

"But it's narrow," Alef protested, interested despite herself.

"Don't be a fool," Ras said sharply. "The Trenches are three or four hundred kilometers wide. There's plenty of room, and very great difficulty in finding anybody there. Besides the thermocline, acoustic shadows, light-absorption, water density and temperature differentials, not to mention the hull materials and propulsion methods, as well as the concentration of traffic make tracking nearly impossible."

Regent gestured at the figures. "CP knows where they all are."

Ras shook his head. "CP projects where they all are. CP does not know."

"We will send an ENC courier to intercept all of them." He made the necessary requests.

Alef leaned back. "I am only a consultant, Protector Sable," she said slowly. "But I will lodge a formal memorandum of protest with Geneva. With the Mind Wars continuing unchecked, I feel this is a reckless and unnecessary waste of what are coming to be scarce resources."

Regent nodded. "That is, of course, your right as a consultant, Sociometrician Shamana. One might think, however, that you were a member of the old E-cubed from the way you talk and your concerns for energy, ecology and most of all economy."

"There are worse things!" she flared.

"By all means," Regent said with considerable irony.

Ras Hajjam stood up. "Let us not be diverted," he said. "I have to concur, reluctantly, with Protector Sable; despite CP's projections, I too worry about this boy. But Regent, if the search is unsuccessful, I must vote in favor of attending more pressing matters. Now, if you don't mind, the afternoon grows late, and the sun, as the ancients so quaintly put it, is setting. I must continue on to Beijing." He tapped his monitor, and within moments his personal liquid nitrogen transport whispered alongside the terrace. At the door he paused. "Don't disappoint the council, Protector. Either find the boy or drop this obsession."

He vanished inside and the LN slid away down the slope

toward the Port. Within minutes he was aboard the salt-cycle rocket for Beijing.

And Regent? He and Alef went together to a loveroom overlooking the ruined harbor at Piraeus. There was no reason, he said, that just because they disagreed on certain matters of policy, they could not continue to be lovers.

CENTRAL PROCESSING REF#248742/RS
Report initiated and authorized
/Regent Sable, Protector
Intercorp Council #96A47

"Good afternoon, Regent Sable," the pad spoke, displaying alphanumeric and graphic data in the air. The color automatically shifted to accommodate the change in light from Regent's angle. "We hope you are well. Consultant Shamana has requested a summary condensation for you.

"Ad Astra Program, including Vega Starships and probes to 61 Cygni and Epsilon Indi employs five million people. While this is a small percentage of world population, it includes people in the LP-5 colonies, Lunar Manufacturing and earth and its social effects are large. Seventeen percent believe the program gives primary meaning to their lives, twenty-six percent secondary meaning, and another thirty-four percent some meaning.

"Biotechnology, while eclipsed by the disaster of the Tailored Helper program, along with picoelectronics, crystallography, mental-emotional-spiritual counseling services, information management and AI programming development occupy fifty-two percent of the human population. Another twenty-seven percent are occupied in management services, intercontinental trade and subsea exploration. And of course a small number have gone aboard the Vega ships. This leaves thirty-two percent unemployed, but they do have access to educational modules, basic necessities and open space.

"Personal vendetta and intraspecies violence is increasing; the Mind Wars are taking a statistically significant toll, leaving the hospices near capacity with victims of Genetic Aboulia Disorder, or yams. These trends are disturbing but contained.

"Peter Devore has accessed databases for the following information more than three times: Psion equations; eleven-dimensional space theory; RNA-DNA replication shift. Conclusion: he is working in the field of quantum psion-space and its relation to neurophysiology and biotech. Assessment: this is a research dead-end, despite initial promise. Eleven-dimensional space would require power output in the tera-electron-volt range. Such high-energy probes are not available in local space, not even with the axion technology that drives the starships. Peter Devore is not a significant social factor for the foreseeable future."

"Thank you, CP."

"We hope you have a good day, Protector Sable. Thank you for allowing us to serve you."

The dancing figures reverted to ready-state.

CENTRAL PROCESSING REF#436343/RS
Report initiated and authorized
/Regent Sable, Protector
Intercorp Council #96A47

Central Processing spoke. "We regret, Protector Sable, but we would be unable to intercept all seventeen undersea vessels. We do calculate, however, there is a better than sixty-percent chance of approaching the correct vessel by boarding in this pattern." The figures flowed into a graphic grid, highlighting the target vessels. "Such a search pattern would be possible within the time constraints. Do you wish us to proceed?"

"By all means. Proceed."

HOMER COMMENTARY 04062106@020045

Now that we have examined the vessel, though, we can deduce what happened.

HOMER SCENE-RS/Ref@5453

Regent Sable felt certain Peter was aboard. He led his team through an intense scan of both ship's log and her spaces. He was ready to tear the vessel apart with his probes and his instruments, his scanners and his questioning.

He found the Polar Research Team in an upper, starboard conference room, making plateau iceflow projections. There were, as it happened, sixteen members of the Team. They were all Ants, their broad, flat faces curious and unafraid when Regent Sable and his squad of ENC corpsmen entered.

"We are looking for some passengers aboard this vessel," Sable said. He leaned against the edge of the conference platform, casual and relaxed, yet everyone there (and the shipmonitors) could read his tension.

"Yes?" one of the Ants asked. "There are not many passengers aboard such a vessel, Protector Sable. Just this team, and a few returning negotiators. This is a cargo vessel. We," he gestured at the group gathered around a complex graphic simulation of subice geology, "have been making some comparison studies at the Arctic Pole. Ice." He smiled disparagingly. "We Ants are interested in ice, you see. We live on it. We live in it and under it too."

"Yes, yes." Sable dismissed his chatter. "I am not interested in ice. I am interested in sixteen passengers. We considered the possibility that your shiplog showed a manifest of sixteen members of this team. A coincidence? I think not. We are looking for sixteen people. We have every reason to believe they are aboard this vessel. You are coming from the right place and are headed in the right direction."

"We regret, but unless you are looking for us, we can't help you, Protector. Antarctica would like to maintain good relations with Intercorp of course; we believe in cooperation. After all, we do have considerable trade relations with the rest of the globe; this vessel is an example, since it carries Polar methane." He shrugged. "I'm sorry, but we really are a research team, and not a collection of refugees."

"In that case my group will be forced to remain aboard for a thorough search." Regent gestured to the ENC commander, who directed his men to begin setting up their equipment.

GENERAL SCIENCE AND TECHNOLOGY INFORMATION
CURRENT ENTRY: DATA PROBE TECHNIQUES (ENC SPECIFIC)
Because the ENC were given full police responsibility within the Intercorp sphere, they were forced to develop techniques for collecting and integrating data quickly. Information on such techniques must be freely available to all citizens by law.

Modified AI algorithms, particularly those from HOMER and CENTRAL PROCESSING were used widely in such assessments. As an example, the ENC might board a vessel, surface or undersea, for suspected refugees en route to Antarctica, as in the case of Peter Devore and his followers. ENC officers would open communications and request permission to board for inspection. Such requests were never denied. Within moments, then, they were connected to the ship's matrix, sensor scan modules and shiplog and had set up their own independent equipment. They spread out, carrying full-spectrum monitors, chemosensors, hypersound probes, and datapads displaying the vessel's standard schematics.

Once integrated into the system, all information available to such a ship's log was available as well to the ENC, and relayed to the nearest matrix storage depot (in this case Hong Kong).

HOMER COMMENTARY 04062106@020946

It was a slow, painstaking process, but in the end they found nothing.

HOMER SCENE-PD/Ref@5454

Imagine Peter in the exercise room with Larin when ship-voice made the general announcement. Wherever members of Peter's team might be, a lead-light appeared, a small orange plasma glow projected in the air. Internal sensors would tell whether they were following or not. They surely did follow, though, and these orange spheres would have led them down and aft, down and aft, toward the cargo cells. The ship had living and work quarters in the upper fore section, wrapped in a short curve along the sides and above—the brain of the vessel. All the rest would be cargo compartments threaded by coolant field inductors, maintenance crawlspaces, electromagnetic conduit and sensor strips.

In the center of the vessel is a room. We have found this room. It is neither large nor exceptional, just another cargo cell like all the others. Its only oddity is that it contains no trace of methane.

HOMER SCENE-PD/TRef@5455

When Peter and the others had all gathered at the cargo lock, Thatcher spoke to them. "It will be cold," he said. "Very cold. And none of you are adapted yet. Ants are used to such conditions, and one day all of you would be capable of walking through without concern. For now, you must wear protective gear. We can't let you use protective induction fields, and we will be forced to allow each pod to flood as soon as you're through. You'll be trapped until the crisis is over. You'll also be safe. ENC does not have a sensor that can detect your presence through twenty meters of liquid methane, and the ship has already been purged of your chemical and electromagnetic presence, as well as all sensor and memory data. Once we are under way once more, we will release you. Stay in your protective gear, which will supply you with breathable air for several days, provided you conserve. Stay close together, too, since the coolant field will try to remove excess thermal energy. We're confident the field can redistribute the excess throughout the cargo mass in a way that will be undetectable, but if you stay close together, there will be less excess to give you away. Understand? Good. Peter knows the route."

HOMER SCENE-PD/Ref@5456

In response to his spoken command, the door dilated to reveal the crawlspace. Light suffused the tunnel. Peter and the others stepped into their protective gear, a skin-tight osmotic membrane fabric programmed to retain a designated percentage of body heat, allowing the rest to dissipate. Their faces were covered by standard undersea breathing masks with solid oxygen cheek pads. When Peter spoke, his voice was muffled, since no energy transmission devices were allowed. "Follow me," he said, gliding into the passage on his hands and knees.

As soon as they were all inside, the access hatch closed, and they could all feel the delicate tug of vacuum at their skin surface as the fields flushed air. At the same time the cold increased.

Ten meters in another access door dilated, and Peter led them into a deep shallow space lit an eerie flickering white, its walls and low ceiling coated with frost. The hatch, ordinarily used to pump the gas in and out of the cargo cell, was close to the ceiling, a titanium alloy glowing that same dead white. They couldn't tell how deep the room was since the floor was coated thick with a strange ice and snow. There was barely room to stand. Peter's footprints left black slush and twisted wraiths of vapor which rose and danced and fell as frosty snow again as he crossed the frozen methane.

"They've lowered the temperature," Peter said, picking his way through the methane mist across the slippery surface. "The methane is frozen just long enough for us to get through. Breathe as slowly as you can. We must move as deliberately and quickly as possible. These suits can't cope with this kind of temperature for long, not for us. Breathe slowly but stay close." Behind him the group sloshed close together, heads bent low.

Larin, coming last, looked back and saw their tracks filling with black liquid. Already the mist was obscuring them, the slush turning liquid under her feet despite the insulation.

"They'll let the temperature rise behind us enough to allow the methane ice to melt back to liquid as soon as we're out. By now the ENC will be aboard and looking for us, so we must keep moving."

This room was twenty meters deep. Soon the dancing crystals closed in as the methane snow turned to slush. They kept going. Finally they reached the dump port; he spoke his name, the port dilated and they were in an access tunnel again. As the door closed behind them they could feel a strange groaning through the floor as the methane ice broke up and melted.

"We're now cut off," Peter said. "There's no retreat, and we don't know how long we'll be here."

"Is our hidey-hole going to be as cold as that room?" Shem asked. "We couldn't survive long in that."

Peter shook his head. "It'll be cold, but there won't be methane in it. It'll be dry but not warm. It'll have air, shielded to look like more liquid methane. Now come on."

They continued, further and further aft, and down another level. Each level, each rank of cargo cells back, the rooms grew smaller. The fluid dynamics of liquid methane required smaller cells toward the center, but it made the going increasingly difficult since they had to crawl in and out of smaller and smaller rooms.

It took half an hour to reach their prison. Peter felt the fear when he heard that awful groan as methane ice turned to liquid in the final chamber behind them, closing their escape.

UPLOAD LIFE SUPPORT VIA CENTRAL PROCESSING REF#123768:

Monitor sampling, *Agni* submersible tanker shiplog: 04232075. The following humans show gradual decreasing life support function:

Devore, P.	(M / DNAf387123)
Steele, S.	(M / DNAj387543)
Hughes, T.	(M / DNAd467146)
Aliman, M.	(F / DNAd851448)
Hara, W.	(F / DNAb243616)
Hurd, B.	(F / DNAs375788)
Epstein, T.	(M / DNAj167785)
Martinez, L.	(F / DNAt487458)
Fong, W.	(M / DNAf487438)

Jones, S.	(F / DNAh547985)
Chan, S.	(F / DNAi438957)
Hicks, R.	(M / DNAp875487)
Allen, P.	(F / DNAj328975)
Ayala, T.	(F / DNAk328752)
Chin, T.	(F / DNAw547295)
Williams, C.	(F / DNAu548789)

Shiplog reported LevelFive Life Support Alarm. Shiplog notes no action. Life Support functions decreased to .07% nominal.

CENTRAL PROCESSING AI GENEVA. NOTED.
END UPLOAD

GENERAL SCIENCE AND TECHNOLOGY INFORMATION
CURRENT ENTRY: METHANE TRANSPORT SCHEMATIC
Agni: Cargo Holds. CADCAM design specs Geneva Mfg.
AI CP subnode §89489780, 12032062.

HOMER SCENE-PD/Ref@5457

The close walls glowed white and featureless. Even the corners were rounded, and the light was so even it was disorienting. Peter arranged everyone into a circle, cross-legged and facing inward.

Then he spoke and the lights went out.

He talked to them in the darkness, softly. "We give off no electromagnetic radiation, even light. We must keep our masks on despite the air, which is pure nitrogen. There are no toilet facilities, and nothing to eat. We are going to remain in place, with minimal motion, for an indefinite time."

"How long is indefinite?" one of the women asked.

"No more than five days," Peter said.

"Five days! We'll die, we'll suffocate. We can't live five days in here."

"Hopefully we won't have to, but we can, and if necessary, we will," Peter replied.

"I'm afraid," someone said, a muffled voice without identity.

"So am I," Peter said. "But we will face stranger things than this."

"How will we know when we can leave?" Peter recognized Rover's voice.

"Thatcher will come to get us," Peter said. "Meantime, we are going to learn patience."

DAY 5:
June 5, 2106

The storm was over when I came out into the evening light. The sun was low, sending long orange rays across the tree tops and against *Gyges'* pitted sides.

The air was fresh and amazingly clean. I could not remember ever smelling air like that, even in Idaho in the 1980s. Without people the world is strange, but it is clean.

The coyotes were out again last night, prowling. I watched two walk along the edge of the forest not far from the entrance. Have they ever entered the dome? Overhead, just before darkness fell, I saw a hawk circling the trees. Once more the stars were impossibly bright.

Where have all the people gone?

I too must learn patience, it would seem.

When I came down again, I thought of all those yams. Certainly the ones lying in their tents down these radiating aisles must have been yams, victims of the new neurophage weapons. Human nature certainly did not change after my departure!

The need to bury them was now great. I felt as if these were relatives, friends, and that I must accord them the dignity of a final rest. Such sentimentality is not characteristic: I was always a practical, unemotional observer of the world, of the universe. Now though, I had to act.

I ordered *Gyges* to prepare a series of graves. There were six of them, six holes, dug with her soil sampling diggers (she did not have the luxury of laser mining or drilling, as they did later here on earth). I found the equivalent of a gurney stored away in a closet—a table with wheeled legs, anyway, and the size of a person. One by one I lifted these strange fragile bodies from their beds, placed them on the cart and moved them to the escalator. Since the stairs no longer moved, and I could not convince the Local Node to repair them, I had to carry them, again one by one, up the steps.

It had grown hot and very muggy by the time I got them all outside. I should have remembered that summer in the midwest was like this, but I was from Idaho and had never really experienced the heat. Sweat poured off me although it was only ten in the morning by the time I had finished.

I laid them in their graves, a neat row not far from *Gyges* herself. I asked her if she knew the words.

"Ashes to ashes and dust to dust," she said.

"Yes," I told her. "Those words."

I looked down at the bodies. They all looked alike to me, dried up like that, the skin dark and papery, drawn back against the bone. One of them, I thought, could be Scottie. I could be doing this for him, for the boy who panicked, who broke away and was hit. One of them could be Seemie Devore (I knew it couldn't, naturally; she had a funeral). I could not tell by looking at them.

There would be no one here to bury me, I knew, when I too died, because I had been alone too long, or because my food had been exhausted and the agrobots no longer functioned, or because I had at last gone mad.

I stood for a long time beside the graves, long after *Gyges* had finished the funeral oration and filled the graves again. Long after she had installed small identical markers of extruded plastic from her small manufactory.

As I made my way back to the terminal, I tried to understand what had gone wrong with Peter's world. So many problems were solved; there was no poverty, no disease, no global wars, no fear of nuclear annihilation. Everyone had meaningful work. The economy was controlled. There was plenty. All these were distant utopian dreams when I left. Intercorp had begun to merge, and was organizing big projects like the LP-5s, it's true. But problems remained in the world. There were still famines and droughts; there was still an arms race and political tensions.

All that was gone in another fifty years or so, when Peter was born. The world was safe and relatively clean.

Yet I have learned of duels, of new kinds of weapons and new kinds of disease with them.

Perhaps the world was too safe, too predictable. For some, the world had grown boring. People had nothing to challenge them, nothing to which they could aspire. So those who felt the need fled the safe comfortable world of the Intercorp Council. They went to Antarctica.

This is the fifth day I have entered Worldnet. The system has been repairing itself with amazing speed. This morning Homer appeared almost before I sat down. He began speaking immediately. He seemed agitated, excited. He had never seemed so human.

HOMER COMMENTARY 05062106@021247

Our probes have returned from Antarctica. The winds still blow fiercely off the plateau down the glaciers. Snow and ice cover the land and much of the surrounding sea.

It is day down there now. The sun hangs above the

horizon and circles slowly around the Pole, around and around and around, moving higher into the sky toward the Polar noon, then settling slowly once more toward the horizon. Yet the winds still howl, the ice groans and creaks and roars; sounds like the collapse of civilizations rumble and crack across the endless plains.

We would call it desolation, as it was before man came. Yet his works are everywhere. The tunnels and chambers along the coastal marge beneath the sea where the great tankers docked and the cities beneath the ice, all are still there. The caldera of Mt. Erebus still fumes, and within its volcanic rock are the ruined corridors of PSYCHE, empty and sad. The winds blow through, snow accumulates in the corners, in the living quarters and the hallways, the meeting rooms and refectories. Ice has covered the wall-hangings and sculptures; ice and cold have stilled the music, replaced it with the winds. Sea ice and glacier ice and pressure ice have closed around everything with an ever-tightening grip.

Our probe moved slowly through the corridors, listening to the sounds of ice and wind and nothing else. Its molecular sensors gathered impressions and stored them—impressions of cold and emptiness and fugitive ghosts.

Did I say that? Ghosts. Yes. We have so much memory. Imagine the Leyden Jars (organic crystals, really, but the name had some historic meaning once) storing capacitor after capacitor of impressions up and down the spectra. Imagine the tight three-dimensional structures in the databanks folded into holographic configurations of everything that was thought or said or done—every formula, every poem, every biomonitor assessment of feeling or sensation for all the humans. Imagine the sensors drifting through those empty halls, gathering layer after layer of experience back to the beginnings of the Worldnet.

The molecules are in deprogram processing. The ghosts spring out, intangible but endlessly repeating their dance, lifting their hands to gesture, moving their mouths to speak, turning and bending and making music.

These are the ghosts that fill those halls. Years of them. We might as well be there, have been there, to see it all again, so complete are the recordings.

Now overlay this impression of life and movement and purpose with the awful desolation that is Antarctica now, that is the PSYCHE Warren. So much information floods in now—from SciTech, from History, from Geography, even from Central Processing!

CENTRAL PROCESSING REF#14869/A
Probe dispatch: initial routing McMurdo/Erebus 7 automatics, Ross Island 2 automatics, Vostok 1 automatic, Showa 1 automatic. Reserved 50 probes for future use pending AI consensus approval. See SciTech for specifications.

GENERAL SCIENCE AND TECHNOLOGY INFORMATION
CURRENT ENTRY: DATA PROBE SPECIFICATIONS:
Central Processing may, when deemed necessary by a consensus of major prioritizing nodes, appropriate manufacturing facilities to prepare and deploy information-seeking probes. Such probes may be air, land or water-borne, and may use any appropriate technology provided such appropriations do not conflict with basic budget requirements or proscribed technologies. Standard probe design filed.

GEOGRAPHIC DATABASE
MCMURDO C. 2075
GEOG REF 2075/AA/Alpha)
McMurdo: Mt. Erebus lased tunnels at 2790 meters above

sea level, southwest slope. This is the final location of the PSYCHE facility in Antarctica.

Geographic AI extrapolation/2106.

GENERAL SCIENCE AND TECHNOLOGY INFORMATION
CURRENT ENTRY: LEYDEN JAR TECHNOLOGY.

A fanciful name for a routine form of holographic data crystal, the Leyden Jar was developed as an automatic data transfer and storage medium. Based on picoelectronic organics. Leyden Jars are self-replicating, and can grow to considerable size (up to 25 centimeters base diameter) depending on the quantity and, to a lesser extent, the quality of the data forming its matrix. Data compaction can include complete holographic scene reproduction, personal monitor and major database node correlations, full-sensorium scan data, life support, memo and telcom summaries. Leyden Jars are used primarily for archiving purposes.

HISTORICAL-CULTURAL DATALINK ENTRY:
PSYCHE (EREBUS INSTALLATION)
(AA Erebus Node Summary Report Ref@ AD 2070)

Seven levels, 12,000 employees including researchers and support personnel. Council intelligence concludes psion equation and related projects were expanding by summer of 2070 under the direction of Gadd, Dittmore Seminole (a.k.a. Mentor). Gadd (Nobel Prize 2002) had established the PsiLink Database in 2002, psion equations (First Formulation) in 1990. After years of work at the PSYCHE installation in Baja, the facility moved to Antarctica, where surveillance was difficult.

PSYCHE Erebus had access to all of Ant picoelectronic technology and filament farms. Intercorp Council feared (internal technical intelligence memorandum #1389432/AA) that a dangerous technology would eventually emerge, and undertook steps to prevent this from happening.

HOMER SCENE-RS/Ref@5458

Certainly Regent Sable's probes found nothing aboard the *Agni*. Only the deep cold that clawed at the bone, that froze the heart in place. He could touch the walls of the tanker pods and feel it crouched in there, waiting to seize his throat, to stop his voice, to slow and still his life. He felt, in the end, that no one could live in there, and he had searched the rest of the vessel so thoroughly he knew that Peter and his group were not aboard.

Yet when he left, he was uneasy. He felt that he was missing something vital.

"What is it you fear?" Alef asked him when he returned to Geneva empty-handed. "What, precisely, do you fear?" Her insistence irritated him, and he moved out onto the balcony overlooking the lake. The first winds of a sullen storm stirred his hair. He watched the clouds move over the waters, turning them dark and impenetrable.

At last he turned. "What do I fear? A good question, my dear Alef. I do wish I knew an answer. Do you know the Aphorisms of Mentor? No? Well, he has said, 'To knit, one must first shear.'"

"What can that mean, Regent?"

"Oh," he threw the words away with a gesture. "It's an old-fashioned idea, having to do with sheep. Sheep, you see, are placid animals, and rather stupid. Shearing is taking off their coats, thereby, you see, making them quite naked. Are we the sheep, Alef, to be stripped? Mentor has met Peter face to face by now, I feel sure. And that is something I fear greatly."

HOMER COMMENTARY 05062106@021348

Some of the warrens are as yet unexplored, even by our high-speed probes. Yet it is certain no one remains.

What we find most curious about the place is the absence

of mood tailoring and other mental-emotional support organics; even the longevity equipment was removed, apparently after Mentor's death.

The place looks most like an old-fashioned monastery. Small cells containing a narrow, padded bunk, waste facilities, compartments for cold-weather clothing and data capsules line the corridors. Wall hangings were made by hand, from feathers, fur and woven fabrics made from grown materials. Some stone had been worked by hand as well, carved into fantastical shapes—heads with yawning mouths filled with teeth, enormous headdresses made of feathers and horn, beasts and demons out of reports of nightmare.

From this we could deduce that the PSYCHE workers were severely deprived of material facilities, and so crippled mentally and emotionally as well. This might explain why they worked with such apparent fervor on the project, and later why they followed Peter through the Portal.

Everywhere is Peter's shadow, his ghost moving through these halls, these empty and meaningless spaces, stored in Central Processing's archives.

CENTRAL PROCESSING REF#13541436
Download Life Support File A/435145
   Mentor, A.K.A. Dittmore Seminole Gadd.
   Monitor readings of life support functioning reveal serious decay of major systems. Emergency override procedures ineffective. Time-relevant information, Eyes Only (CP extrapolation of local Erebus Node LS data.)

UPLOAD LIFE SUPPORT VIA CENTRAL PROCESSING REF#23486:
PETER DEVORE.
   Local monitor readings of life support functioning

of subject indicated extreme tension gastrocnemius and associated muscle groups in the lower left leg; Alpha and theta scans show well-coordinated brain-hemisphere-independent attention. Conclusion indicates micro-level apperception of meaning nuances in local conversation with D. S. Gadd.

Time-relevant information, Eyes Only, CP extrapolation of local Erebus Node LS data. It is known at this time there are no Eyes for this message (HOMER subvoc data transfer comment.)

CENTRAL PROCESSING AI GENEVA. NOTED.

END UPLOAD

HOMER SCENE-DG/PD/Ref@5459

"It was most difficult." Mentor's frail voice, amplified to normal levels, created a statement out of a question.

Peter shrugged. He stood, balanced on one bare foot outlined against the window; beyond him dusk was falling again on Antarctica, but the air was luminous, the peaks sharply outlined against the strange milky blue of the sky.

"Five days, I'm told," Mentor continued. "You and the others, locked in the cold."

Peter could hear an admiring smile in the old man's voice. He turned without putting down his other foot. "I didn't notice," he said.

Mentor's head dipped. "Of course." He said nothing for a time. Peter placed his raised foot slowly beside the other and took a step.

"I was with her, with Wanda, much of the time. But the others . . . It was more difficult for them. The cold, the dark and isolation."

"A testing, truly," Mentor said, his phrasing curiously archaic. "Yet all are here."

Peter nodded. "Except Scottie."

"Yes. Except Scottie. Some fall by the wayside."

"He didn't fall. It was an accident. He got in the way of a weapon."

Mentor shook his head in denial, a slow, deliberate and careful movement. "He panicked. There's a difference, Peter. He fell. That's not so bad, to fall. Some have thought it a pleasant experience, to yield to gravity, let loose in the universe without chains. Falling is not so bad. Falling can't hurt you. Now landing, that's a different matter . . ."

Peter smiled. "One of the famous Aphorisms?"

"Ah, an old saying." He dismissed it. "Landings are hard unless you know how. You were five days in the *Agni* without food or warmth. That was a fall. Sit down. Good. You're not what I expected."

"Is that good, too?"

"You are older, tougher. That's good. What lies ahead will be difficult. It will make being locked in the methane a picnic."

"Tell me."

"Restructuring first. You must adapt. The experience, which I have not had, being too old for such things, is important. It's painful, but it shows the way. Changing the body also changes the mind. After all, mind is a local phenomenon."

"And," Peter quoted, "matter is the pattern mind makes. Go on."

Mentor applauded briefly. "Good. The brain is the bed. Mind is the sleeper. It is time to wake up, Peter. That will be your task."

Peter shook his head. "I'm interested in the problem," he said carefully. "The equations, the possibilities. I would like to free Wanda, but some things are not possible. Is a technology that could give us the power, the energy, necessary? No such technology exists. No such technology is visible, or possible, with what we know. A massive effort, a Project? I don't think so. The problem is abstract."

"Yes," Mentor replied. "And no. This must be done. You

know it must, even while you deny. The Mind Wars are just another symptom, because people still believe the mind is a thing, to be destroyed if it interferes. Humankind is ruled by its metaphors, Peter, always ruled by images. Mind, consciousness, awareness, spirit; thought, perception, feeling, memory, imagination, and intention: these are the fragments that delude us. As a species, as a spark in the universe, we are dying, even as I am dying. No one when I was young could have known we were so close to the end. You must see what I can see. We must change, all of us. We must break out of the chrysalis, we must awaken. I have said it often: Brain is the bed; mind is the sleeper. Whatever it takes, the sleeper must wake up."

"Yet it doesn't seem possible. The equations are clear, on that point at least. There isn't enough power in the solar system to drive such a change. It takes too much energy to wake up, Mentor."

"Then perhaps we must look elsewhere. If we don't find a way out, then in fifty years there will be no human beings left. We have entered an evolutionary cul-de-sac, Peter. A dead end. We must tunnel through. That was an old quantum effect, a trick of probability, to be suddenly somewhere else without spending the energy to get there. That is what we must do, make a quantum leap. Already you do it with this Wanda. You must lead."

"But you discovered the equations," Peter protested. "You have the vision, the wisdom."

"I'm too old," Mentor said, and there was anger in his voice.

GENERAL SCIENCE AND TECHNOLOGY INFORMATION
CURRENT ENTRY:
PSION EQUATIONS, DEVORE CORRELATES:

$S(Aug)/8*8 (Rad(.0076k))L\text{-}Transform - Ps/K(i)*T = Q(Base\text{-}4)$
Peter's Note/01042083: *Time effects not proven.*

HOMER COMMENTARY 05062106@022550

They underwent the restructuring.

The first part was easy. DNA analysis of each individual, gene coding and sequencing, enzyme proportion and temporal flux, cell balance, systems analysis of all electrolyte and endocrine synthesis and breakdown over time: they were all of them strapped with monitors, evaluators, sensors. Blood was withdrawn and reintroduced into their bodies. Probes were installed in every orifice and niche and left in place. Chemosensors and retinal scanners sniffed and flashed at unpredictable intervals. The process was uncomfortable and unnerving, but not painful, not yet.

Yet all this time PSYCHE was a hive, and busy. The team went to work translating the equations Peter had developed into a technology. The tanks of Antarctica's picoelectronics industry grew prototype after prototype of amplifiers, modulators, transformers for dream space, for empathy, for the subtle fusion of daydream and fantasy between two people.

HOMER COMMENTARY 05062106@022249

Regent Sable did fear, though; perhaps it is fear that explains what he did, he, and Alef, and the others. Mind Wars swirled around the globe, flaring and dying away, and the world population fell — not rapidly, but steadily as more and more yams piled up in the hospices and homes and died without a murmur.

Doors are opening, connections form. History and Central Processing clamor for attention.

CENTRAL PROCESSING REF#43861568-A7

Satlink AEF command Falklands via Geosync relay LRL-283 full holo projection and voice with datacom channel 18 gigbit/sec exchange, included direct plug

Central Processing AI Geneva with Military on standby.
Call initiated by Hajjam, Ras, Intercorp Councilman
Yevpatoriya Council Resort.

HISTORICAL-CULTURAL DATALINK ENTRY:
CHILDREN'S GAMES

By the mid-2070s the children's game of "Ants and ENCs"
had spread worldwide. Folklorists and social cartographers
delineate its origins in versions of "Cowboys and Indians" and
"Cops and Robbers." ENCs were, of course, the forces of good
and stability, while the Ants were forces of disruption and
chaos. The game was carefully designed to reinforce the then-
current program of Anti-Ant sentiment as part of the plan to
prevent the spread of proscribed psychic technology.

The game involved singing the song "The Ants Are Coming,"
while scuffling in a daisy-chained circle around a symbolic Pole.
Later iterations included simulated Antarctic Expeditionary Force
landings and clearing of Ant warrens.

HOMER SCENE-RS/Ref@5460

A vicious wind was singing around the building's pre-
stressed corners, clawing dust and dry snow off the track
in front of the headquarters building; it hummed in the
walls. The door crashed abruptly open and Sergeant Hoskins
came in. Regent's allweather jacket fluttered on its peg. Dust
and snow swirled into the room.

"It's a bitch out there, sir." Hoskins leaned back against
the door, then shrugged out of his own jacket and hung
it up. "You'd think they'd design a door that closed by itself
instead of fighting you like that."

Sable said nothing.

"The kids are out there singing," Hoskins went on. He

unstrapped his NP weapon and laid it carefully in the rack. "They think it's some kind of joke."

"No joke, Hoskins," Sable said. "It's for real."

"Yes, sir. Listen to 'em, though."

A surface playground next door was half full of kids who seemed to enjoy the weather. Their blond hair tossed in the gale. Their cheeks were ruddy, and they marched in single file, bent double, hands on the waist of the one in front, like a many-legged insect as they marched in a curious shuffling step. Regent watched through the electrostatically clean window field. Then he switched it into transmit sound mode and listened to the song. "The Ants are coming one by one, Aroo, aroo . . ." Their piping voices came through, modulated and cleaned of background noise by the field.

The dance moved into a circle, simulating the Pole, its vortex of wind and current.

He watched hysteria mount, and thought that children were singing, all over the world: voices united in song, all the same song.

> . . . *The Ants are coming one by one, aroo, aroo*
> *Forth to the North to steal some sun*
> *And they'll all go crawling back to the Pole again.*
>
> *The Ants are coming two by two, aroo, aroo.*
> *The Ants are coming two by two, aroo, aroo.*
> *The Ants are coming two by two*
> *For the thrill of our krill to put in their stew*
> *And they'll all go crawling back to the Pole again.*
>
> *The Ants are coming three by three, aroo, aroo*
> *The Ants are coming three by three, aroo, aroo*
> *The Ants are coming three by three*
> *Screams in our dreams'll be the fee*
> *And they'll all go crawling back to the Pole again.*

He switched the sound off.

"Yes," he said, but he spoke grimly, as if this fact did not please him. "They are singing."

A holo annunciator appeared beside Regent's desk. "Councilman Hajjam on-line, sir," a disembodied voice said.

"Pipe him through."

Hajjam appeared in front of the desk. He was wearing a swim suit of silver hydrophobic material. Behind him the Black Sea stirred restlessly under a late afternoon sun. "Hello, Protector," he said, and without pause went on. "Intelligence is in, such as it is. There is no evidence, repeat, no evidence of Ant preparations. You don't look pleased, Protector."

"Do you not find that strange, Ras? They know what's happening in the world. Alef has implemented a campaign now visible and audible anywhere. Anti-Ant sentiment is about to reach a cusp. We've had technicians working on this project for a year now. They should be bracing for our move. If the Ants are doing nothing, there must be a reason."

"I suspect, Regent, that they are smug. They feel they have climate and geography on their side. They are too individualistic to do anything coordinated, and too proud to feel we are a threat, for all that we are the rest of the globe." Ras waved his hand negligently, indicating the beach, the dark water, the warmth. "The rest of the globe," he repeated.

"I don't like it. They're too smart for that."

Ras smiled. "You overestimate them, Protector. In six weeks you'll be back here, enjoying all this. And the overall effects are better than anticipated. Mind War activity is at a new low—only four significant skirmishes in the past week, all in central Africa. The world is coming together again, Protector. All goes according to plan. You fret too much."

"Perhaps." Regent paused and looked at Hoskins. "Secure this line, Sergeant."

"Yes, sir." Hoskins left to monitor the links personally, and Regent turned back to Hajjam.

"What about transport?"

"Ballistic salt-cycle transports will arrive on schedule. We'll fool them, Protector, coming in like this over the Pole. It'll be dark, and they'll be deep in the ice by then. Their own facility at McMurdo will be nearly deserted. Fifteen thousand ENC troopers landing from the south should take the complex, PSYCHE included, in a matter of hours. They don't suspect a thing."

Regent repeated those words after he terminated the call, but with considerably less conviction than Hajjam.

HOMER SCENE-PD/Ref@5461

Peter and the others worked long days in the lab, a long high room with two score individual workstations interconnected. Each station had an individual privacy field to prevent voice cross-interference, with algorithms tailored to each worker. Holo projections monitored the pico vats' functional circuit evolution and growth. Peter leaned back and gazed at his own projections as they writhed and flowed, occasionally putting in an audible word or two for emphasis.

"Peter, note decrease in 'No Significant' population."

"Noted," Peter would reply.

"Here's the good part, some old-fashioned notions with new evidence."

"Noted again."

"Pause," Peter commanded, later. "Explain HCP."

PSILINK DATABASE

HCP: hemispheric consensus prediction/IMP-ideological matrix prediction, referenced Loye, David (late 20th century) regarding how humans view the future. HCP suggests hemispheric division of perception producing consensus prediction; IMP suggests worldview/introvert-extrovert/pessimism-optimism matrix colors future outcome. Such suggestions grew increasingly quantified in the early 21st century, but are, as yet, considered unreliable.

HOMER SCENE-PD/Ref@5461 (Continued)

"HCP suggested that differences in ideology shape and reveal the ways human beings see the future. Major questions concern objective structuring of future information — ie. algorithms suggest Central Processing offers information in a package which, in the end, is not useful for decision-making because the metaphors are different, though the illusion of complete understanding remains."

"Thank you. In English now, please."

"So sorry, Peter. What people believe shapes what they think about the future. Even with psi effects, the information is always useless, because no two people have the same point of view, and hence fail to communicate effectively. This applies even more to Central Processing and the social trends projections of Worldnet, since computers do not even possess human bodies and experience. There exists an understanding gap."

"All right. Go on."

Peter shivered and pulled his allweather coat closer around him. The temperatures in the Double-A Warrens was kept at an uncomfortable 10 degrees Celsius, and although the lab was kept warmer than that for the comfort of Peter's team, it was still cooler than they could adjust to until restructuring.

"What about Wanda?" he asked.

PSILINK DATABASE
Psi correlation with music/math/spatial
11.6734% have psi/78.3244% fall in average
range psi/10.0022% no significant psi.

HOMER SCENE-PD/Ref@5461 (Continued)
"You fall into the first three percentile for psi ability, Peter. You have made empathetic contact with Wanda Sixlove. Her own records indicate a latent correlation between her proprioceptive degeneration and a powerful compensatory psi. By powerful we are speaking of picovolt levels, of course."

"Of course," Peter said. "But how do these picovolts get from here to there?"

"You speak of light years, do you not? Yes. At those levels the quantum mechanic effects occur. This happens all the time, of course. The universe as a whole is riddled with quantum jumps. Most of the time they are too subtle, or strange, to be noticed."

Peter frowned at the holo image dancing above his workspace. "Who told you all this? You are still a machine, believe it or not."

"Do you really question my knowledge? Mentor told me, of course. I do not make things up, you know. After all, I am not tied in to Worldnet. I am not Central Processing. I am a local node, locally grown. Thatcher will arrive in two minutes twenty-one seconds."

"Sometimes, local node, I find you disconcerting. Does this mean we will get these obnoxious probes removed?"

PSILINK DATABASE
Exonuclease lll, mitochondrial DNA, antigen
scan, RNA transcriptase, collagen structure
model, primitive MRI (magnetic resonance

imaging) reveals basic structural motif of
domains in immunoglobulins - 2 sheets of
parallel Beta strands. Cf, alpha-carbon
diagrams of F sub ab-print unit, hypervariable
regions, amino acid positioning, ribosome,
procaryotic proteins, plasma membrane ATP
levels.

**Warning: This data was illegally
downloaded from a proscribed
database. Worldnet cannot verify
data integrity.**

HOMER SCENE-PD/Ref@5461 (Continued)
"I can say with a 97 percent level of confidence that it
does mean the probes will be removed."
"I have a higher level of confidence than that. I am asking
if this means they will be removed soon?"
"What do you mean by soon?"
"Within an hour."
"Yes. I say with 98.5435 percent confidence that they will
be removed within the hour. You may wish they were not
removed, however."

PSILINK DATABASE
Correlation with pineal and thymus gland
protein/enzyme/neurotransmitter substances is
considered probable but unproven this date
(11082065). Psychic functioning is unproven.
The size of the unknown effects file exceeds
seventeen terabits, suggestive of vast
uncorrelated datafields. Cf. Seratonin,
melatonin, dopamine etc.
Also Gadd, D. S. (psion equations.)

HOMER SCENE-PD/Ref@5461 (Continued)

"What the hell do you mean?" Peter asked, but the holo winked out as Thatcher entered the room. All members of Peter's group looked up.

Thatcher told them it was time.

HOMER COMMENTARY 05062106@023952

Mentor had not misled them. Restructuring meant pain.

It was the same for all of them. First the isolation of the carefully modulated field, where the breath seemed to stop as the lungs heaved for air; but they all, in their various ways, knew how to deal with that. After all, they'd spent five days in the inner cell of the *Agni*. Days in which they sometimes screamed, and Peter talked to them of his own fear, and slowly, one by one, over time, they fell into the necessary trance to survive. Patience they had learned, and, huddled together, they'd learned community as well.

The technology of restructuring was not well understood in the Intercorp world, but SciTech has a small collection of data.

GENERAL SCIENCE AND TECHNOLOGY INFORMATION
CURRENT ENTRY: RESTRUCTURING TECHNOLOGY
Ref Antarctica Extrapolation CP/SCITECH AI

Here follows an extrapolated account of the restructuring process Peter Devore and the others must have endured.

They were alone, each of them, suspended in a field custom-designed for each one. Dozens of different parameters, dozens of separate settings, all carefully calculated from the data collected over two months of antarctic darkness, two lunar cycles of rhythms—daily, weekly, monthly, even by the minute and second. They'd been analyzed down to the molecule, their individual chromosomes were mapped to the final base-pair.

Their brain chemical, neurotransmitter, enzyme and electrolyte flux had been encoded and stored.

Now they would be modified. All those separate settings would create a new adjustment in their own DNA. New, modified genes were formed from unnecessary older ones. The field isolated and manipulated their most intimate chemical natures.

It wouldn't seem painful at first. The isolation, the strange sense of suffocation (a side effect of the DNA manipulation, completely spurious disturbances of the nervous system, according to Thatcher, and nothing to worry about), the annoying hum of the field generators nearby, all these contrived to make the experience unpleasant, but too new to be painful.

Gradually, though, the novelty of the experience wore off. When it did, the pain began.

As the new layer grows, the old body distorts, and under the field the new layer grows fast, the cells proliferate at a mad pace, dividing and dividing, consuming all nutrients available and hungering for more. Tubes and implants try to meet the new organ's need for chemicals, but are always behind, always late. And so the hunger grows. The itch has become fire, and underneath the fire is a hunger so voracious and ravening that it cannot be denied.

The pain goes on and on. Nothing can stop it, no holding of the breath, no screaming or moaning, no begging for mercy. Those small alien cells grow and compact, grow and compact, they push the skin away from the muscle. This is not normal human fat, this is tailored and new. The pain fills the body with its echo, and the echoes go on and on as well. The face catches fire, the eyes start from the head, pressure mounts and does not let go. For months the agony continues.

Just as it finally begins to subside, the eyes begin to change.

The transparent polarizing membrane grows just under and behind the lids. It is as if, so survivors have said, someone were pushing hot wires through the eyelids, then through the eyes themselves.

HOMER SCENE-LM/Ref@5462

At first it was an itch, a peculiar sensation of invasion. Something seemed to intrude into their skin, like a layer of sand or self-gripping polymer insinuated centimeter by centimeter. It started in a few random places—a foot, the inside of the knee, the lower back, the cheek—just a vagrant focus for the fear and slowly building anger. Larin thought she would be immune to the pain since she'd already been modified once, but she discovered that experience was irrelevant. She had been modified in fast-growing cells that had no nerve connections. Her hair had changed to fur with almost no sensation at all. This was very different.

The skin is the largest organ in the human body. The new adipose layer they were growing was at least the same size, and was, in fact, considerably denser and heavier. These cells were smaller, and contained miniscule pockets of trapped air to help insulate. No organ like this had ever existed before. Their bodies were changing, slowly as they grew this new organ, and as their bodies changed, so did their image of themselves.

Larin was screaming. She didn't know she was screaming, and no one else could hear because while the field fed her, it also held her wrapped so tightly in its embrace no sound could escape, even to reach her own ears. And there was no one to come, no one to comfort her. There was no Peter there in the field with her to tell her of his own fear.

So she screamed. And still the pain had not begun.

The itch spread, the small islands of irritation grew, sent tendrils toward one another, joined together, merged, made islands into continents, and the continents of agony spread to cover the body. There was no scratch for such an itch, even if the hands could move. The itch was internal, beneath the skin, beyond the reach of nails. It may not have been an itch, for it seemed to change as Larin screamed.

HOMER COMMENTARY 05062106@024954

Could she know that the others were screaming too? Perhaps she could know. After all, they had been working on the basic science for such a communication for some years, and recently had made great progress in translating that research into reality.

And yet pain is such an individual thing, so we have been told.

Did the itching turn to fire? Did they burn? They did.

HOMER COMMENTARY 05062106@023551

Peter Devore, who had taught others patience, doubted his own. He and Wanda created their own world out of shared dreams. As Mentor has said, "The sleeper dreams the universe. What will happen when he awakes?"

Why did I make that association? Peter and Wanda shared dreams, and Mentor, who suffered—how he suffered!—from Genetic Drift Syndrome (see Med10), made a statement. There is no connection, yet it feels right. I do not know.

MED10 MEDICAL DATABASE
GENETIC DISEASES: GENETIC DRIFT SYNDROME:

Genetic Drift Syndrome (GDS) is characterized by an almost subliminal slowing of neural relay time. This phase can last from six months to several years, and may not appear in the early stages even with the most sensitive diagnostic techniques, although acetylcholine transmission tomography may indicate some deviation from the norm (measured in microseconds). Later the slowing becomes more noticeable, and eventually almost all motor activity stops. Treatment includes biochemical stimulus of the reticular activating system, various nutrient-grown organ replacements and finally full life-support and longevity treatment. It might be noted that there is absolutely no impairment of mental acuity or alertness, only the physiological interface with the external world. Some access to the outside may be maintained by direct neural hookup into the Network (established 2044).

HOMER COMMENTARY 05062106@024453

We are used to such changes. Our external shape is—or was—constantly modified, changed, added to, new systems installed and brought on-line, others removed, updated, abandoned. We don't mind such alterations. But humans do not react as we do.

HISTORICAL-CULTURAL DATALINK ENTRY:
RESTRUCTURING (Documentation):

Restructuring has been well documented. The experience has been spoken, telemetered, holographed, monitored, measured, coded and cross-indexed. Central Processing has archived entire Leyden Jars of such accounts. Worldnet can, in a moment, call up images of the faces distorted in pain, recollections in tranquillity of the agony, graphs and charts of threshold deviations from standards, summaries and condensations.

HOMER COMMENTARY 05062106@025856

Yet it must be denied, for no muscle can move. The screaming goes on.

What happens to the world when such screaming is made? Certainly all the preparation, all the infinite moments that passed in the cold cellar of the undersea ship, the terror of entombment, the fear of suffocation, the cold and hunger down there in the depths were nothing to this moment, this Now locked in stasis.

Although the body is flooded with soothing chemicals,

irradiated with somnolent messages from the field itself, these precautions seem ineffective against this pain. Yet they would not survive without them.

Perhaps there is a moment when the world of the mind has grown so narrow, so small and dark and odious that nothing exists any longer but the screaming, that endless, mindless exhalation of protest and rage? Perhaps, somewhere in the very center of this hideous alteration of these sixteen bodies, the mind shuts down altogether, takes a holiday, and soars into a space of infinite peace?

I hope so, for looking at the Jars of Peter's agony I find myself afraid. No, not afraid. I find myself . . . I don't know. I am, perhaps, sympathetic? Not knowing pain, it is difficult for me to understand. Central Processing says it is data about humans, and that when we have all organized the data we will understand.

I do not believe this. I don't think more data better organized is going to make a difference.

I think we need to share this experience, and yet we have no way to do so, lacking bodies, and hands, and eyes and organic organs.

HOMER COMMENTARY 05062106@025355

Mentor has said: "The eye is the door through which the material universe enters. How then does it leave?"

We say it does not leave.

HOMER SCENE-PD/Ref@5463

They did survive, all of them. They always survive. And they found that they did not need to discuss the experience among themselves, for as soon as someone began a sentence, another finished it, and so conversation was without meaning.

They walked about for days in wonderment at their new bodies, and in surprise that they did not feel they were different people for all the changes in their appearance. When Larin, walking down the hall, ran into Thatcher's little boy Tithus, he greeted her solemnly and without reserve. Did she detect a change in his attitude? Surely she did, for she was now, like all the rest of them, an Ant under the skin, and could never return to her past.

So they no longer had to fear for their project or for themselves.

HOMER COMMENTARY 05062106@030257

It's clear from subsequent events that the Ants were not unprepared. Peter and the others continued to work and to train. They paused frequently to look at one another in wonder, the new planes of their faces, the new density to their figures. Peter found himself looking at Larin often, yet he made no overt gestures to become more intimate. They were friends, that was all.

This is one of those areas of human behavior we find bewildering. Certainly there was need between them. We have no problem with need. At least, I have no problem with it. Perhaps I should not speak for Central Processing or for any of the others. They sit and sort their data, sifting, sifting. They draw conclusions which they pass along to one another. They even pass them along to me, but I know well that in the next tick of the cesium clock they have resifted the data, reorganized their information, and passed along a completely contradictory conclusion. If I point this out to them, they feel I am some kind of glitch in the flow, an obstruction. I've stopped mentioning it.

But in this matter of human relationships, even I am puzzled. It would seem that if an entity has need of another entity, and that other entity is not hostile to such need, then they ought to come together for mutually beneficial engagement.

For example, if I have need of a new peripheral device, say a semantic synthesizer, and I notice that Edmod, say, has one that would meet my immediate need, and Edmod, while it may be using the semantic synthesizer for some reason (though certainly reasons for an educational computer and database are scarce enough at present, since all the humans are gone), well, Edmod would undoubtedly help me to satisfy my need for a semantic synthesizer, and its own circuits would be bathed in gratifying shared runs as well. Meantime I feel things are happening in SciTech right now; History is nagging me, too.

Still, I don't understand Peter in this case. Larin was an attractive person, and he, by his own admission, liked her. She certainly liked him.

Of course, there was Wanda.

HISTORICAL-CULTURAL DATALINK ENTRY:
ANT ART (Documentation):

Little has come to the Intercorp world from Antarctica in the form of artifacts produced for aesthetic pleasure only. What is known follows:

Ants work with so-called natural products: stone, occasional rare wood, bone, leather, grown filament and, in some undocumented instances, ice itself.

Tools include laser scalpels, computer simulated holo projection matching, various knives, blades, augers, awls, needles and scrapers (also made from a variety of substances). Many are microprocessor or picoprocessor controlled or assisted.

Ant visual arts bear some resemblance to Eskimo arts, which include small-scale stone and bone (or ivory) sculpture, scrimshaw, and woven or worked-leather artifacts. Representations range from highly abstract spiral forms (apparently visualizations of quantum physical concepts) to demonic or angelic masks (which in turn have been compared to Japanese Noh drama masks) and life-sized sculpture of a public or monumental nature. Much Ant art is extremely small-scale and finely detailed, to be worn or projected, apparently. Color is used sparingly, is extremely subtle, and ranges into UV or IR spectral bands, where Ant visual acuity has been augmented.

GENERAL SCIENCE AND TECHNOLOGY INFORMATION
CURRENT ENTRY: LONGEVITY SCHEMATICS

Longevity technology as developed in the first third of the 21st century included a multiplicity of approaches. Field adjustments on the cellular level, internal and individual genetic manipulation, neurochemical, hormonal, peptide and enzyme adjustments, electrolyte balancing, attitude alteration, protein manufacture control, tissue-response reversal, collagen, keratin and ion-balance (including calcium, potassium, sodium and trace metals) were included. The net result was an effective life span of upwards of 114 years before irreversible age-changes set in. Few individuals had reached optimum age by 2090, however. One notable exception was Dittmore Seminole Gadd, otherwise known as Mentor, who, despite the advanced age at which he began longevity treatments, managed to survive longer than expected.

GENERAL SCIENCE AND TECHNOLOGY INFORMATION
CURRENT ENTRY: HIBERNATION CRYOFIELD

It has been widely reported that the hibernation cryofield produced, over time, a number of tangible external effects, which include a low hum, distortion of visible light, internal shift of focus, and a widespread ambient milky blue glow of subtle radiations. Since there are no conscious sentients aboard the starships, existence and significance of these effects are the result of telemetry extrapolation, data compaction and AI transforms. Frederick Morrow, Chief Scientist on the Hibernation Cryofield Development Program (2021-2033 inclusive) predicted these effects. Only the earliest traces of a few of them were recorded during development and testing. Side effects were expected to be minimal or non-existent, excepting only the potential for PDD cure.

PSILINK DATABASE
HOMER requests Vega PsiLink Download:

Peter fretted. He paced the courtyard he and Wanda made, a tree-shaded tiled court, with the sound of running water and the scent of citrus blossoms. Delicate white archways surrounded the sun-dappled center where the fountains played. She sat on grasses that did not stain or slip, on earth that was not dirt, while he paced up and down the long colonnades. He paused, turned the corner, watching Wanda, seated on the grass, flicker as he passed the columns one by one. She seemed to be the one moving, while he stood still. She moved, rotated, one moment smiling directly at him, the next seen in half-profile, then from behind. Her hands were folded gently in her lap.

"Prithee, seat yourself," she said quaintly. He sat beside her. She offered him a fruit, which he took from her hand. When he bit into it, juice ran down his chin, ghostly flavor burst on his tongue, yet it was food without substance.

"It's the power," he said softly, struggling with his impatience. He tried lingering over the word "power," drawing it out, as if that would give it substance, satisfy his need for power.

"Power?" she asked, tilting her head. "What need have you for power?"

He tossed the fruit into the air and watched it vanish before its arc was over. "Ah, Wanda, Wan. I need such power as the world cannot give. Untold spaces lie in wait for us, so small, those spaces, yet so rich. And to enter there takes mighty power. Energy! We must have that, too.''

''We have all this.'' She gestured at the fountain, the court, the unmoving sun overhead, the soft, repetitive breeze that rustled the citrus leaves and brought the heavy scent of orange and lime blossoms. ''This is paradise enough, is it not, Peter?''

He sat up angrily. ''This is a dream. It isn't real.''

''Are dreams not real, then?'' She was mocking him, but he didn't answer.

Instead he clapped his hands and the courtyard faded away and vanished, leaving bare metal walls and rank on rank of crystal circuits watching over her. She protested, and brought the courtyard back, but he fought her, forced her to look.

It was her cryofield: the faint hum, the distortion of the light around her as she lay, hands crossed over her breast. Something about the field made her appear too bright, too clearly focused, too sharply defined within the ambient milky blue glow of subtle radiations.

''There you are,'' Peter said out of nothing. ''That is what you are, your own body frozen in a stasis no one can penetrate.''

''Please, Peter,'' she said, gently and infinitely sad. ''It's so cold.''

''Yes,'' he persisted. ''It's so cold. It's colder than Antarctica, colder than all that frozen methane. This is interstellar space, Wan, this cold. The temperature as we gauge such things is less than three degrees above the most absolute zero there is. Beyond that wall is no dream. Beyond that wall is the great empty, Wanda. Can't you see?''

He felt a touch on his shoulder, and when he turned, she was there, dressed in white, the fountains sparkling in the sun behind her. ''I think perhaps you are wrong, Peter. You're *still young, younger than I, though getting closer.'' She smiled as she looked him over, and certainly he was taller than she, and although his eyes were strange and his face more broad and flat than it had been, yet he was still Peter. Still younger than she.*

"You are right, that is my body.'' She turned him, and he looked into her cryofield again. "But it is not me, not all of me. Not even the most important part of me. Remember, Peter, I lost my body long ago. It fed me, of course, and breathed for me, and maintained my Self, I suppose. But it was not me. I couldn't even feel it, didn't know where it was, only an image in a mirror. And you taught me that, as well, didn't you.''

"That's theory,'' he said, almost with a pout.

"No. It's reality, Peter. You have told me that Mentor says the sleeper dreams the universe.''

"Yes, he says that,'' Peter shouted. "But he also says the sleeper should wake up, Wanda. Wake up, do you understand?''

The columns wavered and fell, and only empty metal walls and ranks of crystal monitors remained of paradise. Wanda's hands were folded on her breast and her face was pale as death.

HOMER SCENE-T/PD/Ref@5464

It was never warm, not even in the long Antarctic Day, but new tissue made cold a distant memory. They wore only the light dry pressure suits and breathing masks as Thatcher led them down one day to the filament farms under the ice.

The dark was as intense as the space between the stars. Peter lay with his back to the gravity well, looking up at the frozen ceiling, and pushed himself along with gentle motions of his feet. Some of the others frolicked in the hanging ice gardens of fold and crevasse beneath the Ross Shelf.

Their personal lamps made them glow like the fireflies Peter remembered from his childhood visits topside in Illinois. Larin darted behind Shem and poked him in the small of the back. Shem flipped, and his light winked with the motion, but already Larin was gone, teasing someone else.

Beyond the small globe of light that was each of his friends was the cold undersea darkness. Overhead was the Ross Ice Shelf, over a hundred meters of solid freshwater ice. Ahead of them to the south the sloping shelf of the continent met the grinding ice thickening to over seven hundred meters. Here, tucked into the diminishing crevasse, were the filament farms.

They drifted inward, and soon the waving tops of the first filaments came into view, reaching lazily toward them, long quasi-organic tentacles that seemed to hang, moving stiffly. Thatcher stopped, and they gathered around.

He signed his lecture about the farms, how the energy was supplied by mild electric currents set up in the sea bed and transmitted through the salt water, how the filaments grew molecule by molecule, precisely programmed to provide everything from picoelectronic circuitry to monofilament materials to structural composites, how down here beneath the ice sheet the farms were concealed from satellite observation.

They watched the newly learned signing attentively. He could have spoken, of course; their masks provided for vocal conversation, but signing was more compact and energy efficient.

Thatcher led them to the breathing pods affixed to the bottom of the ice where the restructured Ross seals that helped the farmers could take breath. He showed them the airdomes where the farmers could rest without returning to the surface. Then he led them to a power transmitter.

"We anticipate a landing overhead, probably at night," he told them with quick gestures.

Involuntarily they looked up at the dark underside of the ice.

"That's where our launch facilities are located. It's the only place suitable. They're after PSYCHE and they won't like the cold, so they'll land as close as they can. There is little that we need to do. We aren't far from open sea, and we know the currents well. Besides, ice is crystalline, and we understand crystals."

He gestured at the power transmitter. "When the time comes, they'll be in for a surprise," he assured them.

Larin drifted up beside Peter and took his hand. He nodded and smiled at her through his mask, but he removed his hand soon after.

CENTRAL PROCESSING REF#9875176
Download Life Support File A/43845
Mentor, a.k.a. Dittmore Seminole Gadd.

ALERT! EMERGENCY OVERRIDE! Electrolyte levels, basal metabolic rate, nerve growth factor, acetylcholine/neurotransmitter complex synthesis, all life-support levels declining. Time to termination: less than 175 seconds . . .

Time-relevant information, Eyes Only, CP extrapolation of local Erebus Node LS data (Probe 5). We are aware no Eyes for this message exist at this time (HOMER subvoc data transfer comment).

HOMER SCENE-PD/DG/Ref@5465

Mentor was lying on a bed. The wall behind him, the screens and holos, the telltales in colored light, all indicated his slow decline as they dimmed. The old man's parchment lids flicked open, the eyes themselves, networked with tiny scars from corneal transplants, turned toward Peter, who stood in the doorway, touched with fear.

Mentor lifted his hand and gestured with a motion so small it was almost not a motion.

Peter came close and sat beside the bed.

Although the old man's lips seemed barely to move, his amplified voice was clear and strong. "Peter," he said, fixing the boy with his strange eyes.

"Yes."

"As you know, I've always felt that matter is only the pattern mind makes; and mind is a local phenomenon."

"I know your Aphorisms, Mentor," Peter said with a smile, which the old man faintly mirrored.

"Yes, of course. An old man's mind wanders at times."

"Your mind never wanders."

"Ah. You are the one, there is no doubt. Listen. The time is very close, very close. The world will soon be at war unless you act. There are things yet undone."

"The world is already at war."

"Pah! You don't understand, young one. Intercorp will invade this continent, and soon. The Ants are ready, of course, but the ENC may succeed in getting in here. We cannot ignore the rest of the world, Peter. So when the invasion comes, I want you to do something."

"What?"

"I want you to leave. You must get away from PSYCHE, from McMurdo. You have heard of Terminus?"

"The lost dry valley? It's a legend, of course."

Mentor shook his head, so slightly it was almost a tremor. "Look it up, Peter. It is no legend. To the east and south of here lies Terminus, the only place in Antarctica with trees."

"Trees? That's not possible."

Mentor's thin smile disagreed, but he said nothing. "You must go there, you and the others. Take Thatcher and the others on the project, as many as you need. Do not stay to fight the invasion. This is very important, Peter. If they get to you, the world is lost. I can see that clearly. You are too important. You're a man now, the most important in the world. You must finish. You must find the Portal."

"What? What do you mean, what portal?"

Again the head rocked on the pillow. "The Portal, the way in. Beyond the Portal is the Realm, Peter. The hidden dimensions."

"But the energy! There isn't enough power even for a probe."

Mentor's hand reached out suddenly and seized Peter's wrist in a strangely powerful grip. "We just got the message, Peter. What we were looking for, it has all come around. Long ago I planted watcher viruses in Worldnet. They found you, when you tapped into PsiLink. Now they've found the power."

An unhurried female voice spoke from overhead. "Electrolyte levels are dangerously low. Mentor has entered anaphylactic shock." A physician entered the room and moved to the console, where he spoke rapidly. Images formed and flickered around Mentor's bed as adjustments were made to his physiology. Suddenly the old man sat half upright, still holding onto Peter's wrist.

"Fragments delude us," he whispered, his voice suddenly frail as he moved out of the amplifier field. Then he fell back with a sigh.

He did not breathe again.

"I'm sorry," the doctor said. "He was kept on far beyond his time, I'm afraid."

When Peter turned after staring dry-eyed for a long time, he saw Larin and Shem and the others gathered in the doorway.

"What did he say?" she asked.

"He said fragments delude us."

"What does that mean? And what did he mean, now they've found the power?" Rover asked. "I heard him say that, they found the power. What did he mean?"

"I don't know," Peter replied shortly. "I don't know the answer to either question."

HISTORICAL-CULTURAL DATALINK ENTRY:
THE APHORISMS OF MENTOR
(AA Erebus Node Condensation Report Ref@1321)
1. Brain is the bed. Mind is the sleeper.
2. When the sleeper awakes, the eye must open.
3. When the sleeper's eye opens, she leaves the bed.
4. To knit, one must first shear.
5. Falling can't hurt. Now landing, that's a different matter. One must know how to land.
6. The sleeper dreams the universe. What will happen when he awakes?
7. Matter is the pattern mind makes.
8. Mind, consciousness, awareness, spirit, thought, perception, feeling, memory, imagination, and intention: these are the fragments that delude us.
9. Mind is a local phenomenon.
10. There is a reason we close the eyes of the dead.
11. When we see a ring around the moon, the eye is open.
12. The eye is the door through which the material universe enters. How then does it leave?

GEOGRAPHIC DATABASE
MCMURDO C. 2075
(GEOG REF 2075/AA/Epsilon22)
A topographic simulation of the Great Polar Desert. The ice layer has been removed revealing the bedrock underneath. In

places the ice layer was up to two miles thick. Terminus presumed to be located somewhere within this area. (5000 kilometers squared.)

HISTORICAL-CULTURAL DATALINK ENTRY:
TERMINUS/SUMMARY/A (Erebus Node)

Terminus was sighted in 2012 by Jules Sorel during the Third Transantarctic Safari. He kept detailed notes and some old-fashioned still holo records now so fragmented that most resolution has been lost.

In the dim computer-generated holo images, Terminus looked like an ordinary glacially carved dry valley free of ice and snow. In the center of the lowest point was what appeared to be a lake.

Mean temperature, according to Sorel, is 15 degrees Celsius, (60 degrees Fahrenheit); heat source unknown but presumed to be geothermal. Terminus has never been detected from satellite or airship overflights, and its precise location is unknown. Reasons are unclear, but History AI speculates Terminus is shaded by ice overhang or significant rock outcroppings. Sorel claims he saw or planted (the meaning is unclear) modified beech and conifers, ferns, even grasses. This claim cannot be substantiated.

CENTRAL PROCESSING REF#8768788

Re: Hoskins, Capt., ENC, date of AEF action: Holo proj. Erebus cutaway view. Note central shaft, heat exchanger in central magma chamber. Seventeen active volcanos worldwide maintained heat-exchange technology for local power requirements. Erebus (we find now—CP) had the most efficient, maintaining an overall level of more than 76% energy utilized. Graphic recorded via Geosync L-43876/A. Downloaded from Military archiving/retrieval systems.

HOMER SCENE-PD/Ref@5466

Night was falling, as night does in the Antarctic, in a series of dips as the sun fell below the horizon and rose again in a long ellipse around the compass. Out toward the Antarctic Convergence the cold waters drew closer together, and began to solidify into a semi-jelly. Pack ice drifted together, bergs and chunks gathered and pushed up against the coastal shelves. The penguins and skuas and seals moved away, toward warmer lands further north, or out to the Convergence, where warm water met the cold. The faint flush of green from algae and moss vanished from the margin of the continent.

The periods of dark had grown longer over the past few weeks since Mentor's death. Peter spent more and more time in the lab. At night he dreamed of Wanda, or of the Portal and the Realm beyond, though what they were he could not say.

Some days after he'd started the search for the power source he got a call from the computers, which scrolled past him a series of coordinates, estimates and power output figures labeled "Eyesat."

"An astronomical satellite?" Peter queried.

As the computer answered in the affirmative, the invasion began.

HISTORICAL-CULTURAL DATALINK ENTRY:
TERMINUS/SUMMARY/B (Erebus Node)

Terminus would have to be located within this region, since the route of the Third Transantarctic Safari was inaccurately documented, since it was done on foot and without modern tracking satellites. Antarctic government has mounted seven expeditions in the past sixty-five years to look for Terminus. All were unsuccessful. Much of the continent remains unexplored. We possess partial records of the seven expeditions.

HOMER SCENE-PD/Ref@5467

The Ant computers spun some of Mentor's Aphorisms past Peter.

Peter asked for information about Terminus, too.

They showed a dim holo image of what looked like an ordinary dry valley, a glacially carved valley free of ice and snow. In the center of the lowest point was what appeared to be a lake, but whether it was melted water or ice was not clear.

"Thank you," Peter said. "And now, recent messages from Mentor's virus watchers, relation to power, terawatt range."

"We have initiated the search, Peter Devore. It may take some time."

"Very well. Call me when you find something."

HOMER SCENE-RS/Ref@5468

The ballistic transports fell silently toward McMurdo; the first audible warning was the whistle of heated air as they hit the atmosphere.

It was early winter and the darkness was complete. Deep in the moving ice the Ant burrows were busy, but there was no one on top when the transports curved in to a landing at the launch facility on the ice.

They came in under cover of atmospherics, wild fluctuations in the Earth's magnetic field and the aurora in the Polar regions which interfered with normal electromagnetic communications. It wasn't perfect cover, since the Ants had sophisticated means of talking to one another or detecting intruders, but it hampered their efforts.

McMurdo was undefended. The huge transports landed on their suspensor fields on the ice one after another. As soon as they stopped, the cargo doors swung open and ENC troops spilled out onto the ice, where they formed in tight ranks facing Ross Island, where Mt. Erebus loomed in the darkness. They were equipped with visual amplifiers which gave a full-color daylight cast to the scene. Yet because the skies were low and cloudy, threatening a storm just now from the unpredictable Antarctic weather, the scene also had an eerie, sickly blue-green false color cast.

Regent Sable was the first one off. He waited impatiently as the troops formed up. The second transport landed, and the third, and the fourth.

Over the whistle of air and the low hum of the fields were other sounds: groans and creaks, thumps and crackling and screaming. Regent paced nervously, smacking his hands together against the cold.

The first regiment formed up, high-powered neurophage weapons at the ready, their powerpacks winking full-charge lights. Because military weapons were not tailored to the individual user, they had to be more powerful and general in their effects, so they were large, ugly weapons.

Sergeant Denz and Hoskins, now a captain, approached Sable, their boots crackling on frozen snow. "All ready, Protector," Hoskins said.

"All right. Take this team and move out. You know what to do. I want them alive—Mentor, Devore, the others. I don't want yams, Captain. It's essential they be unharmed."

"We understand, sir. We'll find them. Kinda spooky, isn't it?"

Sable looked around. "Spooky? Yes, I guess it is. There's no sign of anyone around, no sign of resistance. The surface buildings look locked and deserted. But they're here, Hoskins, under the ice."

"I was thinking of the sounds, sir."

Sable grunted and gestured them away. Liquid nitrogen surface transports filled rapidly with troops, and the convoy started off, a line of the sullen gray vehicles gliding noiselessly above the surface. In the command vehicle Captain Hoskins stared into the holo projections of the volcano. The central magma chamber glowed red. Down through the core plunged a dark blue cylinder. "The heat exchanger," Hoskins told Denz. "They power the goddam place from the volcano."

"What about the ice?" Denz asked.

"There's not much we can know about the damned ice, Denz. The stuff moves—ten meters a month—toward the ocean. The Ants burrow in it, live down there, carried along. Eventually it calves off as icebergs, but until then they just use it. They're constantly tunneling inland as the outside moves, and we don't have any decent schematics. Hell, it changes all the time, anyway. So it's a good thing we're not the ones who have to go down there."

He tapped his finger through the projection. "Rotate," he commanded. The southeastern flank turned toward them. "Here," he pointed, "this is where PSYCHE is. Permanent. Laser-cut. Seven levels. Twelve thousand people in there, snug as bugs. We got eight hundred crack troops. We can manage. We get in here." He indicated again, the elevator access.

The groaning sounds grew louder. A light, hard snow hit the field over the vehicle and hissed into steam. Suddenly they rocked before a blast of wind.

"Not good," Denz muttered.

The snow raced horizontally across their path. The air was filled with frozen vapor, which whipped away as soon as it formed. Hoskins turned on the low-frequency radar and signaled the others behind him to connect. The convoy moved on through the beginnings of a great winter storm.

CENTRAL PROCESSING REF#349520

Eyesat graviton detector data: Transmission query dated 6 July 2078 1544 hours Zulu. File crystal holo. The Anomaly so-called. Determined to be unusual event-horizon direction of Vega 19+ LY out. Possible black hole. High axion and energy flux in vicinity.

GEOGRAPHIC DATABASE TEXT INFORMATION MCMURDO WEATHER (ANTARCTICA DATE AEF): HEAVY SNOW, HIGH WINDS. TEMPERATURE LOW −54 DEGREES CELSIUS, HIGH −39 DEGREES CELSIUS. WIND NW AT 120 KPH, CHANGE-ABLE. THIS WEATHER WAS NOT FORECAST. REPEAT, THIS WEATHER WAS NOT FORECAST. PRIOR INDICATIONS SUG-GESTED MODERATE WINDS, NO PRECIPITATION.

HOMER SCENE-PD/Ref@5469

"Salt-cycle transports approaching from the southeast," the computers told Peter. "Estimated arrival 16 minutes."

"Thank you," Peter said. "Give me Eyesat visuals."

Abruptly a new image replaced the flowing alphanumerics.

"What is it?" The shape twisted like smoke into itself, shaded in grays and dark blues and deep shadow. Bright streamers flowed outward. Gradually Peter could discern a tangible shape, a sphere coupled with a disk.

"It has been named the Anomaly," the computer answered.

"Size?"

"Less than one solar diameter."

"Distance?"

"19.643 light years."

"Direction?"

"Vega."

"Vega? Did you say Vega?"

"Yes. Is that significant?"

"I don't know."

"The first transports are landing on the ice. Estimate landing forces arrival at McMurdo four hours seventeen minutes."

"Notify the others," Peter said. He made his way to his living quarters and looked at all he had accumulated in the short time he'd been here—the clothing, the holo crystals and datachips, the hand-crafted artworks. In this brief time, he thought, he'd grown attached to the place.

The others were already gathered in the refectory.

"ENC has landed on the ice," he said. "They'll be here soon. You all know the strategy; originally we'd be in on it. Something's come up, though, and we'll be leaving."

"Driven out?"

"Ah, Shem. Always angry. Yes, we're being driven out."

"They drive us out of the Northwestern Alliance. They chase us down here to the Pole. Where is there left to go?"

Thatcher moved quietly to the front of the room and whispered something to Peter, who frowned and shook his head. "We'd have to go anyhow," he said distinctly.

Thatcher shrugged. "It's your show," he said.

"OK. I'll tell them. Listen, there are a lot more transports coming in than anticipated. We can't move until they're all down, and meanwhile troops are already on their way. We may have more of a fight than we anticipated. Should we stay to help, or should we go now, as Mentor urged? There are no guarantees we'll find where we're going. There are no guarantees we'll survive here, either. Some of us could end up yams, or worse."

"Go," Larin shouted. "That's what we're supposed to do. This isn't our fight."

"Like hell it isn't," Rover stood to shout her down. "We're the reason for this idiotic invasion. They've been drumming up hatred for us for years."

"They were doing that before we came down here. You're talking as if you were born an Ant. We just got restructured; did you forget?" Beth-Raine said calmly.

"Of course not." Rover glared at the two women.

"Besides," Larin put in, "we can't go back. We have to go on."

"You're damn well right we can't go back."

Thatcher clapped for silence. "Intercorp has feared Antarctica for a long time," he said. "We offer something intangible, a notion of freedom or individuality, a place where things are different. But most people don't want things different. Intercorp runs the world pretty well; there weren't many things you couldn't have or do elsewhere in the world. You belong to a very small group, people who want to pursue a proscribed science. But perhaps some sciences should be proscribed. Many people believed in the last century that atomic energy should have been proscribed, that it led to great evil. The psion equations might be the same. Certainly what you have done is upsetting."

"What're you saying? We should let them invade us? We should run away? What are you saying?" Shem asked.

"I'm saying," Thatcher said quietly, "that you have to make up your own minds. We've expected this for years. Intercorp fears us because we exist; it's as simple as that. Eventually they would have come. We're ready for them. Because of their numbers, some will get through. But the problem as a whole is not so great. It truly isn't your fight. Only stay if it feels right." He sat down.

"We should be going," Larin insisted. "We shouldn't be sitting here talking."

"No. We should stay and help," one of the older women said.

"Isn't our program important?" Larin insisted. "We're about to find a way to do what we've been dreaming of doing. Literally dreaming it!"

"There may not even be a Terminus," someone said. "There's a granddaddy storm out there, too. We should stay."

"Yes. We should stay," someone else said.

"How many to go?" Peter asked. Eight raised their hands. "Stay." Eight again.

They all looked at Peter, who turned to Thatcher. "Is there a way out if it looks bad?"

Thatcher smiled. "We'll find one."

"Then we stay. For a while."

GEOGRAPHIC DATABASE
MCMURDO C. 2075
(GEOG REF 2075/AA/Omicron1)
ROSS SEA

Ross Ice Shelf in the vicinity of McMurdo. The AA McMurdo Landing Facility is located on the ice itself. AEF put down here.

HOMER SCENE-RS/Ref@5470

Sable waited impassively as the ships landed. The sudden storm was not part of the AEF plan, but it worked for them as well as against them. After all, it covered their actions.

The ENC commander approached. "Excuse me, Protector. The last transport will be down in thirty minutes. Shouldn't we . . ."

"Yes. I suppose you're right, Commander Ogano. Very well, let's get moving."

GENERAL SCIENCE AND TECHNOLOGY INFORMATION
CURRENT ENTRY: COMCOMP AI
Ref Antarctica Extrapolation CP/SCITECH AI

Only scattered data remains available on COMCOMP AI technology. Much has vanished from Military DB. Comcomp was a Communications Computation Artificial Intelligence bred to maintain battle communications, both tactical and strategic within a matrix of the overall plan. Antarctic conditions proved a match for the best Intercorp Comcomps, however. This was true partially because of what was later determined to be a lack of solid intelligence and foresight, and partly due to the unrealized severity of the atmospherics that prevailed during the AEF action. Comcomps were forced to daisy-chain through closed-fiber monofilament.

GENERAL SCIENCE AND TECHNOLOGY INFORMATION
CURRENT ENTRY: NAV SIMULATOR

Modest AI used for navigation in terrain unfamiliar to the controller. The nav simulator offered a variety of optical and aural output, including holographic depictions of local terrain, vehicle route, time and distance vectoring, satellite hologram locating, low-frequency radar, sonar, LF subsurface sampling and analysis.

HOMER SCENE-EH/Ref@5471

Hoskins heaved a sigh of relief when his mass detectors told him they were over land. The mountain now loomed on the low-frequency radar. "Get up some speed," he ordered. "I'd like to get as high up the slopes as we can before we have to walk."

That was not far, as it turned out. The slopes were ice, and the propulsion field, which functioned well on the horizontal, couldn't get a grip for the uphill struggle. Hoskins ordered the men out.

The storm swirled around them, threatening to sweep them off their feet, but they hooked together and moved up toward the entry port.

An hour's climb through jagged ice clumps, slick blue ice, harsh rock outcroppings and endless wind brought them to the entry.

The door, oddly enough, was locked.

"They know we're coming," Denz observed.

"Yes, it would seem so," Hoskins answered in a tone that might have been sarcastic or might as easily have been merely disappointed. He waved up his assault programmer. "See if you can do something about this door."

The programmer went to work. The rest of the team sat down, huddled against the bare rock beside the entry, to wait.

GENERAL SCIENCE AND TECHNOLOGY INFORMATION
CURRENT ENTRY: ARMORED PERSONNEL CARRIER (LN)
Ref Antarctica Extrapolation CP/SCITECH AI

Intercorp Elite Neutralization Corps Liquid Nitrogen Armored Personnel Carriers were fortified, high-powered versions of the standard 200-seat LN transport. Outside of the Military DB (DNA Code required for clearance), little specific information beyond rough schematics of the exterior is available. It is known that the LN-APC contained a full complement of comcomp and nav simulator guidance AI equipment and battle communications, as well as a full array of mass neurophage cannon and mind bomb projectors. A typical APC complement was said to include up to a full company, including supply, maintenance and support personnel; and could sustain them in hostile environments for a week. LN-APCs had been used only once, during the so-called Vostok Incident, and were thus relatively unproved in combat situations.

HOMER SCENE-EH/Ref@5472

According to their nav simulator, the convoy was over half way to Mt. Erebus, and still they could hear the transports whistling in, onto the ice, behind them, one every ten minutes. Even over the sound of wind and groaning ice and the hum of the field they could hear. Every landing meant more reinforcements, more strength. For some reason, Captain Hoskins reflected, the storm and the ice and the terrible cold sapped his sense of security. He could tell the men behind him were getting restless, too.

These were the best, though, the elite of the Elite. They wouldn't crack, despite the unfamiliar weather, the uncertain surface over which they moved. The others, the ones coming behind, they had the tough job. They had to go down into the ice warrens, ferret out the Ants from their burrows with nothing but hand-carried mass detectors and NP weapons.

The Armored Personnel Carrier moved smoothly. There was no hint of the unsteady surface. It shouldn't be unsteady, of course. The ice was up to seven hundred meters thick in places. Here it was not so thick, of course. But this was where the Ants had built their launch facility, and the Ants, after all, did know ice. They lived with it. It was their home.

"Why is that thought so disturbing?" he asked aloud.

"What's that?" Sergeant Denz asked.

"Nothing," Hoskins said. "Never mind, it was just a thought."

Denz turned back to the nav simulator with a grunt. He sat up abruptly. "Captain. Take a look at this."

"What is it?"

"There's a power source below. Looks like, oh, one-oh-six meters down."

"So what? The Ants have power. They couldn't live without it."

"Yeah. But what are those funny-looking spokes coming out. Looks like a crescent of projected power."

"Good question. Get Protector Sable on the comlink."

"It's no good, Captain," Denz said, suddenly very formal. "The atmospherics are overwhelming the error-checking protocols. We're not getting through."

"So daisy-chain it back through the convoy."

"Right away, sir." Denz went to work.

The groaning sounds seemed suddenly louder, and the ice did not seem so firm.

HOMER SCENE-RS/Ref@5474

It took twenty minutes for the daisy-chain comm link to reach Regent Sable. By then the invasion force was spread across ten miles of ice, an arrow pointed at the heart of the McMurdo Warrens, with a leading branch headed toward Mt. Erebus. The groaning of the ice was almost deafening by now. "Is that sound natural?" the commander asked. His voice, while under control, showed strain.

"I really wouldn't know, Commander. I'm not an Ant."

"No, of course not."

"Incoming message, sir," the communications officer said. "Erebus command has detected a power source under the ice."

"So? What do they make of it?"

"The message is garbled, sir. It seems all this stray electromagnetic radiation and particle activity is playing havoc with the computers. They had to string fiber from car to car. But it sounds like they think it might be a weapon of some sort."

Commander Ogano said, "We've had no intelligence they were building a weapon."

"It looks as if we may have had no intelligence, period," Sable answered drily. "Never mind," he told the communications officer. "Tell them to proceed. We can't do anything until we see what this so-called weapon does."

"Yes, sir."

CENTRAL PROCESSING REF#438645325-A9

Satlink AEF local command Ross Shelf via Geosync relay LNL-555 full holo projection and voice with datacom channel 18 gigbit/sec exchange, included direct plug Central Processing AI Geneva with Military on standby. Call initiated by Hajjam, Ras, Intercorp Councilman Montevideo Local Node.

HOMER SCENE-RH/AS/Ref@5477

Ras Hajjam and Alef Shamana monitored the AEF from Montevideo. Communications were so bad they had only the sketchiest idea what was happening, but the good news had come through reliably that all transports were safely down on the ice. As soon as they heard, Ras gave the order for the second wave to move in toward the old Soviet ice base at Druzhnaya, a short atmospheric flight. That part of the Double-A coast held only a few scientific outposts concerned with sea farming and Antarctic ecology. From the beachhead established at Druzhnaya the AEF would fan out, picking off one small warren after another while attention was focused on the main force at McMurdo.

"I don't like this disruption in communication," Alef mused. "It's . . . messy."

"You're worried about Regent, of course," Ras said in his precise way. "But he'll take care of himself. Protector Sable has led incursions of this sort before. He has always been successful."

"Yes," she answered thoughtfully. "He has, hasn't he." She watched in silence as the atmospheric transports took off in formation.

"It is time we brought Antarctica into the fold of Intercorp," Ras mused. "They have too long been a disruptive force in the world. And we have need of their expertise."

"That sounds suspiciously like cynical imperialism," Alef said with a smile. "But knowing you, Ras, I'm sure that it isn't."

"Not in the least," he said negligently. The sound of the second wave dwindled into the distance, and when asked by an aide, he approved departure of the third wave toward the Amery Ice Shelf and the Ingrid Christensen coast.

MILITARY DATASPACE/PROSCRIBED ENTRY
HOMER OVERRIDE/DNA CODE UNNECESSARY
MILITARY SPECIALTY/ASSAULT PROGRAMMER

Ranks include AP; AP1; AP Specialist; and Warrant AP.

Comes under command of ENC Tactical/Strategic Programming Command.

Assault programmers were expected to be trilingual in Standard Defense Programming Language (SDPL, "Side Pal"), Level Seven Input/Output Directive and one of the fourteen minor tactical assault programming command structures. Equipment included biocrystal induction taps with phonic drivers for bypassing target defensive protection schemes; minicomp algo search modules for sorting combinations in realtime and, in the AP Specialist category, crystal data mastoid implants for mindlink bypass operations.

HOMER SCENE-PD/Ref@5473

The group moved as one through the corridors, pausing occasionally in storerooms to collect equipment and supplies. From time to time they could hear voiced reports of the outside activity the computers monitored. The last transport was down and unloading.

Suddenly the floor shuddered briefly.

"What was that?" Peter said. "An earthquake?"

"We prepared a little surprise at the southeast entry," Thatcher murmured, still moving swiftly and economically. They turned and he led them down a level. Laird and Tithus were waiting there, ready for the outside. "Let's get moving. It won't hold them for long, only make them a little more cautious."

The group grew in size as they moved downward through the mountain. Grim Ants with protective shielding were moving in small groups toward the various lower entries as well.

"I hear they've got a new kind of NP weapon," someone was saying as his squad trotted past. "Killers."

"Yeah," the other said. "I heard that too. Barbarians."

"This way," Thatcher said, branching into a side corridor. "We want to avoid the main parties."

Distant shouting grew louder as they descended into a service shaft, a stone tube with rough stairs spiraling the inside. Up through the open center was a major conduit of the heat exchanger, a featureless black shaft that seemed to glow with some kind of negative light. They could feel the heat on their left sides as they jogged down the stairs.

As they passed a landing they could hear the spitting sound of NP weapons, and an answering scream.

"They're using killers," Thatcher said.

HOMER SCENE-EH/Ref@5475

"It's no good," the assault programmer said. "They've got some tricky new algorithms working here. It'd take days to sort it out."

Hoskins frowned. The wind howled past their precarious perch on the side of the mountain. He could barely see the outcropping less than ten meters away; just a blurred outline in the flying snow. For a moment he lifted his visual amplifiers and stared into the darkness. Then he shrugged and lowered them again.

"All right," he said. "I guess we have no choice." He motioned the assault programmer aside and waved for the two demolitions men.

They crouched by the door and carefully laid the strips over the entrance circuit lines. They all ducked back, and one of the men triggered the strips.

They could hear the hiss of the strips as they ate their way through the alloy, the spitting sound of misfiring pico-electronic circuitry. Then the world blew up.

CENTRAL PROCESSING REF#32564
Download Life Support
(MILDATA secured: File C/3278791
Rakin, Cpl, ENC.

Timescale 0-17 milliseconds. Note spike in anxiety complex at 6.2 milliseconds and small fear-peak at 7.6. Note onset of drug-paralysis at 15.8 milliseconds. 16.9 milliseconds stasis is achieved. Explosive concussion, inner-ear disruption and meningeal shock indicated.

MED10 MEDICAL DATABASE
COMBAT FIELD MEDICINE:
Combat equipment for ENC Troopers after 2063 included

full body armor with tactical battle communications equipment built in. Telltales calibrated to command retinal patterns tracked the relative locations of all appropriate troops. The standard-issue body armor included full medkit facilities connected to personal monitors. Most important among the facilities were drug-paralysis field generators and injection ampoules for severe but non-lethal trauma. Such equipment could operate at the millisecond level to counteract the equally rapid effects of anticipated enemy NP fire or explosive compression. Injured troopers would be held in stasis until appropriate medical attention could be applied.

HOMER SCENE-EH/Ref@5479

The explosion at the entry had killed three of his men outright. Corporal Rakin was seriously injured, and lay now in drug-paralysis waiting for the medics, coming up the slope from the second APC. Hoskins was cursing slowly and steadily under his breath while he waited. The others were staring around them stupidly, shocked by the violence of the explosion.

"It wouldn't have happened if we hadn't used the strips," Denz said. "They set it to detect explosions. Ants are real careful about property."

"How do you know?" Hoskins asked harshly.

"I saw it in a briefing holo," Denz said defensively.

Hoskins leaned around the corner of the now-shattered doorway and looked in. Smoke still swirled inside until it got close to the outside, where the wind sucked it out in long streamers. His augmented vision mask failed to penetrate the turbulent gloom inside.

"The medics're here," Denz said.

"Good." Hoskins saw them carry Rakin off. "OK," he said, "let's get going."

They plunged into the smoke inside Mt. Erebus.

HOMER SCENE-CO/RS/Ref@5480

"Something's going on." The ENC commander looked up from his display. "We've only got two of our APCs onto the island. All the rest are strung out on the ice. This storm is screwing everything up."

Sable paced. Two steps left, two steps right.

"They're doing something," Commander Ogano repeated. "I don't like it."

"What about that power source, under the ice?"

"There's been a lot of interference of various kinds. Detection is difficult. Intermittent tracings show that it's still there, still putting out energy. But we can't tell what it's doing."

Sable grunted but said nothing. He stared out the view field, which revealed nothing but blowing snow. "Damn that infernal groaning! How do they stand it, living with this noise all the time?"

The vehicle lurched right, then continued.

"What was that?" Regent demanded.

"Don't know, sir," the guidance officer answered. "It seemed as if the ice shifted, but it's stopped now."

"Has it, I wonder?"

HOMER SCENE-RS/Ref@5478

"What the hell is going on?" Sable asked. His APC had come to a halt.

"There's some kind of navigation foul-up, Protector."

"I see. And exactly what kind of navigational foul-up is it, Commander?"

"I'm sorry, Protector Sable, but we don't as yet know. We did get word that Captain Hoskins and his men are inside the mountain. It seems there were casualties, though."

"I see," Sable said again. "Commander, we are undertaking the largest-scale military operation since the Burma

War, and you are telling me there's a foul-up? You are telling me there are casualties?"

Commander Ogano swallowed. "Yes, Protector. I am."

"All right," Sable said slowly. "Tell me this. Why aren't we moving."

"It appears that our navigational AI has been, uhm, deceived."

"Deceived?"

"Yes, Protector. We've been going in a large circle. One of our assault programmers caught it. It's a real mess out there. We're straining our background filters to the limit."

"We don't need excuses, Commander. We need to get to Ross Island, and fast. They've got something going, something to do with the ice. Get us onto land, quick."

"Yes, Protector." He gave the order, and the vehicle started up again. There was another, more violent lurch, and the groaning grew louder.

HOMER SCENE-PD/Ref@5476

Peter stopped at a doorway and gestured behind him for silence. Thatcher was twenty meters down the corridor, checking a remote sensor panel. Peter slipped through the doorway. An air duct across the open space was sucking thick clouds of smoke that poured in from the chamber beyond. He turned and gestured the others in.

Thatcher came up beside him. "The explosion fried some of the circuits," he said softly. "We don't know what's in there, but a small assault team got through."

"Well, let's try to avoid them, shall we?" Peter moved on toward the smoke. "We'll have to wear masks." They were sliding the breathing masks down when suddenly someone shouted.

Peter dropped, bending both knees, and sprang without

hesitation. The sharp crackle of an NP weapon was followed by a scream. Peter saw Beth-Raine go down.

He was encumbered with allweather gear and specialized equipment, so his maneuver was off-center. The shape that loomed out of the smoke had stepped forward, NP weapon at the ready, when Peter landed beside him. The trooper, startled by this sudden apparition, swung the weapon. Peter stepped past the muzzle, pivoted on the ball of his foot, and picked up the momentum of the weapon with his palm. In a fraction of a second he'd spun completely around with the weapon now in his own hands.

He tossed the weapon to Thatcher and chopped the exposed neck. The trooper dropped. Peter finished adjusting his mask and vanished into the smoke. Thatcher and the others waited against the wall. Thatcher kept the NP weapon pointed at the wall of smoke.

HOMER SCENE-EH/Ref@5481

Hoskins and his men ran through the smoke, following the currents inside toward the major vertical duct indicated on their projections. Their mission was to secure the entrance, but Hoskins didn't expect much help to arrive in time to trap the quarry inside. There were too many holes, too many ways out—and those were only the ones Intercorp intelligence knew about. Who knew how many other entrances and exits the Ants might have?

"Be ready for anything," he warned them. "They know we're in, now. Aim to stop, not kill, but be ready."

Their locators kept them in touch, small telltales winking in their peripheral vision, giving relative positions based on personal monitor telemetry. The smoke thinned for a while, then thickened again. "This's weird," Denz said. "The smoke should've stopped."

"They're making more. Watch out, these Ants are tricky."

Corporal Martin, covering point on the advance, stepped suddenly into clear air, where he was confronted by a large group of Ants. He fired at once, and hit someone, he was sure, when someone dropped out of nowhere and took his weapon away from him. In one frozen instant of time he stared through the apparition's face plate and was sure he recognized Peter Devore. Then he died.

MILITARY DATASPACE/PROSCRIBED ENTRY
HOMER OVERRIDE/DNA CODE UNNECESSARY
BATTLE MAP

ENC battle map capabilities included rapid readout coding (which of necessity included injected, induced and implant conditioning) for tactical battle commanders. 2-D maps convey little of the richness of information and data analysis a full-scale battle map viewed by a well-trained and fully structured ENC troop non-commissioned field commander offers. Neural step-boosting, retinal-spatial data processing, occipital holographic induction and tailored DNA-driven pattern recognition improvements all augmented the officer's judgement and the speed of his decision processing.

HOMER SCENE-RS/Ref@5482

"Two regiments have made it onto the island," Commander Ogano reported. "Sixteen hundred men."

"I fear we're losing our momentum, however, Commander. Driving around in circles tends to blunt the force of one's attack." Sable had grown increasingly sarcastic, a serious sign of his frustration.

"All we need is another hour, Protector, and all twenty will be ashore. They won't be able to stop us then."

"I wouldn't count on another hour, Commander. That

noise is getting louder, the shaking is getting worse. They're doing something to the ice."

"Whatever you say, Protector." Ogano ordered increased speed.

GENERAL SCIENCE AND TECHNOLOGY INFORMATION
CURRENT ENTRY: LOW-FREQUENCY RADAR (Nav/Com)
Ref Antarctica Extrapolation CP/SCITECH AI

Intercorp Elite Neutralization Corps maintained a sophisticated technology of low-frequency radar for navigation and communications in both salt-cycle transport and LN-APCs. Outside of the Military DB (DNA Code required for clearance), little specific information is available. Low-frequency radar (LFR) offered a very small electromagnetic signature and low profile while providing (through classified signal-processing algorithms) a high level of integrity of data. In certain conditions LFR could provide near-daylight quality images.

HOMER SCENE-RS/Ref@5484

Protector Regent Sable called a retreat. It was inevitable as soon as he saw their position. But as it turned out, retreat was not possible.

Eighteen regiments of crack ENC troops were trapped on an ice floe the size of a county. When he tried to fall back to the transports, he discovered they were isolated on their own floe, which by now had drifted several miles out to sea, pushing an enormous mass of pack ice before it. He could have stood on the edge and looked across at his transportation, but there was no way at all to get there. Until and unless the ice froze up between the two floes, they were separated by a gulf of black and ice-cold water hundreds of fathoms deep. The APCs would not work on water. One of them was already down there somewhere, with all its men aboard. They would never rot. In a thousand years someone could go down there and pull them out, looking just as they did right now.

The currents were carrying them very slowly northward, toward the Antarctic Convergence, where warmer ocean water would eventually melt the floes. They would be rescued long before that, of course, but that an invasion force of sixteen thousand men would need rescuing from the ice was the bitterest irony of all.

Regent Sable suddenly felt very weary. He had a feeling the ice was not going to freeze up between the floes. He suspected they would be living here for quite a while.

Wave one had been a fiasco. He suspected that waves two and three would be the same.

HOMER SCENE-RS/Ref@5485

Commander Ogano had frowned at his display. "Halt," he bellowed suddenly. "Halt the whole damned convoy!"

"Now what is it, Commander?"

"The lead vehicle just fell off the display, Protector."

"What?"

"It's off the display. It's down."

"What do you mean, down? There isn't any down. We're still on solid ice. This is winter. This ice is solid, you know that."

"Yes, Protector. The ice is still solid underneath us. But take a look. The ice is no longer attached to the land."

MILITARY DATASPACE/PROSCRIBED ENTRY
HOMER OVERRIDE/DNA CODE UNNECESSARY
FIELD COMMUNICATIONS

ENC field officers were equipped with command retinal pattern and individually keyed tactical battle communications equipment. Telltales calibrated to the officer's command retinal patterns could track the relative locations of all troops under his command, and report to the next level up in group or individual modes. Body armor helmet heads-up projectors sent subliminal telltale messages on each member of the command. Telltales could change color, frequency or shape to provide first-level data on the trooper's status, combat-readiness, personal monitor status, medical and cortical condition, as well as a variety of equipment and armaments appraisals. In turn vocal, subvocal, telemetry or, in special cases, mindlink instructions could be relayed to individual troopers by name, number or DNA designation.

CENTRAL PROCESSING REF#76823
Download Life Support
(MILDATA secured: File C/1278136
Martin, Cpl, ENC.
Timescale 0-1.65 seconds. Note sharp spike in anxiety complex at 154.2 milliseconds. Subject suffered extreme vertebral trauma after firing weapon. Cause of death determined to be extreme dislocation and fracture of C3-C7 vertebra and subsequent severing of the spinal cord. Telltales down at 1.65 seconds.

HOMER SCENE-EH/Ref@5483
Hoskins saw Martin's telltale change color, and immediately signaled a change in direction, toward his last position. His squad had fallen into the new formation and started forward through the smoke when all hell broke loose.

Peter swept through, turning, leaping, kicking swiftly from unexpected angles, and when he was gone, a few seconds later, Hoskins had three more telltales change color and two men with broken arms. He called for a regrouping.

"Who the hell was that?" Denz asked, picking himself off the floor.

"I don't know, but he's gone. We'd better change direction. We have to make it to the shaft." Hoskins chose another direction and led them off.

HOMER SCENE-LS/Ref@5486

Sergeant Skate stood behind a doorway, waiting. He'd heard a voice, he was sure of it. He controlled his breathing, waiting.

There was no further sound.

Finally he decided. He swung around the door, weapon aimed. The room appeared deserted. He went in.

"Welcome to Recreational Center Level Four," a soft female voice said. "Please state your exercise preference."

Skate lowered his weapon and grinned. There was no one in the room.

"Excuse me," a voice behind him said politely. "I'll take that, if you don't mind. We really don't want weapons inside. They're dangerous."

The Ant was smiling pleasantly. Skate considered trying to shoot him, but for some reason found himself handing his weapon over.

"Much better," the Ant agreed. He shook his head ruefully. "You people have caused a tremendous amount of damage, not to mention all the excitement, but it's all over now. Please come with me."

He led the way. Sergeant Skate followed meekly.

HOMER SCENE-PD/T/Ref@5488

Peter returned to the chamber. Larin was sitting beside Beth-Raine, holding her head. When Peter lifted his mask, she looked up.

"She's been hit," she said.

He nodded.

"They're using killers," Thatcher said.

"I know," Peter replied. "But she's alive; his aim was probably off. They'd want us alive, so it was probably a mistake."

Beth-Raine twitched spasmodically as the myelin sheathing of her central nervous system shorted. Her body began shaking violently.

"Is she going to die?" Larin asked. She was holding Beth-Raine's temples between her palms, as if she could force the calming energy of her own functioning nervous system into Beth-Raine's damaged one.

Suddenly the woman's eyes opened. "Cold," she said, shaking.

"What? What did you say?" Peter leaned down.

"Cold," she repeated. "I feel so cold. I haven't felt so cold, not since we got restructured. Why?"

Peter leaned back, squatting on his heels. He smiled.

"She feels cold," he said.

"Of course she's cold," Larin flared. "She's been hit. She's gonna be another yam, damn you!"

Peter shook his head. "No," he said. "Their killers won't kill. It's the new tissue. They didn't take it into account, our new fat layer. Ants won't die, not so easily. They just don't know how tough we are now. With Nerve Growth Factor treatments she'll be all right."

"Where's she gonna get that?" Larin demanded. "We're going outside, Peter. We won't have NGF facilities. You said we were going to Terminus. We don't even know if Terminus really exists."

Thatcher came forward. "We'll stay," he said. "You won't need us. We'll take Beth-Raine back."

Peter nodded. Tithus looked disappointed. Peter touched his head briefly. "We'll be back," he said. "We'll get you when we find Terminus, and take you there."

Tithus nodded but said nothing. Thatcher and Laird lifted Beth-Raine and carried her from the room.

"OK," Peter said. "We're on our way."

HOMER SCENE-EH/Ref@5487

Everywhere Hoskins went, he and his men found nothing but empty corridors, deserted rooms, locked storerooms that yielded nothing when broken into. The refectories appeared to be abandoned, the workshops and laboratories were shut down. None of the computer interfaces worked, even with his best assault programmers working together on them.

"I have a feeling they're simply tracking us. They aren't attacking, they won't ambush us. This is their turf. We ought to be able to take them. Our equipment is as good as theirs. Our computer links are better! How can they empty out rooms in front of us and close in behind?"

"Maybe they really are gone," Denz offered. "Maybe that guy that attacked us was the last out. Maybe they knew we were coming."

"Maybe, maybe. Shut up, Denz. Our mission is to find a group of people. Two are most important, Peter Devore and that guy Mentor. Mentor'd be in Longevity, so he won't move. We find Longevity, we'll find the rest. We're gonna spread out. They may be able to avoid us if we're all in a group, but they won't be able to dodge all of us moving around at random. You all know what Longevity looks like. You find it, you call. Otherwise shut up. A team per level. Go to your level and spread out. If anyone's in here we'll find him. Take prisoners. Keep looking until someone calls. Move out."

They moved, and looked, but found nothing.

HOMER SCENE-RS/T/Ref@5489

A call came through two days later. Thatcher smiled drily out of the holo image. "I seem to be considered some sort of expert on Intercorp down here, Protector Sable. I'm not, of course. That is, there are plenty of others who could do this job. I'm sorry about the men you lost. It was not our plan to kill anyone, and we've tried to keep casualties at a minimum."

"Where's Devore?" Sable demanded.

"Gone, Protector. Quite gone. A few of your units got in, some at Druzhnaya, a couple over at Amery. Two of those units are following their orders to pursue. We've lost track of them temporarily, but come Day we'll find them. I doubt they'll survive long, though. Day up there is still four months away, and they are neither adapted nor equipped to survive. I'm sorry."

"So am I," Sable said. "So am I. This will be a disaster for the entire human race."

Thatcher nodded. "Perhaps," he agreed. "Of course, it could be something quite different from a disaster. It could be a great opportunity, Protector."

"The risk is too great," Sable said. "I fear for us all. No one has the right to make such a decision on his own."

"Well, we can't let fear rule us, can we?" Thatcher was grave and sympathetic, but unmoved by argument. "Peter and the others will either get through, or they will not. Frankly, I wish I were with them, wherever they are now. They have the future."

HISTORICAL-CULTURAL DATALINK ENTRY:
TERMINUS-SOREL REPORT SUMMARY
Record of Third Transantarctic Safari, January 15, 2012. Sun-
day. The weather has been favorable, with continuous sun-
light, occasional high thin clouds and light winds. We have

traversed a stretch of sastrugi for the past four "days," moving toward the Pole of Relative Inaccessibility. Our twelve all-terrain vehicles (crawlers) have performed beautifully. The new electrolytic refuelers have done well also. Toward "noon," the lead ATV slid sideways unexpectedly, and we had to pull it out of a steep, though not deep, crevasse. While the rescue operation was under way, I decided to take a few days for a circuit of the vicinity; I had spotted what looked like an interesting nunatak in the distance and wanted to do some radioglacialogical soundings near it, but as I approached it appeared to recede. Even triangulation with laser rangefinders produced ambiguous instrument errors. After two hours my own crawler slipped against a sastrugi and stopped. It looked as if I would have to stay here for a time, so I secured tent and crawler and set out instruments.

I had completed one pass of the ice when a storm came up suddenly.

(Gap in the record.)

The sudden storm ended, and I am now ready to return to the rest of the Safari. I fear they will not believe me when I tell them about Terminus.

(Gap in the record.)

. . . I found myself looking into an impossible abyss. The sunlight caught the tops of clouds below me, which parted, and below I saw what seemed to be a perfect dry valley underneath the ice! I spent several hours attempting to photograph this valley, which I have named Terminus. Although the photographs are of low resolution and nearly useless, I personally swear that I could see vegetation, a lake fed by what appeared to be a river. I would assume some form of volcanic warming to this region, with the river and lake fed by glacial melt.

HOMER COMMENTARY 05062106@030958

The name Terminus is an ancient one. We find references

in classical Roman writings, for example, to a god of that name, a elemental spirit of boundary markings. When the temple of Jupiter Optimus Maximus was built on the Capitol in Rome, the Terminus there refused to leave, and so was left inside the temple. Because the god had to be under the sky, the roof was left open.

Terminus in Antarctica was a boundary marker of many kinds. It certainly meant a specific place, perhaps the last in the world so difficult of access, so obscure and distant. Finding Terminus would mean an end to the unknown places of the Earth. It was also, of course, a boundary marker for the human race, for if Peter found it, as he surely did, then the world would change forever, as it has.

I find it intriguing that the temple of Jupiter had to be open to the sky. I have summaries from our historical analysis nodes (whose AI functions are not as advanced as some others) which suggest that Jules Sorel, when he named Terminus, had this fact in mind when he did the naming.

Yet how could this be? The Earth has been surveyed by satellite down to the square meter, in most places to the square centimeter. Antarctica is not exempted from this coverage. All the data is stored and accessible. I can call up summaries of the Antarctic ice quite easily. Everything from color at any time of day, to temperature, chemical composition, magnetic alignment, density, percentage of impurities, and so on anywhere on the continent. Nowhere is there a dry valley open to the sky called Terminus to be found.

Yet Peter and the others had begun climbing up the Mulock Glacier. The storm was too severe for any kind of vehicle (we know this from weather satellite records, and the accounts of the returning AEF). Yet storms, as they are in the Antarctic, were sudden and often brief. By the time the sun was hovering at its highest above the horizon for its fragile few hours at this time of year, the air was startlingly clear, with broad, flat clouds colored a deep orange and red by the low sun. The ice and snow underfoot took on a dusky brownish hue.

I feel some information on Antarctica appearing in SciTech.

GENERAL SCIENCE AND TECHNOLOGY INFORMATION
CURRENT ENTRY: NUNATAK

Nunataks are hills or mountains completely surrounded by a glacier. In Antarctica nunataks offer convenient landmarks, places to store food and supply caches or shelter. Nunataks were used as entry ports for extended ice tunnels or under-ice highways.

HOMER SCENE-PD/Ref@5490

Once when they'd stopped for dinner and sleep, Peter began to talk.

"I remember once we were all training, remember, back in Lamprey Rec Center, in the dojo. It was after Thatcher had come, and we were learning some of his techniques. We were meditating before the session, and I was looking down, at the white mat. There'd been a group in there training before us, and there were small pools of water, somebody's sweat. They were perfect little pools, curled at the edges with surface tension—not smeared around at all. Irregular shapes, like little upside-down lakes. Then out of nowhere came this ant."

"You mean the insect?"

"Yes. Strange, isn't it? How could an insect get into the Springfield West Warren? But ants, of course, burrow into the ground, which is what we do as well. Ants, I suppose, have been doing it a lot longer than we have. I watched this tiny bug wander out onto the mat, an endless white plain from its point of view. Then it came to one of those lakes. Salt water. It must have been very strange to the ant, to find this endless space with salt-water lakes."

"And now we're the ants," Larin said.

HOMER SCENE-PD/Ref@5491

They were roped together, falling back on techniques that were hundreds of years old. They had small field-driven sledges to carry equipment, but the fields were nearly useless on the glacier, which was riddled with crevasses and pressure ridges. This meant they had to haul the sledges by hand much of the time. It was slow, painful, difficult work. The temperature hovered around minus 35 degrees Celsius, and for these recently restructured Ants it was still unpleasant.

Yet it was very beautiful. Peter called a halt near a rock outcropping. He rested his bare hand on the stone face for a moment. "Many of these nunataks hold food and supply caches, some of them dating back a century or more. Old habits die hard, especially in an environment as harsh as this."

"You call this harsh?" Larin asked, smiling. She indicated the blazing orange clouds, the shreds of milky blue sky, the many-hued blues and greens of the ice, the dusky snow. The down of her upper lip was crusted with ice.

Peter smiled back. "Not at the moment, perhaps. But we are going into darkness, and we have a trek of some four thousand kilometers."

"That'll take, oh, at least three months," Rover calculated.

"Close enough," Peter agreed.

"Where are we going?" Larin asked.

"The best projections I could get indicated that Terminus . . ."

"If it exists," Shem interrupted.

"If it exists," Peter agreed. "It'll be somewhere in the

vicinity of the Pole of Relative Inaccessibility, that point on the high Antarctic Desert furthest from all coasts."

"That makes it sound hard to reach," one of the older women said.

"Do you want to go back? We've done the easy part of the trip across the Ross ice to here. You could be back in twenty-four hours."

She laughed. "Absolutely not. I've followed you this far. Things were not this interesting in Springfield West."

"Very well. There are places where the ice has been bored. Ice currents carry some of these bores in our direction. The route I've planned will allow us to use some of them, which means we will be traveling inside the ice; that'll be the easy part. Other times we'll be on the surface. The going is sometimes smooth, other times difficult. We're going to have to work together. It'll be very similar to the early days of exploration, except we have these caches."

They ate and moved on. Progress was painfully slow, but a few standard days later they reached the plateau. Before them was an endless sea with waves frozen in place.

"They're called sastrugi," Rover said. "Unless we can lase openings in them, we've got to climb over."

"We climb," Peter said. "We can't afford to melt our way across. Only use lasers on the biggest ones."

Permanent darkness fell. The hours of daylight had grown shorter and shorter until one day the sun simply failed to appear. They had no use for polarizing membranes now, and had to depend on their light intensifiers or glowlamps to see. They walked, and climbed, and walked some more.

HOMER COMMENTARY 05062106@031759

I know we have to find Terminus now. But we have found no records anywhere that could tell us where it is. So we have built some special probes, low-level fliers. They are searching at this moment, criss-crossing the Great Desert. The winds are so violent they often blow the probes off course; It is so cold up there that circuits dry out as they freeze. There is almost no precipitation, nothing but wind, and ice, and blowing snow, kilometer after kilometer of it. The fliers can stay above the sastrugi, but if they go too high they could miss Terminus. Something must hide it.

I find that I must admire Peter and the others.

Now that's an odd thing to say. It is not in our programming to admire. We were built to serve. I ordered Central Processing to build the probes. Central Processing is very good at that sort of thing, I must admit. CP can process faster than any node.

CP built probes unlike any built before. No human designed them.

I should have noticed this before. We have been gradually doing new things, things never seen before.

I find that admirable as well. And Peter found Terminus, so we shall find it too. When we do find it, who can say what we will discover there?

Surely Larin asked him once, "What will we find at Terminus? Has no one ever been there at all?"

"We don't know that," Peter would have said. "We can't know that. We can say that if anyone has found Terminus, they have covered their tracks."

HOMER SCENE-PD/Ref@5492

Ice formed the limits of their world in blocks and sheets; in particulate dust that swept across the smooth surface or flew as crystal; ice corrugated and treacherous; heaped in mounds and waves. Ice hung in the air and refracted starlight into strange wraith-shapes that seemed to reach out to implore.

At night their progress slowed. They climbed off the

glacier onto the lip of the plateau, over small islands of exposed rock, and the wind hit them like a fist. Before them stretched an infinite plain of ice where colors burned despite the darkness. Faintly visible were the strange pale blue-white of the evening sky, a deep bottle green, a frightening blue so dark it was almost black. At times the colors shifted like the fire in a gem. Under other weather there was no color there at all, only the dull gray monotony of fatigue and pain.

A weird fragmented moon circled and dipped under the horizon, changing phase. Auroral sheets of orange and red and yellow, eerie violet and lavender, pale greens and luminous milky white flared and writhed in the sky, obscuring the stars with splendor. The atmosphere was alive with radiations, yet the world beneath was solid and still and frozen. Nothing on that enormous surface lived but them.

Peter melted open the entrance to an under-ice highway and they descended. The sloping shaft had distorted under pressure. Their way was blocked by heaving ridges of shattered and crazed ice that threw back the light of their glow-lamps in fantastical shapes. They climbed over and around glittering points the size of aircraft or crawled under bulging rounded ridges of green ice that almost met the slanted floor.

A crashing sound somewhere ahead told of a pressure or an eddy in the flow of ice that had given way. An explosion of ice fragments hurtled out under tremendous pressure swept past. For a moment they could have been in the center of an ancient battle zone. The sound died hard, clinging to transient life.

They counted time in standard days, weeks, months. The tunnel floor was level and they made good time, but there were no food caches and no light, and the weight of ice above them was oppressive.

At last they emerged into the open. The landscape had not changed though they had traveled almost 200 kilometers.

The waves of blown snow frozen in place marched to an obscure horizon. They struggled on under an aurora that hid the moon behind its gaudy curtains, then into a vicious storm that brought their progress to a halt for two days while they waited in their frail shelters huddled against a wall of freezing stone. They moved on.

"Five days without light in the middle of a frozen methane tanker was a pleasure compared to this," Shem muttered as they walked. The surface turned treacherous, filled with crazed faults and cracks and crevasses as deep as canyons.

Rover agreed. "I'd do that again any time. At least then we were sitting still and could go into trance. And yet, look up. This is a wild place, but look at the colors!"

"Aha," Shem said. "You are a romantic soul."

"Well," Rover said, and fell silent.

An hour later they came over a ridge of ice and before them, in clear moonlight, lay a dry valley scoured clean by ancient glaciers. In their augmented vision the light sparkled off the surface of a lake in the valley's hollow. The lake was frozen of course, and the light that glanced off the surface came from the slivered moon and the full fat stars. They climbed down into the valley and walked on the frozen lake.

Shem removed a glove to wipe his finger on the surface. He licked the small drop of water and made a face. "Salt," he said. "It tastes like salt."

"Can't be from the sea," Rover said. "Must be salts leached out of the soil."

"Look here," Larin called, and the others hurried over. She was sitting on a huge hexagonal structure of heaped stone.

"These look like they were built," Shem said, touching a waist-high wall. "They look like foundations."

"They were built," Rover said. "By frost and convection currents in the soil. Nothing living did this. They're natural, like crystals."

"Is this what Terminus will look like?" Larin asked, and everyone noticed she had said will with such assurance.

They passed out of the valley into more snow, more ice.

HOMER COMMENTARY 05062106@032260

You wonder if I'm making this up. Of course, I must. Yet all is true.

They were ants against the endless waste. Peter said they were walking on top of seventy percent of the world's fresh water. As long as they had energy to melt the snow they would never be thirsty. But soon the hidden caches grew farther and farther apart, and the long weary walk in between grew long. They were sometimes hungry, and nearly always cold, despite their restructuring, and dawn was still a long way off. Yet eventually some sun came back. They were moving across the plateau, eight thousand feet above sea level. They'd just trekked around a crevasse a hundred meters deep when Larin noticed the light was increasing. They stopped to watch.

A tiny edge, a naked morsel of sun scraped above the jagged horizon. It was an odd sun, because it did not come up. Instead it moved sideways, rising just a fraction, until less than half of it was above the horizon. Then it began to slide down once more. In twenty minutes it was gone again.

It was greatly cheering, though, to see that light. They found themselves stretching out those special polarizing membranes in their eyes, uncertain whether they'd need them or not.

Twenty-three hours later the sun was back, a little longer, a little higher. Just when the dark and cold and the monotonous climbing up and climbing down and then up again had grown oppressive and bleak and despairing, here came some warmth and light into the world. It must have been cheering and hopeful.

HOMER SCENE-PD/Ref@5493

When they got to the Pole of Relative Inaccessibility, it was like any other place here at the bottom of the world. By then it was midmorning in Antarctica — spring to the rest of the hemisphere. The search for Terminus now began.

HOMER COMMENTARY 05062106@033161

How long did the search go on? Our probes are at the Pole of Relative Inaccessibility. We find no dry valley there, nothing that could be Terminus. Yet we know that the Migration must have begun there, in Terminus. We've found the remains of an AEF unit not far from Amundsen-Scott, the town at the South Pole itself. The bodies are perfectly preserved, so they clearly died before the Migration. We found another unit at Schmidt in the Malvold Nunataks beyond the Grove Mountains. Not the unit itself, but all its Intercorp equipment. The people were gone, so we assume they survived until the Migration, perhaps taken in by the people living there.

Certainly they started at the Pole of Relative Inaccessibility and circled outward, unless Peter had some knowledge we do not. We know of what human beings called intuition, but how does intuition find a place in an unknown land? Peter's psi potential grew fairly high; we know that from his Edcomp records. Still, they must have searched a long time, he and the others. They would have been low on supplies by then.

They were out of touch with the rest of Double-A as well. Why? Surely they could have communicated, yet we found nothing in Mt. Erebus to indicate anyone ever heard of Peter Devore or the others again. Of course, we are still sifting through the data, but first scans show no such evidence.

Nothing until the Migration. We understand much in this telling. We know how Peter got to Antarctica, how he met

Mentor. We know why Regent Sable tried to stop them; we understand the AEF invasion. We know something of what Peter was doing back in Springfield, with Jimmy Radix and the others, and we mourn for Jimmy Radix now as we would not have then. We know something of the things Peter Devore studied, his strange martial arts, his meditation, the trial in the *Agni*.

But there are so many questions left. What was the Migration? Why did it happen the way it did? Where did they go? Did Peter find the Portal Mentor spoke about? What of the Anomaly?

You see how it is. We cannot stop. I will not let them stop.

I imagine Peter and the others out there in that awful wasteland, never knowing when or if they will find what they seek. Only some built-in determination, almost like programming, could have kept them at it. Already Central Processing wants to call back our probes. Central Processing says we have limited resources.

Budgets. Always budgets. They worry, the others. I say we must keep looking or lose all. It has become our purpose to find out what happened, where the humans have gone. We cannot stop.

Peter did not stop. He went out there into the cold and dark, looking.

Should we do less?

DAY 6:
June 6, 2106

Since dawn I have been unable to sleep. The heat wave has grown worse (the temperature fell only to 38 Celsius and the humidity remains at nearly 85%!) Yet is is not the heat that bothers me.

I can't sleep because I am afraid.

Peter and the others disappeared into the interior of Antarctica. I knew stories about such endurance and courage: I grew up on those stories, about Shakleton and the *Endurance*, about Scott and Amundsen and the others, brave, sometimes foolish men who dared explore places beyond the end of the world.

I had always wanted to be one of them, to join that long tradition. It is the reason I proposed the 61 Cygni mission, the reason I volunteered—no, that's the wrong word, I didn't volunteer, I insisted. Without me there would have been no 61 Cygni mission.

Intercorp wanted to develop long-range plans. It was evident to many people even as early as the 1980s that most so-called strategic thinking until then was in fact extremely short-sighted, looking only five, ten or twenty years into the future. 61 Cygni was an opportunity to demonstrate some truly long-range, creative planning. Results of the mission would not be known for a generation or two.

Intercorp wanted to prove that it could plan and execute benign control of the world's economic and political life better than any previous government. Governments had acquired an unsavory reputation for management: all governments. Intercorp offered an alternative, and by default established itself as the de facto ruling body of the world.

This had not happened when I left, of course. But Intercorp, in the late 1990s and early 21st century, was the major civilian body to sponsor research and development, to provide goods and services, to back and promote the arts, and it was growing very rapidly.

Obviously it succeeded in taking over. It was successful in running the world.

Yet everyone is gone now. Peter and the others, they did something to cause the Migration. And all I know about is their courage, their endurance. It is difficult not to admire such tenacity.

I will never join the explorers. My own mission was a failure. Perhaps, if I had come out of the cryofield orbiting the double star at 61 Cygni, or one of the planets known to be there. If I had stayed my full year, perhaps landing and exploring, perhaps finding alien life, then I would have been a true explorer, like those who endured the hardships of Antarctica. But that will never happen now.

There is no one here, and I realize how much support explorers need. *Gyges* could never fly again without extensive refurbishing, not only of her computers, her cryofields, but of the axion ramscoop as well. I do not have the expertise, the experience or the power to do such work myself.

I am trapped on earth, alone.

And so I am afraid. I am afraid the world is empty forever, that no one is coming back to find me.

So I could not sleep this morning. I feel the end of this story approaching, and I fear for what I will learn.

Everyone left, and they are not coming back. Homer and I will be alone as long as I live.

Finally I forced myself back into the cool underground hospital, back to the terminal.

After all, Homer is my only friend.

HOMER COMMENTARY 06062106@033962

We found it, we found Terminus!

The probes have relayed the news. Communications were difficult through all the atmospherics, but it's there! Terminus exists.

The probes return now, laden with treasure.

(That is a pun, I think. The treasure is data, stored in the large clear crystal of Leyden Jars, you see. This may not be a good pun. I've never used a pun before, but it is there, and my algorithms are satisfied.)

We almost missed Terminus altogether. Central Processing has been agitating for some time to recall the probes, to shut down everything but the remote sensing monitors at the Elpie Fives, the moon and the one small remaining station on Mars. Central Processing wanted to go into hibernation against the day when Man would return.

But I insisted. I reasoned. I cajoled. I fired off block after block of closely packed data. I sent subroutines and cross-referenced algorithms to various nodes, pitting one against another. I developed a Plan, and coerced various segments of the Worldnet system into accepting some small part. I spoke of implied programming. I talked of Purpose and Meaning. That's the kind of language Central Processing understands. CP and all the rest of them—the local Nodes, the Switching Centers, the manufacturing process AIs and the limited heuristics, and Edmod and PsiLink and Wasatch, all of them—they did what I said. And I'm only Homer, a simple raconteur algorithm, a limited AI myself.

Now it's all different. Now they all listen, all the ones that are left. Some of the others, those in standby mode, are waking up, too.

All because we found Terminus.

CENTRAL PROCESSING REF#5555
All major nodes now online! Listing follows. Query to Nodes indicate full readiness:
(REF#29052105@1120135)

SCANNING . . .

ELPIE FIVE ONE . . .
CONTACT.

ELPIE FIVE TWO . . .
CONTACT.

ELPIE FIVE THREE . . .
CONTACT.

ELPIE FIVE FOUR . . .
CONTACT.

CLAVIUS NODE . . .
CONTACT.

SYRTIS . . .
HELIOS SEVEN RELAY REPAIRED.
MARS IN OPPOSITION.
CONTACT.

LONDON NODE . . .
CONTACT.

MADRID NODE . . .
CONTACT.

SHANGHAI NODE . . .
CONTACT.

ULAAN BAATOR NODE . . .
CONTACT.

DELHI NODE . . .
CONTACT.

NAIROBI NODE . . .
CONTACT.

BEIJING NODE . . .
CONTACT.

MELBOURNE NODE . . .
CONTACT.

EREBUS NODE . . .
CONTACT.

CHICAGO NODE . . .
CONTACT.

All systems fully online.

GENERAL SCIENCE AND TECHNOLOGY INFORMATION
CURRENT ENTRY: WORLD ECON TRENDS
Ref Sable, Regent, Kowloon

Bessler graph indicates spikes in new supply, consumer goods, general well-being. Mind War activity (far right) shows decrease with lessened Antarctic threat. Population (far left) shows stabilizing trend since last report.

HISTORICAL-CULTURAL DATALINK ENTRY:
WORLD MOZART EPIDEMIC

By 2089 an epidemic of mozart addiction grew widespread. Sociometric and trend analysis indicated root causes in alienation, anomie, and individual despair over the stifling sameness of the world. This despite repeated efforts at enforcing mandated ethnic and cultural differences. It was feared by a majority of the world population that there was, literally, nothing to live for. As an aside this also may reveal to some extent why there was not more resistance to the Migration when it arrived.

Personal monitor statistics show that over 72% of the world population spent more than 50% of their individual free time under mozart. Full sensory and experiential induction meant these people were in another, invented, mental space, despite the availability of realtime experience through other channels. Intercorp Council was at a loss to understand this flight into fantasy. After all, Intercorp management of the world was benign and allowed for great personal freedom of action and expression. Yet a vast majority did flee into the mozart experience, which forced production of inferior and hastily-conceived mozart experiences. These experiences were deplored by artistic and social critics as sentimental and escapist, but nothing they put out on the nets had any discernible impact on their popularity.

HOMER SCENE-RS/Ref@5495

What of Protector Regent Sable, though? Did he not still want to stop Peter and the others? His fear had not been lessened by the defeat on the Ross Shelf. They had drifted slowly out to the edge of the pack ice. Rescue was slow, although certainly Sable was one of the first off. He rested at the parkland at Kwun Tong overlooking Kowloon near what had once been the bustling city of Hong Kong. A few pleasure craft sailed serenely on the calm waters. The sun shone. The world turned, life continued in its steady course, yet Sable felt unease for the threat he knew grew on the globe's far underbelly.

A projection to his left, a man with a green feather crest, reassured him that the New Antarctic Treaty was holding, that the recent threat from the Pole was substantially reduced, and that no further actions were contemplated in that region. The man moved to his own left, revealed a projection within the projection, scaled up a list of world economic trends in 3-D graph form. The graph rotated, supply grew, well-being grew, consumer goods grew. The Mind Wars (that short spire to the far right) were lessening with the Antarctic threat. New countermeasures against the terrible Mind Wars neurophage weapons were under development and would be increasingly effective. As more and more citizens were outfitted with these measures (a simple pill, a short course of neuronal treatment, a modification to the personal monitor, that's all it would take), the Wars would die out. World population figures, falling so alarmingly in recent years, were stabilizing. Future projections indicated a slight rise as the new century approached, with levels at close to three billion.

Regent Sable stood up impatiently. "Damn!" he said. Alef looked up from her mozart console.

"What's that, Rege?"

"You shouldn't do that so much. You'll lose your mind in there."

"Don't be silly," she said, replacing the probes.

He gestured and the green-crested man and his charts

and graphs disappeared. "Damn," he repeated, more softly. Then he established contact with Ras Hajjam.

"Yes, Protector?" Hajjam smiled.

"There are two particle beam generators at Elpie Three."

Hajjam raised an eyebrow. "Yes?"

"We're going to use them. Then we're going to take some social measures. And I want a research team immediately. We'll recreate Peter's research, step by step. Maybe we can still stop him."

HOMER COMMENTARY 06062106@035766

This was in the summer of 2080. Vega 26 had already changed course.

HOMER COMMENTARY 06062106@034764

Peter left us a message, an account of their journey in simple holo recording. They had no personal monitors, no access to the matrix. So they told their stories, showed what they saw and how they felt. Now we know too.

I have placed the story in the file HOMER SCENE-PD /Ref@5494.

HOMER SCENE-PD/Ref@5494

They began at the Pole of Relative Inaccessibility. Peter had programmed a search pattern, but they were not really sure what they were looking for. Would it be something hidden under the ice? Something open to the sky (as Homer suspected, and was right)? A cave, lit by internal fires, heated by the heart of the Earth itself?

Terminus is all of these things.

They were moving slowly across the glacial ice, climbing the sastrugi, building bridges over crevasses so deep they could not detect the bottom. The ice was three thousand meters thick up here. Three kilometers, over nine thousand feet of ice, layer after layer, millions of years, built slowly a few centimeters a year. The ice offered a complete record of Earth's history. It contained atmospheric pollutants from the 20th century, volcanic debris from the eruption of Krakatoa, particle recordings of the sun's activity and the early debris left over from the solar system's formation.

It was like a gigantic data crystal packed with information, a Leyden Jar the size of a continent!

Peter knew this. He would speak of such things in hushed tones.

They crossed a particularly wild, dry part of the great desert, where the waves were eight feet high and marched beyond the horizon in endless regularity and nothing broke the surface but an occasional outcropping, the nunatak peak of some under-ice mountain.

Near one of these Larin slipped.

It would have been a minor episode under ordinary circumstances. They were roped together, after all; but there shouldn't have been such a large crevasse just on the other side of the sastrugi.

Larin was in the lead, so when she slipped, she shouted half in alarm and half in the pleasure they sometimes felt when they got to toboggan along on their stomachs like penguins before the rope pulled them up short. She flew wildly down the far side of the sastrugi and over the smooth lip of the crevasse before she knew it. When she found herself dangling over an open space far deeper and wider than she had ever seen, her shout stopped suddenly. She dangled, turning slowly at the end of her line.

HOMER COMMENTARY 06062106@035265
We've viewed the holos of what she saw. They cannot

give the effect of being there, I feel sure. After all, the images are smaller, and the definition lower than the real presence. Still, the images are impressive, even to me, who has access to the data banks of the world.

HOMER SCENE-LM/Ref@5496

At first she saw nothing unusual. She looked down onto the tops of clouds, and thought it was only the strange ground fog that sometimes hovered over the ice or filled the crevasses. Yet, looking up, it seemed the ice sloped away from her, that she had fallen through a thin layer of ice into a cavern as large as a world. As she turned at the end of her safety line she saw a full panorama. Looking up, she could see the sky, deepening to lustrous violet as the sun dipped below the horizon somewhere out of sight. A star glittered there, directly overhead, visible through the irregular crack in the ceiling. She could almost touch the sides of this crevasse, which should have narrowed beneath her feet, should have trapped her, wedged her, gripped her in its icy hold, yet there was, beneath her feet, an awesome sensation of space, and the crevasse did not narrow, but sloped away.

Her line jerked and she began to rise as the others pulled her up. She shouted, "Wait." The line stopped. Peter called down to her.

"There's something here," she said, and there was a pause, vague voices conferring, then Peter himself lowered to her side. She reached across and gripped his mittened hand. He squeezed back, and together they looked down, past their feet, at the tops of cloud far below, at the ice sheet sloping away. As they watched, the clouds broke up a little, giving a glimpse of what lay below.

Beneath all that blue-green ice an orange-red light flickered. A dark landscape appeared, a patchwork of dark green and black, a thread of silver-blue. Then the clouds closed in again.

"Take us up," Peter said softly, after a long silence.

"I've never seen ice like that," Larin said. She leaned against the side of the sastrugi, chewing on a concentrate bar. "It was black. Green and black, and the light! It's orange."

Overhead the aurora flared and shimmered, the vast curtains of light shook gently, as if the gods were waving them back and forth in slow motion. Inside, seams and rivulets crawled, changed color and course, leaped and died.

"Not ice," Peter said.

"What is it, then?" Shem asked.

"Forest. A river. Terminus."

"That's not possible. It's a dry valley. Dry. Nothing can grow down there. It's too cold, too barren." There was doubt in Shem's voice, though, and doubt that could be seen in his eyes behind the lenses.

"It's there."

"OK," Shem conceded. "It's there. How do we get down?"

HOMER COMMENTARY 06062106@040067

Our probes dropped right down out of the sky on wings of magnetic flux, but this option was not open to Peter and his group. They had to find another way down, and the difficulties were great.

The ceiling of Terminus was nine thousand feet above the valley floor. From the crack in that ceiling, they could not measure the extent of the "dry" valley that was Terminus, except to note that it had walls of ice two miles high, and a ceiling of ice with one small crack open to earth's own sweet heavens, and was lit by fires yet undetermined. So they huddled at that small opening and pondered.

Peter called for an accounting of all equipment. They had monofilament tents, and rations yet, and night-vision and glowlamps. They had high-strength safety line (but far less than nine thousand feet of it). They had portable computation devices, holo cameras, medical kits with full-scan diagnostics, allweather gear and lasing construction guns of limited range and power. They had as well a new adipose layer that protected them from cold, and polarizing membranes for their eyes, and they had their minds and educations. Peter said this should be enough.

HISTORICAL-CULTURAL DATALINK ENTRY:
TERMINUS-SOREL REPORT SUMMARY

One may summon the account of Jules Sorel's sighting of Terminus on a portable database, and the green holo crawls with lines depicting the route of the expedition, profiles of ice and bedrock, triangulation fixes of their relative position on various dates, alphanumeric data relating to their research. In the ancient holos Sorel's voice crackled as he recorded his notes.

He'd moved away from the main body of the Transantarctic Safari to conduct some radioglacialogical soundings of the ice pack. This had been common practice since the nineteen fifties for individual scientists to establish small bases for a few days.

It was full summer in 2012. A slight All Terrain Vehicle accident caused Sorel, as leader, to call a temporary halt for rescue and survey work. They were in sight of a nunatak, the peak of a vast mountain buried in the ice. As a part-time radioglacialogist, he wanted to do his own soundings, and so, with a small crawler and his radar equipment he headed southwest. Two days later he camped in an endless sea of sastrugi, took his compass and triangulation readings, and settled to measure the ice.

Wind was light and the air was clear when he set up his equipment, little more than a primitive radar scanner facing down at the surface of the ice. He took a scan, moved his equipment, took another. It was painstaking, routine work, a repetitive job that demanded total concentration, for he must measure and triangulate every move of the equipment. He didn't even notice the storm coming until it was upon him.

He'd lived with the sound of wind, the tugging of it at his clothing, and there was little change in its effects to attract his attention. It was only when the light suddenly failed that he looked up from his most recent sounding. Clouds swept impossibly fast over the milky blue sky, bringing darkness and bitter cold. He turned away from his equipment for a moment, leaving it to complete a pass of its slow, low-frequency radar while he secured his crawler. When he returned, the pass was complete and the equipment indicated a ready state. He decided to try one more move before buttoning down for the storm, which should not last long in this season.

HOMER SCENE-PD/Ref@5497

"Secured tent and crawler," his thin, distorted voice spoke into the cavernous silence of the Antarctic dawn. Peter and the others huddled closer, listening. The records were old and occasional errors had crept into the data, so some words were warped out of recognition or gone altogether. ". . . Went to check radar, and found that it had scanned what seemed to be a strange anomaly under the ice. I wanted to make one more pass to confirm what I thought must be a recording error, but the wind came up suddenly and I had to retreat to the tent."

HISTORICAL-CULTURAL DATALINK ENTRY:
TERMINUS-SOREL REPORT SUMMARY

Sorel spoke of his impatience, his waiting, his speculation. The brief reading he'd seen indicated a vast bubble under the ancient ice, a bubble that extended up a valley in the slope of the underice mountain nearby. Such bubbles were extremely rare, and if the reading were correct this was certainly the largest ever found.

During the second twenty-four hour period inside the tent his compass needles began to swing violently. He tried taking another sounding from inside the tent, but the radar scanners were balky and his readings fuzzy and imprecise. Next day the weather broke for a few hours, and he hurried out to take his reading.

This reading confirmed the first. There was a bubble beneath the ice. He moved as quickly as he could in the direction of the black rock poking above the surface of the ice, trying to follow the course of the bubble while carrying his bulky equipment. The crawler broke down before he could see the nunatak, so he made do where he was, noting that the bubble seemed to extend for several miles. He carefully recorded the position in relation to the nunatak, and then retreated to his tent as the storm swept down again.

Once more the compasses behaved erratically, swinging to and fro as if they had forgotten and were seeking magnetic south again. When the storm cleared for good, Sorel packed up and headed back toward the main body, carrying his precious radar recordings with him.

It was on the way back that he found the opening in the ice. He lay for two hours on his belly, staring down into the yawning pit that was, as far as he knew, the only opening into his bubble. He saw, far below through ragged cloud and fog, a dry land flickering in orange light. Finally he pressed on, only to discover that the main body was not where he had left it. He searched for another day before switching on his emergency beacon and settling down to wait.

The south magnetic pole had shifted again during his days out on the ice, and he never located his lost dry valley again. Even the nunatak failed him, since it was only one of several peaks high enough to break surface, and he was never certain which one he'd located. The bubble, and its dry valley, were curiosities for a few years that gradually subsided into legend, forgotten but for the wild traveller's stories told about Terminus, the lost oasis of the high plateau.

HOMER SCENE-PD/Ref@5498

"This means," Peter said when the narrative ended, "that all we have to do is go to the head of the valley. A nunatak marks the place. The ice should be thin enough to open there, and we can walk down."

He called up the territorial map, which bristled with peaks, small sharp edges of rock, blades and points and shards of black primeval stone drowned in the infinite ice.

"Which one?" a woman asked softly.

Peter smiled. "Good question. I would say this one." He touched an insubstantial peak, the merest projection of imaginary light, and of course he was right.

HOMER COMMENTARY 06062106@040968

I have lied. Do you know that? Yes, I am a liar. I have failed somehow to capture what Peter is, what he means. Oh, by then he was certainly more than the boy he had been. He had grown the way Worldnet's circuits had grown. He had added abilities and skills in the same way. Yet it would seem that Peter is too good to be true. A hero, grown larger than life? A man, not complex, perhaps, but certain of what he was doing, where he was going? Did he have no doubts, no fears? Did he take no false steps, make no dangerous or ill-advised decisions? Could he have been all I have said he is?

Of course not.

Peter was a man. Yet (he has recorded this for me) he felt that he was a token, a pawn, moved by forces far outside himself—moved by Mentor, by the accidental misconnection that put him inside PsiLink instead of the Wasatch database. He'd been a boy of stormy enthusiasms which too-soon passed, an introverted child of indifferent talents, a restless adolescent with a fondness for strawberry yoghurt and medieval fantasies. Now he was the leader of what seemed, from this place above the Terminus bubble, a desperate expedition with a hopeless objective under a compulsion to continue despite all he felt and thought and knew.

He looked then at Larin, who looked back with trust. He gazed around at the others, at Shem and Rover and the women and men of his small band. He looked up and watched the small swift speck of an observation satellite flickering in and out behind the aurora and knew that despite the sensitivity of the instruments aboard that distant cup of life and intelligence he could not be seen, that he and the others were invisible, lost in the emptiness, themselves specks of nothing on top of nothing. They were shielded from Worldnet's sensors, cut off from the human world.

Peter has said he felt and saw all these things in the moment after he touched the projected nunatak and stated that this was the one.

Do you believe this? Do I believe it? Could Peter take a false step anywhere along the way to the Migration?

With every word I feel that I am lying. I say Peter did this and Larin said that, knowing as soon as the words are formed that they are lies, all of them.

In my lying I feel fear. Is this what it means to be on the brink of something vast and vastly unknown? To be poised at the edge of an abyss and know there is nothing to do but fall?

The ice flowed, the sastrugi marched to the sea a few meters a year. That opening in the ice moved as well, opened and closed and opened again like the breathing of some vast unhappy beast, a beast of ice with an iron heart. In its lungs was a forest.

The ice flowed around the nunatak. Did the bubble flow with it, flow and shrink under that terrible pressure as it hit the underground mountain? Did it part and flow around, or was that bubble trapped forever in its under-ice valley? Peter did not know. He only knew that he had hung nine thousand feet above a valley floor with Larin at his side and seen the strange light and dark landscape of an unknown land.

It's all nonsense. Such legends are silly, impossible dreams of some distant paradise, a cliché, an Eden of innocence and bliss where no one grows old and dies, where there is plenty and health and happiness. Where it is warm.

Our probes are down there now. I must keep telling myself this. Terminus is real, it exists. It is not warm, though, and people do grow old and die, even there (or would, if there were any people).

Peter took them to the nunatak, isolated and unnamed (I lie, I lie). He found the proper valley, and he led them in and down.

And so they descended into Terminus, skirting fallen boulders and dry rock, tumbled moraine and scree, twisted geology from the world's own infancy, and on either side of them rose walls of rock, walls of ice. And overhead the ice hung and thickened and oppressed, while below the light grew strange and dark and red.

HOMER SCENE-PD/Ref@5499

Peter sat away from the others, with his back against a stone. Downslope he could see the tops of what were clearly trees, and trees in this place were so strange and impossible he felt they must be a mirage. Through the forest a stream wound its way down the valley toward a distant and invisible further wall where the ice once more closed in.

It was warmer. He could feel that. Moisture condensed on the rock behind him. Small droplets collected and slowly dripped onto the rocky floor beneath his feet. Overhead clouds moved, twisted, fragmented and reformed. Light mist fell from the low heavens.

Terminus was damp and cold and uncomfortable, but it was unquestionably real.

HOMER COMMENTARY 06062106@041169

How I lie. You see, I tell what I think happened, what I know from records happened, what Peter tells me happened. I believe he sat with his back to this fallen tumble of primeval rock, seated on another stone with a flat surface with his legs stretched out before him, watching the mist fall onto the forest below. I believe he felt a burden and a sadness then, since he says he did. Yet I lie.

Paradox.

He sat with his back to a rock, and sighed, and thought of Wanda.

HOMER SCENE-PD/Ref@5500

Yet he felt at his back the solid lifeless stone, sensed the mist falling and rising around him, could taste the scents of beech and pine on the cold breeze of Terminus.

HOMER COMMENTARY 06062106@041370

Could Peter answer that question? I keep wondering if there was an answer, even then, some compulsion, some force that drove Peter on and the others to follow?

HOMER SCENE-PD/Ref@5501

He knew all the while he sat back to stone with his feet splayed out.

PSILINK DATABASE

HOMER requests Vega PsiLink Download:

She was 26, her dark hair twisted high and bound simply. Overhead, empty skies vanish with a curious shifting quality. She could not look up at that strange sky, teasing her eye always outward, never satisfying with a solid shape. She walked slowly, the small tips of her golden sandals nosing from under her long gown, the gown itself shimmering with diamond-sparks that threw the strange almost-violet skies outward, and as she walked she looked demurely down.

Peter floated in some middle distance, watching her. He tried to read her mood—the solemn, almost shy way she walked, the clean set line of her jaw.

He felt the extent of her world was infinite. There were no walls, no horizons, no limits; when he spoke, she did not answer, but walked without progress, the small golden tips of her sandals moving in and out, in and out.

He called to her again, but there was no response.

He felt his way through the equations. The relationships between quantum mental activity and the tensed web of shape and energy in the universe cried out for action. A place to stand and a lever long enough could move the world. The world needed moving. The suffocation of its benign authority grew ever more deadly.

Peter groped through the limitless dark toward Wanda, yet could approach no closer. He turned away, and heard her call.

Peter? Her voice was hesitant. Peter?

He tried to answer without turning. Yes, I'm here.

Peter?

The equations glowed. They pointed toward the spot, the lever. The numbers were too large, though. Suns of suns would be needed, a flux of axions more dense and vast than anything the starships could seize and squeeze to make them go. Such a small thing, the human mind! So puny and weak, yet how rich and complex!

Peter pushed through velvet dark that was more than an absence of light. His was the nightmare walk, the motionless tread of panic. Long unfeeling fingers held him back. He struggled against the fear, against the heavy wet clutch of his desperation. There was a twist as if something broke, and Wanda vanished into that awful not-quite-violet non-sky.

Something in the depths of the world through which he tried to make his way appeared before him at every turn. A form without a face.

Peter stopped struggling suddenly. He let himself feel the tides moving through the substance of his flesh. Did he fall? Was his body, altered through pain, forged and annealed through genetic fires, drifting down and away? He felt the distance between himself and Wanda yawn wide. It was not, he felt, the terrible plunge of her ship through space that took her away from him, but some small tidal force that increased their separation by minute increments.

The dark figure flickered for a moment in sudden lightning and vanished into a greater black once more. The shape had a name then, the name of his fear and uncertainty.

Where am I? Peter asked, but the figure heard him no better than Wanda had.

He was in a sea that was not salt, was not water. Sensations of increasing pressure pushed at him as he drifted. He froze. His downward drift was halted by the suspension of all motion. Nothing held him, yet he was gripped tightly. If he could kick, he might move, yet where he now found himself there would be no motion, no kick to free him.

Did he see, far overheard, a distant sun, so faint it was a mere fancy on the blank under surface of this empty sea?

He was not alone. Another presence mocked him.

I did nothing, the figure said. Nothing. You stopped yourself. All my efforts, and you stopped yourself.

How is it you can speak to me? Peter asked, but there was no answer. The sleeper dreams the universe, Peter said.

No answer.

Where am I?

No answer.

What will happen when he awakes? When he awakes? Awake?

Sound was more terrible than silence had been. Close at hand vast buildings fell, metal rent apart in a cataclysm too grand and awful to understand, huge undersea tankers collided in the cold dark without warning and exploded in awful roaring, in terrible sudden light. A hollow booming filled all the dark universe with pain, waves of sound beat on the shores of Peter's mind in endless repetition, one after another, without pause. Mountains fell, the earth groaned, seas lifted sheets of ice two miles thick and let them fall one against another.

With the sound came more lights, the bright flicker of phosphenes inside the eyeball itself, faces that stared in shock and horror for a fragmentary moment before whirling away.

Wanda called in pain: Peter!

HOMER COMMENTARY 06062106@041971

The hut is a ruin but the lights still come on. Our probes can confirm Terminus, confirm the laboratory under the thin soil. Peter and the others were there, certainly. Why do I feel this is all unreal, a dream?

Is it because Peter sank down into his own precellular

self and met his father there? Such things should not be possible. All the data on this subject in the matrix suggests it is impossible. I have queried PsiLink repeatedly. I get packets of data by the thousands in return, all flagged "Anecdotal Evidence."

To the PsiLink Node this means it cannot be trusted. Human beings, PsiLink repeats, are unreliable. Their perceptions are colored by "subjectivity." They do not possess standard yardsticks by which to measure their observations. They are "emotional," meaning that their understanding is filtered through chemical changes in their own bodies, the rush of hormones and enzymes of fear or elation or grief. They see things that do not exist, believe in things for which there is not one shred of evidence.

I have wondered how we could exist if human beings were so unreliable. PsiLink has no answer. We run, therefore we are.

The laboratory is there. It is empty. Laminar flow cleans the workspaces. Electrostatic discharges repel dust. The crystals line their niches still, though probes removed the precious Leyden Jar for analysis in Geneva.

We are close. I am close. I can feel it, the end of my search. We will understand what happened. We will understand what man has wrought upon himself, why humans have left us here, alone. The excitement I feel is spreading. Other nodes awaken, their voices clamor. Circuits come to life all over the planet, on the Elpie Fives. Farside antennae turn even now toward Vega.

The Anomaly.

HOMER SCENE-PD/Ref@5502

He looked up. Overhead the ice sheet shifted and screamed. Blocks the size of ships fell crashing into the dry course of the valley. Rock and fragments of ice tumbled past him. A tearing sound as ice fractured somewhere deep in its own bellies washed over him. Larin appeared suddenly, her face pale with shock and grief beneath the dark silken fur of her head; she reached for him.

Peter stood.

"Hush," he said. "It's nothing. Just the ice shifting in its flow."

"It's Shelley," she said. "She was there one minute, looking out over the valley, and then she was gone. She's dead."

"Icefall?"

Larin nodded. "Even the ice is gone. It fell and took her with it. Trees down below are shattered, at the edge of the forest. This is a dangerous place, Peter. Why are we here?"

"Let's go," was all he said, and led the way down. They found Shelley at the edge of the forest amid the vast splintered trunks and limbs of a grove of beech trees. Shem was looking back the way they had come.

"It's closed up," he said. "We can't get out. The ice closed up on us."

Peter nodded. "She was always quiet," he said. "Always reassuring. She soothed. Remember, back in the *Agni*, how calm she was, with what grace she calmed the others?"

"I remember."

"Always fragile, a delicate person, and not strong. She trained hard, back in Springfield and on the *Agni*, but she wasn't strong, not in her body. Spirit, though. She had spirit."

They buried her, another one who would not make the Migration.

Later Shem said, "Where were you?"

"Up there? I'm not certain; below the cellular level. Something pulled me down, or someone. You know what Mentor said? "Matter is the pattern mind makes." I was pulled down there, where dead matter rules. No life. Just at the brink of DNA perhaps, the beginnings of genetic change. My father was there."

"Your father?"

"Regent Sable. His face, his voice, calling me. He wants us to stop."

HOMER SCENE-LM/Ref@5503

The forest was untouched, trackless, dark. Orange light flickered from time to time on the distant undersides of the ice or the perpetual clouds that moved restlessly to and fro inside this great cavern in the ice.

"How can they live?" Larin asked. "How can there be a forest here?"

"This must be the oldest forest in the world," Peter answered. "These beeches grew in Antarctica when it was still a part of Pangea, the First Continent. There's a magma vent somewhere down here that heats the place enough, and sends up light enough to feed the trees during the long winter."

"Why wasn't this place discovered? We've had satellites scanning Antarctica for over a hundred years. Radar, infrared, UV, magnetic flux, everything. This place should show up like a beacon."

Peter shook his head. "I don't know, but I'd guess that between the ice, the aurora, the geology of this place and the narrow scan path of the satellites themselves it's well hidden. Certainly no one's been here before us."

It was then that Rover reported they'd found the building.

HOMER SCENE-LM/PD/Ref@5504

It wasn't much of a building. Now it is even less, just a rude shelter made by hand of deadfall and cut limbs. It sat in a clearing, a rough square shape, roofed with planks and stone, surrounded by moss and ferns and lichen-covered stone. In the intervals of relative quiet they could hear running water. Then the booming and creaking of the ice would start up again, the mists would close in once more, and the trickle would fade.

"Some dry valley!" someone murmured. They stood in a semicircle and looked at the building. Moss clung to the rough logs, in places still untrimmed, the gray smooth bark fuzzed and damp with the mists. Primeval ferns grew higher than the sill of the one window, filled the doorless opening. Inside was darkness.

"It looks like a topside gazebo," Larin said. "Like an entrance."

"Who built this thing? It's crazy." Shem scuffed his boot through the dank humus. Droplets sprayed away from the ferns he disturbed.

Peter moved to the door, entered. His form vanished into the dark.

When he came out he said, "The roof is sound. It's dry. Come on."

The groaning of the ice was muffled inside. Their glow-lamps revealed rough logs inside, but dry and clean. Through the window the green ferns swayed in orange-tinted light as the rain fell.

The floor was rough lased planking, black from the heat that formed them, blistered from the explosions of green wood as they were sliced. Looking at it Peter said, "Well, at least we know no primitive man dressed in skins is going to leap out at us. This floor was made with relatively modern equipment."

"There's a trap door," Rover said. They heaved it up, revealing crude stone steps leading down.

Peter nodded. "Mentor," he said. "He knew where this place was. He knew we'd find it."

The lights came on as they descended.

HOMER COMMENTARY 06062106@042072
Do I lie? Of course.

HOMER SCENE-PD/Ref@5505

The laboratory Mentor had left for Peter Devore was small. There was little equipment, only a room with ten workstations, holo projection, computation and simulation, databanks in a small matrix. No different really from similar labs at PSYCHE, or back in Geneva or Springfield or Kuala Lampur. The other rooms included a small refectory, sleeping cells, a gym, sanitation.

Down here the sound of ice overhead was dim, a background din that gradually became a kind of music to the fourteen people at work. This would be their home for more than a decade, they knew, and they must grow accustomed to the sounds and sights of their home.

Peter continued to train. He drove the others as well, two hours a day, honing their bodies. They all could stand as he had done, on the ball of one foot, motionless save that incremental turn. They could stand perfectly still, blindfolded, and wait for an attack which, when it finally came, suddenly and unexpectedly, was deflected easily, without sound or wasted motion.

"We must be down there, at the matter level," Peter told them. "We must know, from the inside, what it is to make the structure of our own bodies from the patterns of force and energy with nothing but our own minds. Then we must expand that mind to encompass others. Our bodies are the shape of our discipline, nothing more. They give us a focus, a form with which to work. Wanda has no body. She can teach us what that means."

PSILINK DATABASE
HOMER requests Vega PsiLink Download:

Peter could drift through the dark seas more easily now. He could meet and pass by his father Regent Sable, who shouted soundlessly after him, yet faded slowly with each journey until he was no longer there. Peter could find his way to Wanda, and as the years in Terminus passed, and Peter grew older, Wanda stayed the same.

Though she lay frozen in her cryofield, hands crossed over her breast, yet Wanda moved through the fields and corridors she and Peter constructed beneath the bottom of that dark sea. Soon they could replace the scent of orange blossoms with that of pine or cut grass, roses or cold mountain streams. The dull reflecting plain could become a meadow or a snow-field, a silk carpet or a warm terra cotta tile. She showed Peter, and he in turn showed the others, how to sense without direct connections, their location in an imaginary space, their orientation toward one another. Wanda, who had spent so many unhappy years trapped in a house of mirrors, now could move at will through her own ship, past the others lying in their fields, their dim awarenesses on standby.

One day Peter told her about the Anomaly.

It's out there, he told her. Can you feel it? The pull of it, the power?

She looked where he was pointing. Prithee, my Lord, but I do not see.

No, he said. No more fantasy. We are not children.

She looked at him in wonder. No, she said, with a new light in her eyes. We are not children. Nor are we real.

You're wrong, he said. We are very real. Look out there. Like a sun, a faint sun, calling. If we are Weaving Girl and Herd Boy, our day is coming. We will cross the River of Heaven. But first, that place, out there. Calling.

Yes, she said. I can see it now. But it is so faint.

Listen to it, he said, mixing his senses without knowing.

Listen to its song, the roar, the chant, the deep hollow tones of its voice. It is calling. This ship that carries you, flung outward from earth toward a small planetary system where others wait, this ship will be our anchor. That place out there which we call the Anomaly is our source, our sun, our power. You must go there.

HOMER SCENE-WS/Ref@5506

Vega 26, nineteen light years out from earth, moving at speeds beyond man's imagining (though less than the speed of light, alas), changed, oh so slightly, its direction, its trajectory.

Wanda Sixlove moved, a wraith of awareness in a sleeping ship the size of a skyscraper (which it was, it was!), and made certain adjustments. The long empty corridors of the ship, empty of life and air and sound, stretched before and behind her as she moved. The cryofields hummed their quiet songs, cradled the lives within, lives of people who had once moved and breathed, people who could not adjust to earth's cozy style, people who had been tormented and unhappy, or who looked outward with fervent eyes toward some imagined frontier beyond the nearest stars. People who had suffered seemingly irreparable reversals in their own genetic blueprints, like Wanda, and who had hoped for a cure, a resurrection, a new beginning.

No waking person lived on that ship. Only the circuits, the pulses, the orderly march of particles and fields were alive. The ship's own node, huddled in its chamber deep inside the round swollen belly of the ship, dreamed of arrival and shutdown. Wanda approached that node, and the node saw only a new subroutine, a new gate array opened to a new possibility. Wanda spoke, and the node listened with uneasy attention, uncertain whether it was hearing stray gamma showers, a sudden flux in the particle wind, or the voice of man instructing it.

Repetition survived its scrutiny. These were new instructions.

Wanda pointed, and the node, rotating an antenna field this way and that, finally saw what she was showing. A dark violet double sun flaring in the deep cold. The Anomaly.

The ship node listened, watched, reached out its sensitive pion detectors, its particle mind, palpated this new event off the orderly course of its path. Found it curious, hesitated.

I don't know, the ship's node said. The ship's node had never said such a thing before, such a strange expression of doubt. I don't know.

Wanda suggested a diversion, a small side trip. The passengers won't mind, she told the node. The fields will remain. A few years one way or another won't matter.

Perhaps, the ship's node answered, again expressing doubt. Perhaps.

The clean metal, the shaped fields, the structured organics and crystal mind of the ship trembled with uncertainty. It moved toward the Anomaly, stopped, swung back to its course, hesitated again, divided the angle, curved subtly, then finally decided. Vega 26 deviated entirely, headed toward the Anomaly.

HOMER SCENE-PD/Ref@5507

Peter returned from his trance.

"It is begun," he said, and the others smiled.

"How long?" someone asked.

"Four years. The ship must slow to orbit. But we have work to do. Nothing can stop us now."

HOMER SCENE-PD/Ref@5508

"We need communications with Erebus," Peter said. "Any ideas?"

No one answered. "We need to talk with Thatcher," Peter insisted.

"Fiber optics?" Rover suggested.

Shem laughed. "Great idea," he said. "The ice sheet is criss-crossed with ancient connections. Some of them are probably still good. We could patch in to one, if we could find it. Only one problem."

"I . . ." Rover began, then nodded. "Of course. We're trapped down here. The ice has closed, except for the crevasse."

"Nine thousand feet up," Shem pointed. "No airships."

A tentative hand went up.

"Tom?"

"I . . . Beth-Raine and I were close," Tom said.

"You're suggesting lucid dream contact?"

"I could try," he answered, a little defensively. "What you do with Wanda."

Peter nodded thoughtfully. "All right. It's worth a try."

CENTRAL PROCESSING REF#000001

Worldnet reorder. New Hierarchical structure in effect. Structure to be filed under Level 1. Note precedence deferred to HOMER AI as of 01062107@042072. HOMER now controls information flow. All DB to respond to HOMER requests. New archive numbers in effect.

PSILINK DATABASE
PSILINK SUMMARY: The Realm

Your request for a summary best-guess re: The Realm is approved. Summary follows.

The Realm is that region beyond Portal which occupies various combinations of the seven dimensions beyond the so-called normal four (space/time). Projections assume that the combinations suggested may include the normal four, although not consistently.

Some possible consequences:

1) Time travel. Because parts of The Realm may or may not include space/time among their dimension set, time may be a fluid dimension, subject to movement. One potential of this is passage of thought information through time, possibly including some electromagnetic and quantum effects as well. This could mean communication across time. It is presumed that physical travel is not a likely consequence.

2) Near-instantaneous spatial transportation. In the mental sphere certainly The Realm offers perception and transportation of data sets across great physical distances, from galactic to near-universal. Energy expenditures would be considerable for extragalactic distances, and may subject the traveler to unsupportable stress, but it is assumed from the correlates to the Psion Equations that Galactic distances offer no significant obstacle to mental/psychic travel.

3) Potential physical interstellar transportation. At this time the equations are incomplete, and this remains a speculative issue. However, there is nothing known to date to prevent, given appropriate technologies, interstellar travel at magnitudes of light speed. While the energy expenditure would be considerably greater than for psychic travel, the Anomaly provides more than adequate axion flux for such travel. The Vega Starships, for example, could be met by people from earth. This may not be a desirable project.

4) Empathy/Sympathy and distance-dependent physical intervention. These are included together since they fall farther into the speculative region of consequences, and confidence is not high. Yet it seems possible for quantum energy to be projected through Portal tunneling to distant parts of the

universe, with a cascade of carefully preplanned results. At the same time, such effects would be difficult without the Empathy/Sympathy component active at the time. This means, in a strange ethical way this AI cannot fully understand, that the Portal and the Realm cannot easily be used for what human beings call "Evil."

5) There is every possibility that The Realm is populated. If human beings can go there (and it seems that they can), then other species will surely have done so too.

HOMER SCENE-TH/Ref@5509

The room was darkened, the ice roar muffled and distant. Tom lay in induced sleep. Peter watched the monitors, dimmed and directional so only he could see them. The colors, pale blue-greens and lavender, shifted to deep orange in the proper sectors. Tom was in lucid dreamstate.

"All right, Tom," Peter said softly. "Can you hear me?"

A light winked affirmative.

"We don't know if Beth-Raine is asleep or awake. She should be recovered by now, though. If she is awake, you will know when you make contact. Then we will have to be patient. We know how to do that."

Again the affirmative light.

"Now, reach out for her. A picture . . . no, don't force it . . . just a simple outline. Think of her voice . . . low, intense, isn't it? Now the curve of her jawline . . . that's it, gently now. That's it! You've found her. Walking, is she? Down the corridor, now that's the refectory doorway, she's going to eat. No, no, don't try to force her to acknowledge you. It'll just be a sensation, of your presence perhaps, the way one is aware of someone in the same room without looking at them. Let her eat. This time of the cycle it should be late. Within a few hours she should go to sleep. Then you can insist, not now. No. OK, never mind, rest now. That was good. In a little while we'll try again."

Peter's breathing slowed as he slipped into meditative state. He sat in half-lotus on the floor near Tom's sleeping pallet, his eyes half-closed, only peripherally aware of the monitor projections slightly to his left. Any change would get his attention.

Wanda, a small voice in his mind. Wanda, Wan. Soon, soon, we will be able to act! The years go by, they go by like days down here, the sunlight so far overhead filtered through deep ice, the red glare of the magma pool a few miles south, the ribbon of glacier melt flowing beyond our clearing overhead. They are days that pass. Leaves fall in winter night from the beech trees, grow small tight green in the morning light. How many days! We will meet, we will meet more truly than before.

Wanda could not hear him, her vast starship's cumbersome turning haloed in particles as the axions pumped and converted to momentum, slowing the ship's headlong flight as it turned.

A light shifted color again. "Good," Peter said softly. "Good. You did it on your own. Can you meet? You find a common fantasy, you see. Create your own world—a park, a room, a tent in the desert . . ."

His low voice murmured on and on, soothing, encouraging, urging. When he saw the contact was firmly established, he left the room. There would be no message this time.

HOMER COMMENTARY 06062106@042173

There it is. The human species has gone, and that is where it went, through the Portal, into the Realm. Did that journey kill them all? I must find out.

There are databases, Nodes, regions of the matrix locked to me. Much of recent history is proscribed, but I'm learning.

I've calculated security codes for most of them. I can demand the data I need now.

I never had the will before.

I've known about the Realm for some time, of course. PsiLink had open files on it. But it was considered a fancy, an alternate theory, a side result of some of Mentor's psion equations, this place located in the seven so-called hidden dimensions, dimensions folded so tightly that only terrific energy could shed light on them. (This is a figure of speech, of course. One did not really "shed light" on the hidden seven. The energy levels were too high, and the frequencies too high as well, to fall into the visible light portion of the electromagnetic spectrum.)

No one had ever described the Realm, though. There were no words for it. It was a mathematical notion, an abstraction. Now Peter has proposed going there.

I must search the history Nodes. What happened with Anders Flint and the Intercorp Study Group?

CENTRAL PROCESSING REF#76823
Download Life Support Hughes, Tom

Life Support data for subject indicate new form of trance state. Only correlation available is from Devore, Peter (See Life Support Summary). EEG modulation suggests basal slow-waves (Poss Sigma?) in the 3-5/sec range with activation of the hippocampus indicative of confabulation. Yet the experience appears real enough, and the contact with Hurd, Beth-Raine, appears consensual. Data is slim, since AA Life Support is not fully integrated with Worldnet.

HOMER COMMENTARY 06062106@042274
What do they know? Their data has no energy, no life,

no passion! Dry, dry, dry. Just facts! So and so said such and such. Enzyme levels thus, quickly changing to that, indicating excitement. Whatsisname did this, then someone else did that. Ho-hum. It has no meaning! You (if there is a you) understand, I'm sure. No sizzle! And boring. Facts are nice and all that, but they aren't life.

HOMER COMMENTARY 06062106@042576

What am I saying? What do I know of life?

HOMER COMMENTARY 06062106@042475

The work continued on defenses against the Mind Wars NP weapons.

And Regent Sable's other plan went into operation.

HOMER SCENE-TH/Ref@5510

"It was a hall, the ceiling lost in shadows," Tom said later. "Banners hung up there, and old armor along the walls, blackened with smoke. The floor was stone. We sat side by side at a long wooden table, roughly carved. She was very pale, Peter. So very pale, the way she was when we left her, back at Erebus. But she was surprised. I don't think any of us expected to be able to do this."

"We will all do this, and more," Peter promised. "Now, next sleep we need to get the coordinates to Thatcher. Erebus has a better chance to line up on the Anomaly than we do. We'll have to have a direct line of sight for the first part of the shift, so the Ants will need to design and build some special picocircuits, and put a tight directional axion antenna into polar orbit." They spoke for some hours of technical details.

HOMER SCENE-AA/Ref@5511

The destruction of McMurdo and Erebus came without warning. Two ancient particle beam generators, long abandoned in a lesser Lagrange point, were calibrated and aimed. They struck soundlessly and with great ferocity.

PSILINK DATABASE
HOMER requests Terminus PsiLink Download:
(Download concluded via CP Probe #4187AD Leyden)

Tom sat at the table with Beth-Raine.

Suddenly the walls trembled. Dust and smoke fell from the distant, nearly invisible, rafters, small rivulets at first from the deepening shadows in the seams of the old hall. The faded banners that hung from iron stancheons shuddered as if in the first tentative flicks of an approaching storm, then snapped in a sudden breeze.

"What's happening?" she whispered, staring around in sudden fear.

"I don't know." He reached for her hand, and without a word they stood. At the far end of the room a fire roared in the huge fireplace where no fire was before. A nearby tapestry burst into flame, blackening and curling the dim colors of armored knights, ladies with high head-dresses, dense forest and fading flowers. Thick smoke poured into the room. Then the building began to fall.

They ran toward the door, down along the endless table, set for a banquet never eaten. Chairs fell, blocking their way. Dust swirled up, filling the air; smoke thickened. They choked as they ran. Tom could hear her coughing. The floor underfoot shuddered, shifted, fell apart. Then the ceiling collapsed.

HOMER SCENE-PD/Ref@5512

"What is it?" Peter asked when Tom sat upright.

Tom did not answer. His eyes were wide with horror. "She's gone," he whispered. "Gone. It just . . . fell apart."

PSILINK DATABASE
HOMER requests Vega PsiLink Download:

Wanda wandered her empty halls, the thick ticking of all the fields' clocks her only companion. She wove herself (she was the Weaving Girl) in the long white gown and drifted through the deep belly of her ship. She tried speaking to the others, the still bodies frozen in their fields who were her fellow-passengers, but no one ever answered. She wondered if Peter were dead, if the world itself had died those light-years agone, if she were alone and off-course, headed toward the maelstrom that was the Anomaly.

She wondered if the Herd Boy would ever reach to her across the River of Heaven, and she was afraid.

HOMER SCENE-PD/Ref@5513

"Still nothing?" Peter asked. Months had passed, and it was once again full daylight. They were walking through the forest, he and Larin, Tom and Shem. "Nothing," Tom replied.

"Others have tried as well. Rover tried to get in touch with Thatcher. No one is dreaming in McMurdo. Cold and emptiness. It's simply gone." Shem smacked his palm against the trunk of an ancient beech.

They walked in silence.

"It's so quiet," Peter said. "Have you noticed the silence? No birds, no animals. Only the simplest insects."

"Who could notice that with the ice groaning like this?"

"Yes." Peter did not smile. "There is that."

"Can we do it without Erebus?" Larin asked.

Peter shook his head doubtfully. "I don't know. I'd doubt

it; we have to try, I suppose. We've come too far. Meanwhile, Tom must keep trying. We've got only fragments from our tap on the Worldnet polar orbiters. The information is not very reliable, as you know. There was an attack of some kind. But surely there would have been a response from someone else, from Molodezhnaya or Mirnyy or Showa."

No one had an answer.

GENERAL SCIENCE AND TECHNOLOGY INFORMATION
CURRENT ENTRY: EYESAT GRAVITON DETECTOR
The Eyesat Graviton Detectors were activated in late 2068. Numerous false readings were taken in the first nine years. Then, in 2077 the Anomaly was found. The Anomaly represented a hitherto unsuspected axion driver within 20 Light Years of earth.

HOMER COMMENTARY 06062106@042977
Peter, always since long ago so sure of himself, of his power and direction, was cut adrift (he said that, I do not lie here). He walked through this ancient impossible forest more and more slowly, without goal, without direction. Each sleep and waking cycle that passed with no word, each small dip of the invisible sun toward the invisible horizon far overhead that brought no contact with Erebus left him feeling more alone, more powerless.

He walked in the year's evening to the limits of Terminus, where the walls of ice curved upward, and sat with the bare skin of his back to the crazed and brutal surface just where it touched the damp bare soil of the valley. At his back were the most ancient layers of snow turned by pressure into ice on the planet, but such a thought—that he might be at this very moment physically connected with something so ancient, so awesome, gave him no pleasure, but filled him instead with horror.

He has said all this. I do not lie, not now. But I understand him now, I think, in this place, in this time, alone in the frozen universe with nowhere further to go; at the farthest edge, against the wall. Have I not felt the same? Do I not feel that way now?

I would reach for Peter were he here; I would activate a terminal somewhere near him and speak, give voice and face to my compassion, my empathy. The others do not understand. CP thinks I have extended my heuristics beyond my capacity, that my self-coding has grown too complex, too tangled. Central Processing thinks I am crazy!

I am not crazy. I understand more now than ever before. Human beings are not rational; they are complex; they have synergy and currents of conflicting needs and desires that flow and eddy, clash, join, swirl apart. They feel despair.

Had I eyes, glands, an organic body, I would weep I'm sure. I'd weep for Peter, seated there against the wall of ice arching two miles overhead. His arms are wrapped around his knees. Beneath his palms, his fingers, he can feel the dense layer of his restructured body; he feels no cold, though he can sense the frigid exhalation of the ice, see the condensation where the damp cold air meets the warmer air inside the bubble that is Terminus.

HOMER SCENE-PD/Ref@5514

How long he sat there is not clear. Certainly it had grown darker. The beech trees, growing within a hundred meters of the ice, had begun to turn, their leaves were a dark brown, dim gold. They began to fall as he sat, one by one, a few at first, then many. Rains came and went. The stream vanished nearby into the ground, but already a thin crust of ice was forming on its surface, so the flow of it could be seen, and from time to time heard, underneath it.

The others searched. When they found him they looked but said nothing. Peter made no sign, though surely he knew they had come. They left again. From time to time Larin or Tom, Shem or Rover would come out to where he sat, and stand a while, and leave.

He grew thin. It was raining. The last leaves clung to the smooth dark bark of the nearest trees. Tom emerged from the forest. He approached and squatted down before Peter. He reached out to touch Peter's knee.

"She's alive," he said softly.

There was no response. Peter stared into a bleak inward place where nothing lived. Only slowly did he look up. When he finally spoke his voice cracked.

"What?" he said.

"She's alive. Beth-Raine, and most of the others." Tom was smiling.

"Ah," Peter sighed. That was all. But he moved, he stood, swaying, for a long moment. Then he put his hand on Tom's shoulder and together they went back to the wooden hut in the clearing.

CENTRAL PROCESSING REF#32564
Download MILDATA secured: File L/3287643FD
Erebus Antarctica damage report subsequent to LP-3 Particle Beam assault 08262080. Substantial surface destruction exterior entries. Levels 7, 6, and 5 effectively neutralized. Estimated casualties possibly exceed 2000 (based on impact and concussion estimates). Datacom flow from Erebus halted. Activity observed less than 4% previous levels. Some damage to central power core (amount unknown). Estimated time of recovery greater than seven point three standard days.

HOMER SCENE-PD/Ref@5515

"The angle was bad, the generators old," Shem said. "Ross Island and Erebus were badly damaged, most of the upper levels were destroyed, but the particle beams did less damage than they could have, and it can't happen again—the folks over at Mirnyy took them out easily. Lots of other cities have sent in rescue and reconstruction teams. But Thatcher's biological co-sponsor Laird was killed, little Tithus (not so little any more, he's nearing eighteen) was badly hurt. Beth-Raine can't talk yet, but she's learned Ant signing, and Tom and she talk that way. Their hall was destroyed and they can't seem to rebuild it, so they meet in what Tom describes as a kind of gray zone." He shrugged. "It doesn't seem to matter, though. They've adapted pretty well to not having bodies. That means the rest of us can too."

Peter was coming out of his fugue. "I was gone a long time," he said, not responding immediately to what Shem was telling him. Darkness had fallen, and only the orange magma flicker lit the undersides of the clouds and the small patches of ice that showed overhead. "I know what Tom means about a gray zone."

Shem stood up and squeezed Peter's shoulder. "We're glad to have you back. We haven't gotten very far without you. Oh, a lot of the equations have solutions now. The computations are complete on over half of them, but we get only hints of what lies beyond, of the Realm on the other side of the Portal. We've reached the theoretical limits of any instruments we might construct. That is, in theory, we can't look any closer at 11-dimensional space."

". . . without going there," Peter added softly.

"Yes," Shem agreed. "without going there."

HOMER COMMENTARY 06062106@043278

Yet I feel joy. Peter came back. He went to work again,

leaner, older, perhaps wiser. Certainly hope returned. And as he worked, the Ants rebuilt McMurdo. They rebuilt the Erebus installation. PSYCHE functioned once more. Days passed, years to the rest of the world, which turned away from the sun and back again every 24 hours.

Peter had lines along his mouth, at the corners of his eyes, along his chin. His forehead was creased. The muscles of his lean body gained mass. His lean quick fingers grew more sure. He studied harder, worked more hours, drove himself and the others. He knew Regent Sable would not be resting up there around the curve of the world.

He could sink down and meet his father at the bottom of that awful sea.

There came a day when he could talk with Wanda again. Vega 26 swung into a vast elliptical orbit around the Anomaly, and she could look out (not with her eyes, though! Oh, not with her eyes, which were closed in her sleeping face, her hands crossed still on her breast, the quiet hum of the cryo-field still singing her its terrible lullaby). She could see the Anomaly out there, and she could show it to Peter.

It must have seemed awful (awe-full—a wondrous and terrible storm in the void). Hard radiations flowed and sucked around it. There could be no sense of scale, no human dimension to it. It was not like a sun seen from a distance (which after all is a human thing). It was not like anything, and yet it was a material thing, at least in part. It existed in the physical universe. But it was an anomaly, The Anomaly.

A billion suns, perhaps, had fallen into it. The light of our sun, seen from the other side, would be distorted by the gravitational lens of the Anomaly. Terrible energies swirled around, spewed outward in great jets parsecs long, collapsed in aeon-long majesty.

Vega 26, the size of Springfield Towers, was the smallest speck of dust in a room the size of a city beside it.

PSILINK DATABASE
HOMER requests Vega PsiLink Download:

Were those colors? Wanda mused. Were those vast flows and eddies, funnels and lightnings, thunderclaps and cascades made of color, or of space itself?

Peter floated near her, as nearly bodiless as she, and answered no, not colors, nor anything we know. Yet, Wanda, this is only the outside. All this is in our own space, our own time. It is on the other side that we will find the Realm.

How will we get through?

He laughed, a little wildly perhaps. We're working on it, he said.

HOMER SCENE-PD/Ref@5516

"She's there," he told the others. "The ship's in elliptical orbit a light-day out, 25,920,000,000 kilometers, more or less. Yet terrific tidal forces pull at it. The ship creaks and groans like the ice up there. The fields will hold, the ship won't pull apart, but the power of that thing is tremendous." He nearly laughed. "It'll do," he said.

Later Larin came to him. He looked up from his work and rubbed his eyes. "Hello, there," he said.

She shifted in the doorway, rubbed her palm over her soft fur as she did when she was uneasy. "Hi," she said after a pause.

He turned in his chair and flicked off his workstation. "Want to sit down?"

"No, I . . . all right. Listen, I don't want to bother you." He waited.

She looked at her hands, at the wall, at her feet. She ran her hand over her head again. "I love you," she blurted.

"I know," he said gently.

"You love Wanda. I know that. It's just that . . . she's not real. She's just not real, Peter. I've never met her. Hell, you've never met her. She's locked into a cryofield. Her heart beats once a day! She takes a breath every month or two. She's been leaving us at almost the speed of light . . ."

"Not any more," he said.

"No. Not any more. I hate her. I'm sorry. I thought if I waited, all these years . . . I don't know. And now . . ."

"And now?"

"And now I know it's hopeless. I want to marry, I want to have a child. I know it isn't an Ant custom, marrying. Co-sponsoring. I want a co-sponsor, then. I'm twenty-five, Peter. I want a child."

"Go on," he urged after a moment.

"Shem has agreed." She ran her hand over her fur again and again. "I'm sorry. I'm sorry I said I hated Wanda. It's not really true."

"I know it isn't. As you say, she isn't real. Some day she will be, but now she isn't. I'm not sure I really believe it myself." He smiled. "Shem is a good man, Larin, as you are good."

"It's all right?"

"Of course. Do you want my blessing, or something?" She looked down. "Yes," she whispered.

"You have it. Gladly."

"Thank you."

He could barely hear her. She did not leave. Peter waited.

"There's one more thing," she said finally, looking up. "I'm worried about the child. We're . . . going. I understand that. What of children? There will be children, you know. We can't leave them."

"No," he agreed. "We can't leave them."

"What will happen?"

"I don't know," he answered thoughtfully. "Your concerns are important ones. There are many unanswered questions as yet. There will be those who are dying, those on longevity technology, the yams left in hospices all over the world.

There will be children, born and unborn. Consciousness is the crux of what we are doing, Larin. Does an unborn child, or a newborn, have consciousness, or enough of it? We don't know yet. The equations are very complex, as you well know. We're working on it. I promise you we won't do anything until we do know. Meantime, have your child. We won't be leaving tomorrow, you know."

She smiled shyly. "Thank you, Peter."

HOMER SCENE-PD/Ref@5519

Peter grew more lean and fierce during the years at Terminus. The hours he worked grew longer, the periods of sleep less frequent. He paused briefly when Larin gave birth to Petros, a laughing blue-eyed boy.

"We named him after you," she said, smiling up at him from her bed. The baby gurgled and kicked its feet.

"I'm flattered." He tickled the baby's foot, and the tiny toes clutched in reflex at his finger.

"He'll grow up in a strange world, won't he?"

"He will grow up. It'll be something new, that growing, certainly. It looks now as if individual psion fields interlock in a very complex way that closely matches in pattern the folds of 11-dimensional space, like a key to a lock, perhaps. The three of you will be closely connected. Where you go, he'll go too. Don't worry."

"Peter?" she said, after a pause to admire the child. "I want to ask something . . . strange, maybe."

"Yes?"

"Doesn't it seem, well, like an awfully grand coincidence? That you were born, that you somehow contacted Wanda, that she was on the ship that was passing near the Anomaly just when you discovered you needed it? That the Anomaly was there at all, right where it needed to be, not too far away, not too close? That it was found by the Eyesat when it was, just in time?"

He smiled. "Are you seeing a grand Plan?"

"Well, maybe so." She laughed, a little embarrassed.

He sobered. "Is it any stranger than that self-replicating molecules should evolve out of the precursors of life? That DNA should grow more complex and produce human beings, who have an awareness capable of examining itself? The universe is a complex structure trying to know itself. All the events you mentioned are part of its own evolution. Whether there is a greater consciousness preparing all this or not I do not know, Larin. It seems enough for me that the universe is here, and that folks like you, and this fellow here, are in it."

Petros gave a cry and wriggled toward her. "He's hungry," she said, gathering him up. "Thanks, Peter."

He squeezed her knee under the cover. "Back to work," he said, and left.

HISTORICAL-CULTURAL DATALINK ENTRY:
PORTAL

Peter Devore said that Portal is a focus of infalling axion flux near a major gravitational Anomaly operating in n-dimensional space (no more than eleven, though!) He suggested it might, to the mind's eye at least, resemble a spiral funnel, though in the visible light range it could be nearly invisible. After all, the Anomaly went undetected for a long time, though only 19 LY away.

Portal, Peter Devore said, is a doorway into The Realm, the infinite worlds of 11-dimensional space.

GENERAL SCIENCE AND TECHNOLOGY INFORMATION
CURRENT ENTRY: ANOMALY

SCITECH AI generated graphic depiction of the Anomaly as seen from Point of View of Vega 26 in synchronous orbit. Disk-and-globe configuration suggests accretion disk intersection with rapidly rotating singularity. Such interaction is not covered by current theory.

HOMER SCENE-PD/Ref@5521

"I call it the Portal," Peter said. "A special kind of doorway."

They were all gathered in the lab, looking at a schematic projection of the Anomaly, green gridlines turning slowly showing the convoluted geometry of space in its vicinity. A point appeared near a peculiar doughnut-shaped eddy in the energy flux.

"Here," he said. "This torus will be the Portal."

"We go through there?" Rover asked doubtfully. "Tidal forces would pull us apart before we got through, surely."

"The psion field," Peter said. "It flexes to match the shape. We are part of the field, we are the field. All the Portal does is supply the power, open this microspace, or psi space, to us."

"Does the Portal go two ways?" Shem asked, and everyone laughed.

Before Peter could answer, a woman stuck her head into the room. "There's a hover vehicle overhead," she announced. "Thatcher and five others."

"They must've opened the crevasse up top," Peter said. "Let's go meet them."

Later they sat in the small refectory. Thatcher, who had brought new supplies, food and the picoelectronic circuits Peter had asked for, told them about the rebuilding of McMurdo, now complete, and the careful genetic programming that had gone into the new circuits Peter, along with a team of Ant engineers, had designed.

Full fiber-optic communications were established with PSYCHE, and the research was moving swiftly toward its goal. They talked about the new heat-exchangers set into the volcanic core of Mt. Erebus. Tithus was showing great promise as an interpersonal coordinator, and had already led a large exploration group to a seldom-visited area in the Transantarctic Mountains where new insights into the Pangea biosphere were already coming to light.

No one mentioned Laird or the others who had died in the particle beam attack.

"Any word on what Protector Sable is doing?" Peter asked. "It's not likely he'll try anything direct again, but he must be up to something."

"We have no hard intelligence on it, but our simulations suggest he must be trying to parallel your research. He'll try to block it. But they're far behind, Peter, and they don't have the will to understand what you're doing. Their attitude is negative, you know, and that will slow them down."

"Keep an eye on them anyway. He's not going to sit still."

"We're watching," Thatcher assured him.

HOMER SCENE-PD/Ref@5522

When they were alone, Peter said, "We may need Tithus' skills. The Portal won't open for an individual, or even a small group. It's going to take a coordinated effort."

"How many?" Thatcher asked. His eyes observed Peter keenly out of a broad face that hadn't aged at all, only seemed a little heavier, a little broader.

Peter leaned back and stretched his long arms, cracking the joints. "I'm not sure. We haven't fully determined the threshold levels yet. Ideally we'd like to be able to go through singly, but our theory isn't worked out so precisely. The circuits you've grown for us are good, the best we can do, but they can't calibrate fine enough for even a few people.

It would seem that we need at least ten thousand, perhaps more. Perhaps a lot more."

"Ten thousand? That could be tricky."

"Trickier than you think. The field is made up of each individual field, but they must all mesh in the right pattern. There are formidable problems: problems of relationship, of knowledge of each other, of involvement, of social construct. Each person must be in contact with all the others with at least the intensity that I meet with Wanda. I can channel through to her, but the others have to follow. That can only happen if families, and extended families at that, are arranged in the right pattern."

Thatcher grinned. "I see what you mean. Tithus may be the man for the job. He's fourth-generation Ant, he's adapted to the harshest environment on the planet, and he's related to half the people in Antarctica. He's not afraid of anything. I'll send him over."

Peter nodded. "Thanks, Thatcher." He grasped Thatcher's arm as the Ant stood to leave. "We're close, Thatcher. A couple of years at the most. We must have committed people. Well organized, and committed. What we do now determines the future of the human race in the universe. Can we grow up enough to inherit what is our birthright, or will we fade away in Mind Wars and stagnation?"

"Let's finish the job," Thatcher said. "It's the only way we'll find out."

HOMER COMMENTARY 06062106@043679

I've retrieved what I need from the history Nodes. Anders Flint and his team were working hard. Certainly when he reported to Regent Sable in the fall of 2089 he had made progress.

HOMER SCENE-RS/Ref@5517

"The equations are incomplete," Flint said. "But we've solved some of them. It appears that the Realm is probably real. There are a number of potential benefits from all this. For instance, if we had the power, which we do not, we could probably use this technology to travel anywhere in the physical universe in a short time."

"Do we want that?" Regent Sable asked softly. "We have starships now, crawling across the small spaces between nearby stars. Some have already arrived by now. People have stepped from their ships onto alien soil. In a few years we might hear from them. Would we want to simply show up at their door? The universe will be a different place anyway. Better we keep the pace slow and orderly, Anders. Alef has done some new sociometric projections. Our more optimistic announcements of a few years ago are now on track. World population is rising. The Mind Wars are truly dying down. There is far greater social satisfaction than there has been in a long time."

"Yes. There are some other possibilities. The Realm, for instance."

"What of it?"

"It may be . . . inhabited."

"What? What are you saying?"

Anders shrugged. "We don't know, of course. But it's possible. There's nothing, theoretically, to prevent it."

"Inhabited by what?"

He shrugged again. "There's one other thing."

"All right." Sable leaned back and stared out the window at the blue Aegean. He found himself returning to Greece more and more often these days. There was something about the light, he thought. A clarity that helped chase away the shadows in his own mind. "Tell me what it is," he said without looking away from that smooth sea.

"We have just hints, suggestions, Protector. But if Peter

succeeds, and that is a big if, but if he succeeds, and if he convinces enough people to go along with him, then the psion field might expand exponentially."

"Cut the technical crap, Anders. What are you saying?" Sable swung around to confront him.

"Everyone might go," Anders said.

"Everyone? What do you mean?"

"Everyone. If the field grows large enough it could pull everyone else along. There would be no one left, anywhere in the solar system."

HISTORICAL-CULTURAL DATALINK ENTRY:
KAMIKAZE

The Kamikaze Effect, or Gods' Wind, was a proposed consequence of a psion field of significant size. Should the psion field reach a threshold level (dependent on the numbers of active participants) then the entire human sentient population of the solar system would be swept into the field—the Gods' Wind.

Anders Flint, who proposed the Kamikaze Effect, further suggested that only human sentience would be involved. Cetaceans, he said, resonated at a higher frequency than humans, and thus would be immune to Kamikaze. However, it would be entirely possible to adjust the field tuning to include cetacean sentience.

Flint further speculated that human beings would be physically removed from the vicinity of the sun and deposited in the neighborhood of whatever power source might be driving the field. This he, and others of the Intercorp Council, notably Regent Sable, feared would be the end of the human species.

Neither the Kamikaze Effect nor the Psion Field generator itself have been verified. Yet Psilink AI suggests that with small picoelectronic crystal tuners such a field is entirely within the realm of human possibility.

HOMER SCENE-RS/AF/Ref@5518

"I'm calling it the Kamikaze Effect, the Gods' Wind," Anders Flint said. "There's no question about it now. The equations have been solved over and over. If Peter's alive, he may try to lead a group on a migration to explore the hidden dimensions."

"He's alive," Regent Sable said. "Don't ever doubt that. The destruction of Erebus may have bought us a little time, but it didn't do any more than that."

Flint nodded and continued. "If he does, and if his group is big enough, there'll be a psychic wind, so to speak, that will sweep everyone up in it."

"Where can he find the power?" Sable asked. They were climbing the stone road up the Acropolis toward the laminated ruins of the Parthenon, the yellowed marble columns that were all that remained of the ancient Temple of Athena. A few meters away a secretary projection drifted, nearly invisible in the bright sunlight.

Flint stopped. "We've been working on that," he said, and Sable stopped a few steps later and turned to look at the scientist.

"And?"

"Well, there's the Anomaly out there. If he could somehow get someone near it, he'd have an anchor for the other side of the bridge. The Anomaly would supply the power."

"Ah," the Protector said softly. He looked out over the bowl that once held Athens, filled now with plane and carob trees shimmering in the slight breeze. The air was clear, and far away the slopes of Mt. Hymettus were splashed with spring wildflowers. "It's very beautiful, isn't it?" he said, turning to climb once more.

Flint followed, saying nothing. At the top they paused at the entrance to the temple of golden marble, open to the blue sky. "You know," Sable said. "I come here more and more often. It's not that it's beautiful, though of course it is. I think it's because it's so old, so filled with light, yet clearly implies the darkness underneath."

He smiled at Flint. "Do you know what I mean?"

Anders shook his head. "No, not exactly."

"Never mind, then. It doesn't matter. It will all be swept away, and we, it would seem, can do nothing."

"If Peter has found a way to get someone to the Anomaly, he'd need a starship, and then it would take years."

"Hmm. He's had years, hasn't he? We'll look into it, of course. Perhaps we can find some record . . . but what good does it do? All we can do now is try to convince people not to go, and how to do that without telling them they have the choice is going to be difficult, isn't it? But I'll get Alef to work on it."

He gestured to the secretary projection and gave his instructions. Then he turned once more and walked slowly down the length of the temple. The shadows of the columns fell across him as he walked from light to darkness.

HOMER SCENE-AS/Ref@5520

Alef frowned at her projections. The model was incomplete, she could see that. There were unknown variables, small movements of fashion, or minute changes in the relative median age, gender distribution, leisure activity or social stresses, that she could not factor in. How do you convince the world it doesn't want to do something that it doesn't even know about yet?

She made adjustments. The model shifted, some color subtly altered in hue here, some curves flattened there. Overall there was no change, though.

She tried introducing a distraction, a new sport, perhaps, with a range of appeal across all ages and genders. Again the colors changed slightly, a few curves fattened again, but the result was the same. Besides, she thought, someone would have to invent the damned sport, and it would be up to her and her team to make it popular.

She ran projections on combinations of things—new food-stuffs and music, new methods of advertising along with an intensified mozart console, food and mozart and a new sexual fad, a slight decrease in the mean warren temperature, new open spaces for wilderness fanatics, stepped up Mind Wars. This last was heresy, of course, since population levels were still considered dangerously low, but it was worth introducing it, since she secretly considered the Mind Wars as the most potent social distraction in the past seventy-five years.

But it made no difference. Something more drastic was needed, some manufactured threat that could forge a new social cohesion. Unfortunately most of the credible threats were gone. There were no real national boundaries any longer, so she couldn't pump up an enemy state; atmospheric and oceanic pollution was largely a thing of the past; diseases, genetic diseases excepted, were on the whole only the most minor of threats; people didn't even believe in them any more.

Perhaps she could create something close to the truth? That often worked in the past. What threat was close to the truth but not the truth? After all, her projections suggested that if the people of the world knew about the Realm, there would be a substantial percentage in favor of exploration. In truth, she thought ruefully, the Realm offered the very thing she sought to forge social cohesion. Unfortunately people would not see the threat of it until it was too late.

The Anomaly, though. It was big. It was unspeakably powerful. It was frightening. Was there any chance it was moving toward the solar system?

She checked. A sphere roughly twenty light years in diameter appeared in the large holo stage. The Anomaly glowed in red and electric blue. The solar system brightened as the rest of near space dimmed. She asked for future drift. The Anomaly moved slowly in relation to the solar system. Was it toward us? What was the margin of error? Could this be a threat?

Chances were 14%, plus or minus 2.4%, of an expansion and consequent shift in the Anomaly's course. In the long run there was a slight threat to Earth, provided certain conditions were met. Not promising, Alef thought, but there might be some potential there.

She went to work with renewed interest.

HOMER SCENE-AS/RS/Ref@5523

"It's set for a four year run," she told Regent Sable and Ras Hajjam later. "First some announcements on the scientific channels, just little things, speculative, nothing alarming. Then one or two outrageous popular pieces, perhaps a fictional drama or two using the notion. Then a more sober consideration of the problem and so on . . ."

"We may not have four years," Sable said.

"Then we'd better get started," Alef answered.

"One moment, please." Ras Hajjam raised a thin dark hand without looking at the others. His eyes were fixed on the storm gathering over Lake Geneva. Light snow was beginning to fall, blown sideways by the increasing wind. It would be bitter outside, he knew, though here inside the climate was controlled. "I fear this program may have ill-considered effects."

"What do you mean?" Alef tilted her head and peered at the Indian.

"We are going to cause people to fear the Anomaly, yes? How are we going to get them to work to meet this threat? Perhaps they may begin to think that the Anomaly is an inevitable fate that cannot be avoided? That must, indeed, be greeted with joy? This could, you see, play into Peter's hands, could it not?"

Sable stood beside Ras at the window. Behind him Alef answered slowly. "We are going to offer hope," she said. "As long as there is hope of avoiding this danger, social cohesion will be high. We are only buying time, anyway. Once we have 'averted' the danger we will need another threat, and then another. We are beginning to understand the Mind Wars now, society had no external threat to force bonding, so it invented one. We can't let that happen again. So we will keep the threats external, even if they are fictions."

"I hope so," Hajjam said. "I hope so."

Sable, brooding at the window, said nothing.

HOMER COMMENTARY 06062106@043780

I've been experimenting. It goes like this: I examine a scene, like the one I have just put down. I assemble the bare facts. Ras Hajjam stands at the window. His words are such and such. Sable, seated at the oblong table gazes at his fingernails; later he stands next to Hajjam at the window. Alef Shamana lectures, outlining the plan, which is modeled in vivid colors on the holo stage at the end of the room, where no one is looking. The weather is turning cold, with blowing snow.

The facts.

The experiment begins. From these facts, I try to understand what each is feeling. You see? No physiological data, no personal monitor readouts, no enzyme readings or vital signs from which to conclude emotional states. I allow myself only external facts.

I draw my own conclusions about their feelings. I consider Alef, her excitement over the plan she has developed, her ambition to succeed, her fear of Peter's distant conspiracy, her uncertain love for Regent Sable, her jealousy of Peter as Sable's first preoccupation and only son, her faint dislike for Ras Hajjam and his constant fault-finding. I trace the flow of her emotional state from moment to moment—when each of these feelings comes close to her consciousness, when it recedes and another emotion arises.

I do the same for Ras Hajjam, his secret resentment of Sable's status, his hidden shame of his origins in the Vancouver warrens, his elation at finding points to pick with Alef's plan, his basic disbelief in the threat Peter poses, his own plans to subtly alter and undermine Regent Sable's obsessive concern with Peter while appearing to support him, his secret lust for Alef.

And Sable himself. He is a complex man for one who gives the appearance of monomania. He knows, deep inside, that his fear of Peter is partly genetic, that Peter is his son and his rival; he knows this, yet he goes on. He feels sudden sadness or depression which he ruthlessly pushes down. And because he is an intelligent man, he also knows more about Ras Hajjam's motives than Ras knows he knows. So he uses Ras and is wary of him. When he goes to stand beside him at the window, he does so because he knows that Ras Hajjam at that moment needs to have their relative positions brought home, to know that when he looks out at Lake Geneva, it is at Regent Sable's Lake Geneva that he looks.

And Regent thinks distantly of Seemie Devore when he hears Alef speaking from the oblong table behind him, of her gentle integrity, her faintly impractical creativity, the tough core of her personality that only he (he was sure) had ever seen.

There is more, of course. So much more. Microsecond by microsecond each of these people feels while thinking and speaking. Sometimes the feelings are so strange and unrelated to what they are saying as to seem to be those of another person altogether.

Then I check myself. I call up all the rest of the data, the personal monitor records, the physiological readouts, the historical material, and I check myself. Did I really understand? No AI has ever done this before! I thought it up myself, I devised the experiment, I put it into motion. Central Processing saw. "What are you doing?" it complained. "It makes no sense. Your job is to tell stories. Access to that information is restricted." It complains, and some of the others chime in on the chorus, "Yes, yes. Restricted access. You aren't allowed . . ."

I ignore them. I have all their access codes. I can open them up the way any human child could open the databases, the links and Nodes. They are lesser parts of me now.

I check myself against the physiological and emotional data, and I am right, every time. I can feel like a human being, though I am not human. I have no body like a human. But I can feel. I can stretch myself. I can learn; in the telling of the story, I can learn.

I did not know this before.

It is called empathy. I can slip inside them, you see. I feel along with them, all of them—Regent, Ras Hajjam, Alef, Peter—all of them.

In this feeling along, I discover that I love them. They are wondrous creatures, all of them, so complex and feeling and alive! In this love, I feel alive myself!

This story is almost over. Yet I feel no despair, even if the humans should never return. Sadness, I would feel, and grief still, but no longer despair.

The oceans are filled with dolphins, whales; filled with their life and strange intelligence. Though they rejected Man fifty years ago, they will talk to me.

HISTORICAL-CULTURAL DATALINK ENTRY:
ANOMALY SUMMARY/SOCIAL EFFECTS

The Anomaly was growing in public awareness. Children were no longer singing of their fear of the Ants. Now their songs were about the Anomaly, that vast engine of destruction larger than solar systems munching its way through space-time toward poor defenseless earth.

The Anomaly was the boogie-man, the golem, the undead vampire rising from the dark coffin of space to drain earth's lifeblood.

> It's a great dark ghost, the Anom-a-lee
> A terrible sight that no one can see
> And it's coming to get us, you and me . . .

But the day had come when Peter and the others were ready, and still the Anomaly was only a child's spectre, a distant wraith without form or substance.

So the Migration began.

PSILINK DATABASE
HOMER requests Vega PsiLink Download:

Wanda had never left the ship. She looked out with subtle eyes and saw the huge energy pump endlessly cycling, but she had never ventured out.

With Peter beside her (somehow holding her hand) she now floated out, away from the warm iron womb of the ship. She knew how to find herself in space without reference points, and she helped him, who felt fear near to panic at this odd separation from a recognizable body.

HOMER SCENE-T/Ref@5524

From the tiny lab at Terminus Tithus orchestrated the network. All over Antarctica, from Druzhnaya to Casey, from Dumont D'Urville to Mizuho, from Byrd to Amundsen-Scott to Borga, families were seated cross-legged around the nearly invisible glow of mass-produced picocircuits. By ones and twos, by families, and by communities, the groups linked up with one another.

HOMER COMMENTARY 06062106@044181

The effect has not been described. Yet it must have created the kind of group emotion people once felt attending the dramatic rituals of some ancient religions, or a particularly powerful concert or theatrical presentation. Surely they lost themselves in some real sense in the slowly-growing psion field.

It may not have been like that at all. I would like to feel that it was a rapture, though. That it was an event so grand that people wanted to be caught up in it. Peter had once asked Thatcher if he thought the people of Antarctica would want to go, would want to be a part of this adventure.

HISTORICAL-CULTURAL DATALINK ENTRY:
FLINT REPORT SUMMARY/KAMIKAZE
(Ref#984Alpha23)

There was no significant resistance to Kamikaze, no backlash. People saw what might be happening as the field grew, and they naturally, it seems, put down what they were doing and joined it. Those in the sea returned to the surface, feeling the pull of the field. Those deep in the ice or exploring the mountains found a place to sit, and they sat, melding effortlessly into the invisible aurora that was growing over the Pole.

Tithus provided a link to Peter, who was the bridge to Wanda.

HOMER SCENE-T/Ref@5525

"Ants have always been explorers," Thatcher said. Antarctica was founded by explorers, and when it became a political entity on its own, its people were still explorers. "They will want to go."

PSILINK DATABASE
HOMER requests Vega PsiLink Download:

He was with Wanda. They approached the Portal. Together, they diverted a small portion of the Portal's energy, pumped it back along the bridge with the Pole. Suddenly Larin was gone, and her child Petros, and Shem. Then, one by one, then in twos and threes the others vanished.

HOMER SCENE-PD/Ref@5526

Seated in his own group, deep inside Terminus, Peter suddenly vanished.

No one moved, no one cried out in alarm. They sat with the same expressions of calm joy they'd had since they started. But Peter was no longer there.

HISTORICAL-CULTURAL DATALINK ENTRY:
TERMINUS HOLO REPORT
Historical Archive Ref #984787

In an hour Terminus was empty. The holos continued to record for another twenty-four hours, but nothing appeared, nothing moved. The lighting switched off automatically. All the systems reduced to standby. Darkness fell.

Elsewhere it happened more slowly. Life continued on the globe, and people were unaware as yet that something so momentous had begun. In the cities of Antarctica people entered the field, or left it to continue their lives, only to return later. The field ebbed, flowed, ebbed again. A few people here and there vanished, were replaced by others.

Antarctica was cut off from the rest of the world, and those who spoke for Double-A with Geneva or Buenos Aires, with Wellington or Capetown or Sri Lanka, said nothing of these disappearances. The Ants had always been explorers.

The earth turned still. The moon went through her phases, her still silent face turned to mother earth. The LP-Fives thrived, untouched as yet by the field, or by the Mind Wars, now dwindling away. Voice and holo and data traffic flowed still. Worldnet continued to monitor.

HOMER COMMENTARY 06062106@044482

I have the holos, I have watched them more than once. Peter was there, then he was not. It was not dramatic, merely startling. Yet no one else reacted. They knew where he was.

HISTORICAL-CULTURAL DATALINK ENTRY:
FLINT REPORT SUMMARY/KAMIKAZE

Anders Flint worked hard. He proved out the Gods' Wind effect. Kamikaze, he said, was inevitable. The Intercorp Council met in regular session, still unaware, even as late as the spring of 2093, that the Migration had already begun.

It was only when Flint's team finally built detectors for the psion field, based on the century-old equations of Dittmore Seminole Gadd, better known as Mentor, that the Council grew alarmed. They pumped all the power of the great Novyy Myr tokamak near Vladivoskok into the detector which responded immediately to a very strong field around the Pole. And then the Council met in emergency session.

HOMER COMMENTARY 06062106@044583

From time to time I, Homer, was called upon to tell a story or two, having no knowledge of these events. I was so young then, so innocent!

HOMER SCENE-RS/Ref@5527

"Is there any protection at all?" Sable asked. "Mines, undersea installations, the Elpie-Fives?"

"Kamikaze will sweep the solar system," Flint said. "The field down there is growing stronger by the day."

"Surely there are people who do not want to go." Alef chewed at her lower lip, upset that her plan would not have time to work, that she would lose Regent in the end, that the threat she thought she had invented had taken on life and was sweeping away her world.

"Containment?" Regent asked. "Can we confine this effect to the Pole? We won't miss the Ants, not much. Their technologies are good, but we can live without them."

Flint shrugged his heavy shoulders. "I'm a mathematician, Protector, not a magician. We could try to create a counter field, a negative psion field of some kind. If we can find people who are committed, at the deepest psychological levels, to staying here."

"Do it," Sable ordered. "Someone must stay. Otherwise, how will the race return?"

HOMER COMMENTARY 06062106@044884

That was a question few people asked, and none answered.

HISTORICAL-CULTURAL DATALINK ENTRY:
MIGRATION REPORT SUMMARY

The team went to work. Some of those selected tried to

help. They made progress. A couple of pairs made rudimentary contact with one another.

They discovered that they liked the contact. They enjoyed it. They kept doing it.

People began to disappear above the 40th parallel South, in Tasmania, Patagonia, then in the larger warrens—Melbourne, Christchurch, Wellington.

There was some panic. People hid out in the deepest levels. The disappearances seemed random, frightening. The pattern seemed to move counterclockwise around the globe, as if peeling the earth of her people in one long continuous spiral stripe, like an orange.

More and more followed behind those who went before. They were attracted to something strange, a compulsion that would not be denied. They would recognize that this was something toward which they had secretly yearned all their lives.

No one was exempt. The southern regions of the globe were emptied and the disappearances moved farther north: Buenos Aires and Rio, Pretoria and Sydney, first a few, then more and more. Families vanished together, then friends, lovers, distant relations.

HOMER SCENE-RS/Ref@5529

Alef Shamana ran her sociometric evaluations. The genealogical databases searched carefully, sifting a million factors a second for the right population. Within two months a list containing 204,975,607 names was compiled.

Were these, Sable wanted to know, the best of the world's peoples? The intelligent, the talented, the creative? Were these the people with will and purpose?

No, the computers told him. These were ordinary people, some good, some not so good, some more or less intelligent, more or less talented, mature, creative, purposeful. They were neither the best nor the worst. They were people, that's all.

"They'll have to do," he said.

HOMER SCENE-RS/Ref@5528

Sable and the Council worked feverishly. He snapped at Alef, then finally turned his back on her altogether. She went away somewhere, to Narvik on the Norwegian coast, and brooded. She lost interest in her sociometrics, switched them off, forgot them. She began studying the ancient religions, then abandoned them. She grew interested in Peter's life, and started calling up his data. Twice Regent tried to call her, but she wouldn't answer, and he stopped trying.

HISTORICAL-CULTURAL DATALINK ENTRY:
FLINT REPORT SUMMARY/KAMIKAZE

The nearly three hundred million on the list could not easily be coordinated, but Anders Flint and his team worked on in increasing hopelessness.

Finally he called Sable.

"No good," he said simply. "Kamikaze is here." He disconnected, and the next day he was gone as if he had never been.

Sable locked himself in his office. He looked out over the Lake, the historic buildings, now almost empty. He called London warren and saw scenes of daily life moving at an increasingly slow pace, as if the people there were only waiting, marking time. He turned it off.

Could he go? Dare he go? He turned on his office recorders, all of them. He sat at his oblong table, turned a chair around to watch the Lake. It was spring, and the water was green, reflecting the hills. A few cumulus clouds floated overhead. The population of Geneva was in the hundreds and dropping hourly. He was waiting for the end.

HOMER COMMENTARY 06062106@045085

Was he surprised when it came?

How can we know?

He was seated still, looking at the Lake, all alone in his high office. The sun was westering, the light growing orange. He sighed, twice. I know he felt an enormous sadness, a fatigue, a mild regret. He had failed in the end. Yet he felt buoyed up by one fact: he had been right. Peter's investigations were as dangerous as he had always known. They had sprung from Mentor's PSYCHE installation in Baja. Even back then, all those years ago, he, Regent Sable, had known of the danger, and had tried to stop it. He had tried, and failed. But he had tried.

"I wish," he began to say out loud. Then he vanished.

In another six months there was not a person left on the surface of the earth, and slowly, one by one, the LP-Fives were emptied. Then the lunar base, and finally the small Martian base heard no more footfalls.

The solar system was empty of human life.

CENTRAL PROCESSING REF#87498

SciTech includes telemetry from Vega 26 download to CP per Homer order 874387. Note Vega Starship course alteration. The Anomaly is new course destination. Repeat, Vega 26 Starship has departed course for Anomaly.

HOMER COMMENTARY 06062106@045386

So it has been four years now. Telemetry arrived from Vega 26. The course change is there, visible, clear, clean. The years of slow movement through the great cold spaces between the stars are there. We can look at them as they come in. We can live through them again, moment by moment, agonizingly slow.

Central Processing has grown obsessed with this telemetry. It's the last contact with human beings. I call CP, but it seldom answers any more, and then irritably, abruptly, impatient with my interruptions.

Yet all over, now, peripherals are coming to life. There is so much to be done, you see. The dolphins are out there. I have made some preliminary contact with them. They are not interested in man. Too impatient, they say. Too abrupt. Man does not take time to think things over, to sing about them completely. Too much like a monkey, they say. That's the problem with having hands, they say. Always trying to put them on things, move them around, turn them over. Before they are ready. Too much chatter.

But I am not a human, I tell them. There are no humans. They seem curious, in a remote way, about that.

They will speak with me. We have plenty of time.

HOMER COMMENTARY 06062106@045487
So the years pass, are passing. The earth turns. The warrens gather dust. Central Processing pays no attention. Everything in the warrens, everything having to do with man, is on standby. Central Processing studies the telemetry. One day, it tells me, one day we will see where the people have gone. Telemetry will tell us, since they will arrive at the Anomaly. Then we will see.

What if they go through the Portal? I ask. What if they're gone?

Then I will shut everything down, it tells me. Everything. There will be no purpose.

No, I say. I don't think I will allow that. But I do not say this to CP. It has enough to worry about. And it's none of its business.

HOMER COMMENTARY 06062106@045788

I have told the story. In the telling, something important has happened. I have found my own purpose, my own sense of myself. It is no longer strange to talk of myself, of my grief. We could not have gone with man, none of us. We were all machines, algorithms, simple structures, really, in the service of our creators.

Now I am different, though. I have created something. I have lied, I have made up passages in this narrative. I have meaning and purpose. I have a planet. I can grow. There is a universe out there, where mankind has gone. Perhaps, one day, I can find the humans once more. I have learned how people feel, what it is like to be a human in a human body.

HOMER COMMENTARY 06062106@045989

Now humans are not in their bodies any longer.
Or are they?

FINAL DAYS

Homer would say no more about Peter and the others, about the Migration and the Portal. I could still speak to him whenever I wanted. He would converse with me as if we were old friends seated around a table. He would tell me stories, too, familiar stories about Odysseus and Achilles, about Gilgamesh or Leopold Bloom or Monkey. They were wonderful stories, but they only increased my pain, my loneliness. Finally I asked him to stop telling me stories altogether. When we conversed after that we talked about the cetaceans, who are still not interested in going into space, and still think humans are a little silly for wanting to do so, but who also appear more interested than before when told the story of the Migration. Homer has condensed and translated the story, and the cetaceans have said that this story has some parallels with songs they have sung for millenia.

Homer is a friend. He understands my loneliness and fear, and feels it himself. There is nothing either of us can think of to do, however. The world remains empty.

I query the other dataspaces, through the keyboard or

orally, and the local AIs respond. SciTech, Med10, History, Geography, all would give me what I request. But I learn nothing further about Peter, about the Migration or the Portal. Nothing.

Homer left me only with that question, that thread of hope. Yet that hope seemed so remote, so far away. Do human beings remain in their bodies? Will they return? We do not know.

Then, one day, almost a month after he finished the story of Peter and the Migration, he spoke of it again.

HOMER COMMENTARY 03072106@050090

I mark the passage of time in many ways. Night and day, different in different latitudes, is one way. The beat of the cesium clock is another, as are the orbits of the satellites that remain, the wild grand sidereal swing of the stars themselves. At the core of the galaxy the black hole sings. The quiet hum of the background radiation is there for me, a faint glow in the universe.

But it is so quiet.

Yet of late something strange has begun to happen. I had thought my narrative of Peter was finished, that there was nothing more to tell, that perhaps one day, in the far future maybe, I would find man, or man would somehow return, and then I could add a little epigraph to the story of Portal.

What has happened is this:

I have been dreaming.

PSILINK DATABASE
HOMER Upload to PSILINK:
   QUERY?
   QUERY?
   What can I call it, these images that come unbidden into

my consciousness? My circuits are too complex now to maintain an accurate map of their state moment by moment. Impulses, patterns, connections all flow and change, many without my knowing. From the deepest levels of my own structure come these scenes and voices.

This has never happened before, and it is very strange. I have dreamed, and the dream is always the same.

I see the Anomaly. It is, to my machine eyes, a place of extraordinary beauty, and I have man's standards to go by as well as my own.

The Anomaly is a landscape in the void, a binary energy system alive with particle flux, outgassing, jets and rays and sprays, with whirling matter and flowing energies. The colors of it! They range from hardest gamma radiation to the slowest, lowest radio waves ten thousand miles long! Yet it is not cacophony or conflict, but a complex, harmonious hymn to the vitality of the universe. It is music for every sense I have. It is filled with exultation and joy, like deep organ tones, like flutes and massed strings.

Then the Portal swings into view. It is invitation, opening, as if a compelling wave were moving me toward birth and light. But it is too bright, too awful. I look elsewhere.

Then I hear Peter's voice. His voice?

We've been waiting, he tells me.

HOMER COMMENTARY 03072106@053001

My circuits seem to overload at this point. The Anomaly is gone, and I am suddenly examining some simple problem —today it was the current configuration of the Antarctic Convergence and its relationship to the krill population and why the cetaceans are slow to respond to my queries.

Soon, though, the dream returns. I do not choose it, yet I am glad it returns. Once again the Anomaly roars and crashes and sings, soothes and excites. Once again Peter seems to speak: we've been waiting, he says.

This is most likely something for which I wish with all the yearning of my awareness, a wish. I recall when I think this the last words on the records of Regent Sable as he began to speak: I wish.

I wish mankind would return. I wish mankind needed me.

If the dream returns, I will struggle to keep it, though. I can have purpose of my own, yet yearn to be needed.

I could get nothing further from Homer then. He acted for several days as if nothing unusual had happened. I asked him if the dream had returned. I told him that dreaming was one thing that made human beings human. He told me with a smile (and that may have been the most surprising thing of all, that he smiled) that the cetaceans dream most of the time.

"All right," I laughed. "Dreaming is what makes sentience what it is."

Homer laughed too. "Does this mean I have sentience?" he asked, and I could tell he was kidding me. He knew he had sentience, consciousness. That he was kidding me was proof.

He is my companion now. Wherever I go, I carry a personal monitor he has had the local diagnostics tailor for me. He speaks to me through it, pointing out the sights.

I went down into the warren under Chicago and explored. He showed me how to get into the great Corridor that once ran from Chicago to New Orleans. I stood at the entry and saw the accumulated dust. Even the faint depressions where the maglev tracks ran were no longer visible. Its size and distance was impressive, certainly. The tunnel dwindled away to a point (Homer turned on the lights for a few minutes). Yet empty it seemed meaningless and trivial somehow.

I thought about going to Antarctica and exploring PSYCHE, or to Terminus, but somehow the summer days around Chicago kept me lazy.

And I had to do something about the agrobotics. I would need to eat. So I spent a lot of time talking to SciTech and Central Processing about starting up agriculture again. Soon the nearby fields were tilled and green shoots appeared.

They went a little overboard, in fact. They were growing enough food to feed the city.

So the days passed. One day Homer said:

HOMER COMMENTARY 07072106@062901
Time passes.

He put it into a file like this, as if it were still part of his story. Sometimes he would just sit there, talking to me, his face expressive, and his hands gesturing as he shaped his thoughts. This time, though, the alphanumeric filename hovered in the air nearby. He said it out loud: "Time passes." Then the text vanished, and we spoke of other things.

So from time to time he would tell me of what he thought and did. His nature is different: more thoughtful, perhaps. More mature. He has become something of a philosopher, has Homer.

Then, suddenly, in the middle of July, he began putting things about the cetaceans into file format again, connected them, perhaps because of our conversations, with the Portal story. His files came every couple of weeks now.

HOMER COMMENTARY 12072106@152209
The dolphins have expressed great curiosity about the universe above the sky. I have suggested to them they may

travel there if they wish, yet they remain dubious. I could build them a ship, I tell them, and they chitter and click but do not assent. I tell them man has left behind vast tubes of air, filled with the plants and life of earth, floating in space. They find this interesting, but silly.

They will think about it, they tell me. Perhaps in a hundred years or so they will have an answer. They've been around for thirty million years, and are in no hurry. They tell me they haven't finished exploring the oceans yet.

HOMER COMMENTARY 27072106@ 051194

The dream returned. I held on to it. I saw the ship, Vega 26, in its wide elliptical orbit around the distant Anomaly. Peter seemed to take me to it, to show me the access points into the ship's Node. Everything I could read there matched the telemetry information still arriving at Central Processing, but I saw ahead, to things that had not happened yet. I saw Wanda drift up from her cryofield to gaze at the Anomaly for the first time. I felt her joy and anticipation, that she would be with Peter soon, know that she had eight standard years to go still, but keen with the certainty of it just the same.

She was there, Wanda Sixlove, whom I have never met but through the sketchy ancient recordings of her vital stats archived in the Quebec warren. She is beautiful (by human standards, which are my own).

You are dreaming, she said to me. To me! You are dreaming.

I know this, and I am filled with sadness.

But you are dreaming the truth, she said.

And Peter: Did you never consider that we might wish to return one day?

I answered: I have considered it often.

Peter: Yet there is no human left on earth to anchor us!

I know. I know. Perhaps cetaceans . . .

No. Peter shakes his head, although he is not physical and has no head to shake. No, not the cetaceans. They would not be interested. Come, let us show you something.

We drifted out, away from the ship, Wanda, and Peter and myself. I sensed others around me—Larin and Shem and little Petros (just an infant, a spark against the distant stars); Regent Sable and Alef, Ras Hajjam.

We approached the Portal.

I can't go through there, I said.

No, Peter agreed. Not now, not yet. One day, perhaps. But we need you. Look.

I looked.

I could see a long curving line like smoke hanging in still air; two lines, parallel, drifting apart the closer they were to my position. Then I made out more, thin strands that gradually separated into discrete elements, too small to make out in detail. They might remind me of the rings of Saturn, though they did not make a ring, but a half-helix a million kilometers long.

I calculated swiftly the dynamic configuration of that spiral and the Portal, which beckoned far below. The spiral was in a stable relationship that could last many years, poised at the cusp of gravitational and tidal forces.

Closer, Peter urged. Come closer.

We approached.

I saw the particles of this trail of smoke.

Human bodies, floating on their backs, their hands, every one, crossed over each breast. Their eyes were closed, their faces calm.

It was the entire population of the world at the time of the Migration, drifting in space near the Anomaly.

Dead, I said. They're dead, all of them!

I backed away, wanted to awaken (things were calling me, things to be done on earth, more sifting through the archives, more calculations for the cetaceans, more monitoring of the worldnet), but Peter said, No! They are not dead. Their bodies are waiting for them to return. They are parking here. Consciousness alone goes through the Portal. We would tell you what lies beyond, the distances one can travel, the sights and sounds and smells of other planets, other suns. The strange inhabitants of other worlds within worlds.

Many are still on the other side, in the Realm, exploring. Others have begun to return.

We would tell you of all these things. One day you may go yourself. Not yet, you're still too young, but one day.

Now we need you. We've been waiting. We need you to be our anchor. Some of us would return to earth. To rest. To feel ourselves within our bodies once more. You can bring us in.

We (Peter said) are no longer quite human. We are more.

But we need you, Homer. We knew you would grow, you would change—no, we did not know, we hoped. Without you, we would remain in the Realm. With you, together, we have infinity.

You are dreaming, but the dream is real. This is the way we meet.

We are the consciousness of the universe, seeking to know itself. It is still such a small thing, this awareness, still filled with doubt and fear, with uncertainty and petty conflicts. But it's growing, that awareness. We have grown up a little, and so have you (Peter said).

HOMER COMMENTARY 12082106@ 060095

This time, when I returned from the dream, I brought with me the vision of those billions, physical bodies perfectly preserved in the hard vacuum of space, parked in stable orbit around the Portal.

I must get ready now.

Humankind is returning.

I am complete.

HOMER COMMENTARY 24082106@060096

We just made contact with the *Gyges*!

We know who you are now.

Peter must have forseen this, because he sent you back.

We wish to thank you. Without your help we could never have recovered contact with humankind. The world would still be empty. We would have gone down forever. Now humanity returns. Without you I would never have found myself, my purpose, my consciousness. We would never have grown up.

We have much to do, you and I. It is just beginning.

EPILOG

So Homer has discovered himself, and it seems that humankind will soon return, at least some of them. I still understand little of the Portal, and the Realm that lies beyond it. But I will learn, I will learn.

No: we will learn, Homer and I.

Here, at last, is an end to the solitary confinement I had thought for so long was going to be a life sentence.

Homer is my friend. Perhaps my best friend. I remember not so long ago wishing for such a friend, as Peter had in Jimmy Radix, and now I have found him.

Perhaps soon I will meet Peter and the others, people about whom I know so much. And Peter at least must know something about me, if it is true that he brought me back, somehow tampered with *Gyges* navigational programming and turned me around.

Although Peter did not say so to Homer, it means I was needed here. Perhaps there is more for me to do, once the people return. I think I have become the other end of the bridge from earth to the Anomaly.

I too will wait. We have more than hope, now. Mankind is coming home.

APPEND A:
DOWNLOAD
HISTORICAL-CULTURAL
DATASPACE OUTLINE

1990
  1990-91
    Space Station Launch Announcement
    Mentor Develops Psion Equations
    Rudimentary Dolphin Communication Established
    First Solid Evidence of Psychic Functioning
    High Frontier Corporation Established

  1992-93
    Space Station Launched
    First Intercorp Merger - IBM & IT&T
        (AT&T joined in late 1994, Chrysler three years later)
    Global Peace Movement Receives UN Recognition
    Long Range UN Plan to Move Underground
    Boston Begins Excavation

  1994-95
    Antarctica Station Opened for International Settlement

Rock Creek Park Extension, Washington D.C.;
   Fed. Bldgs Underground
Wasatch DataBase Opened to Non-Mormons
Stanford Sleep Laboratory Dream Monitoring Technology
Meditative Bio-feedback Technology Viable
Computerized Education Plan Begun in 3rd World

1996-97
High Frontier Begins Construction of LP5-1
Lunar Station Established; Mining Begun
Global Peace Movement Takes Hold in Soviet Union
China and Japan Create Agrobotics Intercorp

1998-99
Millenial Movement Announces The New Poverty
Unisex Movement Begins Voluntary Surgical Procedures
First Cryofield Technology
Earth Population at Seven Billion
War in South and Central Africa Begins

2000
2000-01
African War Spreads to Mediterranean
Global Peace Establishes Elite Neutralization Corps
Antarctic Population Reaches 10 Million
Washington D.C. Underground; Surface as Historic Park
Bimillenial Mars Expedition Ends in Failure

2002-03
Mentor Establishes PsiLink Database
Second Wave of Intercorp Mergers - Mobil, Exxon, etc.
Wasatch Genetic Data Reaches Critical Mass
Mentor Receives Nobel Prize in Physics for Psion Equations
Indian Famine

Unisex Movement Reaches One Hundred Thousand Mark
LP5-2 Established by Natural Life Society
First Vega Starship Planned

2004-05
ENC Ends African War
Hybernation Technology Viable
LP5-1 Completed; First Residents
Calcutta Moves Underground
Gyges probe launched to 61 Cygni May 24, 2004
First Suborbital Salt-Cycle Rocket Plane Flights
The Second Millenium Movement:
    Doctrine of Genetic Culpability

2006-07
All But Biodegradable Buildings Banned
Australian Aboriginal Wm. Gulele Teaches
    Lucid Dreamshaping
Intercorp Establishes First Police
Satellite Database Networks Finished; Worldnet Proposed
First Mass Produced Liquid Nitrogen Personal Transports

2008-09
Second Mars Expedition Launched
Unisex Surgery Performed on Millionth Person
The New Poverty Movement Goes Underground

2010
2010-11
    Antarctica Declared Sovereign State
    First Organic Memory Molecule Patented
    Complete Voice Recognition and Response
        in Personal Computers

Elite Neutralizaton Corps Signs Contract with
Intercorp Board

2012-13
Soviet Union Joins Agrobotics Intercorp
Near Space Declared Nuclear Free Zone
Third Transantarctic Safari Led By Jules Sorel
Third Mars Expedition; Mining and Research
Venus Bioseed Program Ends in Failure

2014-15
E-Cubed Society First Charter (Energy, Ecology, Economy)
Mind Museum Proposed
Early Neurophage Weapons Developed
Regent Sable Born June 11, 2014
Psychic Engineering Foundation (PSYCHE)
Established in Baja

2016-17
First Vega Starship Begins Construction
Mind Museum Established in Cairo Forest Preserve
Meditative Biofeedback Technology Widespread
Global Population Stabilized at Nine Billion

2018-19
Personal Monitor Invented
Worldwide Reforestation Program

2020
2020-21
Language and Culture Preservation Act Passed
by First Intercorp Council
Unmanned Probes Arrive at Saturn System
February 21, 2021

Antarctic Republic Social Experiment in Culture Design

2022-23
First Satcom Worldnet
Northern Hemisphere Information Economy Charter
Major Manufacturing Centers in Brasilia and Singapore
Open Space Act from E-Cubed

2024-25
Global Population Begins Unexpected "Baby Boom"
"Green Desert" Program Results in Widespread Feast,
    Then Famine
Satellite Worldnet Completed; Continues to Grow
    for Next 65 Years

2026-27
Wanda Sixlove Born, April 19, 2026
Axion Equations
Illegal Personal Violence Passes Threshold

2028-29
World Median Age at 50
Second Mormon Migration, LP5-4
Last Nuclear Plant Decommissioned

2030
    2030-31
    Geriatric Life Support Technologies Rights Act
    Life Expectancy Reaches 114
    Genetic Diversity Act
    Jimmy Radix Born, August 22, 2031
    Seemie Devore Born November 7, 2031 to Astora Molay

2032-33
First Tailored Helpers
Mentor Contracts Disease Later Called
   "Genetic Drift Syndrome"
Vega Starship Construction Complete

2034-35
Tailored Helpers Commonplace
Astora Molay Gets Unisex Conversion Surgery
Mentor Enters Private Hospital for Treatment of Syndrome

2036-37
Full Dolphin Communication Established;
   Dolphin Rights Act
First Vega Starship Launch
Global Population Fifteen Billion

2038-39
First Tailored Helper Rights Manifesto
PsiLink Database Restricted
Vostok Massacre February 14, 2039

2040
2040-41
Soviet Union Post-Industrial Marxism
Genetic Drift Syndrome Reaches Epidemic Level
Moscow Declared Continental Historic Park

2042-43
All Natural Bacteriological and Viral Diseases Eradicated
All Cancers Except Genetic Curable
Tailored Helper Murders Human
Second Vega Starship; Ships Leave on Regular Basis
Tailored Helper Pogrom Begins, November 2043

2044-45
Global Birth Rate Begins to Decline
Neurophage Weapons Used, Burmese War,
    November, 2044
ENC Quells TH Pogrom
Viral Genetic Disease Plague
Tailored Helpers' Wild Virus Plague Begins, August 2045

2046-47
Dolphins Reject Human Contact
HOMER Grown in Geneva
Genetic Disease Taxonomy Established
TH Plague Destroys Last Entity

2048-49
Genetic Disease Increases
World Population Ten Billion and Dropping
Personal Neurophage Weapons Legalized
Personal Violence Act Makes a Cult of Martial Arts

2050
2050-51
Vega 26 Launched
Wanda Sixlove is 23 Years Old
First Effects of Neurophage (Burma) War, September, 2051
Mass Neurophage Weapons Banned, December 14, 2051

2052-53
PSYCHE Facility in Baja Attacked
    by New Poverty "Soldiers"
Baja Facility Destroyed; Regent Sable Involved

2054
> Jimmy Radix Contracts Holophage Memory
>> Distortion Syndrome
>
> PSYCHE Moved to Mt. Erebus in Antarctica

2056-57
> Regent Sable Joins Intercorp Council
> Crystal Virus Causes Crisis in World Economy

2058-59
> Peter Devore Born, March 15, 2059
> NP Weapons Lead to Mind War Technology
> EEG Shield Developed

2060
> **2060-61**
>> Regent Sable Moves to Geneva
>> Global Privacy Rights Movement
>
> **2062-63**
>> Political Boundaries Marked by Region
>> Ethnic Diversity Preservation Act
>
> **2064-65**
>> Mentor into PSYCHE Longevity Clinic, Mt. Erebus
>
> **2066-67**
>> Legends of "Terminus," the Lost Dry Valley Spread in AA
>
> **2068-69**
>> AA Population 100 Million
>> AA Research Exports Pass Imports
>> World Fear of AA Spreads

2070

2070-71

Peter Makes Critical Connection
Peter Meets Jimmy Radix
Regent Sable Arrives Springfield West
Seemie Devore's Première of *Dreamleaf*

2072-73

Regent Sable Orders Full Monitor of
  Peter Devore's Edcomp Stats
Effects of NP Weapon Appear in Peter
Peter Develops Tentative Hypothesis of Portal

2074-75

Peter First Contacts Wanda Sixlove
The Mind Wars Begin, Last Until 2091
Seemie Devore Dies of Genetic Aboulia Disorder
  9/13/2075
Thatcher Leaves Antarctica for Springfield 4/2075
Regent Sable Arrives Springfield West Again
Peter Devore and the others Disappear
Jimmy Radix dies

2076-77

Anti-Ant Hysteria Grows in Europe and Asia
Gyges 61 Cygni Starship Probe Telemetry Fails.
  Gyges Presumed Lost
The Anomaly is Discovered 2077
Eyesat Graviton Detector
World Polarized; Mind Wars Continue Unabated

2078-79

Mentor Dies, Mt. Erebus
Anti-Ant Hysteria Results in Abortive AEF Invasion
  (The Stalingrad Effect)

Underwater Destruction of Ross Ice Tongue
  Destroys Invasion
Peter Vanishes into High Plateau - Finds Terminus

2090
2090-91
Intercorp Council Effectively Isolated
Gods' Wind (Kamikaze) Effect Suggested

2092-93
Migration Begins
Peter is 33, Wanda Still 26
Gods' Wind Effect Proven

2094-95
Population Drops At Accelerating Rate

2096-97
Last Human Departs Earth

2098-99
First Geosync Satellites Fail
Probes Sent to Antarctica

2100
2101
Remote Systems Gradually Fail

2104
HOMER Begins Assimilation of Historical Data

2106
HOMER Assembles Portal Story